Staci Collins

The World Beneath:

A Story of Love and Physics

Copyright © 2008 by Staci Maria Collins

First trade paperback edition 2007.

For information regarding special discounts for bulk purchases, please
contact info@narrativeedge.com

Manufactured in the United States of America

ISBN: 1-4196-7240-1
ISBN-13: 978-1419672408

Cover design by Tina Campillo, www.tinacampillo.com
Initial cover image by Jay Johnson

For more information, go to www.stacicollins.com.
To purchase additional copies, go to www.booksurge.com

Dedicated to

My late, esteemed parents
Peggy Jean Burgess Collins
And Edward Daniel Collins
And always, my love Johnny

ACKNOWLEDGMENTS

This book is also dedicated to the staunch Americans of New Orleans and California, and all who came here on their powerless own. I hope it infotains them and their descendants who've found hope in this great land of hard-won opportunity.

It turns out this writing stuff is harder than it looks. My gratitude to my five main writing teachers over the last seven years – Mimi Albert, Jewelle Gomez, Karen Joy Fowler, Carol Edgarian and Tom Jenks. Without them all none of this would be readable. Acknowledgement to the fellow writers who offered feedback above and beyond the call, out of the generosity of their hearts: Kathy Kim, Joe Evanisko, Jackie Luckett and Diana Prufer.

For the revelations of the main ideas, much credit to Michelle Meehan, Monisha Mustapha, David Rhodes, Shauna McKenna, John Havard and Barbara Beasley. And my appreciation to those whose reading and feedback made the work get better: Monica

Jones, Pam Hoyer, Marissa Carus, Michelle Long, Suzanne and George DeVos and Rita Updite. I'd like to acknowledge the experts who shared the realities of banking, newspapers and Swiss German with me: Michael Beardsley, Glenn Mayeda, Mario Galvez, Katie Bloomer. Finally, my thanks to the librarians at the California Historical Society, Bancroft Library, and the San Francisco Public Library.

David Bohm – a quantum physicist conducted all of the early experiments and developed all the theory mentioned herein.

This story hits the tip of the iceberg of some amazing true tales:
Michael Schneider *A Beginner's Guide to Constructing the Universe* (Harper Perennial)
David Peat, *Infinite Potential* (Addison Wesley)
Anton Zeilinger, *"Quantum Teleportation"* (Scientific American)
John Cassidy, *dot.con* (Perennial)
Cliff Stoll, *The Cuckoo's Egg* (Pocketbooks)
Robert Thurman, *Mandala:The Architecture of Enlightenment* (lecture)
J. Krishnamurti, *Krishnamurti's Notebook* (Harper & Row)
Mu Soeng Sunim, *Heart Sutra* (Primary Point Press).

L. Downie, Jr. and R. Kaiser, *The News About the News* (Vintage)
Eric Alterman, *What Liberal Media?* (Basic Books)
Mary Gehman, *The Free People of Color of New Orleans* (Margaret Media)
Christine Wiltz, *The Last Madam* (Da Capo Press)
Gwendolyn Midlo Hall, *Africans in Colonial Louisiana* (LSU Press)
Sybil Kein, *Creole* (LSU Press)
Curt Gentry, *The Madams of San Francisco* (Ballantine)
Douglas Henry Daniels, *Pioneer Urbanites* (UC Press)
Lynn Hudson, *The Making of "Mammy Pleasant"* (Lynn Hudson)
George D. Lyman, *Ralston's Ring* (Scribner)

Finally, my best regards to my clients who, along with my parents, taught me all I know about the American Dream.

One always learns one's mystery
at the price of one's innocence.
Robertson Davies, Fifth Business

One

To begin with, I never believed in the American Dream – not that it smelled like new cars and credit cards, or looked like slick gadgets or designer shoes in mansion-sized homes – or that you could live like a king guilt-free – certainly not a girl of color – a *voodooienne.* Whole thing caught me by surprise really; slipped me up when I wasn't looking. Came right into my heart through the open back door I didn't even really know was there.

So, that first night, all night, I stared out the plane's smudged cabin window to a trail of lights through the dark – the prairie route the old pioneers had once followed – 10,000 gold seekers 'round the Bay in 1849 – 50,000 in the hills, a few thousands of them Indian, Mexican, Chinese and free colored men, women and slaves praying to be made rich and free along with everyone, as I hoped now to become rich and free beside the dot boom.

And I hoped to find out what had happened to Lilla Cadot – a younger sister ancestress who'd come out during the Gold Rush, and been lost. Her recovery I hoped would be my own.

"Stewards, prepare cabin for landing."

The cabin lights dimmed. Dotcom central stretched before me far as I could see – a land of electric lights – dawn, and a new millennium hinting at its edges. It had taken 16 years to get here. My heart began to pound.

That's when my darling daughter Cariña's final goodbye sliced in, "You're a liar! Daughter to a whore! Not my mother – not even a very good maid. Moman L says so." Her rosebud lips screwed up in disgust and rage.

But just then my senses went black – no sight, sound, scent – not even the rough airplane fabric beneath me – all ripped away – as if out in space with my slapping heartbeat my only company.

"We'll meet again in San Francisco, *dauphine*. You must unite the Ten into One to turn the curse – to win your *succés fou*." My Moman Féy's words from her last night on the banks of the Mississippi wisped past my ear

I blindly stabbed the seat's arm several times before connecting with the button to lean back.

My row-mate glanced up from the screen she was shutting on the beat-up laptop she'd typed on the entire trip. "You all right?'

A flush of appreciation dissolved vision and void. I nodded at her with gratitude. Out of habit I crossed myself and searched for something in the world to steady me – my eye caught a colorfully-lit skyscraper with a neon red dial clock. *The Tribune* black letters read.

"That's Oakland," nodded the small, young woman whose curls escaped ignored from her dark ponytail as she slid her early notebook into her boxy, 50's style black valise with white stitching that sat open between her feet. Then she bobbed her head up toward the window, "San Francisco's across the bay."

"Yes." Though many of the pioneers of color had eventually moved over here – some of the oldest families still lived in the star-lit hills.

"Assume you're here for pleasure?"

"For journalism – student – or will be...at San Francisco State. I want to cover the dot boom. Get *splashed--,"* the plane bounced once onto tarmac, "by it."

"Better do it fast."

"What do you mean?" I push-buttoned the seat back up before the stewardesses appeared.

She sat her satchel in the seat between us – the middle latch was in the shape of a cowboy hat. "The boom's overdue for going bust."

"Really?" The stock market for months had kept outwitting doubters, even the Wall Street Journal, and more and more Americans, like me, bet our futures on it.

"You've heard the theory of the Greater Fool?"

I shook my head, smiling.

My seatmate turned. "You buy a stock you know is insanely valued because you trust a fool greater than you will buy it at a profit. You can guess the catch." The plane stopped and the lights flickered back on. She stood and grabbed down her bag and black pea coat. Her suitcase was covered with overseas tags.

"You're the last fool," I said.

She shrugged and nodded.

"What's your dotcom? Maybe I can cover you."

She laughed. "I never said I worked in dotcoms."

"Oh?" I knit my brow. "I just assumed..."

She pushed into her heavy jacket. Light glinted off a left lapel pin outlined in silver – a grey cowboy hat. It matched the latch on her briefcase.

"Like your hats..." I nodded to the case.

"Thanks." After considering, she reached in her pocket and handed me a card. Then she grabbed her case, turned and walked down the aisle.

I grinned down: Annie French, Free Programmer, email and voicemail. Be kind of nutty if she were one of Moman Féy's Ten.

A bird I didn't recognize right away as an endangered condor, circled above Coit Tower on old Chile Hill, now known as Telegraph Hill. There, from the start of the Gold Rush, "wayward", "seditious" or indentured women from Mexico, Peru, and Chile had lived. Others from China, Australia, France, the Eastern Seaboard and Storyville had all made their way out to these blocks. I watched them loom larger as we inched 'cross the Bay Bridge into the City.

We Cadot, ourselves, for 15 generations had been two kinds of women. Those like Féy, who'd left me to be mistress to another woman's man – and my grandmother, Moman Laetitia, or Moman L as I also came to call her, into whose strong–fingered palms I was born.

Whether unpacking raw hat forms and accessories for our downstairs Ladies Hat Shoppe and Meeting Place, chopping up pepper, onions and celery for our Friday night crab feeds, or delicately drying the old Royal china which we used always and only for the Ladies' tea and coffee, in her thick, ironed Creole green apron, Moman L would say, "In this world, Jim Crow may be gone, but there are still two classes of people: owners and servers. Some Cadot might have once been the devil's servants, but now we've served honorably our Ladies and our Marigny for generations – we treat them like owners, remind them of past dignities – and by God's good grace together we've kept this store and home and our station in society. Pick well who and what you serve – it's His salvation here on earth...What separates us from..." her tight nod always meant women like Féy, and presumably women like those on old Chile Hill.

Féy had proven out Moman L's warning. When I was 12, she'd actually jumped from the high stern of the QE II on which she was singing her way home to Paris. Her body'd never had a hope of being found in the deep-trenched mid-Atlantic, even if the ship had been able to stop quickly. Among the Ladies, of course, we'd not mentioned it – we never mentioned Féy.

So I'd lived Moman L's strict Catholic path until, hitting the prom trifecta with Davis, my Creole green eyed, 23 year old, well-known prom date. After several nips of Maker's Mark bourbon from his etched, silver flask in between fast songs, a very grown-up itch began to dance 'round inside me. A slow Brass Band number came on, and when he grabbed my waist to pull me close, that itch suddenly blossomed into a full-grown desire that I'd never known before – or since.

So that night in his caddy, after half a bottle of fine French champagne, I gave him my first time out the gate and hit the jackpot again, eventually bearing my daughter, Cariña, just 'round when he was marrying another; a better positioned girl – daughter to Moman L's best friend and leading Marigny Lady, Alva Decoudreau.

We never talked about that with the Ladies either.

We never talked about how Féy could have come back from the dead to bear and abandon this second child as she had me.

In fact Moman L and the Ladies sudden and complete takeover of Carina's loving care and precious heart, along with their icy eyes to me, had directly frozen my will, and my heart.

And over eight years I'd not thawed it out. Now here, though I dreaded encountering a ghostly Féy, I would. I'd do whatever I must to become Cariña's loving and loved *moman*.

The Laotian shuttle driver with a round, toasted almond face put back his radio mike and said, "They say we've got a jumper, folks. Might be a while." No one else spoke. A jumper on the Bay Bridge seemed odd when the Golden Gate's red lights flashed orange through low, dense fog. It was the biggest suicide destination in the world.

A large black shadow flashed. I shot up a black leather-jacketed arm. The driver leant forward and peered up, "Did you see that? That bird flew at us – there it is again!"

The shadow swiped again. Peering past my elbow, I saw the condor's bald head turn. The black eyes bored and pulled me in. The car windows went black; the passengers' rustle died, along with the driver's shouts, the conditioned air – as usual only my heartbeat and a black universe remained.

Then the void split wide, this time to mingling Chanel and Jean Naté, fresh as it had been 23 years ago.

"You are marked for a reason, *dauphine*. I'm here to show you." My Moman Féy sat 10 feet away in the gold plush loveseat in one of our old guest *boudoirs*.   Third-story of our Creole townhouse with the infamous curlicue backstairs, each level marked with a wrought iron "C", gateway to octoroon and quadroon pleasure for generations of mayors, businessmen and city elite; its backdoor entrance on Rampart 'round the corner from Esplanade it had stood open for almost 200 years.

I sat on the gold bedspread watching her in the floor lamp's dim, tasseled light beneath the Louis XV gilt mirror – all now kept silently by Moman L, for Friday "wicked Nawlins" tours to supplement our income and customer base.   Féy, a featured topless performer in Paris's Folies Bergére, had made her first visit home since my birth, for this, my fifth birthday.

Her eyes shone with other worlds – and illegal laudanum it turned out.   Her creamy arm extended beyond her flame tulle nightgown through which everything she had could be seen.

"Jeanne," she called me in French as she rose and moved toward me, her face alight, her gold jewelry shimmering.   She swept in close and in the middle of her chest I saw a five-sided star birthmark – just like those on my neck and lower back.

"It is written," she knelt, took my hand between hers, "in the Cadot letters of eldest sisters over 12 generations. We three: 13th, 14th and 15th," her red-draped arm reached 'cross my lap to take my wrist up, "have a destiny. We all, even you, daughter to a dark king, wearer of the twin stars, must die before we live."

She lifted her chin, "In San Francisco, you'll turn the Cadot curse – become the first to achieve *succés fou* – the real American Dream, *dauphine*. You'll become free to truly live."   She ran a finger 'round my neck to the star birthmark in its hollow.   "But you must master the twin powers. Or the dark sea will take you."

"Holy Mary," the driver jammed on the breaks despite our slow roll, cracking open my sight, "Did that bird just look in here?" I saw him glance at me, at the five-pointed star nestled in my neck, my no doubt otherworldly eyes. All my life folks had crossed themselves upon seeing the mark I couldn't remove. He turned away, and whispered most certainly a prayer.

Now the condor circled above the entrance to the city, above Rincon Hill, home to San Francisco's first elite. William Chapman Ralston, an Ohio river-man by way of N'awlins, had mined millions in silver from the Comstock Lode, built the Palace the first Stock and Board Exchange and filled many pockets with gold through his Bank of California. And he'd had his first mansion here. The bridge span dissolved to a white two-story mansion surrounded by lawn, a carriage pulling up. But even into this impossible sight, the condor swept. Condors split open the sternums of the dead for others to get at, I flashed. Presumably there were even more dead back in Ralston's time.

And then I recalled the first black bird I'd seen – spiraling up above my head on Royal Street in the French Quarter – the year I was seven and these incursions of the past began.

On the street beneath the blackbird, Féy and I'd just arrived in the street in front of Benvenue's where the oil painting of an orange bridge hung in the window, when thwack, splash – two water balloons had smacked me and I'd scrambled back, my leg crashing into a pothole marked with an orange cone.

Across the street the Faucheaux boys' yelled from a second story window, "*Voodienne! Sorciére!*"

A terrible smell rose. Moman L'd always said 60 miles of drains lay beneath the Quarter, most of them built by our Creole of color forefathers and slaves. Something wet rushed 'round my foot, rose slowly up my leg. I wriggled, but I was stuck. Féy hurried over, but instead of yanking me out, she pressed her thumb awkwardly 'gainst my inside left wrist – at my pulse – her fingernail pinched my skin a little bit and I squirmed. She only pressed harder as she smiled at Sophie, "Girl's headstrong. Clumsy. Let her stew in her own juices just a little bit."

Through the store window behind Sophie, her mother Fayette's eyes glinted over a squashed smile. To get to her long-promised Dream of being an owner, Fayette had sued to be "white" instead of "colored" on her birth certificate, removing the stain of her great, great grandmother, Margarita, a slave until she bought her freedom, then her children's – from their half–brothers. Since then she'd fought staunchly against our kind of Creoles. She'd kept our shop out of the Merchant's Association for years arguing we were just outside official French Quarter boundaries.

But what happened then in front Sophie and Fayette between Féy and me – only way I can describe it is that her thumb somehow ran invisible dark water all through me – up my arm, 'cross my shoulder and down from behind my birthmark to the one on my tailbone – on into the water in the hole beyond. A river of unspeakable things I knew at an instant.

Dirty green water bubbled up against my bottom bringing with it the smell of burning metal. But when I raised my right fingers they were dry. Yet the water spread like a flash flood down Royal, wherever it covered, dirt road and bare wood walls shone through – a wet window to the past.

Once the vapor water reached the horizon, hurrying toward me, I saw a long gown and three thigh length suit coats, rough leather boots – a group of five pioneers – from old Chile Hill.

"Jeanne, when all hope is lost, there is your path to me," Féy's voice hissed. "Now, stay back," she warned the ghosts, "No closer yet. Or I'll not come again when you need me."

The five froze. A Creole-looking man and woman looked concerned; a well–fed, dark man just looked irritated. A lean white man crossed his gloved hands over his chest with a smirk; a small Incan woman rocked back, her black eyes enraged.

"There he is," the driver's voice melted them away as my wresting my hand from Féy had then. All these years since, they'd never again appeared. Féy'd come twice more before the end.

So now between two police vehicles, seeing a man's wet, pink head hung between silver–clad shoulders, with his hands cuffed behind his back, I wondered had he been a last fool? And had he come back for his family? And now I was finally here, would Féy really come back for me? And bring her pioneers, her Ten? Take me to *succés fou*? Or would I become the last fool? Worse, now as a student journalist just coming here to seek her fortune in the late 2000 dot boom, perhaps I'd already become one.

The moment I set foot on the concrete beneath the Hyatt Regency on Davis Street, beneath the exhaust, old metal burned from the smoke of the old foundries South of Market, black carriages with horses and mud flickered in next to taxis and cars, as if the city's past itself had risen up to greet me. Muddy board sidewalks sloped up seven brown grassy hills.

Wharves crisscrossed a watery Yerba Buena cove. Bells rang announcing a bonanza on the Exchange. Ahead of me a black dockhand peered 'round a wharf shack that was today a photo store. I could feel his racing heart as he pointed to an ebony man in dark tatters and whispered a terse direction, maybe to hide from slave catchers.

Just then a cab honked twice dissolving the past and bringing along a headache. Gratefully I dropped in the back seat. "Chile––Telegraph Hill." I might as well get it over with before leaving downtown. If there was anywhere Féy and her Incan friend would be, it would be there I imagined.

The driver, a middle–aged black man who looked learned beneath his African cap, shifted, "It's a big hill."

"South side, please." At his headshake I added, "Just a quick tour before heading to S.F. State."

"Coit Tower?" Confederate Lillie Coit who'd commissioned the tower had, like many San Francisco women of society, worn pants, rode horses, played poker on the docks, and smoked cigars – all after the fashion of the loved and despised Peruvian women, often dancers – as I imagined my Incan woman had been.

"No, below that, the streets." He nodded and pulled out.

From my coat's inside pocket I loosed the small frame Féy'd first found on her third visit – for my tenth birthday – hidden behind the upstairs linen, the wedding photo of Lilla Cadot and James Collins, 1873, San Francisco, the man and wife of my vision. She stood in a full-length tightly gathered skirt with a tailored, padded long-sleeved blouse and a long, full train. He wore a thigh-length suit coat with two top buttons. They both had on white gloves. They did not touch. All my life, no matter what secret I'd poured into their young, stoic faces, they'd remained impassive, never moving, never needing anyone.

I unhooked the back, shook out the photo – behind it another was hidden – a group in front of a ship – the *HMS Lawrence II* spanning its middle. The first two were Lilla and James. Next to them an older, darker, stouter man with a small mustache, then the dark Spanish woman, head covered in black mantle, large black eyes intent –the condor's eyes. And on the end, above his smile, a white man wore a Van Dyke beard, hard eyes and top hat. On the back was scrawled, Signing Day 1873.

"On tour?" The cabbie shot from the front seat.

"I've waited years." Outside at Davis and California, the abandoned ship the Henry Lee flashed, as did hundreds of others still buried here, still laden with cargo, abandoned for gold in the old Bay as soon as they'd anchored.

Commercial, today a closed-off flagstone alley of metal tables, exchanged with a wide wharf where two French girls swept their hoop skirts up and into a padded carriage. They might have been prostitutes "of the lowest sort" deported here in Napoleon's son's fake lottery of 1849.

Down Sansome, nearing the hill, passing Pacific Street's brick windows – still the original foot above the street in the old Barbary Coast, I glimpsed a sign: Big Matilda, "Three hundred pounds of black passion.... all hours...50c each: three for a dollar." And a black woman on a low, uneven stool turned to stare with the condor's eyes.

Again the dark sea rose to crash over me and I was again on Royal, staring at Sophie Benvenue's little dog tight against her buxom chest. Féy's finger was still at my wrist, but she laughed toward Sophie, holding out a Virginia Slim in her free hand. "That smell," she exhaled, "is just awful." Her hand went up with just the right amount of waver. Féy'd never show public distress – she thought it common. "Jeanne, you all right?"

In my head she urged, "*Dauphine*. See Sophie's real living. Even owners have to serve. We all serve somebody."

Up came the black wave, washing over me – and then I saw – Sophie in a sedan backseat with a dark chocolate high school boy – his purple football jersey and a broad grin all she wore as he moved in and out of her.

I shook my arm, but Féy's grip tightened and then in a second dark rush I saw Sophie's hand on her belly over a dark child – one not yet known of – a child who'd be given away soon as he hit the earth. At that I wrested away my hand and mind.

Now I rushed, "You know what driver? Let's go straight to State." No way I was ready to confront Féy or her world.

He watched me through the rear view, "We're almost there."

"Yes, yes, never mind. Turn back, please."

The driver stopped at a light at Broadway. We'd have to drive by the hill to get back. My heartbeat rose. A shanty house flickered in 'cross the street. I shut my eyes, didn't open them till on the 280 freeway past Potrero Hill.

To our east Ralston had often raced horse and buggy 22 miles down a plank road against the San José train, to his Belmont show estate. But the thought stayed inside my mind – the past didn't rise. When we reached the former dunes of pink and white San Francisco State, I decided it would be a bit before I brought it all back.

Two

Not able to afford State's dorms, through the journalism office I'd found a room in exchange for nighttime care of its owner, 87-year-old State alumna, Verna Dennis.

The house was in Ingleside, an area of big homes 'cross 19th Avenue. Driving that first day down Delano, past the neighborhood's large stone balustrades, solid Buicks and Cadillacs drove by – not flickering even a moment.

Claire, the tiny Filipina day nurse, explained through the shadowed hall to breakfast room off the kitchen, I'd do all the food shopping and cooking for all of us; she'd do all the cleaning though she might need my help getting to the top cabinets or moving heavy objects.

We came into the back sitting room. Through the corner plate-glass picture windows, sunlight filtered in to shelves of flowering plants and succulents.

Mrs. Dennis, a thin tan colored woman, lay in a hospital bed amidst neat stacks of Los Angeles Times, National Geographic and Life, Ebony – some of them going back 40 years and stacks of them on every flat space. "Welcome, Ms. Cadot," she pronounced it perfectly; and still lively grey eyes regarded me through pearl-handled glasses.

Sight unseen she'd allowed me to come – after a twenty minute phone call. She was a journalism alum. "Thank you for having me. You've made all the difference."

"I hope you'll do well here. For us both."

"Yes, ma'am."

"Now I'm reading. Tonight, we can talk. I'll have some authentic Creole dish from what's in the freezer – show her Claire." And she vaguely waved the largest pearl ring I'd ever seen, and went back to her yellowed The Nation, listing the Vietnam War and the Power of the Pill on its cover.

Claire explained that both she and Mrs. Dennis needed all the good fat they could get to keep their weight and strength up. This was the main reason she'd hired me. So that first afternoon, I prepped catfish etoufee — while it simmered I read the Chronicle, the Mercury News and the Tribune at the small kitchen's square folding table, beneath floor-to-ceiling walnut cabinets.

Mrs. Dennis had late onset Parkinson's for which she took medication, so it took her an hour to slowly chew and swallow her meal, which she'd precede or follow with her daily vodka tonic – though this day she finished the one from the day previous while she made me tell her all about myself. By the time I was finished, she was done and falling sleepy.

After cleaning up, I slept fitfully to C-Span on the long gold couch next to her, close enough to respond if there was any problem. Ear plugs hit the top of my shopping list. Claire came in promptly at six-thirty.

So at nine in one of State's most rundown buildings, I was grumpy, nervous and on Excedrin when I sat in front of a 50–something, good–looking, dark brown man with a crisp green and bright white Izod over knotted arms and sharply creased Dockers – Clive Jones, a senior editor at SFEye.com, a new

Chronicle and Salon.com competitor.

"People," he growled to the 50 or so students squeezed 'round a double-windowed, white and beige classroom, "Journalistic values are what?" Clive was called the Chicago Tracker for his persistence on the Fred Hampton murder case in 1968. He told us that for his efforts on Mr. Hampton's behalf, he'd also been fired. It had taken him fifteen years to work his way back, ten in the West.

"Fairness and truth?" A young Asian kid said, reminding me of the twin powers. Did the two somehow work together?

Clive acquiesced then looked at the class. "Anyone else?"

After a silence, a brown man with mature eyes in the back spoke up, "If it bleeds it leads." I caught his eye and smiled. He smiled back.

"Getting warmer."

"Sell papers," said the white kid slouched next to me, legs splayed out in front of him, his baseball cap turned backwards.

Clive stopped at him, stared down and the kid moved himself upright. Starting with him Clive scanned us, "History's first draft must sell. More and more it must not piss off parent conglomerates and all their friends. At S.F. Eye we don't have that worry, but you all might not be so blessed." His index finger pointed at me, "But still, what is the truth about news?"

I crossed my fingers, "The truth will out?" Truth about him was he slightly mesmerized me.

He smiled before looking away. "If you find proof, irrefutable proof, someone, somewhere will print it – but it could be dangerous. Power doesn't like to be checked. Are you ready to risk it? Do you have the stuff? Many of your colleagues have shown they do not.

"Read Salon, the Chron and the Mercury News every day. Also a smaller press – a blog or community rag. Expect a spot quiz on a headline story each week. And you'll each have a beat."

Clive's challenge excited and terrified me. For now at least there'd be no more hiding.

After class, the older, wise-eyed brown man, Chuck Handley, came up to me. "Lot of work for an elective," he said. "I'm an accounting major. Thought investigating might help me. Want to grab some coffee?" His green eyes brought back Davis, and the black wave rose, but I laid a hand on his arm and just nodded.

"So what brings you out here?" Chuck smiled as he leant back in one of the grey metal chairs outside Café Rosso's squat single story – bull's-eye under the second oldest continually operating web video camera, though we'd no notion then.

I paused, "I suppose it really was my high school column, Invisible Heroes. Well, I started in 7th grade – profiling merchants, choirs, soup kitchens, small diocese, Black krewes. By junior year it got me a plaque hung in our front nook for 'shining the light of love truly on the Lord's meek', and then two profiles made it into the Times Picayune."

Invisible Heroes had helped me reclaim and reshape myself in Moman L's image after Féy'd left me on the dark banked river. "One of those brought me to the Graham Foundation Awards in New York City, which led to my scholarship – and now to here with Clive, with you."

"Wow, I'm impressed," Chuck's hand brushed my arm and he brought his latté suddenly to his lips as if embarrassed.

"Still you might be better at investigating than me," I hunched over my Americano, "I spent a childhood learning to shade my eyes from the awful truth."

"I did the same before I left Salt Lake. But eight years running trips down the American River cured me – a class four rapid can't be tricked."

His quick glance at my chest sent my heart racing away from the cold past, toward a warm future.

That weekend Chuck joined us for a cocktail and picked out a random issue of Atlantic Monthly with which to tease Mrs. Dennis. With just a glance at the cover, she said, "Have you never met an AP reporter, young man?"

She correctly detailed which article she wanted to read – on the Bobby Kennedy's trip to the poor towns outside Tuscaloosa – then she told him of her career and then they began discussing what she saw as the spiraling state of journalism. Chuck argued it was different, no worse. I chopped, spiced, simmered and studied in the kitchen.

In this way we quickly spent most every fall weekend when Chuck wasn't out of town leading or taking bike or river trips.

For Thanksgiving, Chuck went on home to Utah, and I cooked for Mrs. Dennis, her sister, Claudette, Claudette's son Walter –long-time manager of a boat repair on Wharf 27 – and his wife, their two pre-teen daughters and nine year old son.

In the dining room dotted with pre-Colombian sculpture and large amethyst geodes gathered by Mrs. Dennis when covering Brazil where she'd learned Portuguese and become an AP mainstay, we ate my jalapeño cornbread, cheesy grits, Creole coq au vin, shrimp jambalaya and turnip greens off her Spode China. It brought back memories of home – or how it might have been had we ever allowed used our own special things for ourselves.

After a couple of glasses of Bourdeaux in thick, leaded crystal and many compliments to the chef, I finally relaxed and said, "You know Mrs. Dennis, in 1873, Edmonia Lewis had her first major sculpture exhibition here. Her brother's gold–mining fortune had put her through Oberlin," I blushed, catching Mrs. Dennis's eye watching me, "Just...out here you've done what many of us back home still dream of."

Mahogany-skinned Walter, eyes sharp over his crisp magenta shirt, caught his wife's eye. Catching my glance at them, she looked away to her son's plate.

I spoke in Walter's direction hoping to apologize for whatever toes I'd stepped on, "There was even a Black man named William Leidesdorff, a captain out of New Orleans, who from here became American Vice Consul to Mexico in 1845. He introduced the steam ship to the Bay and earned the title 'most valuable resident'. And unfortunately, after his death from brain fever his land along the American River was found to hold gold worth millions. But there were others – black women millionaires, real estate moguls; they are the reasons I came out here."

Claudette wiped her mouth. I rose and began to clear.

Friday afternoon, Mrs. Dennis sat with C-Span playing on the T.V. Walter left shortly after I came in and from the weekday visit and by his unwillingness to look at me, I gathered something was wrong. But when I came in to say "hello" to Verna, she read as usual. That night I chopped the holy trinity – celery, green pepper and yellow onion – for a Creole bouillabaisse and called Moman L who'd taught me all the cooking I'd ever known.

In a tone not soft but not as hard as usual, she asked, "Jeanne, you coming home for Christmas Reveillon?"

My knife poised above a yellow onion, uncut, but still choking me up, "I'll try."

When I entered at 4:45 with the day's vodka soda, the room was gold with late sun and Mrs. Dennis again watched me, with an odd, intent look. The television was off.

"Jeannie," she asked, "You've one last assignment for your class with Clive?" She'd known Clive from her last years out here for the AP.

I smiled, "One last chance." I was at a solid A-/B+ from not working any nights – something I'd nearly reconciled myself to.

"Well, in return for all the meals you've given me, I'll give *you* an exclusive."

"Oh, Mrs. Dennis," but she held her hand up to stay me.

"Today I just changed my will to fund scholarships to State for girls just like you – in art or journalism. I've had a wonderful life, this house and my retirement are all because of what State made possible for me. I'll make it possible for other girls. You write it up. It'll get you that internship with Clive. You can stay here, but next year you can't any longer work for me."

"Wha-at?"

"Read it." She nodded at some papers. "That's your copy."

Sure enough, the Verna Dennis Scholarship Fund. It would start after I graduated.

Mrs. Dennis's fund turned out was for one point five million dollars – enough to generate ten scholarships a year. Turned out she did this even though she'd been victim to an on-campus, racial assault during her years. But the street boys had not gone to school at State and had been poor as she'd been before she'd gotten in, so she'd long ago forgiven them. And she'd written as much in State's Register.

So the piece and Verna's picture went front page at school and when the *Chronicle* and local morning shows called, I gave it to S.F. Eye exclusive. On it I got an A+.

The term's last day Clive asked me to accompany him to State's oddly mauve parking garage. "Verna Dennis called and gave me an idea. What was it you said at the Graham Foundation awards?"

Pausing, since we'd never spoken of the cat-called 'affirmative action' as I'd walked to accept the award, nevertheless the words came right out, "All I've ever desired, as each of us, is to find or make some place my skin, class and sex won't limit me. Those things, rather than my work, may be why I got this award. But I doubt it. Whose award this truly is, those I interviewed, their grandmothers and mine, all the men and women of service who come and go unrecorded, unrecognized. It is their stories I will continue to represent. Whether or not I deserve this, I am confident they do."

"You hit it," he chuckled as we entered the garage. "You know, profiles rarely win Pulitzers." He stopped, "But investigators who put something on the line, do. And the S.F. Eye wants a new take on everything – even obits."

I leapt at the chance, "Everybody has secrets they don't want to take to the grave. Guarantee not publish it until they're passed. Let unheard folks leave their own public last word."

"You do it for us exclusive? No other free lance." I nodded, too scared to speak and jinx it. He put out his hand then scooted it back, "I mean doing all obits and the occasional deathbed interview? Till we see how it goes."

"I accept," I grabbed his hand, trying not to grin like crazy. I called in the good news to Moman L. "Please let Cariña know," my voice stayed strong, "I'm coming home for Christmas."

I'd walked in through the Quarter and now stood outside Benvenue's on Royal – one day before Christmas. An older, plumper, less intimidating Sophie Benvenue had been in the window where Fayette had once stood. There was no Golden Gate painting, or any sign of the old sewer hole or the green tinge. Except for that first day in San Francisco, I could almost forget my old pioneers – forget Féy. The girl that had needed them then seemed not even to be me any longer.

Sophie looked at me twice and wondering about her child I smiled then rolled my bag on – the Faucheaux boys' window was closed, only a few tourists dotted the banquettes. The smells of garlic and sugar pervaded the air. Few tourists, but many locals had come on home now to see and be seen.

Five blocks down, across the double wide boulevard I stopped outside the front entrance of our Merciér Ladies Hat Shop and Meeting Place at Rampart. Just as always, about 15 hatted and gloved Marigny Ladies perched like colorful birds across folding chairs and window seats in our large front nook just beneath an old and majestic live oak.

Moman L, had inherited the group from her mother, Marie Cadot, who'd founded the Ladies during the depression "to safeguard and uplift our folk," and because folks then needed more than hats.

The Ladies of the front *and* back stairways had saved each other then, and the store, our house. But Moman L, strict

Catholic seemingly from birth, had gotten rid of the girls up the curlicue stairway long before I was born.

She'd reminded me each weekend before she'd ever opened the door, "We, like our customers, are Ladies, Jeanne. Don't forget yourself and they won't forget you." I wondered now if they ever spoke of me or whether I'd joined the silent ranks of Féy. Still I pushed open the front door and tinkled the chimes. Bright heads turned to me and then many pivoted back to Moman L, others bent, few forced a small smile.

Though previously, the Ladies had not allowed in women under 30, third Cousin Cecile who'd won her first award for her hat designs as a Tulane sophomore, was credited with bringing the store through its recent renaissance, including now going online. She now faced the scarved, perfumed and hatted Marigny Ladies, and she cleared her throat.

"Jacqueline and Davis Saturday," Cecile finished, checking a clipboard. Cariña, my darling girl, sat between Jacqueline and another woman in the window. Moman L sat in the far front as always. She was wearing oxygen. "Jeanne, you're here."

As I passed by some of the Marigny Ladies leant back from their chicory coffee "warmed" with bourbon, and meeting notes, or peered over their eyeglasses. But Moman L her best friend Alva move toward her daughter and had me sit next to her. Her hollows had darkened, her back hunched a little, but she still had the same starch and chicory smell when I hugged her.

Cariña stole glances at me and I waved at her, acknowledged Jacqueline who held a tight smile on her lips. Alva had announced her engagement to Davis just days after my strip had turned pink – three weeks after prom. I'd just wanted to not go away as a virgin – I wanted to come out knowing something of the world – to leave something special of me in New Orleans. That was eight years back and I certainly had.

Cecile gave me a slight incline and went on finalizing arrangements for the after Christmas Merchant's Fair. She'd managed to gain the Hat Shoppe entrance in the Quarter's

Merchants Association. Fayette must have passed. Watching her, younger than I and already on her way to being an owner, to being Cadot heir, my heart sank.

Moman L rested after the meeting and Cariña and Cecile closed and prepped the store for tomorrow's big shopping day, while I chopped and cooked dinner, letting the familiar skills bring my confidence back.

Setting down at Reveillon dinner with Moman L, Cecile and Cariña, right up front they praised my cooking. "Seems you've learnt something right out there in California," Moman L said after a bite of crab and shrimp jambalaya.

"I cook for my room and board." I told about Mrs. Dennis's scholarship and how it led to Clive's job, avoiding that I wrote death notices and interviewed the dying – and that in old downtown the world would still break apart on me.

"Good work – *Momma*," Cariña suddenly said in her small, precise tone. All went quiet except the polite clink of Moman L's dishing tongs.

"Well, Corinne—Cariña," I stammered, taking back the name changed at birth by Moman L. "Cariña... my da–darling daughter...thank you," I blinked back tears. I'd thought Moman L would take that secret to her grave. I coughed; drank a deep gulp of water; then croaked, "And how are you holding up? How's school? The bad girls leaving you be?" I cleared my throat as my inner turmoil calmed.

"All that's fine, Momma. Jacqueline and Davis are very good to me." She smiled, willing me to just accept it. My 8 year old was toying with me.

"You know Hollywood stars have begun to wear Cecile's hats." Moman L said, "We're hoping she'll soon find a nice gentleman." But Cecile, whose hair was cut remarkably short, knitted her brows an instant, then glanced at each of us, and finally looked down at her plate, her lips frozen.

That's just how it happened. That single word, Momma,

spoken twice with a child's deceptive smile – no other comment.

After dinner we opened gifts on the parlor's burgundy couch beneath the ceiling tall Christmas tree. They'd layered every ornament we had on it, covered it with tinsel that caught the light and sparkled where Féy'd danced for Alfonse, her Argentinean choreographer at the Folies – and the main reason she'd left me.

The ebony wave rose bringing me toward what had happened right here, but thankfully Cariña screamed in delight opening Moman L's unlikely gift of Paris couture. And I was back in – opening my own outfit. Cariña made us try them on then and there and model together in front of the tree for pictures.

Her effervescence, our glee at being happy together, kept the wave of the past frozen above us, lifeless, like the ghost pioneers suspended in the old city.

Moman L took snapshots from our overstuffed plum armchair. Holding Cariña's hand tight for our first shot together as Mother and Girl, I felt reborn. By the end we twirled and posed carelessly where Féy had once spun in a mass of gauze and jewels. Leaving the next day I hurt physically when I lifted my arms to hug her goodbye. So holding her tight, I made her promise we'd start a daily evening phone call.

Throughout the spring, those calls became my anchor – my day's bright light and purpose. After each close of the tail-spinning stock market that sucked down the last of my dreams of stock options, and my illusions of not being a fool, Cariña would always brighten my day.

After hearing about my triumphant reunion with my daughter, Mrs. Dennis insisted I call Cariña each afternoon – from upstairs in my smoky pink pearl guest bedroom.

After our hello's, sitting then pacing, I'd ask, "Well, what do you think about drugs?" or sex or cheating or shoplifting – always current topics, nothing about the past, nothing about our family, nothing about servers or owners.

"Please, mother. I'm a Cartier."

"You're a Cadot, Cariña. Beware foolish pride."

"Yes, Moman." With each call she became more relaxed and I became more certain in taking Mrs. Dennis's advice. A few of my obit profiles got in, none of them splashed much.

During finals and one of the first Enron blackouts in late May, Claire, one morning, found Verna Dennis dead in her sleep. Her voice quavered when she called me out of the shower.

That evening Walter came in with the family lawyer. Their voices and faces were drawn in the living room, as he said, "You've got 30 days Ms. Cadot, to make other arrangements. Your services are no longer required for my aunt." The way he said aunt told me not to expect an invite to her memorial, that I'd better say goodbye while I was here.

Upstairs after saying nothing unusual to Cariña I called Chuck, "My home here is gone." Graduation was in three weeks.

Three days and another blackout later the phone rang while I sat in robe and slippers eating two fried eggs, perusing classifieds amidst Mrs. Dennis's suddenly lifeless and cluttering stacks, being finally recycled slowly by Claire in her two weeks notice.

"Jeanne – she's gone. Moman L's passed," Cecile said. "She refused treatment." What? So close to Verna it could have been written. Gone without a word? But I recalled Moman L's fallen cheeks when she'd learned of Cariña. To her I'd already died long ago.

Cecile encouraged me to stay put. "We're fine, really. I can handle it, Jeanne. Cariña's got Davis and Jacqueline, her brothers. She's very strong you know - beyond her years - special. I'll be in touch on the will." She expected to be heir.

Cariña said, "She's happier now Moman. She's finally free from her pain."

And I broke down. At her tender age, my darling daughter knew more of my acting mother than I ever would. But the past took pity on me and stayed put. Still, I couldn't go home for the services, and prayed each night for forgiveness.

The night of the two memorials, Chuck came by, quietly helping me pack up in his steady, contained, competent way. But when our eyes met, we averted our gazes – without lively Mrs. Dennis, we felt naked, awkward. We'd had few conversations of our own we both realized, yet we knew we'd very little in common other than Mrs. Dennis. He left early, and we made no next plan to meet.

About a week later a registered packet from a New Orleans attorney arrived in the mail. It sat atop my mauve bedspread while I called Cariña, showered, changed, made dinner and then phone calls to apartment listings, then did my evening reading. I only opened it at midnight, lights all out but my reading flashlight, when I lay in my three-weeks-to-be-lost bed. Deep breaths kept my heart steady.

Mssrs. Metoyer and Rubicon
Attorneys at Law
13549 Esplanade
New Orleans, LA

Dear Ms. Jeanne Cadot Merciér,
It is with great sadness I write of the passing of Laetitia Cadot Merciér from natural causes in the New Orleans Parish of Louisiana on June 3, 2000. We have enclosed, as per her wishes, her last will and testament naming you as her sole heir and executrix. In the attached you will see her property divided as follows...

I got home, furnishings, possessions, including the Cadot letters, all 12 now being translated, annotated and preserved at Tulane. As I'd expected, Moman L had not sent a copy of hers to me. Neither had Féy left a letter behind. But Moman L had enclosed her rosary, that she'd worn and prayed with each day and which I kissed and wrapped 'round my troublesome wrist.

The feel of the worn carnelian beads brought back her long, strong fingers, her chicory and Eau de Lalique scent – and before I knew it, the dark wave deposited me.

On a sunny afternoon 'cross from the Ladies I'd helped Jacqueline, then a 17–year–old, unwed Creole beauty, to put on one of our new silk *tignons*, and my fingers brushed against the inside of her wrist.

First black, then clear as day, old Monsignor Paul hovered over Jacqueline in her crib. Wine lingered, his warm fingers cupped her feet and ankles, the wool of his robe nudging against the bare bottoms. He murmured prayers of sustenance, for strength, but slowly his hands edged up Jacqueline – my – legs.

Grown-up Jacqueline swiveled of out my hands and craned back from me, her eyes darting to my neck's bottom then my eyes, mouth taut as if she'd been caught or bit, "You all right Jeanne?"

Suddenly I could feel the Ladies disapproving eyes on me.

Moman L with her preternatural hearing turned, lifting her broad chin, and her eyes took us in from head to toe. "Jeanne, everything all right?" Moman L's voice sounded light, but ready to get heavy.

"Fine, ma'am." Several ladies didn't bother hiding their lifted eyebrows and pursed lips though their eyes averted.

"What'd you do then girl? Speak up." Alva scowled behind her.

"I said it was nothing." And I'd left for the back. That afternoon I'd avoided everyone, even myself.

So that night at Midnight Prayers – the Lord always hears pleas better from the middle of the night – Moman L, apron off revealing a soft, gingham patterned dress, sat on my bed, Bible in her lap, and took my chin between her strong fingers. She rattled my chin before tucking it away. She kissed the iron cross at the end of her old carnelian rosary.

"Moman L—...what's wrong?"

"*Bondje,* Jeanne," she crossed herself. From the back of her Bible she pulled out a letter on oilskin. She unfolded the page.

"Thanks to your mother I hoped never to have to tell you, but after today seems I must." She unfolded the page as though it weighed 50 pounds. "Mama Sarr herself writes in 1732.

"'In 1730 Bambara slaves logging cypress grew sociable with the Chickasaw who too longed to live free of the French. The Bambara swore they'd rebuild their crossroads empire here in the bayous. So the Indians taught them their bayou ways.'

She read the old Creole French as easily as English. Her moman, Marie, had read each of these letters to her many times over the years – traditionally that's how we'd passed ourselves along, ever since Mama Sarr traded herself to learn the alphabet and wrote the first Cadot biography. Moman L's eyes moved up to memory.

"From their strongholds they planned to take over New Orleans. By late summer all was in place. But Mama Sarr's eldest, the first Marie, then still a slave and young, bragged to a French soldier he wouldn't be alive to slap her much more.

"Her talk raised his suspicions. Investigation brought the eight rebel leaders to be broke on the wheel in Place D'Armes. They called them 'the betrayed Eight'. The girl herself was hung in front of them." Moman L stopped. "That much is already in history, *piti*. What's not...it's said, in retaliation, all her kin was damned.'" She squinted over her pearled reading glasses.

"'Let her family's seed be damned with only girls cursed with dark history's love. Let it destroy their families, let them be abandoned stoop and altar, let it whittle them to ones.'"

I breathed in slow. "Is it true?" I knew from Féy that Henry Lavalle, Moman L's only love and Féy's father, hoping to reap the benefits of national service, which had long freed and raised up our Creole men, had been killed in the Korean War before they'd even had a honeymoon – common enough then. And my father—but that was one of the things I did not think of.

"Girls for 15 generations and all of us have been left one way or another ...just like most."

I inclined my head to see the text, but Moman L snatched it back and replaced it in her bible. I folded my arms. "What does she mean by dark history?"

She lowered her head to kiss her crucifix. "It's the curse. We cannot touch anything or person that we see — we cannot speak to them or serve them. Even if they are somehow alive, telling them will not change or even appease the evil outcome — perhaps only hurry it along. Best we can do is to escape our 'gift'."

"So you have it?" She nodded, her fingers rolling beads. "My Moman?" A tear rolled down her cheek. "Moman L…" I reached to her. She pushed my hands away.

"I see folks' last rites, Jeanne. Only glimpses praise the Lord. But I saw your grandfather's every time he held me. All your mother could ever do is go far away. Better *not* to follow after her."

A pang of loneliness caused me to blurt, "Can I see the other letters?"

She watched the pendulum of the Black Forest cuckoo clock Féy'd brought. She sighed. "Your Moman read these letters over and again. Then she was lost *before* she died, you see? The curse is self–fulfilling. We've had only one child for two generations — we are 'whittled to ones'. It's your job to marry well then breed. I will not have you spoilt like Féy. And we'll never speak of this again. *Oui, piti*? You promise me?" Resolutely she withheld her touch until I nodded. Then she patted my thigh. "Let us pray."

I'd prayed God would make me attractive and fertile and no longer interested in history.

A sharp laugh from the outside on the street brought me back to the typewritten page. The will's date was the day after Féy'd died. In a recent codicil, Cousin Cecile got the right to lease and run the Ladies Hat Shoppe and Meeting Place. But I kept the right to all our things and the letters. It was a god send and that night I slept peacefully for the first time since she'd died.

The next day, I called Cecile, who to my query said, "Seems everyone these days wants 'crowns' from traditional New Orleans Creole milliners," she said. "We ship to L.A. and Atlanta and Japan. We'll be worn this year at the Image Awards. I want to open the second floor as a Creole museum."

I had her promise to ship me out a few pieces, and then I leased to her our house as well as the store.

That weekend Chuck accompanied me downtown. Though we were both still embarrassed, his arm still gave me anchor.

That very day, standing next to Chuck at plate glass windows that looked down to the old wharves become skyscrapers, I remembered Bridget "Biddy" Mason and her family of 13 who, when her owner tried to remove them back to Texas slavery in 1855, were ruled "free forever," and then Mrs. Mason had gone on to become one of the richest businesswomen in the state and one of its largest landowners.

So ignoring Chuck's warning about bloated real estate values, with nothing down I bought a 15th floor condo on Rincon Hill, the edge of the old city, beneath where the condor and near suicide had greeted me. Cecile's check would pay for the mortgage each month. Mine would nearly cover maintenance and living expenses. Perhaps up here I could finally be the strong, successful mother I daily dreamed of for Cariña.

Walking out with Chuck that afternoon, a few blocks north of my place toward Coit Tower and the city's dark past erupted. However, with creating a home amid constant deadlines, increasing political and dot bomb fears, today's world soon held long as I didn't go too near to old Chile Hill.

Early graduation morning, looking into Cariña's room all made up like some sort of voodoo charm, I said into the phone, "Shouldn't be long now, Cariña, my darling. You and I will together revive the Cadot."

"It'll be a bit." At her precocious words, my throat closed.

Truth be told, I was nowhere near the custody agreement threshold. The red couches and black lacquer end-tables covering my floor, were all still on my credit card. As were my framed Tanner, Bearden and Barth on the walls, the suits in my closet, and most of my used BMW Roadster, whose purchase like this apartment, had been a muddy, impulsive act of faith, of unwarranted confidence in my future.

"I'll be there *soon*." She didn't respond.

That day at lunch at Club Jupiter in SoMa, Clive asked, "How about a job as editorial assistant? Not a reporter's pay or stock options, but twice what you've got now – and you'll be able to submit free–lance outside."

With seven profiles published, I'd yet to get a front page. So, shaking hands I said, "Clive, you won't be sorry. I'll look for a Verna Dennis style scoop."

And that's what I failed at all summer.

In the shock of September 11th, without a blink or breath, re-maxing out a recently paid down MasterCard, I flew home wondering just as everyone 'round me, in what world we now lived.

Davis met me. As we drove down the I–90, his fine Creole green eyes – so like Cariña's, got to me right away. "Jeanne, you look good. You burning them up there in California?"

Gazing at his still young skin, pioneer photos and tales in Tulane Tilton library flashed, as did a proud and public prom invitation upon my return from the New York award ceremony, a pink orchid corsage, and our first eager kiss in his Cadillac's front seat facing the Mississippi.

"Coming along, Davis, just fine. How you all doing out here?" I tried to conjure Chuck's strong arm to lean on.

He stretched his chin. "We're just fine here. Thriving. In fact, Jackie, Cecile and I were wondering – you know with the Twin Towers and all…"

My heart suspended its beat.

"Well, it's just that we all love Cariña just to death. And she us. And I owe Jacqueline for all these years."

"What are you trying to say?" I avoided the vision of him pleasuring himself to young women in Catholic school uniforms, while he was deflowering me in his Seville's back seat.

"We've been talking about…adoption." He sped past an El Dorado.

Adoption. To Davis and Jacqueline – the Cartiers. So that was the new world. With my face hot as flame, I didn't speak the rest of the ride.

Cariña and I went for a walk late the next afternoon to Marigny's postage stamp park. Two boys rode by lazily and a bum sat on a far park bench. "So Cariña, my darling daughter, everything alright here with Davis and Aunt Jacqueline?"

"It's best with *Popa*—and the boys. And I love *sometimes* staying with Aunt Cecile and Moman L at the store."

I spoke slow, "Moman L?"

She smiled. "The dead aren't as far gone as they seem."

I'd heard this before in the red parlor from Féy, but I pushed it back and squatted to look up at her. "Did someone tell you that darling?"

She looked at me with flawless skin and shook her head.

"You know moman's here for you always, don't you? Are you looking forward to come to visit?" My voice cracked.

"Oh Momma, I can't go out there."

"What? Why not?"

She reached out to shift one of my new curls, for the first time bleached gold. "I'm the 16th Cadot, the connector."

"You're…what?"

"Just wait Momma." She tucked another lock. "Follow the twin powers. Wear your Christmas outfit."

"How do you know that Cariña?" I grabbed her arm.

She reached out and rubbed the inside of my wrist. "I saw them all my last birthday."

"All who? The Cadot? Féy?"

She gulped and nodded. I traced her face – its contours seemed aged – not lined, but structurally tired – she had remarkably thin cheekbones, but her gaze met mine straight on. San Francisco society matrons had learned to smoke cigars and wear pants over heavy boots from their daughters who'd learned it from the hookers…but this is too soon, I thought.

"Cariña," I spoke softly. "First time I saw my dead I was 10, just a year older than you. And it was right there – on Royal. We Cadot are tied to the dead and gone, but that doesn't mean we can't live." Her eyes widened and I glimpsed the girl in her.

I clasped her shoulders. "I'll be back for you soon and I'll take you with me, show you things in this world you've never imagined." I lightly tapped her chest. "Help you find yourself in the here and now. Then if you want to live here, fine. But first you must see some of the wide world. You mustn't grow up until then. Do you hear?" I loosed my grip, remembering how Féy's tight clasp last night alive had frightened me.

She nodded, swallowing.

"All right. Fine." She smiled a little.

Davis took me back to the airport.

I said, "No adoption. No way." No way I was giving up my only family – and he should know that. He and Jacqueline now had four sons.

His lips flattened. But then his eyebrows acquiesced as if he in some way understood.

When we invaded Afghanistan in late October, things seemed to right a bit. Davis had not yet served me with papers and slowly I began again to breathe.

Then two weeks after Enron's December ruin, Clive called Metro into his old world styled office. Despite his open window letting in a rare, Indian summer breeze, my skin prickled.

"Listen up folks. Our dot millionaire has lost all he's willing to." He raised his hands over the inhales and groans. "West

Coast Media Corporation has bought us and coming up from L.A. is Todd Hunter – architect of The Sheet." Now he spoke over protests, "West Coast's greatest success. I don't know him. But he's shallow, ruthless and next year we're a tabloid. We're officially on the dark side. Better gird your loins."

The groans dropped into silence. The Sheet *L.A.* never carried outright political issues. But would that work in San Francisco?

A week later Todd, sporting dark, spiky hair and an Armani suit, looked like a pro linebacker and out of place in our low ceilinged, seaside blue, SoMa offices. He announced, "I'm excited to be here. And you should be, too. A revolution is afoot. New media is going to turn traditional media on its head – with standards of truth and openness and sizzle are going to blow news into another level – requiring a new level in ourselves – and in our stories.

"To get the ball rolling, in two months a few reporters will be high–profiled – The Sheet *S.F.'s* 'Dream Team'. They'll do breaking stories, long–term exposés, international and social issue or political pieces. The kind of pieces that turn journalists into heroes, and news bureaus into legends. The kind that brings in subscribers who bring in advertisers."

A ripple ran through the staff. We wanted to hate him, but the dream was tempting – since most of us had just had our dreams of homes or our best life crushed.

But Todd wasn't done. "The team will be selected in three months. Take a look at who I'm looking for. Susan?" A put–together Texan with wavy auburn hair and killer body stepped forward and Todd cited her work in L.A. attracting high profile secrets, the kind of stories that normally would never be told.

I thought back to the twin powers. Among both the living and the dead, servers and owners, one could be ambition – and the other one, sex. At least I needed to try them, to try something sizzling.

The next two weeks, 15 folks were let go. Todd looked right past my smile in the halls. Rumors were 10 more bodies lay on the slate. Speculation ran wild about whom – even with Clive.

Past midnight on Christmas – Davis, family and Cariña being in Jamaica for this first holiday without Moman L – following Cariña's precocious advice, I tried on Moman L's last year's surprise Christmas couture and posed in Féy's old ornate silver mirror that Cecile'd sent out at my request.

Amaranthine tulle ran down to thick, satin pants with long, discreet side slits – like Féy, but more vivid. Gentle narcissus petals gently cupped my breasts, long green stems minimized last of my baby waist. I half expected to see her, but instead heard Moman L's frequent admonition, "Women without good work are just one step from being some man's whore."

But Cariña's words, and Féy's old, soft lilting, "Women bare less than most think with their bellies and their breasts, *dauphine*. Power always recognizes itself," drowned out Moman L and soothed my soul.

Then into my mind's eye floated our curlicue backstairs. So that evening I prayed to Féy, .asked for her support.

Three

"Dauphine," Féy's voice had startled me awake I'd thought, but then she and I'd soared out from the Golden Gate, through pre-dawn fog – 'cross the dark, empty bay toward Coit Tower. "Tonight it begins." Cold had whipped over my stretched out arms – covered in slick, black feathers. She'd stared at me through the condor's beady eyes.

The tower had loomed large and shadowy in the pre-dawn fog with only a few lights visible behind it. As we neared I grew terrified of what she might show me and Sophie's abandoned son haunted. I tried to veer away toward the hills, but Féy'd somehow blocked me. "Be strong, Jeanne. I'll stay with you long as I can." Then she'd guided me away from the tower down over the wharfs toward the quiet bay. "Moman L had her reasons for turning from the past. But our curse is not all dark, not all hopeless. We offer witness – and sometimes accidental expiation, atonement for those who can't rightfully ask for it. Still down into the dark sea, is where you must learn to go – and to come out again." She dove down and took me with her.

Just before we hit the water, in a blind panic, I'd wrenched away from her just as I had as a girl. I'd shaken myself awake to a headache and pastel plum sheets bunched in my fists, my mind and brow bunched tight with it. Today was far too long and important for me to start it with something that insane. I'd not even let myself think on it again until now, in full morning.

"Jean—*nie*," the high alto voice brought me back to the present, at almost noon. 100 feet in front of me underneath blood-red, satiny covers on a stately black oak, four–poster king bed, was Anna Kincaid – a high profile I'd finally won. She went on in a conciliatory way, "I didn't see you walk over. Would you please go back to the door and cross again? You can tell a lot from a person's gait."

Great granddaughter of Alex Kincaid, one of "Ralston's Ring", financiers of the city's first stock exchange and behind almost every early building and institution, Anna was known for making folks – and horses – jump. Since death of her father, Anna and her mother Pauline had run what he'd built into Kincaid Semiconductors. In her youth she'd been a ranked equestrienne. Now, at 58 Anna lay dying of breast cancer.

Across a massive floor toward the door, a pony-tailed, white-aproned Latina maid backed the cart away – but a smile lit her lowered face. I stared off through a slit in a black draped large window, down the wooded hills to the bay, gathering myself before I glanced to those black-blue eyes. "Look, Ms. Kincaid," the molded ceiling's echo captured the clicks of my Manolo knockoffs as I headed straight toward her. "You asked to see me. And I imagine you don't have all the time in the world. Nor do I. So shall we talk?" I pushed a large, carved, dark chair to her side.

She smiled then nodded. "Good. You'll need that."

"Pardon?"

"That sass you've got," her eyes leveled with mine. "You'll need it if you're going to find the truth." She sipped through a straw. "Would you like some tea?"

"All right." Her thumb sat upon a self-delivery button for the I.V. behind her—"Morphine sulfate" on the bag. "I'm no stranger to secrets, Ms. Kincaid."

She regarded me with clear baby blue eyes that contained sorrow worn so long it had become a familiar necklace, amidst a face fasted to its bones, its essence. "What, you are...25?"

"31."

She smiled; asked more softly, "Tell me Jeannie, what's the worst thing you've ever done? Ever lied on a story?"

"You ever lied to the press?" I'd spoken louder than I'd intended, more forcefully, hoping to push the gloom back. But I could see the gleam of a story in her intent, blue eyes, "No, I haven't lied."

"I'm not who most people think I am," her eyes glistened. "How do I know you won't spin me, leave out crucial facts? Like every other reporter."

Despite myself I bristled, "You've read my work." I'd sent her everything over the last few weeks.

"A bit cloying, sycophantic.... but there's...some yearning."

"Well, obit—my profiles are not investigative, but we strive for bal..."

"My obituary," she pronounced each syllable, sounding it out. "You can say it. I do. You know when I first felt my lump I cried. I knew about it for months before I told anyone. I wanted to die, I prayed on it. Can you understand that?" Her face set in a challenge.

Féy's early morning words wafted through my mind. So this time I dove, "I left my daughter behind me in New Orleans after hiding my true identity for eight years. Now she and I are the only ones left in our direct family and she knows me better than I do her – or myself. But I'm trying my damndest to change that."

For a moment her face froze. Her own daughter had died in Switzerland a year or so after her husband, and she'd only one child left alive. Her eyes filled. "I'm sorry, Ms.—"

"No, it's all right." She waved my pity away. "We are in

similar situations, being the kind one never forgets – or gets over...but I am worse off – you see I *do* know myself."

I leaned forward. "Ms. Kincaid, in my years of profiles, I've learned that our deepest truths usually only make it with us to the grave. If we're lucky, we tell our lovers at midnight...we might never even tell ourselves...or we blurt it out to complete strangers." Her laugh rang welcome as Moman L's St. Louis church bells. "The question is, as I'm sure you know – how forgivable do you find your own truth?" I blinked at this rant that seemed to come from somewhere beyond me. And she eyed me a bit.

"You're his choice," her voice broke then wandered, "You would have been. He always loved the underdog."

So that's why I was here. "Your husband?" I stood and moved closer. She'd married Edward Berne, controversial physicist ultimately exiled by Hoover's House Un–American Activities Committee in 1954. But after his and her daughter's deaths in 1973, she'd retaken her maiden name and position in the Kincaid family. Kincaid Planetarium, Kincaid Technology Center, Federal Judge George Kincaid, Supervisor Paul Kincaid, they were an institution in Santa Clara County.

Suddenly the far door swung wide revealing an imperious woman in a wheelchair, her patrician face held together by anger who, despite the distance, took in my pad and poised pen, and stared as though I was a dark stain on a new white shirt. "Get out! God damn you Anna." She thundered, though where all that voice came from I'd no notion. "No interviews. No journalists!"

"Mrs. Kincaid," I guessed, rising.

But Anna gripped my arm and hissed, "You want my truth? Shall you judge whether it's forgivable? I killed Edward just as surely as if I'd lit that fire myself. I thought it the only way to save my family. But I was wrong. Find my diary – at *our* family's home – our Heart's Home. Help him before it's too late."

"I said out," the angry aged queen's voice rose as she rolled 'cross the 100 foot wide floor.

"Well, thank you, Ms. Kincaid. Truly, it's been an honor." I spoke a little loudly. "I'll be in touch." And blessing the room's size, with a little smile at the oncoming Pauline, shaking her hand with both of mine, I brushed Anna's wrist.

The familiar black rushed up with a smell of burning. I popped through to Anna with her high cheeks drawn in, her eyes red from tears, her lips tight and trembling, sitting at a speckled-white Formica table. Behind her, feathered orange kitchen curtains distinguished dark walls from the night sky. A small candle lit her face from below. A thick manila envelope sat next to her. She looked back and forth at a black journal and a – forest green passport?

Finally closing the book, she lifted her face and startling blue eyes seemed to stare at the future. They held condemnation of everything, including herself – and despair. It was a look that I knew well how it felt. I felt my heart crack a bit. Then something rippled and blurred the air like green water rising, as it had on Royal.

Space rustled then thickened into a watch fob, a hand, a cuff, a sleeve with heavy buttons, a single breasted thigh–length suit coat and next to it a full–length, fancy dress – in broadcloth and muslin. The room filled with figures, as if all the old portraits had come alive. Lilla, James, the Incan woman, the stout black man and the white man with the mustache, but many more behind them. Some reached forward, others pounded fists. Suddenly stepping out front in her most delicately sewn, bone sheath stood Féy, eyes smiling, arms wide, holding them back, "Jeanne, it's time. Don't fight them when they come to you."

A physical yank jerked me back to the present, "I said get out, god damn it." Pauline Kincaid glared up at me, her one hand on my arm, the other out for my notes; she stopped herself from grabbing at the pad I'd instinctively snapped up from the red satin. A headache slammed in, stepping me back and bringing my pad to my chest as if to protect them both.

Pauline's gaze took me in from head to foot and suddenly Louisiana didn't seem so far gone.

But seeing my distressed disorientation, her pressure lifted on my forearm. "Are you quite well, young lady? Can you hear me? Nothing she says can be printed. Your paper couldn't afford it. You'd better to have some discretion."

"Jeanne," Anna's voice wisped my name in French from behind. I turned. Her face in the soft gold lamplight looked smooth, as she must've been in her youth, "Seek to know the truth – despite where it leads. Then your heart will come back."

I blinked, "Thank you so much Ms. Kincaid. I'll just show myself out." Pauline watched me and signaled the maid to shut the massive door and follow me out.

Down the hall my heart skipped with anxiety and glee. So Anna'd participated in her husband's death – and let the guilt take her to an early grave – and she wanted some expiation. Then she would not tell Pauline my name or paper. Most likely Pauline was not online news savvy.

And the appearance of the pioneers suggested Anna was of Féy's Ten. And though we'd not spoken of that this morning, or of the twin powers, clearly Anna was an owner. Perhaps the line between owner and server was not as hard and fast as Moman L had said. Perhaps Féy had been right about her.

Glancing up outside at the door, another servant I imagined backed away from an upstairs window leaving a curtain to settle. Assessing as the pony-tailed maid's soft, brown eyes, I pressed my cell number into her hand, "For anyone," I nodded at her then up toward the window, "who loved Edward. Ask Anna – alone – she'd appreciate it so much."

Waiting for my nerves to calm, gazing through the California pines and laurels down to the bay, I kissed the cross 'round my neck from Moman L's rosary. If Féy was right I might see her some time again, get her explanation.

Winding down into the little town of Woodside, I plugged in

my earphone, powered up my phone and turned the radio low,
singing to cheer myself up, chase away that gloomy dark sea now
that guidance through my world had shifted from Moman L to
Féy, "Oh, won't you take me to Funkytoowwn?!"

"Jeannie—" Recognizing my number on his phone, Clive
didn't even wait for my hello, "where the hell are you?"

"On my way home Clive. You won't believe what I got," I
beamed, "An admission—"

"I'm here with Susan." Hearing the ambient noise of a
speaker phone, I bit my tongue. Last week Todd's protégé's
article on the coffee elite had bumped my second approved
profile. Clive's tone was awkward, first time I'd ever heard that
and I turned down the radio and sat up straight and focused,
"Um, Jeannie, Susan here is gonna be..."

"Like your mentor." Susan's low Southern drawl wasn't a bit
fazed.

"What?" I braked behind a lane-shifting car.

"Mentor, darling. You know, show you the ropes. Todd
thinks you've got potential, but need some...well, like a
journalistic makeover." That bright tone suggested her bright
smile beamed through the phone. "You can run story ideas by
me and I'll help you to 'showcase the sizzle.'"

Now Clive's baritone had subdued anger driving it. He'd left
the last paper that had messed with his reporters. But today was
a new day and his dot dream, too, had gone up in smoke, though
his kids and their college needs remained. "You'll go to Susan for
investigative advice or when anything possibly hot comes up –
call *me* and her. She'll review your copy as well as me. Okay?"

"Okay, boss man." But my pounding heart belied my casual
tone.

"Good. Now what happened at the interview?"

I squirmed behind the wheel as I came down 'round the San
Francisco airport. "Oh, she admitted some regrets."

"Fuck regrets. Give us secrets."

"You know of course she's one of our largest advertisers,"

Susan spoke coolly as though reminding us to wash our hands before dinner.

Clive was as silent as I.

"I'll do what I can, boss man." Pressing end, despite my discomfort with a "handler" and what that meant for me and Clive, my pulse galloped – Todd had noticed me.

Back at the office I threw my red leather tote cross my office chair and turned on my green iMac, grimacing, having caught a glimpse of Clive 'cross the cubes and watching him turn away from me. If he saw me now as a threat then what did that mean?

The email came in: a corporate broadcast reminding of the bay cruise tonight – our holiday meet and greet with Todd – and subsequent griping jokes from staff – until one came up with no subject. It read,

> Jeanne Cadot,
> With the money due you, your debts have been paid.
> The Grey Hats

Hilarious. The Sheet staff had been notorious with their pranks since Todd came in. I went to delete, but my eyes ran 'cross the message once more. There was no signature, no blue text, no reply–to.

I grabbed my purse and pulled out a credit card and turned it over, but before I dialed, my mind's eye dangled darling Cariña. Every month with Cecile's check I barely made my mortgage. And once she'd been late causing me to panic as I'd not enough credit to cover the payment, having rung up 30 grand with student loans, my car, clothes and condo furnishings.

I hung up, printed the email and attachment, marked the message unread junk. I'd call later. I could say I'd never seen it.

The day's obits took me the rest of my shift.

That night, on my way to pick up Chuck, who'd moved downtown after graduation, I drove down Kearny toward Chile

Hill, first time since arriving. Driving here wearing Moman L's haute couture and Féy's antique peridot drop earrings, to go out for the first time on the water had me nervous as virgin on prom night.

The full moon rose through cloud cover above the East Bay hills reminding me of another shaded moon above the Mississippi's shore. But I dashed my eyes away.

Back in the Rush there'd been saloons and gaming houses all along Kearny. Six brawls each day, a successful murder here at least each week. I eased up for a light at California—beneath the giant black and mauve Bank of America building, San Francisco's tallest. So far so good keeping my world on top, but then...

The air wavered, grew thick and green just like on Royal or at Anna's. All down Kearny board sidewalks swam in – on them The Morgue, The Slaughterhouse – rough–board brothels, fandango parlors – a hundred ways to lose your hard–earned gold. Men loitered or passed outside sporting Van Dyke beards and hats like my five though I didn't recognize anyone. Poking from some facades were barmaids, shirts cut low or buttons loosed as their expressions – owners requiring them to drink with the customers. Some looked unrepentant, some worn. Some laughed with disdain, a few leered with bravado, but the tones were so exaggerated as to suggest a well hardened act.

Next to me instead of a speckled plaza, a roof of redwood deadfall lay 'cross what looked to be a cellar dug in the ground. The Devil's Dance Hall a charcoaled sign proclaimed. I remember it described by 1850's police as "the wickedest place in the wickedest city", it was a clubhouse for pimps, junkies they called hopheads, and thieves whose specialty was robbing drunks after knocking them out.

Suddenly the Incan woman from Royal in her voluminous grey, mud-splattered skirts beneath a bowler hat walked out from some unseen door to the place, a cigar clamped between her lips. She pinned her black eyes on me and began walking.

I gripped the wheel I no longer saw, and shut my eyes, shook my head. When I opened up again, the scene had shimmered away, leaving the sparkly, Bank of America plaza.

A cab behind me honked. My watch read 7:20, the boat would leave in 10 minutes. Cursing, I hit the gas, ignoring timed flashes of the mad, hatted Incan woman keeping pace with the car until she stood working her cigar on a muddy corner in front of a buxom gal with pretty, but stained peasant blouse. In my rear view mirror she stared after me.

I screeched into Chuck's driveway on Chile Hill – Sansome above Enrico's, the Green Tortoise and the closed Finnochio's. I shook my chin, squinted and tightened my jaw to put to rest the glimmering wooden shacks, large canvas tents, packing–case shanties and few two–story buildings. Coming out of one I saw Féy and the Incan woman, behind them a group of pioneers.

In front of them, rising from his retaining wall Chuck removed his hand from his sports coat—brown plaid with flecks of desert sand.

"Hey there Chuck–a–doodle–do," I lilted hoping the scene would vanish.

He looked at me as if worried I might have had a few. I had downed a bourbon neat after ·putting on Féy's earrings. "Need me to drive?" I rattled my head. He bent his 6' 1" frame to fill the entire passenger side. We left a light black skid as we squealed away from the coming throng.

"Sorry," I pursed my lips, "Will be my first time...on a boat...I mean since I was born. I'm a little nervous."

Chuck shot me a second look. I'd not shared any of my past with him, nothing of Féy, Cariña or Moman L and I wasn't going to start now. He nodded, nursing his own secret I suspected.

In silence we pulled into Pier 26 beneath Coit Tower under where Féy and I had flown this morning. Soon as I saw the *San Francisco Belle*—three full decks garlanded with white lights—my pulse began to dance. Salty dank filled my nose; nerves spiked down the nape of my neck.

A seagull cawed as we approached and I looked up. The full

moon rose above Treasure Island behind scattered clouds, just as it had 19 years back. When I brought my gaze back down I stared at the *Belle* gently bobbing, but I saw the *Mississippi Queen*. I turned from it, grabbing Chuck's elbow.

At the foot of the ship we stopped for a photo. During the flash I saw green gauze behind the light – and the shadow of numerous pioneers. Silently I swore. This night would be hard enough without them.

A Latin swing version of "Winter Wonderland" started onboard.

"You ready?" Chuck's grip on my waist brought me back.

"As I'll be." I took a deep breath.

Congo drums beat loudly in my chest when 'round the corner we came to the sparkly grey gangplank, so short you could almost miss it. I smelled burning metal beneath the salt, and saw green mist wrap the ship. My mouth dried as written on the Belle's midriff, *HMS Lawrence II*, the name of the ship in my old secret photo, shimmered in and out. I gripped Chuck who looked at me sharply.

"Wait." I forced my gaze down and let the head rush rise, but it did not evaporate, rather opened into a thick, wide consciousness, with seemingly Chuck, Féy and Lilla all egging me on. So with stomach clenched and mind's eye firmly on Cariña, I crossed myself, kissed my rosary, and then we crossed.

Chuck held me stiffly. Cold bubbled through my legs to arms and torso as I passed over the bay and through the ominous green membrane. I didn't dare to look down or look at Chuck.

Once we entered the main chamber, linen–clad tables with orchid centerpieces flickered into view, along with sparkling sterling and crystal settings all down the main hall. Halfway down a white–suited band played against a wine red curtain – similar to that of our old parlor – and ornate iron lamps reached up to brass–plated ceiling tiles.

Darkness loomed outside – no skyline – but small, green-tinged fires dotted dark hills. I stopped.

Offering the perfect rear profile a woman stood in bone chiffon deep in conversation with the Indian woman who, though shorter than Féy, was draped and shapely in stitched black, and the tall, Van Dyked white man whose eyes flicked up to me. They stopped arguing, all turned and Féy pushed a young, welcoming smile past a look of frustration.

She'd looked the same the night she cruised away forever. My heart raced. I didn't see Lilla or James, but were all these others my Ten?

Behind her the grey and black–suited pioneer crowd mingled around a white–linen, be–flowered table, laid haphazardly with dishes and food. Above it a banner hung, "*HMS Lawrence II Inaugural.*"

Chuck's warm hand joggled my elbow and the top lit Ferry Building and Embarcadero skyline grew back in outside the windows. White and burgundy–draped buffets ran down the center, a sport–jacketed band set up in front of parquet dance floor. Red linen tables scattered the deck filled with some reporters sporting black armbands to symbolize unity with the downsized 15.

Glancing at my feet I saw no vapor 'round them and was relieved. I held onto Chuck waiting for reality to settle – starting with the fact of the unseen wall seemingly grown between us. Now we didn't even share the awkward connection of embarrassment.

Out of the corner of my eye near the main bar, a white–gloved black man in a tuxedo, his hands rolling a hat, stared at me. His gaze felt cool, but his face was in shadow.

Next to him Clive walked with Mavis, bureau office manager, an ample woman the color and smell of dark French perfume. Catching sight of me, she nodded and smiled.

I turned to Chuck, "Be right back." Passing a waiter I noticed his uniform was wine red. And he'd no high white collar with a front V and tightly knotted tie.

Past the bar there was still no sign of the staring man, so I ran up the stairs. When I got there a row of three lavatories faced me. The rest of the floor was dark. I looked inside each small room. Nobody. The last I slid into myself, stared into the mirror at the star birthmark, tonight looking like a pendant. Well, let's get over with. Now would be an appropriate time. But the mirror didn't tinge, will it as I might.

It wasn't till I'd refreshed my blush and my coat fell back revealing the curve of my left breast that Féy appeared translucent upon my reflected face, "Don't be scared, *dauphine*. I'm here with you."

"And why should I trust you? You jumped in the middle of the ocean rather than be with me. Now you're back – with them – you're all stalkers."

She downcast her eyes, when she looked up again they were softer, "I was twisted up inside, *dauphine*. No good for anyone. A last fool."

"How do you know that?"

"I'm with you often now. So I can be there when you need me."

"Then who was that pioneer man downstairs?" I demanded. "He looks familiar."

She grimace-smiled, "We're told little to nothing of our sight – we must discover its purpose ourselves. I found mine in the letters. I know you must look through your shame and I'm not strong enough yet—" She vanished.

Left with my own split brow and famous dimples of the Cadot mistresses and whores – I scrounged in my tote for my emergency shot of Maker's Mark.

As the shot tingled down my arms and legs, I pulled off my coat. Wavy white silk narcissus petals cupped my breasts. I could feel the fine yellow sequined pistils against the mesh. My 5 feet 8 inches didn't look or feel like my own. It looked like...Féy, some early backstairs Cadot?

I pinched my cheeks hard, applied more powder, lipstick, and Chanel over my warmly beating heart, then humming "Oh, little town of Bethlehem" along with a faint rumba, I pushed out the cabin door.

Coming down the stairs I ran into Todd, impeccable in double–breasted, navy, pinstriped Brooks Brothers. He was walking up the steps with Susan and some redhead knockout; both wore plunging necklines. His eyes flicked over me with a set grin, but then he stopped. He extended his hand, "Jean?"

"Jeannie...Cadot." His warm gaze and palm ease me into a reclined stance like Féy's so long ago with Alfonse. "Metro with Clive. Obits? End of life interviews?"

He nodded. "From New Orleans?"

I leant my head and breathed deep to calm my heart.

"Clive speaks well of you. I see why. You look...great. Is that...?"

"Valentino."

"Valentino?" He sounded surprised. "What are we paying you?"

I smiled. "It was a gift."

I could see my cachet rise with his eyebrows. "Ah, then your husband?"

"No sir."

"Oh. Well, your boyfriend?" He held up a palm. "Sorry. None of my business."

"My grandmother."

"Really! And your date?"

"I'm with...a friend." I hoped we were still that.

"Oh, I see. Then maybe later – a dance? I'd like spend a little time...Clive speaks well of you." I saw the redhead shoot Susan a look and I stood a bit more arched, slightly held out those delicately cupped breasts. After a very polite nod, with a little push on Susan's lower back, Todd continued up the stairs. But not before he ran a hand down my arm. Cloaking myself in a smile I descended.

Downstairs Chuck was nowhere to be seen, so I headed for the coat check where I heard my name rumbled.

I wheeled 'round beaming, "Mavis. Darling. You look good as a chocolate praline. And this ship...the band. Fine work." The ship's motor revved and the boat moved from the dock with nary a lurch. I kept my eyes from the windows.

Mavis, once S.F. Eye's – now The Sheet's office manager and unofficial counselor, and my closest thing to a friend, stretched her well–made–up eyes. "And you, my dove. Look like you need to be quenched. What man we going after tonight?"

I grabbed the outstretched bourbon neat she offered. "One guess, Mave. Can we get to this? I've a feeling I'm going to need it tonight."

She inclined her head and we chanted, "May those that don't kill us make us rich." Then we lifted our glasses. The rush of warmth immediately quelled my discomfort.

Clasping her, we turned our backs on the cloakroom's tanned skins on hangers and crossed the foyer toward the main chamber.

Rectangular windows ran 'round the sides of the bottom deck. In them white linen tables and copper fittings occasionally glinted, but the view beyond that was the Ferry Building, the Embarcaderos, the Pyramid and Pier 39, even the orange lights of the Golden Gate.

Mavis leaned in, spoke close over the smell of Givenchy and smoky bourbon, "One ought to at least warn a person." She indicated my outfit, "When one is...stepping out." Mavis had long ago taken me beneath her comfortably jaded wing.

I raised my palms, "Oh this? Read Dream Team, Mave. My sizzle is showcased...Render unto Caesar...When in Rome, etc."

Mavis cocked one brick red eyelid. She'd worked with Clive for 10 years and sometimes I wondered if she reported back to him. So I squeezed her arm and down my cocktail.

At the u–shaped bar a bartender in red vest came over to us, "Two Maker's Marks, rocks, please."

New spirits in hand we walked upstairs to the observation deck. I saw Todd, and stiffened when Clive—French-collared purple Oxford beneath his Italian black—walked toward him.

My left thigh spasmed; I rubbed my frosty glass against it leaving a tiny damp mark.

"So, tell me," Mavis jiggled her drink. "How's Chuck?"

I wrapped my fingers tight 'round my glass, "Pretty sure he's got something to tell me."

"What's that, Sweet pea?"

I turned. "Take a good look Mave. Is this the face that launched a thousand relation-ships?"

"Funny. Those eyes sparkle like they've got gold in 'em. And those plump, kissable lips, that birthmark." She cocked a brow, "You know Stephanie would pay for those?" Then she blushed, but hid it, "She's told me so."

Giving us both time to recover I worried my head, scouting the room. I still didn't see pioneer man. In fact I saw nobody.

"But you've got more than that, Jeannie. Maybe it's being Creole, but there's a grace, a purpose…and you spent an awful lot of time with a man who didn't seem to *recognize*. I'm glad to see *you* finally are." Her highball waggled.

"Mavis…" I reached out and touched the double-paned window and when I did the green tinge rippled out as though I'd put my finger in a pond. I drew it back. "I'm not to have a man. At least not yet – I may be able to change it – the Cadot curse. That's why I'm out here."

Mavis's reflected turned down lips and skeptical brow said, "Oh, really."

And so I turned and we took seats at the long table behind us. I kept the windows in my peripheral view. "I've never spoken on it, but tonight, I'm trying out some new things as you see." I waved three fingers sidewise—sign of the *sorcière*. "One of them's as much of the truth as I can bear. In 1764, Marie Madeleine Cadot, still a slave, being beaten, boasted of an upcoming slave revolt. With her report, slaves *and* freed were captured, torn apart on the wheel.

"Since then we Cadot have been 'All girl *piti* cursed with dark history's love and so left stoop or altar.' It's been a fate within which we've learned to stand. In 15 all–girl generations, only a handful of Cadot woman have married, some tragically like my Grand Moman, a few others to great shame. The rest of us have been spinsters, mistresses...or high-tone prostitutes."

Mavis just stared. After a moment I bent my head left. I nodded toward Todd who now chatted to Susan. "You know she's been made my mentor."

Mavis's mouth shrugged. Still her eventual smile carried sad respect, as if she'd just learned I was older than she'd thought.

Taking our drinks out to the windy front deck, to avoid looking down, I glanced up to a window on the captain's deck. The man in a high–collared, long–coated black tuxedo raised a lantern to his face. In the full, bare, greenish light I knew him.

Henry M. Collins had started on the Ohio River just like William Ralston, only he'd been Free Black from back East. He'd made a small fortune here as ship's steward between the city and the Gold country, until he'd raised enough to become San Francisco's largest Black landowner. Also one of the state's best fundraisers, he'd started *The Mirror of the Times*, the first African American newspaper in the 1850's. He'd also been part owner of the first *Lawrence*. He must be James's father – could he also be part of the Ten?

"Mavis," I felt each syllable as it came out and dissolved the man, replaced him with a smokestack, since the Belle's bridge was further back as befitted a bigger ship. "Have you ever heard that there are twin powers in life?"

"AC/DC you mean? Electric or magnetic? ESP and physics? Gay or straight? Street or board room?"

"I always thought power was like a light switch – on or off; alive or dead, owner or servant, but I'm beginning to wonder." She half–laughed and I turned back to her, grimacing, "Let's hope it's male and female. Tonight I've a barracuda to catch."

"Well, you've got the right bait. I do know one thing about power on earth."

"It radiates from within?"

"I know you can fake it. Wear that dress like you're all that and you will be."

"It's a pantsuit. But I sure hope so. I've got to get to Todd tonight. Speaking of visions, Mave, you see that?" I rose and moved toward the rear of the ship, beyond which passed Alcatraz, and I saw a man, greenish white and struggling against a mighty sea. The sight surprised me, since our ride was so calm.

"What do you see, Sweet pea?"

The whisper of green moved steadily through the water, rough in his time, calm in ours. I turned wildly, instinctively going for help. Suddenly, in the lime windows, formally dressed men and women crowded in great agitation, speaking to each other in anger. Metal burned somewhere and green vapor rose up from Bay.

The man struggled – I could see clear as day when he went down. He didn't come back up.

"Jeannie," A blurry Mavis waved in next to me. "I don't see a thing."

I downed my Mark and blinked my sight clear of tinge and dead; took her hand from my warm, damp bare shoulder. "No Mavis, I see now it was just the beacon – a trick of the eye. Come on, now, I must need sustenance."

As we stalked inside to a table, I remembered – William Chapman Ralston, who swam daily in the Bay, often to Alcatraz, had drowned the day of a run on his bank. He and Henry Collins weren't in the original photo. So, if all Ten were dead, perhaps I only had to figure out the remaining three.

Relieved, I ate, joked and drank my way through a smooth garlicky Caesar salad, a spicy chicken cacciatore and fluffy rice with dark green broccoli. Mavis knew how to get the best and wasn't going to mess around when people's jobs were on the line.

I snuck a glance now and then at the windows and saw green past lick at the edges, but more Chianti contained them.

By the time we crossed the room to rejoin Chuck, I felt a bit the roll of the ship, but the green past was easily blinked out.

With drunken bravado, I even tossed a head toward the windows, as if daring them to bother me.

"Jeannie, well, well," Mike Carruthers sat next to Chuck. Bureau staff called Mike "Blowhard" for his unending, seedy stories; a collection he termed 'Life in the Big Shitty,' tales that celebrated the worst of humankind. He'd covered investment banking for 10 years and over there they loved his bawdy English bits. Chuck talked with him to get the dirt on the street. He must have been sharing a bad one, for after nodding "hi," Chuck flushed and kept his eyes down.

Mike, on the other hand, could not take his eyes off. I had to grin.

"You look *fine*," he said, settling one arm over his chair back as I took the empty seat next to them. "I was just telling your boy, Chuck," he clapped Chuck on the shoulder and Chuck winced. "I was just telling Chuck of my new favorite videos - regular women stripping for the camera. Luckily women's clothes are so easy to get off. Thank you for so nicely proving my point."

"You boys make it so hard...easy." I tightened my jaw hoping it would right my words.

Mike laughed. "But what you're doing, it's worse than affirmative action. To a pair of breasts we're reduced to our sexual DNA. We *must* want it. And you lot take full advantage." He ogled me again. "Not that I'm complaining."

"You want it. And then you hate it – because you want it. And did you hide your strength on the golf course last Mon—, no Tuesday, Tuesday night?" The liquor was beginning to be hard to hold. But Mike had gone with a competitive Sheet group that had begun meeting each week at the driving range. According to Mavis, Todd was impressed with his swing. He was shoe–in for the new Dream Team.

"You girls want to play in a man's world?" He clapped his chest, fell back against his seat. "You got to learn our rules. Like learning the language. Tonight you're doing great. I love our new tabloid world."

The words chased each other out of my mouth righting my speech. "25 million of us are managers and professionals. And some of us have been for centuries. I'd say we're more than just 'hot bods' or racks'."

"Oh really, and what great value have you added to our economy this year, Jeannie? I mean aside from that dress. How much money have your obits and occasional, sad, sycophantic profiles put into anybody's bank account?"

His words slid like cold blades between my ribs. Just then I caught sight of Todd three tables over. With him sat Clive and Susan, heads together. "Blowhard, when you're right, you're right." I rose, steadying myself against the boat, the swimming past, and the liquor.

Appearing from nowhere to scoop my elbow, "Talk to Todd next week," Mavis hissed low, turning me away.

But in that moment, the skipping of a Paso Doble, tipped up and out of me a Gold Rush historian's most famous line, "There are also some honest women in San Francisco, but not very many," I announced, "I'll dance with him tonight."

I popped a peppermint and wobbled up, wrestling free of Mavis's grip. A slight ship's sway knocked me off balance. "Come on now Féy," I whispered, "This is your turf, not mine."

This time when the black wave came I did not fight as it washed me back to our red parlor, long before any Christmas tree. This memory must have come from Féy – whatever skill I owned in evading the dark sea now had been built from the days and years I'd spent avoiding this.

It had been one of those Southern nights where the damp heat never ebbed, not even past midnight, and the lazy ceiling fan in the second floor red parlor created the only, thin breeze. I'd been reprieved from evening Bible read because Féy had come to town with Alfonse.

I'd awakened to a burst of laughter, a clink of glass and a man's low, sometimes barking laugh. The door to my room –

Moman L always left it ajar – had swung open. The heat had stifled, the laugh had rung. So I'd slipped out.

Moman L lay steady breathing in her room at the end of the hall. She kept the door open, but she wouldn't wake with her earplugs and nighttime pills. She preferred to give her fallen daughter's *placer* a wide berth.

I tiptoed down the long grain floors. Féy had the parlor's old *fleur de lis* floor lamps lit, and had draped the ceiling tall stands with filmy scarves. An oil lamp burned on the mantel. The red wallpaper shimmered off gold. Thick red velvet curtains closed off the view to Esplanade and potted ferns laced them with shadows.

Féy'd worn a sparkling gold–magenta turban and sat on a backward chair facing her audience of two. One bare foot laced the chair's leg, the other had dangled free, and glimmering scarves had cascaded all 'round her. Drums had beat softly on the Victrola – an African beat with strings that I'd never before heard.

"You know, Monsieur Ballantine," Féy's dulcet voice, just shy of a laugh or song, teased in time to the rhythm. "You best be careful. The dead are not always so far gone as they seem. Especially in New Orleans." A low voice chuckled from the young man fully reclined in our plum velvet easy chair.

Behind him a tossed finger released a sharper voice, "Begin Féy."

Without taking a beat, she began to move in time with the sweet minor accordion, in harmony with a violin melody straight from the streets of Buenos Aires I dreamed. A leg hooked, an arm made a slow arc. As the accordion began complex chords beneath the fiddle, she moved faster. She stood and twirled, spun the chair, interwove in and out of its legs, swapping hands invisibly. She and the chair, the accordion and the violin, all became a whirl of gauze and gold. My head felt dizzy. Finally, as the fiddle leapt up an octave to sing its melody, she raised the chair high above. Glittering scarves twirled and twisted until you could see her at the center no more. She spun with the violin's mad finale. At the music's sudden end she dropped 'cross the chair's lap, chest heaving.

One of her sparkly nipples escaped. My hand flew to my mouth. She wore only filmy scarves and gold chains 'cross an otherwise bare, glittering chest.

The young, low–voiced man, rising, burst into hurrahs. Féy sprang up and ran to the one who didn't clap, a hard–looking, handsome face against the brick fireplace. In front of him she bowed. Again my mouth flew wide.

And from there I pulled my slightly more sober self back to the dark, then the *Belle*. The dance had been the point tonight.

The quartet untwined their heads as I approached.

"Jeannie," Clive raised his brows, assessed my stance, accentuated by the boat's loll.

"Clive," my chin fell. "Todd. Havin' a good time?" Polite murmurs came through. Todd leaned back and slowed his chewing. The champagne-fizzing through me increased. "That's wonderful, terrific." I leaned in close to Todd and purred in my best Southern voice, "I wonder Mr. Hunter, would you like to have…that dance?" The words felt slow in my mouth, but they plopped out in order. I could sense every eye at the table on me, happily even Susan's date – a man who sat next to her in a black suit. My vision wavered.

I tried to focus on Todd as he brought his napkin to his lips and murmured, "Excuse me," but a shadow behind him caught my eye and I rose back up.

A line of dark–suited men and long–skirted women stood en-greened in the windows all 'round the deck. There were many more than Ten. They watched Todd and me patiently. As we walked past them to the dance floor, they flowed out onto our deck, flooding the place with an invisible, turbulent sea giving off a green vapor. And in their midst, facing me, in her bone white sheath stood Féy, slowly turning green from the hem up.

When we hit the dance floor to a spicy salsa, behind Féy

James appeared with his hand on Lilla's back – they both stood terribly still. Todd's arm circled me much more formally than had Davis, and the tall Van Dyke bearded man rolled in working his handlebar mustache. As we began to spin, the well–fed, dark man stood vested, dagger–eyed and straight–backed, his hand on the Indian woman's back, her head inclined to one side. They were all waiting for something from me. I was on stage in two times. The impossible sea rose to my knees. Old-time dancers got into position 'round us.

Still Todd's guiding hand showed me I had his full attention and that my reality still played on. Luckily the band shifted gears into a Little Drummer Boy rumba. Best as I could I fixed on Todd. He spun me with a grip mercifully tight, his frame hard.

As the water rose 'round our at first slightly awkward whirling, Féy, clear as day on the simple, old deck, eyes on me, appeared behind Todd and began to sway. It recalled old times, me mimicking her 'round the red parlor.

The living were all but gone as the ring of dark suits turned and danced over our blurred green tablecloths. I pivoted my attention back to Todd's tight hands, the march of the timbales.

The music segued into a cha–cha. I closed my eyes and sped up my feet – watching myself dance-chase Féy backwards past the mantel, the curtains, the plum chair. My body received the trumpet's blasts like heat. Féy's voice rang in me, as it had then, "You must push yourself, *dauphine*. To have real living." Todd spun me and let me go alone.

Black sleeves, shined cufflinks, rough cotton, and bone white chiffon, gauze and skin, as well as our old oriental rug, they all moved in – I couldn't gain my bearings back in my time.

"They can't touch you directly, Jeanne. They can only hitch a ride or give a message to someone who loves you – who has a right. It's easier for them here on the sea."

Of course, on your tomb, "But what are they waiting for?"

"You must learn to never fully submit."

After what I hoped were Féy's best solo moves, Todd

thankfully found me again. We began the same series of steps over. In my mind now I danced with Féy back in our old parlor.

"Inside you, Jeanne. Your hidden shames - you're stronger with them than without. We know this once we pass. Name them and their power ebbs — *own* them and their power becomes your own. It's true for a country, a person, or a family."

"But how do you do this?"

"Embracing the truth, Jeanne, even the less pleasant parts, shall make you free — as the Bible says. But it won't be easy."

"What do you mean?"

"You must find a way to accept the truth of your life — not the dream." At the end of his series again, Todd let me go.

And I danced amidst the grey suits, who edged ever closer. Some of them mouthed things insistently to me, others pointed at various things, but it simply increased their green-tinged eeriness. I wanted to fight, to kick my way back home. And that's when I felt something like a rush in of that old dark river, this time bringing warmth with it.

When the brass section began to bleat, I swept my leg in pure defiance and I saw a red tablecloth flash. So, my hips snaked my anger, adding a dash of anxiety about Todd and an entire table appeared. I circled my hips to disappointment about Chuck and Clive, and I caught a glimpse of them both standing with hands on their chairs, their eyes and necks craned at me.

The band accelerated into a *merengue*. I skipped my despair about leaving Cariña, about Moman L dying without a word. I stomped feet to Féy's suicide; undulated arms to her topless chest; wrist-flicked out her leaving me in the old sewer to get filled with shames. Each wave of my emotion cleared the past away.

My palms slapped. I ran a hand down my slick torso, wrenched my head to the right and leant back. The outfit's long side slits opened, and air cooled the length of my thighs. My red–lacquered fingers beckoned like Féy's to Alfonse all those years back. I arced toward the night sky, shimmying, calling down my time to rain on me. The tulle became a hot net against my chest, stomach, hips. The trumpets triple tongued.

I pumped out the thwack of the Faucheaux boys' thrown water balloons and Fayette's guilty smirk. I threw the Cadot curse and Cariña's distance out my fingertips. Then re-opening my eyes, suddenly my world was back though blurred, as though the green vapor had risen to the top.

The band suddenly dropped into an Argentine tango. Thick ripples the color of Mavis flowed from the stage.

And right then a shadow crossed my face, a cool and loose hand took mine. Through thickened air, I saw a French–cut, single–breasted black suit. I caught eyes the twilight blue just before the sky goes dark – a hue deeper than Anna Kincaid's. I told myself it was Todd. It just had to be or I couldn't think what, or who or from what time. I screwed my eyes tighter. Still, it didn't lessen Todd's touch, which relaxed in pace, reassured me.

First firm on my left hand, he encircled my exposed back with his right. His hand spread against my bare skin, his fingers wrapped my waist. Wherever he touched my muscles slowed, the boiling receded, the emotions and images calmed.

He placed his fingers lightly on my left hip and revolved me into a close, brief spin before turning 'round again. Before I knew it we paused and glided spun, in the old street tango, the Orillero – a favorite dance with Féy.

Now fireflies flickered all through me, a night sky replaced the *Belle's* faux brass ceiling tile. And with Todd's touch everywhere guiding me, the flow between us blanketed the others, the concerns, the emotions. All became our shared movement, the dance.

He drew my hand in along his surprisingly cool, dry face, settled it onto his shoulder, and then he wheeled me out then back again. The band stretched and bent. With his right hand, he pressed along my back. His forearm ran up my spine cradling my head. He lay long over my torso and lowered me down.

Once there, he bent as if to kiss and caress my throat. Instead, his palm hovered; he blew cool air all 'round my chest. Opening my mind's eye – I saw faces leaning in, smiles insistent, grimaces demanding, the condor's black beads pressing.

After a second watery current out of me, Féy leant between the others, her neck tense, her chin insistent. "Do you see now, *dauphine*? That's real living – perfect tension. Riding the twin powers." Behind her they all leaned in further. All of us were being pulled down into the watery green sea – down into the dark past. Suddenly I wanted to scream.

So once he brought me back up, I threw my arms 'round Todd's shoulders and pressed my face deep into his black velvet lapel.

Eyes shut, his arms wrapping silence tight 'round me, I swirled in black. No more encroaching ring, no more memories, green vapor, dark wool suits, bone white sheaths, no more shames, or black beaded eyes - only Todd and I turning in the pitch-black night. I pressed deeper into the void, willing, with all my thumping heart, to stay there. It was the last thing I remembered.

Four

In the early morning light before waking, vague, undulating black shadows separated away from a twilight blue background then reunited again. It reminded me of last night's blue black eyes and I leaned in, but a strident doorbell cut through the cool hands, dark swirling, and thick velvet lapel. I snuggled in even more seeking escape, calm before the storm I sensed coming.

The bell buzzed again. I opened my eyes. The twilight blue remained – all 'round me. I sat up. I was alone in a wide room ending in floor to ceiling windows onto my same view, but clearer as if they'd just been washed inside and out. A navy couch faced the windows and balcony beyond them. The light blue sheet fell forward. I was naked except for my amaranthine bikinis; my Valentino strewn 'cross the unused side of the bed. I heard voices – two women's – coming toward my door. Grabbin' the sheet to me, scrabbling up the one-piece, I tried to piece together how I got here. I remembered little or nothing after the black velvet lapel.

There were two sharp knocks and the door pushed in. "We'll be out in two shakes of a Castro boy's tail," a gravely voice said. "Good morning, Sunshine. I've brought gifts." Pushing the door wide from a lush velour jogging–suit adorned with 14, 18 and 24 carat gold chains, Mavis held out a tray with coffees and a pastry bag. From her hand dangled a pair of jeans, top and sandals – all mine. I'd never been happier to see a gal.

"I just came to return your car and keys and I stopped by your apartment on my way up. How are you feeling today?"

I accepted the coffee first – Peet's black, it was bracing and it cleared my mind right away. I shimmied into my coral tee and remembered the frantic solo of the previous night. As I jumped up to put my pants on, I tossed my head and mouthed, "Who again?"

"Oh, I told Ms. *Witt*, Marcia, we'd be out in a minute."

Marcia Witt who ran 'round with the Getty's? Her mother, Marlena's obit had run on those crisp, barren days after Moman L had died – she'd lived in Europe and San Francisco. So her daughter was a friend of Mavis's? Clive's? Perhaps Todd's. Shimmying into my shirt, I grabbed the coffee again. Mavis offered the pastry bag. "Can we do that down at my place?"

"I can't stay too long. Stephanie's downstairs. We're off to the Cliff House for lunch and I want to run by Nordie's first." Mavis and her roommate, Stephanie, were inseparable and more than just friends, though she never spoke to me of it.

Really I did not want to talk about last night at all. "It shouldn't take long." I adjusted my belt and smoothed out the bed. "Should I take these sheets off?"

Mavis shrugged. "I'm sure they have help." She walked 'round the room as I hastily straightened the sheets and blankets.

On the low end table in the far corner – beneath hardback books covered in two week's dust, out stuck an old black and white photo. The minute I saw it I hit the stack of black Mathematics titles with my elbow, knocking the picture free and the sleek, metal alarm clock radio over in the process. "Oops, I got it."

On the deep navy carpet, there lay a shot of a couple dressed for their wedding: he in the mid–thigh, square cut coat of the 1860's, she in an infinitely quilted and gathered trained dress; both wearing white cotton gloves. I blinked. It was my Indian mujer, her eyes pierced over a tight Mona Lisa smile, and the dark well–fed black man. Husband and wife. Just like Lilla and James. So was I in the home of one of the three living?

Mavis turned from the window where she'd been comparing the view to mine. Rearranging the stack, I flipped the photo. "Benjamin Harris, 1868; m. Cati Corteo" scribbled 'cross the top. Restacking the books, smoothing the sheets, and grabbing my dress, stilettos and coffee, I slipped the photo into my jeans pocket before leading the way out of the deep blue room.

Marcia Witt stood looking out her own wall of windows in the living room, in wool pants, pink cashmere sweater and pearls. She held an oversized burnt yellow mug with thick brown brushstrokes to her chest. She turned at my throat clearing, gazed me up and down much as Pauline had, with eyes matching the mug's brushstrokes. "So you're up. Ready to go? Or do you want some juice, coffee?"

"No I'm fine," I lifted my paper cup. "Hits the spot this morning. Thank you so much Ms.—"

"Please...Marcia."

"Marcia...for offering me a bed. I live only two floors below."

"Yes, I understand."

"It's not as gorgeous as this. This, this is truly lovely." I glanced 'round. Dark walls stretched from the white stone fireplace where a small fire burned, past three white leather couches squaring off a gleaming black wood coffee table.

"Yes, it's quite nice," she looked like Sophie Benvenue so long ago, beneath the humor laid sadness, as though she'd just learned a family member hadn't long to live.

"Are you really all right, Marcia?" Mavis moved toward her.

She waved her off. "Really it was our pleasure."

Our..., "You are truly kind for helping a woman in ...need. It was like I was drugged or something..." or haunted, I thought. I pointed my finger back over my shoulder. "Afraid straightening the bed I knocked over some books. Is that daguerreotype of your family?"

She frowned and shook her head, "I don't know what you mean."

"There was an early picture of a married couple with the books," I glanced 'round but saw no other photos.

She smiled indulgently, admitting nothing. She was used to the press.

"Well, we'll get out of your hair. Thanks again. You were most kind. I didn't know about the sheets?" I walked toward her hand out. She took it firmly, which caught me by surprise.

I gave her a strong squeeze back and met her eyes. Marcia Witt would be prime rib for Todd, especially if she hadn't been his date. "Perhaps some time I can return the favor? You two can come two flights down for a drink?" And I can surreptitiously return this picture. "It's not this nice of course, but it is interesting to see the view from a different height."

She smiled, "I imagine it would be." We dropped hands. When we released I let two fingers just lightly cross her wrist causing a little surprise electricity, "Oops, sorry." But I saw nothing.

"We'll see ourselves out." The door shut on her staring at my back. "Whew," I said once the elevator doors closed. Mavis and I both half-chuckled. "I can't believe I slept there so deep." What I really couldn't believe was that I'd lifted that photo just like that, as if it were honest. Surely in Féy's world a little crime was acceptable — maybe even a twin power — you could do a little sin as long as it did a little good.

"Well, you had quite a night." Mavis said as the doors slid open and she put out her hand to hold them.

"Hope overall it was entertaining. Was it too awful?" We

walked down the hall. Against my door leaned a cream colored envelope. I picked it up – blank on both sides.

Mavis used my key. Then she skipped them onto the red lacquer stand in the open hall – beneath an oil painting of brown–skinned mother and daughter that stood out against the cream wall.

I tossed everything but the stolen photo on the white tile counter past dishes waiting to be put away and led Mavis down the three steps to the living room. "God, it's good to be home. Why couldn't I have walked down here last night? What the hell happened out there?" Though, of course I remembered the attack too well. I sank into one of twin red leather couches facing each other 'cross my low glass coffee table. No fire was laid in my white stone hearth, where no fire had ever been. I'd never yet wanted to have to clean up after it.

"What do you recall?" Mavis asked, settling herself on the sofa then methodically unrolling the pastry bag. Actually I was pleased to see it. Mavis loved her "tea" and stories. If I'd totally bombed she'd not be so enjoying herself.

"I'm piecing it together now." With decaled, cherry red, three-quarter inch nails, she handed me a napkin-wrapped chocolate croissant. "A few bourbons, perhaps one glass of wine too many, a few dances with Todd, the last one an *Orillero* – a street tango." Wonderfully cool hands on my waist, firm, but perfectly contoured, each finger feeling me with every inch, eyes the color of the sky just before it goes black – eyes you'd want to swim in. The wave rose, but I pulled myself back, "That's about it."

"Do you remember your solo?" Mavis's tone lightly warned.

The liquid shimmy slammed back, as did the preceding strange rush into me, "Yes…" Féy possessing me – I hated to think on it.

"How about being carried off?" Vague flashes winked of a cushioned bench; my head against a strong shoulder.

"No? Well, you winked at the crowd. You waved as he

carried you out. Made it all seem an act. Most thought it a stunt to get   Todd's eye. We told them all that you'd sprained your ankle and been exhausted. He was a perfect gentleman. He sat and talked with you till we docked. Susan and Marcia kept guard."

So half an hour alone with Todd? Susan must have hated that. But what in the world had we talked about until we'd docked? "You know, Todd surprised us all...." I stopped at her expression.

She turned her latte slowly, watching it. "Todd."

"Oh no. Did I drool, snore?"

"Nothing like that, but, you see, sweetheart...it wasn't *Todd* you danced with – at the end."

"It wasn't...?" For a minute this news hovered just beyond my comprehension then Todd's face snapped back into place – his eyes were grey.

"Well, no, sugar," Mavis looked up again. "It was a man name of Echo, at least that's what's on the note." She reached into her bag, pulled out a precisely folded sheet. Once opened she pulled back and read haltingly, "'give this to *la belle dans...*' "

"*Danseuse?*" my voice dropped off. Féy'd been a *danseuse*.

"That's what it says," Mavis squinted. She avoided her reading glasses whenever possible.

"It means beautiful dancer."

"Ooo, la, la."

"Yeah, yeah. Give what?" My flat tone belied my cantering pulse, the air turning in my chest. I flicked at the croissant. Could this all be Féy's doing? Last night, this man and the Grey Hats?

"10 digits," Mavis waved the paper. "The magic number. Now, Jeannie," she pulled the note back from my reach. "I think we've learned that you have a tendency to leap before you look."

My heart began to skip. Something about the number seemed familiar. "Do you know where he's from?"

"No. But Marcia had keys to his place."

"I didn't see a ring. Nor clothes, shoes, bags, make up, jewelry, anything feminine." My face warmed with the memory of the sanctuary of his lapel. I looked at Mavis, "He sure could dance." She set the number down facing me. I nodded, too scared to pick it up.

For a moment we didn't speak. Then, "So where'd he sleep last night?"

"I think he said he was going to his office."

"Burning the midnight oil, huh?" That wasn't the action of a love struck man, but it also reminded me of what *I* should be doing. "So how'd Todd take it?"

Mavis bobbled her head. "Your solo was a bit...with your eyes closed, we weren't exactly sure what would happen. You looked...not entirely the girl we've known for three years."

"Mave, I was possessed or something. I think someone – like Blowhard might have slipped me a Rufie. You heard how he talked."

She lifted her chin and paused. She'd seen her share of journalistic binges, and she knew what drunk looked like, "But with Mr. Great Legs? When he swung dipped you then spun up? Worthy of applause – didn't you hear it? Todd clapped hardest." She chuckled, "Looked like he'd like to do the same to you some time."

I gave her a sardonic grin. "What about Chuck?" I casually took my first nibble.

"He walked on home. It was so close." Some other news lingered in her eyes, but Chuck wasn't one of the Ten – nor Todd, nor Blowhard. But Mavis did look a little worried.

"Mavis, I don't normally drink, you know that. But last night – something happened that's been foretold my whole life. Remember about that curse? Well, it turns out I might be able to change it."

"Sweet pea...." Sad disappointment grew 'cross Mavis's face, reminding me far too much of Moman L.

"So just who is this Echo? And what kind of name is that?"

Mavis shook her close–cropped, magenta-red head, her matching lips tight. "I don't know, sweet pea. Susan brought them. They sat and chatted with Todd until the dance. During the two of yours chat after, we found out they had a place right here – Marcia offered to take you with her. I used your car to bring all the office's supplies back this morning." Mavis didn't own a car – living on Russian Hill she rarely needed one. Still something about her tone made me ask. "Did we dock all right?"

She paused like she was thinking. "Oh yeah. No problem...little early."

"Because of me – oh, my word."

"Now you know how hard it is to keep newsmen off land.... And after your floor show," she teased, "Well, as they say darling, the wad had been shot."

She finished her mocha, but I could no longer eat. All we could hear was my brass and glass wall clock's steady tick, reminding me of my debt, my dignity, reputation, my daughter and all the things I'd risked to follow Féy and some crazy destiny, both of which had let me down as always.

"Guess you don't want to go shopping?" Mavis rose.

"I won't be shopping this year." I beat back surprise pricks of tears by pushing myself up. "I've got to get Cariña."

I helped Mavis up and she patted my back, "Hang in there, sugar. I know what happened last night is the sort of thing to throw a young blood off their game, but now that you've got your barracuda's attention, the question is what's next?" Her hand rested on my shoulder, as we moved toward the door.

"You mean an encore?"

"I mean you might want to turn this into some killer story. And not about being drugged by Blowhard. Or wear an ankle brace for a bit." She shrugged.

I made a face. "I'm on the story. But mum's the word until I get something, all right?" No doubt Féy would say this was real living.

"Sweet cheeks, I'm always—"

My mouth set to ask her if she'd ever heard of real living, I opened the door. 'Cross the hall Chuck stepped off the elevator with his touring bike beside him. "Oh. Hello Chuck."

As my heart sank, he and Mavis exchanged a passing nod. Pivoting with brows raised, one wine nail pointed at Chuck, her burgundy lips mouthed, "Be good," as the elevator doors shut taking her down.

"Hi, Jeannie," Chuck said, moving his bike into my hall. "Came by to pick up my stuff."

I nodded, leant back against the doorjamb. I only glanced at his eyes then his bike bags. "There's not that much."

"Jeannie," Chuck spoke as if he'd memorized a difficult speech, "About last night. I'm sorry I just left. I knew you were among friends." He waited for me to speak.

For a moment I was back in front of Sophie and Fayette, my foot drenched, my tights torn.

"I will want to stay friends," he said, "in the long run. For now...you see I've met someone. I meant to tell you last night..."

"That's wonderful, Chuck." And I pushed away telling myself I'd known this would happen. But after finding his few things and shutting the door on the closing elevator, I dashed to my office and grabbed up the phone.

Next to the red cushioned window seat with papers stacked haphazardly against jersey pillows, I slid open the balcony door.

A seagull sat on the far end of the banister, head beneath its wing. I watched him, hearing the city's ambient noise float up along with car horns, an occasional shout, a door slam. Then over the high railing I stared down. Nothing much was between the street 13 stories below and me. Completing the foretold trio of deaths? Could that be why I'd really come West? I hated that thought.

I didn't exhale till I heard her voice, "Cariña darling, Happy New Year. You all right?"

"Yes, Momma, fine. Happy New Year."

"Happy New Year to you my darling. This year we'll be back

together again." I hadn't visited this Christmas. Instead all monies went to paying off the MasterCard. A car's alarm cried. "Cariña?"

"Yes, Momma."

I winced against her drawl, more pronounced this year. ""How are you really, darling? Those boys being good to you?"

"All right." Her new, teen's indifference tugged at my heart.

"You sure, darling?" Her silence chided, while a sailboat scooted beneath the Bay Bridge. My fingers thudded against the cold painted steel. "I might have good news Cariña. Yesterday and last night I met some important contacts. I think they might really help us, darling, get back together I mean. But, first I need to know...have you...seen anything new...about me?" The seagull on the banister took off.

"What do you mean Momma, you mean about what's happening out there?"

I took in a sharp breath, "What is happening?"

There was a silence. She giggled. I did not.

"Cariña, if you know something."

She hemmed.

"Cariña!"

She verbally shrugged, "You're waking up."

"How do you know?"

She huffed, "I go to sleep and sometimes in my dreams sometimes the wind blows."

"What do you mean?" My voice stayed calm, though I feared what she meant. Like that strange current in and out of me last night – I shivered.

"The wind fills me with stuff. I wake up next day knowing certain things."

"Certain things?" The seagull flew by at a steep decline a few feet in front of me.

"Don't worry."

"Cariña, if the wind ever brings something that scares you – or anyone that tells you things. Is there anyone?" Teen silence blared. "You know, I had my first vision about your age. It terrified me and I never told anyone. I never spoke of it. After my second one I did, but for years I just ignored it."

"There's just so much."

"Oh, Cariña, my sweet. So much of what?"

"It's the noise."

"You mean of..."

"Of all the people. I can't always make it stop." Cariña heard in her dreams' wind people's life desires, all in one fell swoop. She'd grow to use it waking, to great advantage.

"Cariña, as Moman L is my witness I will find a way for you to turn those voices off. You hear me? I will wake up. I promise. And then I'll come to get you."

South of the skyscrapers an immense barge crept low in the water stacked with Asian stamped boxcars, filled with goods from parts exotic. "Did you wear your present yet?" I'd sent a Young Versace midnight blue lace and velvet gown – outlet find of the year – for her Christmas Reveillon dinner.

"Not yet, Momma. *Ma mer*—Jacqueline said I can wear it tonight. We're going to drive the lights before the party."

The City Park lights—had she almost called Jacqueline *ma mere*? Oh that would not do.

"You'll look beautiful, Cariña. Don't forget to take a picture tonight, right darling? Then save the dress for when I come....I know," I soothed her silence – since Moman L'd passed, she hated having her photo taken, like an old woman believed it captured part of your soul, "Just capture a piece of your soul for me please darling? I promise to treat it right. Happy New Year, Sweetheart. I think this is going to be the best year yet. This is the year we get back together. This is the year I teach you how to stop those voices in your head. You call me at any time – I've a special ringtone for you – and I'll know – any time something gets too difficult, you hear me Cariña? You can tell me anything. Your mother loves you every milli–second. You're a Cadot."

"All right." As we said our goodbyes, there was the

beginning of trust in her tone. I came back inside a little damp. The fog wouldn't burn off today until noon or so.

Cariña in that soft, glowing blue dress would be my new version of Echo's eyes. And hopefully she'd remember me in the midst of so many others – like Jacqueline. That had to change.

I snatched up the stack of credit card bills on the table and dialed the first number, staring at the skyscrapers. Was a phone in one of them ringing? Balance zero. Last payment $5,561.57, December 30, 2002 via wire transfer. I ordered a trace – same story at all five. Balances paid down to zero – also at my student loans. If the money was stolen I'd be in a world of trouble.

I forwarded the un-junked email urgent to Kris Bharatavan, a free–lance hacker I'd met through a profile. Sheet tech Jimmy's voicemail said he'd return after New Year's.

A Grey Hats search recovered over a million listings. Besides being hats, Grey Hats are hacker teams that make public their attacks. With names like "Legion of Doom", the Pranksters, they were mostly high school-ers, but there were rumors of more mature teams with members both inside targets and out. As rampant were the conspiracy theories on why corporations, especially banks, wouldn't want us to know of them.

From the plane Annie French's grey hatpin blared in my memory. She'd said she worked *in* dotcoms, not *for* one. I scrounged for her card, sent an email asking casually if she'd anything about a new, local hacker group called "the Grey Hats".

Hackers in the Ten – or was this just coincidence, suddenly two stories approach me on the same day as a man? Good things come in threes. Sitting back from my desk I searched the fog.

Anna'd said she'd caused her husband's death – murder or suicide and the proof was *her* family's home, presumably that meant her home with her husband and kids. The news articles on Kincaid Corporation had revealed Anna and Pauline's competitive past, but not much of their personal history.

Of course Edward Berne wasn't listed in any local phone books, but the University might have a record of the Berne's former address. They were closed for winter break. Nor did I find any information on Anna's surviving child, Eric Berne, still in Switzerland where the Berne's had once lived. The final notice of her husband, Edward, wasn't in Current Biographies or Newsmakers – too small and too old. Frustrated, I googled him. A number of websites came up. One quoted him writing:

> Quantum study shows us, on the subatomic level, reality is a vibrating whole. There exist none of the Cartesian dichotomies that plague our current understanding of reality: matter and energy, observer and observed, male and female, visible and invisible, even self and other. On the most fundamental level all of these entities are one.

Well, if that didn't beat all. Surely that extended to the living and the dead, the past and the present – the twin powers. So beneath these opposite or complementary powers, they were actually one?

Berne was a sort of guru for physics undergrads who wrote with fervor of the "New Physics" or the "Big T.O.E.", the single "theory of everything" – that explained it all – a physicist's God it seemed. It, like our Catholic one, had never been proven.

Robert Oppenheimer – the father of the atomic bomb – had headed Berne's first lab till he left for Los Alamos taking Berne with him to study the plasma – a fourth state of matter Berne had discovered. Though not found on earth, at 20,000 degrees Celsius, inside most stars, as distinct from solid, liquid or gas, plasma constituted over 99% of the matter of the universe.

They had used a plasma to create the Uranium isotope U235 for the atom bomb. But 18 months into the Manhattan Project Berne had left. Online threads had speculated Berne had followed the wishes of his pacifist girlfriend, a known Berkeley Communist. So in the early 50's when, along with others from Oppenheimer's first Lab, Berne had landed before the House Un–American Activities Committee, he'd declined to testify.

Oppenheimer, for fear of losing his station, had declined to testify for him. So following the hearings Berne had worked 13 years in exile: Sao Paolo, London and finally Bern, Switzerland.

But in 1965, Berne was back at Berkeley under Enrico Fulani to work on something called "entanglement" – particles entangled 'cross time and space. I sat up. There were no phones or addresses on the site, but I urgent emailed the site's administrators and the most prolific online message posters and then looked up the Who-Is registrant, Max Conrad on 9th in San Francisco. He didn't answer his phone, but I left messages everywhere.

I turned to search on the *Lawrence II* or Henry M. Collins. Due to the holidays the historical libraries would re–open the following week. I hoped Kris, Annie, and Berne's followers weren't gone for days.

Ten minutes later, the shower's hot cascade brought down the memory of Echo's hands running up and down my body obliterating all thought. This time with the memory came desire as bold as with Davis. Being the start of a new year, this time I didn't push away.

Waking from a brief, uneasy nap after sunset, the city came to light, and the deep blue sky heralded experience just beyond its horizon. So I called the number Mavis left.

"Huh," the voice sounded waking, wary.

"Hello, is this Echo? I'm sorry. Did I wake you?"

He yawned. "Who is this?"

"This is Jeannie Cadot," I said pronouncing my name slowly for him without any accent. "The one you rescued on the dance floor Saturday night."

"Oh, right," his voice softened. "*La belle danseuse.*" After pause, a sigh, "I've been thinking of you…your dress – our dance – our conversation."

He seemed to have a slight French accent and my neck pulsed, "Well, really it was a pantsuit. Valentino."

"Of course." He gave a slight chuckle. "But, you are alright?" His accent explained his strange nickname, Féy'd also had given herself a nickname.

"Oh, yes, I'm fine. I'd not been on a boat since...my childhood – and I guess I drank a little much. I didn't even know I remembered the street tango. Though my mother danced – the *Orillero* in fact – I guess you could tell that."

I took a breath, hoping he'd say "Yes, remember we spoke of it." But nothing came forward from him.

"Yes, well I...just, wanted to share my gratitude for the dance...and you escorting me so...grandly from the floor—do you call it a deck?"

He said, "Tango has been known to induce...altered states."

"States, you say."

"Some places you know it's quite the rage."

"States? Or tango."

He laughed. "But, 'honing in' on strangers is not a thing I often do. I couldn't resist you so red and welcoming—" he stopped abruptly.

I flinched. "I hope Marcia did not mind?"

"Marcia? Um. We did not talk about it."

"No?" When no further explanation came, I rushed, "It's just that...I wanted to offer a thank you lunch or drink, and I...didn't know if she might mind." With even that small truth my heart skipped against my ribs, again as it hadn't since talking with Davis. I pulled out the stolen, old photo to steady myself.

"I'd like that." His accented voice deepened, rolled down behind my knees.

"I'd love to show you I'm not always 'in trance'. Tomorrow night? Your condo?" Once copied, I could put that photo back before he missed it.

"Tomorrow," he rushed, surprised.

"Oh?" Blood pulsed once in my temples. "Well, when is good for you." It dawned on me Marcia might be visiting from out of town.

He paused, "Already you know I can't resist you."

Despite myself I was pleased. "All right. Tomorrow."

"The Cave at 8:00?" In the Tenderloin – not far from our offices – a dive – where you go when you're hiding something. I spoke warily, "I know it."

"Good," Echo clipped. "8:00 then?"

"Sure. Yes. All right." Hey, I've got this photo.

"Look, I've really got to run. I'm on deadline."

"I'm familiar. I'll see you, then...then." I rolled my eyes.

"Yes, you will. *Ciao. Ciao, bella* Jeanne. I am pleased you called." He said softly.

I set down the phone, and placed my hand upon a flushed face.

Maybe it's much too early in the game, Ella's creamy voice floated. *Oh, but I thought, I'd ask you just the same. What are you doing New Year's, New Year's Eve?*

'Round midnight, I sat in my first firelight looking up to the lights of downtown San Francisco. Tonight I'd eaten Palomino's takeout with a demi–bottle of Moet champagne, pretending my debts really were history and that Cariña would soon be with me this year.

Holding up my glass, in its fire–lit reflection, I saw behind me the cream–colored corner hanging off the kitchen counter. I'd forgotten it – so I rose.

The textured envelope had a watermark, and the card at first glance seemed to be a kaleidoscopic foil mirror. Only when turned, dozens of holographic stars burst forth. Inside a message was typed.

"KinCo IPO stolen from Edward Berne, American Dreamer. Seek to know the truth, despite where it leads." This was Anna's line. But there was no handwriting at all outside or in. IPO meant initial public offering. I'd not seen that on the now privately-held Kincaid Company's website. But if true, it made Anna's 30-year-old story much hotter. I unfolded the enclosed pages.   Twelve paragraphs of E45B32F082C983... insensible, alphanumeric strings.   So perhaps Anna was working with the Grey Hats.

I dashed straight back again to the office and opened the up the old frame – out fell a slip of paper written in Féy's hand.

She'd given them to me that night on the Mississippi when she'd said, "In San Francisco, we will be together again, *dauphine*. But you have to want me."

I had to admit her tactics had worked – ever since the dance, I had two stories to follow and leads on Lilla, felt warm inside, even had a love possibility.   Could it be her shame-embracing approach had some merit in it?

The black river rose, but concentration on the slip of paper staved it off.   Fifteen digits scrawled 'cross it.   They were all one through nine, including no letters.

So after re-fitting the frame, I sat the cream colored card on the coffee table.   The hologram's tiny stars sparkled.   They seemed full of hope.

Five

New Year's morning at 6:28, I paced outside Clive's closed door. He was on his phone – lots always started up on New Year's Day. Caffeine burned my empty, worried belly. I still had not decided exactly how to bring up my debt. But I knew I must. I could not afford to lose Clive's trust.

At 6:30 sharp, Clive opened his door. "Nice dancing Saturday," he growled when I entered. "Don't." He raised his hand, "I don't even want to hear. Unless there's something I need to know?" I shook my head, shrugged.

He nodded. "I recognize mini–crimes of passion, God knows." He chuckled. Clive had lost his job with the Chicago Sun Times in 1968 when he'd taken up with M'Shele, a lead lieutenant in the South Side Panthers. It had taken him decades to earn back the right to laugh at his past. He looked at me over horn–rims. "You made your bed, Slugger. Now...I'd rather not go into detail." He aimed a long finger, "But...now you really have to approve everything with Susan."

As my face flamed, he added, "You'd better make nice with

your new colleagues. Your stunt didn't win you many friends."

Many friends outside of Todd and Echo, and probably Blowhard, but still I grimaced, "Oh yes, boss. Absolutely. It won't happen again." All I could do for some seconds was gaze at his closed, dark walnut face. I squirmed. "I've to talk with you about something else – a story. I wasn't entirely honest with you the other day. With Susan."

"No?" Click, click – the randomness of his mouse tapping always caught one off guard. That's the way he liked it.

"Anna Kincaid admitted to having her husband murdered." I reveled in the sudden silence. Then click, click...click.

"On the record?"

"She didn't say not."

Click. "When did he pass?" Clive was not easily excited.

"'73," I mumbled, making great show of standing the New Year's card on his desk.

"This?" he grabbed the card, looked inside. "Who's it from?"

"No signature, no return address, found outside my condo door yesterday morning." I inhaled; slid over the Grey Hats pages of code and email. I prayed he wouldn't look at the date, which of course was the first thing he did. He frowned, weighing the two days I'd had it – the holiday. "I think there's some revenge plot going—."

"You had this since before the cruise?"

I tried to swallow, but my throat had dried out, so I croaked, "It was in my junk file." I cleared my throat, "Excuse me."

Slowly he looked back to the card. "So you think Anna sent it and paid your debts?"

"Don't know. But she said the truth was in her diary. At *her* family's home, which I take it is not her ma's – where she's dying." I paused.

"Is it true?" he asked.

"Haven't found it yet, but her husband worked over there at Berkeley – they'll be open again soon. They have records." And I'm seeing her son tonight. I danced with him night before last, slept in his guest bed. But I couldn't force the words out anymore than put my head into a noose.

"No, I mean your debts. Have they been paid?"

Again my throat constricted, I cleared it. "Matter of fact, they have.."

"That a lot?" Clive's casualness belied a deeper interest. He felt fatherly for me which I appreciated. Perhaps he suspected Cariña – though I'd only told Mavis, not wanting to explain my exile.

"With student loans….about 30 grand."

He whistled, sat back in his chair holding up the email. "What are these? Records?"

"Don't yet know, but I've a guy to get on it." Least I hoped Kris was back by now – he'd not called me yet. I picked up a Barry Bonds–signed baseball. Clive held box seats at Pac Bell Park.

"Someone you can trust? KinCo's one of our first advertisers."

I thought of Kris, who accepted only cash and refused to join any company, even a dot.com, helping out the "man", "We can trust him. Could be a big crime. Big proof. I have access – exclusive."

"And you're implicated," he leaned forward, toyed with the sharp crease down his right leg. But I'd gotten his hand off that damn mouse. "What else you got?"

I opened my reporter's pad. "Nothing on the stock offering as yet – but I've an insider to try." I sure hoped Chuck would help. "30 years ago Berne died in a fire in his home laboratory. It was recorded as an accident."

"Wait a minute," Clive raised his click finger revealing a gleaming Cal school ring. "What was her husband's name?"

"Berne. Edward."

Clive spoke slowly. "Edward Berne. Wasn't he at Berkeley?"

"Yes, yes he was," I'd forgotten Clive could wax nostalgic. Hopefully some of that would transfer to his eagerness for this story.

"Berne died in a fire. Early 70's. At home. An accident...I remember." His hand stretched towards a Cloisonné bowl full of Altoids; he chucked a few into his mouth. "He ran a pretty radical physics Lab in the 60s. I was at the Daily Cal. Berne's work was up for the Nobel Prize, we ran a couple of stories. They were the science gurus of the movement, I remember the motto...'Seek to know the truth, something.'"

I dropped my pad. He sank back into his leather chair; his voice got smooth, "I remember their vehemence and fire. Not the distant, brainy types you'd expect. So someone has suggested this stock offering is based on Berne's work from back then?"

"But why would his work become so relevant now? Could be a wild goose chase. Except..." it's been foretold all my life.

"Your debts have been paid. By someone who wants to buy themselves a reporter." At this point I should've told him at least about Féy and her strange warnings when I was a child, her incredible effect on men, and the oddly named fellow with the accent, but Clive sat back, "Well, looks like you got yourself a real story this time, Slugger." He smiled before he stood, and came 'round the carved edge of his old world desk. "Don't even think of a spending spree, Jeannie. You'll have to give it back. Get a trace. Shut down those cards." He sat on the desk's corner and touched my arm, "The Kincaid's would be hot news down in the Valley. Find those Grey Hats fast and keep it quiet. And tracking the IPO story? Keep it soft. Do you hear me, Jeannie? Loose lips sink stories...and reporters."

I tightened my jaw.

He went on, softer, "And Jeanne, listen up. You're not gonna like this, but I want you to work with on this with Susan. You be the legs, let her guide and write the story."

For a moment I thought his head had exploded. "Wha—what?"

He looked up, "I talked with her the other night. She knows Todd, knows what his hot buttons are. You want to be published? Learn everything you can from her."

"I...I"

"Jeannie, it's the first draft of an unflattering history of major advertiser for our new tabloid publisher. You've never reported on a hidden crime. You need guidance."

"Just give me a week, Clive. Susan will leak this immediately to Todd. Let me work with Mavis."

"Mavis!"

"Don't you think she knows more about this city, news and how to run this bureau than *Susan*? Who do you trust most?"

Clive's mouth kinked. "You work with Susan. And check in with me, *frequently*. Tell her today and don't forget to show her all this." He frowned back at his screen.

I narrowed my eyes. I couldn't believe Clive – my main partner out here – gone or at least now powerless. "I'll tell her," my voice chilled, "But do me a favor and don't get between us? Don't make her my rival. Let me handle it. I'll keep you informed."

Clive nodded. "Jeannie, on this story. And after last night - you trod the narrow and straight. OK? We're already exposed. You want excitement, adventure, romance, read a novel."

I sucked my bottom lip as though I'd eaten raw lemon, "Don't worry boss–man; no more Valentino's – or tango's." Still, I scratched him off my list of Ten.

"This story might be good for you, for us. Might be the kind you hope for."

I stood up, turned to go.

"Oh, one more thing? Create a paper trail. That should be enough...should anything..."

He didn't need to finish – should it turn out the funds had been stolen, it could ruin my credit and my career.

I glanced back, but he was already eyes a–light for the next big thing. As he always did, I pointed my trigger and middle finger at him, "Power to the people." I spoke low as I aimed at his mouse, and closed the office door.

I went to see Jimmy in IT. The only Times staffer with blue highlights and a pierced tongue and nipple rings that poked through his usually threadbare, dark t-shirts, Jimmy stared at a large, flat computer screen as I walked in.

"Jimmy," I joggled him, "Did you get my New Year's message?"

"Hiya, Jeanne." He swirled 'round in his chair and pushed his headphones back. I heard something like tinny Nirvana pumping out of them. "I was just chatting about it with my buddies. This thing is fuckin' bizarre. Check this out." He pivoted back to the screen and pressed buttons until my inbox appeared.

Twice a day the computer took digital photographs of all the stored files on the network as part of the new security system. The screen highlighted a single message. Jimmy double clicked. The message opened to the Grey Hats email and he scrolled down to the bottom, then he held a multiple key combination. "This reveals any hidden codes or attachments." Suddenly a small blue icon with skull and crossbones appeared. "Don't click it," Jimmy whispered, then swung over to another, larger screen to his right. "Here's the secure version." He pressed a key and program code filled the screen. Looked just like the wire transfers – EAC3420FD598... Programming code?

"Well done," Jimmy chuckled softly. "Very well done. See this?" He pointed to a section. "That's the beauty part." He ran his finger sensuously along the screen.

"Headquarters to Jimmy," I said.

"Oh," Jimmy swung back to me. "It's a worm."

"A worm?"

"A program that crawls through a network looking for something. In this case it was looking for your machine."

"Ah."

"Yeah. A worm usually crawls through a network operating system: MS/DOS or Unix. But this one...it's in assembly language – talks directly to the machine – beneath the OS and it's invisible. The system shows no record of having run it."

Jimmy swung back to the code. I sat back against his desk, thinned my eyes and crossed my arms.

He hurried on, "Your typical worm has two sections. The head – the part that searches and reproduces itself – and the tail, the part that does the dirty work. This one has three parts: a head, a body and a tail." He again caressed the screen.

"Jimmy," I prodded.

He spoke dreamily, "If it didn't find your PC, it deleted all traces it had been there under the name of another utility program. If it hadn't found you we'd have never known we were hit. Odorless. Trail–less. Traceless." Jimmy grinned and slapped his hands on the table. "Fucking nice work."

I grumbled. "There's nothing you can track?"

"I'm shopping the code," Jimmy said. "Not that many can program in assembly language these days. But I don't hold out much hope. Though I've never seen this design, it's pretty standard. But there's no signature or comments, acknowledgments. Just code. Weird."

Damn. "You ever heard of this group, the Grey Hats?"

He shrugged, shaking his head, "But is it true? About the debts?"

I pursed my face as though saying, 'yeah right.' "Jimmy, can you keep this just between us? Clive's worried about getting scooped and I'm not everyone's best friend right now."

"That was some show for the old folks." Then he nodded solemnly, zipped his lips, "Mum's the word."

"Keep me posted," I shot over my shoulder on my way out the door. "Happy New Year."

Twenty minutes later I stood in Susan Caldwell's cube with a file in my tight, right hand. My heart galloped, but I steeled myself against it as two smart, perfect blue marbles settled on me. A thick Southern accent drawled, "Why, look who's here. Our not so tiny dancer. Have a good time Saturday night?"

I flashed my best crocodile smile. My voice clear, off—handed, cut through, "I wanted to thank you." My pulse hastened, "for watching over me. That was kind and unexpected."

Susan's eyes looked surprised for a second. "I was wooing a new VIP, Marcia Witt." My brow smoothed, "You made quite the impression on her date."

I spoke over my heart's sudden hammering, "I danced with him." I faltered, realizing I'd spoken before thinking.

"Yes, I saw. Didn't get his name?"

I tightened my grip on the file. "An executive secretary named Belinda Wheeler's long-time cabbie father was an institution here before he passed last month of prostate cancer. Belinda was distraught. Then she discovered a lump in her breast, just after she'd gotten her pink slip from Tele.com.

"Knowing me from my interview with her father, she told he she has memos signed by Jim Cooper discussing transfer of company funds to offshore accounts—just days before Tele.com's bankruptcy declaration. Clive wanted me to have you guide me on it. But, if you don't want her information…then don't give me that name."

Belinda had been Jim's jilted lover. After he started dating Kate Hunter – Todd's sister – she'd filed harassment charges they'd dismissed after an investigation. I'd found this from a public search, but I'd taken those pages – and the memos with the fuzzy Cooper signatures – out of this file.

Susan considered. Her perfect eyes drilled into me. "He told everyone he was called Echo, but Marcia said he's some mathematics guru who came back from Europe to help his mother die. Nobody knows him. And he wants to keep it that way. He's very rich – probably nine figures. And he's fierce about his privacy, especially with the press. Who isn't these days?" She shrugged.

Her words blew me open. "W–what's his name?"

"Eric Kincaid. But you didn't hear it from me." She stuck

out her hand.

A shock wave extended my arm with the folder. "Thanks," I managed tunelessly. Her smart eyes laughed at me, as I scurried down the hall. Echo's – now Eric's – twilight blues danced in my head, mocking, along with Anna's, Pauline's. Cool eyes, cool planing hands I could still imagine on me. Eric–Echo was Anna's son. He'd taken his mother's family name.

At my desk, I typed in Eric Kincaid.

Bingo. Website for a stock market forecaster, based in Europe; client page a Who's Who of stock brokerages: JP Morgan, Merrill Lynch, CIBC, Salomon Smith Barney, Goldman Sachs, Lehman Brothers, even Gianinni Securities, Chuck's firm.

There was no picture, but the address was Saanen, Switzerland. Forbes, the Economist, and the Wall Street Journal praised his elegant algorithms and fruitful models. Shearson's website called him a forecasting genius.

I sat back. So he had his father's brain. Easy enough for someone like him to program a 'worm' I supposed or drop a card in a hall – paying back Cati and Benjamin's stolen photo. I couldn't wait now to see again those impossible eyes, to have them reveal what all they knew and had in store for me. He, Anna and the deceased Berne, could be the last members of my Ten.

At 11:25, I marched into the lounge and ran right into Mavis who preferred to eat early. She carried a nail file. In the microwave her bowl of chili heated.

"Hey girl, how you feeling?" she asked.

"Hey yourself," I said. "I'm all right. In deep this time."

"Oh, my dear, do tell." Mavis rose and removed her chili.

I asked, "No more diet food?" Mavis had been off and on Jenny Craig for years with little change. I think she did it just to keep people off her back.

She shook her head. "Girl, fat gives food and people staying power." She focused on her chili. Ever since her husband Walt had died suddenly—eight years ago—leaving her childless in a new city, she'd gained more than a few pounds. As a native Manhattanite transplanted through her husband's military career to the Presidio, when things went rocky for Mave she dove deep into food and theater. With her wooden, bangle bracelets, tropical plants and the Lorraine Hansberry Theatre, being indispensable with Stephanie and at The Sheet, she'd wound up all right.

"Did Echo happen to mention his last name?" I asked casual like.

"I didn't get that. Why, did you talk with him?"

"Matter of fact I did." I said. "We're going out tonight." Omission created pressure where my head met my neck.

"R–e–ally," Mavis gave the word three syllables. "Isn't that nice. I'm sure you kids will have fun. Going dancing?" She twisted her lip at her magazine and I cut my eyes.

"What happened this morning was even more interesting." I nodded to the balcony's sliding door.

We walked out on a low balcony overlooking our alley parking lot. Not much ambiance, but a lot of privacy. I slid the door closed.

"Mavis, you know my motto." She nodded and we sat. "A secret shared is a secret lost. But I'll explode if I don't confess. So what I'm about to say cannot leave this patio."

At her assured bob, I went on, "Remember that interview with Anna Kincaid – well, she admitted to more than a just a few regrets, she admitted to successfully planning and carrying out her husband's murder." I let her absorb this. "Seems her husband knew Echo very well. In fact, he's Echo's father," despite our privacy, I mouthed the final words.

I heard Mavis's loud exhale. She put down her spoon and turned wide and waiting eyes up to me. "Who was he?"

"A world–renowned, controversial physicist killed in a home lab fire," I spoke quickly. "Got a tip – probably from this son Echo – that the folks at Kincaid Semiconductor are trying to capitalize on his stolen work to the tune of millions."

Mavis whistled and picked up her spoon. "And you told Clive?"

I nodded. "KinCo's a huge advertiser. Till we know something we'd like to keep it quiet."

Mavis sat back, arching well–drawn brows. "Anything else?"

For an answer, I stabbed my salad.

"Mm," Mavis said. "Are you worried he's targeted you?"

I regarded a forkful. "Well, his grandmother seemed to hate me. And somebody possibly involved has paid my debts. A little over $30,000."

She almost swallowed her surprise with her chili.

"I've only got sketchy information. The whole thing may still turn out to be a hoax."

"Hm?"

"Tip came through an untraceable worm over the Internet." I'd keep the card to myself. "It's probably a fake."

"But you say your debts?"

I nodded. "Turns out this Echo's some sort of investment guru. Wonderfully successful, of course," I bit down hard on a mouthful of green.

"Well, well, well. So you think he paid your debts? Nice courting style."

"Mavis," I swallowed fast. "We're not courtin'. But he might be framing me."

She considered. "But why do you think it's him?"

My birthmark itched to tell her about the Lawrence, the dead, but I wasn't that hopeful yet, so I said, "Pretty sure it's too great a coincidence. But either way, it's a promising lead. And maybe..."

"Jeannie," Mavis set her spoon down. "You don't know anything about this man. Remember Ted Kaczyinski? Wasn't he a hermit?"

I laughed. "The Unabomber lived miles from anyone else by himself in a tiny shack, mostly unemployed. This man is tops in his field. And he's no Momma's boy, not with that touch, that voice, those eyes."

"That Marcia."

"He's not attached to her."

"Did he tell you that?" He hadn't really, but it didn't matter. I had to know this truth, even if for reasons I could never share.

I punctuated with my fork, "Story is mostly about his parents. And there's no evidence of any crime as yet." My tone hardened. "I know a lot of things have changed at this paper, Mavis. I hope you aren't one. Clive wants this hush hush."

Mavis met my gaze and winked, "There's no shakin' Mavis no matter who your daddy is." We both laughed with relief. The dead pressed against my throat again, itching to have me speak of them. But I couldn't risk her thinking again I was nuts; on the contrary, I needed her approval. So I added, "Clive asked me to work with Susan on this."

Mavis nearly choked on a bite of hot chili.

"When I saw her just now, I told her of some other story – a goose chase. I told Clive I'd rather use you for council. She'll run to Todd. I know it. She's less than a year from the Dark Side." Most reporters after a few years went to work for corporation.

Mavis nodded, this time blowing cool her steaming bite.

"I would really appreciate it if, just for a week or so, you would advise me and keep me from having to blow this by telling Susan. I have reason to believe this whole thing will work out."

She caught my eyes, "If you leap and get caught, it'll be your ass in a sling. Second, you might not like what you find."

"Don't jump to the finish, Mavis," I waved away her objection, "After all, now we don't know anything about him... So will you help me?" I lowered my head against the clicking of Mavis' tongue. She could tell I was holding back.

"One week, young blood. And I'll be checking. You better keep Clive away from Susan."

I beamed.

Back at work I stuck my head in, "Susan's aboard." Clive

nodded without looking up. I began to feel excited.

So at my desk, I wrote to Miss Peters at Tulane that I would wait to take custody of the letters, but would love to receive copy of any text mentioning or from San Francisco or mentioning a Ten or Ten–into–one, or any twin powers.

Finally Kris Bharatavan, the free–lance security whiz had sent word. We made an appointment for that evening.

Luckily in January, nights came early. The city's 1930's street lanterns glowed in the soft, early dark. The damp roads glistened. Air moist from a fresh rain tamped down the usual gritty urban sounds and smells. Avalanches and Sierras jammed the streets. The past flickered, but I found I could keep my attention from it.

I jogged 'cross Columbus, then up a block and a half to duck into a small building on Grant tucked between garishly lit tourist shops, bright yellow windows cluttered with electronics and mirrors, and a small, busy restaurant filled with Asian elders.

Kris' apartment had as many roaches as North Beach had people. They scurried to the corners as I bounded up the stairs. His door stood ajar when I reached the top.

Kris walked out of a small kitchen just beyond the door. "Did you find the hidden attachment? It's up," he said, mouth full of cereal. "It's cool. Take a look."

I followed his loose afro down the hall. His gold bathrobe hung open over loose, colorless culottes and a gold tee with a multi–armed blue figure. His belt trailed on the floor. A small lift in his step barely suggested he, too, was excited.

I peered at screens full of financial terms – Transfer Reference number, Source Establishment, Routing Code, Destination, and End Transfer.

"Your numbers were hexadecimal code. They decoded into this."

"Financial transactions," I read the screen.

"Wire transfers," bespectacled Kris spoke over his chewing. "The first set is downloaded records of twelve transactions to

multiple accounts from a single account. From 1972 to 1975.
Each for a million or more."

I withheld my whistle and scanned the screen. 1973 was the
year Berne had died.

"The second and current set itself looks divided in two. A
large transfer of 97 million in to start with; then transfers out to
all different accounts for widely varied amounts."

"They're for two, three, four million."   And the amounts
were all round numbers, but Kris continued not noticing my
eager relief.

"To over six dozen different accounts all on the same day –
February 15th – a Saturday – this year." The first and last
transfers are cuts off in the middle. This could be a portion of a
larger batch."

"Can you print this for me?"

"Already done." Kris handed me the pages. "But before you
take off...This code is hexadecimal, base 16." He swung down
into his chair and rocked 'round to look at me.

I crossed my arms and straightened my gaze.

"That's assembly language – the one that talks directly with
the circuits. It's hardly known anymore." He toggled something
and two black boxes of code filled the screen. "On this first one
– this tag in front references the larger data file they came from.
Like the home address of these records." The boxes flipped
positions. "But the second shows no such I.D., as if these
transfers were never recorded.

"But they haven't happened yet."

"The waiting ones would still be stored somewhere."

"You mean that these weren't processed through authorized
channels?" Here it came – the illegal transfers that had paid my
debts and would take down my career.

"Not only not authorized, but possibly not even known
about. This program speaks only to the circuits – not to any
operating system software – so they might not notice until they
reconciled the accounts. But if they can take data out – they can

also put it in, so maybe not until someone complains. So where are these from?" Kris had never asked me for a source before.

"Kris, I can't tell you."

"Jeannie," he placed his hand over his heart, sounding hurt. On the other hand I wanted Kris on my side and he might know someone, "On your God there?"

"On Krishna, I will not tell a soul." His black eyes warmed.

"Ever heard of the Grey Hats?"

His lips considered, "Dual point hackers? One guy in, one guy out – they do it to expose weaknesses in systems. There've been rumors of small–time free–lancers, but only urban myths..."

"Well," I stared at the printouts.

"I doubt you'll ever find these fellows." Kris said. "They wouldn't be careless. I'm surprised even this leaked."

"Frankly, so am I. Why would you broadcast your own theft? If I hear or read anything of this – you're cut off for all time you know. And I'll name names." Ah, dawned on me these transfers could be revenge for the KinCo payments 30 years ago. But the account numbers from the different years didn't match, let alone the amounts.

He waved me away. I dropped his bills – he preferred cash – and slapped a satisfied, munching him on the shoulder on my way out the door.

Back at Columbus, beneath the hill sure enough the green vapor rose. But my vision settled by Pearl's Jazz Club down Columbus. Whatever power I was using, it was doing me wonders.

On the way home, after wishing Cariña a sweet rest, I called Chuck. When he answered I said, "Hi," in a soft voice. After a bright response, there was awkward silence.

"It's about work," I assured him. "And it's fast. And maybe quite big. I wonder if you know anything about a Kincaid Semiconductor IPO." Through a long pause, a TV news program—probably Wall Street Week—played in the background.

"Why?" he asked.

"We got this tip."

A broadcast voice said, "The stock should tsunami."

"Oh Chuck, come on," I urged. "Would I ever reveal a source? Besides, I've got wire transfers for you."

"What wire transfers?" His interest sparked.

"Well, the tip suggested they have some bearing on the future of KinCo's new IPO."

He paused for long seconds. "Where'd you hear that?"

I turned toward the juniper bushes just outside my downstairs entryway, "Came in the mail—anonymously. Only here's the thing Chuck, I can't tell whose account numbers these are – if they're indeed Kincaid's."

Chuck took a breath. "Jeannie. It'd be my ass if anyone suspected. I'd lose my job. My certification. My licenses."

"I know, I know," I agreed softly, as a navy coated couple went through the door. "It's a risk. But what if you back KinCo's IPO and someone brings a lawsuit? This guy Berne has a lot of fans still. There's certainly some not-so hidden evidence. Starting with what we've got. Hope we're the *only* ones."

He was silent.

"Come on, I'll bet you want these transfers. Maybe even need them. I just need corroboration on this stock offering and these account numbers checked." I held open the door to my building.

"I—I'll think about it."

"Think fast, Chuck? I'll fax them to you at home."

My pace raced my pulse as I skedaddled six long Tenderloin blocks to the Cave – ten minutes early – to establish my space.

To get to the Cave, one walked carefully in three and a half inch heels through an alley cellar door, down a steep, industrial ladder, into a hulking gloom from which objects began to appear beneath thick wisps of smoke – low, spacious booths, pool tables, neon, and close-captioned TV's bookending a long wooden bar. In the back the jukebox played. The place really came alive much later judging by the hole in the back wall that led into a dark space with a stage.

As I walked to the last booth I spotted two businessmen in muted pickup with a Goth and a punk, behind them my mauve suit glimmered in the bar's mirror. I'd be all business tonight. At the last booth, I strode clear into those blue–black pools over a nearly finished pint.

Though tall and lithe, his embossed St. Moritz tee was faded; his well–used tailored wool jacket didn't look like any millionaire's. His face looked vaguely Southeastern European, with an extended shadow beneath the skin. His hair fell below his neck in kinky, rough curls tied by what seemed an ordinary black band.

"Echo?" At his nod I smiled, "My last interview wrapped up early…"

He laid down the financial page, which he'd marked up in red geometry.

"Getting some picks?" I gestured with my chin as I sat, tried to make moving the bulky case look smooth and graceful.

"Go ahead," he smiled and folded his long fingers and tidy nails 'cross his red design. .

"I beg your pardon?"

His eyes flicked to 11 o'clock behind me, a small smile, a nod yes. "You want bourbon?"

Had I told him in the forgotten hour? More likely Mavis had explained my state the other night. I nodded, my lips shut. He passed the order.

"Thank you so much for the other night. That night…I wasn't myself…something came over…"

His cheeks reddened as if from cold.

I half–laughed, "…got beyond me – to be honest."

He reached in to squeeze my hand and his touch brought back the pitch bliss. "It was an unusual…" his voice was a quiet rustle, "...experience for me...but I'd consider a repeat."   His praise ran into my cheeks. I removed his hand, scooted back a bit. "So why did you want to see me?"

His eyes crinkled and he leaned back, too. "You don't remember?"

I watched him a moment. "Matter of fact I think I do, Eric." An image of our heads together on a forest green couch, him whispering – me answering back softly – rose up.

He let out a chuckle and the memory ran and hid.

The waitress arrived, placed his martini just so with an authoritative twist and slid past him an ashtray. She'd done this before. He picked up his drink as she slid me bourbon neat – I smelled the Mark. This fellow didn't miss a trick. "You want me to investigate your father's death."

"Ha!" Challenge laced those eyes.

I scrabbled in my bag, pulled out the card.

He came forward and squinted at it before he scoffed and drew back. "Where'd you get that?"

"You don't know?"

He shook his head and asked, "Do you know what it is?"

"Why don't you tell me?"

"You first."

I glanced at it again. "Is it a universe?"

Both our shoulders tensed.

"Am I right?" He tipped his head, went for a cigarette. Though illegal, 'round the bar smoke rose from various spots.

"Well, what is it?"

He lit his butt, "A hologram. Kind of thing my father and other crackpots studied. Look it up."

"You know about the sites to him on the Internet?"

He snorted.

"Think any of them would send me something like this?"

He considered, "Why?"

I showed the card's innards to him.

He read it. His eyes flashed once before he lifted them.

"That true you think?" I asked.

"I don't know."

"You've never met any of his followers?"

"Miss Cadot." His formality stung.

"Jeannie, please."

"Jeanne," his emphatic French pronunciation reminded me again of Féy. Be just like her to recruit poor Anna's son just when she knew I was doing a story on them. Hadn't she said she was with me all the time? But what was I thinking? Did I think Eric was a *sorciére*? "I've not spoken of my father my entire life. Why would I speak of him to you?"

"You know I come from a long line of Creole women." I watched the smoke curl from his perfect arrowhead nose, down 'round razor cheeks, up rugged chin to rough lips. "One of us lived in San Francisco during the Gold Rush."

He weighed this on the end of his cig, "Tragic quadroon or mulatto?"

My blood rushed out the truth, "I'm the 15th in our line – African, French, Spanish and Indian who settled the French Quarter before 1811. Long before in fact."

His eyes changed from smug to curious. So had we discussed Féy in our lost hour? "And you are?"

He shook his head, "Californian."

I nodded, "The Kincaid's—"

"My father's people also go back to before the U.S. came in 1848."

"Oh. So…" my thoughts skidded to the picture of Cati and Benjamin.

"They were descended from a Peruvian and…one from your side of the fence. He'd escaped here early."

It was now or never. "Echo, by accident I knocked over a few of your books at your house. This fell in with my things." I laid the picture of Cati and Benjamin carefully in front of him. "I had a great great aunt who lived here. I thought they looked familiar. Seems they knew each other." I lay the photos of the

HMS Lawrence and Lilla and James down next to his.

His index finger ran over the partners' faces. And the Cave's noise faded, all my senses telescoped onto the Mark's smoky kick, Echo's clean wood and cigarette scent and his words.

"Before the Americans came, my family, half mestizo – native Indio and Spanish – half African, rose to be Governors, vice consuls, steamship owners, colonels, most favored sons. But in 1849 they lost all rights, and status."

Surely this was evidence of the Ten. "Did you know about any of their business ventures?"

"Just that she was from Peru, a dancer – maybe more – and so shunned by polite society. Still she married Benjamin Harris from Massachusetts and they had my great grandfather."

"Do the Kincaid's know about this?" I quickly added, "Did you know I interviewed your mother the other day? She didn't mention this."

His nod was curt. "She wouldn't."

"Does she know of your father's family?" But he went back to scribbling. "What's that?" I waved my drink at his red outlines.

He grinned, "I'm a...." he paused, "or do you know already that?"

"A forecasting *genius*." His laugh caressed my ear. But the entire page was covered with equations. "So what are you tracking?"

He took a healthy swig and signaled for another round. "What is that, which, being known, everything else becomes known?"

"That's what I'd like to know." I'd like to know it about more than just his page.

"The One behind the Many. Physicists and mathematicians have searched for the grand theory of everything for years." He laid his palm up on the table in front of me, inviting.

I took another sip, staring at his hand. Surely two nights ago I must've brushed his wrist. I remembered nothing but inky freedom.

He shook his bared hand, "Come on. Take a risk, journalist."

I laid my hand on top of his cool skin, palm down, fingers just beneath his wrist. My insides settled. Other patrons disappeared. The Cave's permanent beer smell vanished. Even our gum-snapping waitress didn't break the spell.

Casually I stretched my fingers to sweep his pulse – but came no black, no sudden scene. When I glanced up his eyes held a look of longing. So I relaxed. He didn't move until my hand rested like a weight. Then his other thumb brushed my neck birthmark.

"The Pentad from the five, the number and shape of life." Lowering his free hand, he traced from my wrist up along my pinkie. "First described by the ancient Greeks six centuries before the coming of Christ. Think of the human form: five appendages from the torso, limbs end in five fingers, five toes, and five senses – each in the shape of the pentad."

He ran 'cross the tip of my ring finger to the middle nail. "DaVinci's famed standing man describes a pentad." He drew a line down to the tip of my thumb. "And not just our bodies but the five's beneath every flower, leaf, fruit, plant pinecone, stingray, or cat's paw."

He lined down my thumb to the wrist then cut back 'cross to the part of the wrist where he began, "From the 5–sided star springs the star and the golden spiral, the shape of eardrums, of DNA, and of the heart muscle." Now he circled my palm, "snail shells, galaxies, waltzes, tangos. The spiral and the pentagram connect us to all life in the universe."

Sandwiching my hand in his, he repeated, "What is that, Jeanne, which, being known, everything else becomes known? That's what we're all seeking. For me it's math."

His voice washed over the demarcations left by his finger. "Do you know the meaning of the Ten?" I whispered.

He smiled. "So you don't remember? We spoke of it."

"Did we?" But I was musing on what it would be like if he

kissed me, telling myself probably this was a mix-up caused by Féy.

"So you're doing a story?" He let my hand go. Cold air rushed 'round it and without thinking I hid it in my lap.

He downed his drink and signaled for the check, pocketing the old photo, leaving the card on the table. No, no, my mind yelled. "American Dreamer – ever heard of it?"

He shook his head.

"It's a new twist on exposés." I lied. "We search out and interview anyone striving for the American Dream, whether or not they succeed. I'd like to do one on your father, his experiments from 30 years ago. We think that's what they were referencing on the card." His eyes now looked like the bay some days – cold, murky, sad when he glanced down at the old photos.

Then he pulled a wallet from his soft leather jacket. "I've got tickets for the Firebird, Friday night. You want to go?"

"By then you'll have an answer?"

"Six? We could have dinner first."

"I—I'll have to check." I pressed buttons on my Blackberry though I knew I'd nothing scheduled. "Uh, I've a cancellation. Six o'clock?"

"I'll pick you up."

My heart pounded against my chest. "13F."

He dropped some bills, rose and winked, and for a minute I wondered whether he'd been acting all this. Still all I could think was we had a second date – meeting.

He put on a hat from the seat next to him, and brought my hand to his lips. I tried not to imagine our bodies linking tight.

15 minutes later I climbed back outside. The waitress had refused to say more than, "Mr. Berne?" So he used both names. "Been here a few times. Nice man, good tipper."

His spiral remained inscribed on my palm. Though he may have done the same to our gum snapping waitress and countless others before, still, the remembered coil felt full of hope and significance – seduction and tangible destiny.

Six

"Received your message," My low tone played Mata-Hari with Chuck early after a refreshingly dreamless sleep. "Is it Kincaid?"

"Do you promise you won't mention me or my firm?"

"Industry insiders, right hand to God."

His hand muffled his voice, "The 1970's source account number matches to some old ones we used for KinCo." His voice was focused. "The target accounts…."

I held my breath.

"Well, one links to one of the Kincaid personal accounts still on our books. Hold on," he spoke up, "I'll be there in a second."

"Is it Anna's?" My heart rose.

"Numbered Swiss accounts are anonymous."

"But surely you know."

He didn't respond.

"What about the second set's accounts?"

"They don't look familiar."

"Oh, come on Chuck."

"Well, the source account is Swiss. So is the hub account. But not ours. Not any well-known Swiss bank. I can't search for them without a reason. And I won't lie or steal for you."

"Will you let me in to see?"

He paused, "What's going on, Jeannie?"

"There's a tip those transfers help prove KinCo's upcoming IPO or at least the technology powering it, belongs to the inventor murdered for it – 30 years ago..."

Chuck whisper whistled.

"KinCo *is* having a public offering?"

"It's a cardinal sin to leak any news during a blackout."

I paused, "If there were a blackout, how long would it be till Go/No Go?"

"With the dot bomb implosion, high tech market's well past bearish. We'd probably wait to see the Prize results in October."

"Prize results?"

"The Nobel prize?"

"Thanks, Chuck." My warmth flowed into the phone. "I'll get back to you long before that. And, Chuck? Thanks. Even for your escort to the party...I am awfully sorry about...."

He sighed. "Water under the bridge, Jeannie. Just keep me informed and *unknown*."

"Promise," I said. So someone in Anna's family had benefited to the tune of millions 'round the time of Berne's death – and the Grey Hats had sent out the evidence secretly hidden in an email. And then in a card, someone was moving large sums again – could they be connected? But why would the Grey Hats send me a card? That card was much more likely from Anna.

In the office, I searched out Shel Goldberg, Sheet science editor. He'd never heard of Berne. But he had heard of entanglement and of a Fulani and Coomb who'd completed the "First quantum teleportation of a photon. Thought to be short listed for the Nobel Prize in Physics." His red Afro bobbed. "Quantum micro–processors will squash current computing speeds, which will exponentially improve fiber optic communication, allow 100% secure encryption of on–line messages, crazily advance data analysis, simulation, nuclear and weapon systems."

I covered my excitement. Grand theories, seductive millionaire geniuses, Swiss banks, Nobel Prizes, nuclear and atomic weapons systems – how could it not be my ticket to *succés fou*. But KinCo sitting for 30 years on a technology Berne had been killed for? I needed to know why.

Clive was busy clicking and barking when I showed up. In the same move he hung up and fired at me, "Tell me something good, Slugger. Did you find the source of those transfers?"

"Oh, more than good," I jetted in as a junior editor poked in his head.

"Cut 2 inches before you come back," Clive bellowed.

"Well, nothing on my transfers yet. But it looks like some Kincaid got rich 'round the time of Berne's death." I dropped the decoded pages down. "To the tune of 12 one million dollar payments. And someone might be redistributing that wealth – and more."

"Any leads on who?"

"Not yet, but I found Anna's son – the hermit. Claims he knows nothing about this, but I'm not certain I believe him. Either way he could get me to her diary." My patter I hoped covered up my little omissions, about Susan, about who Eric was, and my rather unprofessional interaction with him. "Elder Berne's a little legend on the Internet – so quite a few suspects could link him to the Grey Hats. Perhaps they're getting revenge. I sure could use some time free."

Clive nodded, "Take Fridays – two of them."

"Two? Come on Clive. This story's been buried for 30 years. Give me ten."

You're nuts." He raised his hand, "Take five – final offer. We'll have an intern to cover you. Lili Soe – runs the Chronicle archives. Back in the day, she was a Metro E.A.   She might know something." He paused and walked toward the door. "With her don't use the cover.   She'll smell it…. oh, and bring her Star litchis – not chocolate covered – she loves them straight out of the jar."

Despite having no earthly notion what a litchi nut was, my mouth puckered.

Lili Soe, a solid, 60–ish Asian woman in a shirt of red and orange hibiscus flowers, heaved a book on top of a short stack of bound newspapers, clapped the dust off her hands and sneezed twice into the back of her wrist, "I'll take real paper any day." She tossed her head towards her computer. "I still believe there's a little man in back sending messages…" She sneezed again, crossed her arms over her chest and walked to the counter that separated us. She peered at me through lowered bifocals. "Who are you and what you want?" Her Brooklyn–accented voice that suggested she was a smoker, a jazz singer, or both.

"Jeannie Cadot, Metro, The Sheet." I extended my hand. Lili left it to swing in the breeze. "I'm researching a piece on Edward Berne, Sr., the physicist," I said. "My editor, Clive Jones, said you were the person to talk to."

"He did, huh?   Still trying to get me fired.   Always was a bastard." She offered a slight grin.

I smiled back.   All of us competed against the Bay Area's paper of record.   The rise of Internet and cable news didn't help their mood any.

Lili stared at me. "So, what do you want?"

"I want to get to everything I can on a man named Edward Berne and his death in 1973," I said. "Besides clippings I'd love to get a look at a photo file and notes. And talk with you, if you don't mind. Clive says you're the living archive 'round here."

Lili crossed her arms. "Can't help.   Got to be a member of the Chron staff.   But feel free to take a look at the coverage – that's public. Papers are filed over there by year." She pointed to a large block of filing cabinets.

Suddenly remembering Clive's suggestion, I pulled out the Star litchis. "I forgot," I turned back. "Clive mentioned you liked these. Hope they're the right kind?" I held the jar out to her, and watched as she reached for it.

"Om," Lili's eyes relaxed. "Casing the Wounded Knee takeover of Alcatraz my stash of these were sometimes all we had to eat. Nice to meet you." She extended her hand. I took it and grinned.

"Edward Berne, hunh? Why you digging that old story up?" Lili asked slowly after deliberately devouring three whole litchis in a row and methodically wiping her hands with a folded Brawny. "Got to deal with that family and that ain't easy. That's why the whole thing was kept quiet back when."

"Oh, yeah?" I flipped open my notebook.

"Check out the column inches. Coverage only ran over a week, maybe 15 inches on the whole story. Our team had a lot more than that. But that old man Kincaid – he was very influential. We all got reassigned just eight days after the fire. In so many words, they communicated," Lili's voice dropped, "that to do otherwise would negatively *impact* our jobs."

I scribbled furiously. "Why, do you think?"

"Well, they said," Lili walked back to her round metal garbage can, warming to her story, "it was to spare the poor widow and her two small children any more undue harassment. They'd already been through enough already – blah, blah, blah." She tossed in the crumpled towel.

"But the reporter didn't believe that." She walked back toward the counter, "Takes a hell of a will – doesn't it – to sit still long enough to allow flames to kill you, melt your fat. Edward Berne – and that Vietnamese monk – are the only ones I remember." She stared. "And I've been in this work for 35 years."

"Why do you say he just sat there?"

She paused, shrugged, "Something about the police reports I think." She cleaned her glasses with the hem of her shirt. "Still, hopefully he was dead of smoke and gas inhalation long before." She put the glasses back on and flipped her left arm casually, her eyes surveying the library. "It's not much, but it's all mine. You go over there and look up those stories. You get 25 minutes before we get busy. Berne died October, 1973."

"Thanks, Lili." She had one heck of a memory. Lili returned to squint at her screen.

Coverage of the Berne incident had run for only one week in October 1973, just as Lili'd said. Three short articles were buried in the bottom half of the Metro front page. The longest was the first.

> Four fire units battled against a blaze in Claremont last evening. Killed was Edward Berne, prominent Berkeley physicist and husband of Anna Kincaid, only daughter of Alec and Pauline Kincaid, of Menlo Park's Kincaid Semiconductor Corporation.
>
> Berne was believed to have been home alone working in his basement laboratory. He worked most recently on laser holography at the University of California at Berkeley and was known to seclude himself for hours in the basement–constructed facility. According to fire department sources, special steel alloy casing turned it into an incinerator while protecting the rest of the house.
>
> The Piedmont fire department responded to the call. "Gaining access was the most dangerous part of the operation," a firehouse spokesman said. "Because of the airtight, steel lining, if we let in too much oxygen too quick, the explosion might have taken even neighboring homes.

Having to wait until temperatures were safe for entry, we were unable to save any inhabitant."

According to Chief Wolcott the fire team found laser debris and quartz crystals in the rubble. There was no sign of forced entry and no suicide note. Berne is survived by his wife and their two children, Eric and Heather Berne. A private ceremony will be held at the Bar Elev Temple. In lieu of flowers, the family requests donations to the Cal Scholarship Fund.

A day later, Berne's obituary dovetailed with the websites. It added that Enrico Fulani, the Nobel Prize contender, who had then been Director of the Berkeley Physics Department, had begun an inquiry in 1981 'round an applied entanglement experiment. Berne resigned shortly after, died a year later.

In two days more a blurb was buried in page two of Metro. The byline read Staff Writers. The item stated that due to the devastated state of the remains, there was no medical examination or coroner's report. Police called the fire accidental from malfunction of various laser devices. They didn't mention what spread a fire in an all—metal space. I couldn't think what accelerant could stick to metal walls.

At the counter, Lili eyed me, "Find what you're looking for?"

"You were right. There's not much. Given the scandal, the fire, why wasn't there a bigger investigation?"

Lili shrugged. Behind her desk sat pictures of grandkids.

"I know his wife and son. She's dying. She says there's something more to the story. She asked me to find it."

Lili was quiet. Then she slapped down a yellowed business card on the counter. 'Sid Shafter, Editor, The Vallarta Expat' was clearly printed on the front. "He moved down there a while ago. Shouldn't be too hard for a bright young cub like you to catch up with him," she said.

I scribbled down the info, "Why'd he go—"

Lili held up a hand, "Except for Sid and Clive, you didn't hear it from me. I haven't even talked to you. But tell Clive he owes me more than just lychees." Strange how you can feel you're looking up to someone who's considerably shorter than you. Lili winked and turned back to her computer signaling the close of our interview.

Back at my desk, Blowhard popped into my mind. He'd have a Swiss bank contact. I twisted my mouth as if I'd tasted something sour.

"What can I do for you?" Blowhard's eyes traced me from head to foot. I imagined it took all his strength not to lick his lips, so I got right to the point.

"Did you put something in my drink on the ship?"

"Wha—at? What kind of man do you take me for?"

"Oh please. Well, if you answer this, perhaps I'll believe you. If a friend of mine needed some information from a Swiss Bank, what would they have to do?"

This brought his features back into place. "Well, it helps if you're God."

"What about *unofficially*," I spoke casually.

"Yeah?" Blowhard turned in his chair and laughed. "You know anonymous banking for them is a national heritage? They consider themselves almost holy for fuck's sake. And the government watches them like a hawk. Only very, very occasionally might one give anything up. You got 100 grand and three months? Or a cool quarter million will speed things up. I could make some calls. What do you got?"

I marched away ignoring his twice-repeated, "What you got," that followed me down the hall.

Seven

"You brought her litchis?" At first, Sid Shafter made me repeat everything. The tuneless clack of ice punctuated his silence and sprightly Mariachi music played in the background.

"Clive suggested it," I hurried.

Silence melted into soft chuckle. "Sucks 'em down like grapes." I sighed in relief. "Shit, you're looking into the Berne case? Good luck." He exhaled.

Sid could be the source of the tip. "Oh yeah? Why?"

"That bitch, the Grande Mere." A slight slur dragged down his speech.

I scribbled Pauline v. Sid. "That would be Mrs. Kincaid?"

"Might as well call the bitch Your Highness." He slurped. "Otra, por favor. She officially took over the family mantle after her old man kicked. He wasn't a bad guy, paid industry-high wages, hired unions, kept the company private, proud, generous – old school. But once she assumed ownership of the factory, the family – things were different," he laughed.

"A real go–getter."

"More like Attila the Hun." Sid bellowed. "In the 70's *she* broke the back of the union, blackmailing the chief negotiator with dirty pictures to not oppose breaking their contract. Went public and dumped 350 poor sods out on the street. In the 80's another 75 workers gone, this time management and now they're private again. She and her clan make another bundle."

"So she's a tough lady."

"Tougher than a witch's tit." "I'll bet that whole family was in on it," Sid continued. "Putting the screws to Berne."

"What do you mean?"

"A conspiracy," ice clinked again in my ear.

"Conspiracy," my hope flattened. Clive had spoken of washed–out beat journalists in Mexico spouting tales of widespread corruption and betrayal over tequila shots. He said current wisdom held that the real conspiracy was what brought those drinks to their lips over and again.

"Hell, yeah," Sid practically shouted. "Look, kid. It doesn't take genius to see that Berne worked on unleashing nuclear power, speeding up silicon manufacture, sending information faster than the speed of light. He's never had a large experimental accident. So there he is working furiously on some experiment with monster applications – and he reportedly gets some breakthrough, but right after he's forced to resign, goes home, builds another lab and works like a madman until an accidental fire takes him out. There's rumors about some unpublished proof, but I couldn't find any."

"So what do you think happened?"

"That bitch made sure that case got shut down pronto. No besmirching the family name. Kincaid, that is."

I paused, remembering her anger at finding me. "So Grande Mere called in a favor?"

"Got those files sealed tight as her heart. Even my regular sources wouldn't help. But that was just for starters. Three weeks into the story, they fired me. They didn't defend me, or even just take me off the story – they fired me. No questions asked. Bastards."

"Jesus," I said. "Didn't you appeal?"

"The managing editor went to all Grande Mere's hoity toity affairs – so did the Union Rep. Grande Mere could've cut that off with a wave of her bony finger. Not only that, but I was out on the entire West Coast: LA, Frisco, Seattle. I could have sued," his hate dissipated, "But then I never would-a worked again. You know this business."

Legal budgets were expensive so newspapers could be pretty unforgiving. Still one could usually find some ally.

Sid continued, "The only offers I got worth anything were in Detroit or Boise or Akron. So I said to hell with being landlocked and here I am, writing on tourism in Vallarta, making other expats think they belong." There was a long pause followed by a noisy smacking of lips. "Next question?"

"Who told you about Berne's breakthrough?"

I could hear the smile in his voice, "It's pretty common knowledge among his fans."

I spoke quickly. "You mean the websites. Do you know this Max Conrad?"

But he went on as if he'd not heard. "He was working on some highly classified stuff that could help KinCo. Pauline took him down. I wouldn't be surprised if their whole 'marriage' was a sham. Tell you what, kid. Check out those police files if you can get your hands on 'em."

"Why?"

"First officer on the scene told me there were no remains. No ashes, nothing."

"So you think he wasn't there? That he's not dead?"

"Maybe he's in Puerto Vallarta." He was about to hang up.

"Wait, Sid. Why'd they seal the files?"

"They said juvenile involvement." His voice vibrated.

"You mean Anna's kids?"

"I saw them at the service of course. That boy, eight maybe – he kept silent, like he knew something. The sister, she was a pretty thing…flighty, not tracking. In shock I guess."

"Not long after, she ended up dead. Do you remember the first officer on the scene?"

"They'd be retired now. Maybe even gone."

I looked back over my notes. "You got those any of those photo file pictures?"

"Yup," Sid said after a moment.

"Use this messenger account." We exchanged particulars before I hung up. So Berne had had a late career breakthrough, Pauline could easily ruin or kill me and Eric had been tracking back then – all according to a conspiracy theorist eager to find a partner for his crazy notions. But his old photos would help.

At lunch, I stopped for cash. My balance was $98.65. In another 10 days I'd get a check to save – if my debts truly were paid. No news on my traces was good news for me, but before long I'd have to push on them again. Clive would insist. I ought to check those Feb 15th wire transfers, see if one was coming to me.

Luckily Clive was gone when I returned.

Eight

We sat over a Bourbon sour and martini at a small place actually in North Beach on the bottom of the hill, known mostly by locals – too dark for the 'wanna–be–seen's.' "My editor asked me again about that profile on your father."

Echo's eyes froze over his shiny, smoke tie. "Why do you suppose he did that?"

"Well," I went in softly. "It seems the 30th anniversary of your father's.... passing...is coming up. Clive—my editor—knew of your dad at Berkeley. He admired him." Out of the corner of my eye I saw the swish of an old, long gown and I tightened my jaw, shook the image away.

Echo watched my mouth. His eyes solidified.

Tiny beads of perspiration left my palms clammy. I went on gingerly, "As I said, we believe that your father might be an American Dreamer."

"Oh, really?" he said.

"A striver, wrongly accused," I said. "Life destroyed. Remember my new column?"

He signaled yes.

"Your father was controversial, wasn't he?"

Echo shrugged his features.

"At Berkeley he was a rebel, gave speeches...eventually resigned?"

Though at a glance Echo looked casual, intensity laced his eyes and taut mouth.

"Well..." Now I watched him closely. "Sounds like your father fits into our profile." His eyes barely flickered. "So my editor thought we might check it out. Profile your whole family for a feature."

The din of the restaurant became thick 'round us. This time there was no velvet cocoon, but thankfully that eased the green edges.

"What exactly do you want to know?"

I stared at his steepled fingers. "Oh, anecdotes mostly," my hand flipped as if to say, 'It's nothing'. "His science, his career, and of course, your family life. You had a sister, didn't you?" I reached for my pad.

He stayed my arm. "Hold on there, Jeanne. I won't subject his name to any more disrespect." He sat back and crossed his arms. "And you don't lie very well."

Dropping the notebook and pen back into my black newsboy bag, my palms went up. "Echo, it's a profile – really. We want to know what your father dreamed of, what happened at the end. Other folks still profit from the plasma, the entanglement theory, why not his final experiments? You seemed to want to talk about him last time."

He slowly wrapped his fingers 'round the handle of his glass.

"Echo, it must have been just awful for you." I touched his hand briefly, felt the calm black rush into my fingertips.

"The impact on me is not...important." His face set like stone.

I heard Anna's voice, *It's what he wants...would have wanted.* I replied softly, "It was to your father. Your mother, too. She seemed to feel deep regret when we interviewed."

He jerked his neck back and brought the glass to his lips. For a while we just sat. Then I leaned in and lowered my voice, "After our dance Saturday night – I thought you wanted to talk to me. I thought you'd chosen me."

His eyes shot up.

"It was such a coincidence waking up in your place, and then finding that picture, and the way it felt being with you....like we'd been together before..." How cliché I must sound. "So I did some sleuthing of my own." He almost cracked a smile, but sadness stayed settled in his lines. "You've just come back from Europe?"

He dropped his chin. "Maman wanted to die here at home."

I squeezed his hand. "How awful it must be losing the last member of your family so young."

"You have also lost your parents?"

"They both died when I was 12." As I suspected he would, Echo caught my eye. So perhaps he did know of Féy – or had I told him that first night? "Well, my mother died and with her all the information I had on my father – he never knew of me." I took a big sip to push down the threatening past. "But don't cry for me – I've dreamed of coming to San Francisco since I was ten. And now I'm here."

He just smiled, as my garlic sea scallops and his rare Filet Mignon arrived, along with a bottle of Chianti that he coaxed away from the waiter. Pouring me a big glass, Echo said, "Tell me more. I like it when you convince me."

"Well," I flushed a bit, "Your father would say we're entangled with our pasts. In every interview I've done the past lives on – sometimes kills. Like with your mother."

Something flickered 'cross Echo's face, but his voice was bland, "Oh really?"

"She lives in regret – especially about your father. She suggested it influenced her choice to pursue care."

I watched him closely. His eyes caught mine with bitter

satisfaction. "And what about me?"

I gave it some thought. "I think you carry your past with you for love. But it's dragging you down. That's why you *should* do this piece. Then you can let your burden down," my voice caught a frog; I gave him a wry smile.

"And what about you and yours?"

"My past?" I took a sip of Cosmo to clear my throat.

He nodded.

"Everything I am is a result of strangely good, bad luck and hard work."

Echo refilled my wine, but I caught a latent smile in his eyes.

It was exciting to hurry through the well–dressed crowd on the broad sidewalks of the Civic Center to the Opera House. Eric pulled me up the wide steps and then red–carpeted staircase to the boxes to the syncopated Russian chords that announced the overture.

We sat behind his friends and could see musicians in the pit below us, but could move ourselves in relative privacy. As a child, once in orchestra seats with Moman L for a travelling Peter and the Wolf, I'd imagined myself up here above the fray.

Echo's spiced cedar scent, his proximity next to me, the gaily–dressed, graceful Firebird twirling 'round the stage, all made a magical space, similar to our previous dance. So, though I shouldn't have, I shifted back against the hand he rested on rear of my chair, and his fingers moved to caress my neck where the hair ends.

His touch brought the black tunnel to the green fog, with a hint of frying metal subtly shifting the orange and red sequined dancers to green-tinged grey and black suits on muddy board sidewalks. But this time even the burning metal smelled welcome, the rushing voices did not frighten, nor was there any hint of Féy.

When Eric's hand moved to graze my upper arm as he leaned in for the second movement, the vision flickered in as if its signal had been boosted. Back on the *HMS Lawrence II* Cati and the tuxedo'd young waiter walked out the main chamber to a tiny galley where Lilla stirred a pot and James chided a waiter whose shirtwaist had escaped his cummerbund. So our relatives had worked the ship and Kincaid had bankrolled it?

Eric shifted and the scene rolled again. Now a brown grass hill, muddy planks sharply sloped to two, crude board buildings, one two stories tall with a tiny balcony. As I'd seen when I'd picked up Chuck for the Belle. In past a rough board door and long bar, past a few tables and chairs, and an out of tune piano, to the back, where at the biggest pock-marked table sat Cati, her head mantled, her husband, Benjamin, standing behind her, fingers in his vest pocket, the white man standing above them both, two fingers on his lips, and now Lilla and James came in.

There were papers on the table and Cati signed them, followed by each in turn. Try as I might I couldn't overhear their conversation or get close enough to see the contract I presumed. I leant forward, leaving Eric's hand. The scene disintegrated back to the bare stage studded with giant, bright green trees.

Eric's fingers ran up my back, but the scene didn't return. During intermission we met his friends' friends Jane and Johnny.

"Well, that was just wonderful," breathed a glowing Jane, "I haven't seen that combination of strength and grace since Baryshnikov. Our little one loved him, I could feel her kicking." She patted and smiled at her very pregnant belly.

Her husband chuckled, "Perhaps I should get myself some tights."

"The not–quite–ready–for–public–viewing *corps de ballet*. I'll get bedroom seats," Janie teased.

They seemed as if they'd not known a harsh moment in their lives, and it brought back hope. "I dream for a life as beautiful as that ballet. At the end I'd like my life to have been romantic."

Without pause Echo shot, "What we have much more of is tragedy, drama. And yet we prefer to pay strangers to see it acted out on stage. To see meaning we'd never dare approach in reality. Most people," he slowed and met my eyes, "want others to live for them. Like celebrities. It's not lack of opportunity, but lack of courage that is the greatest threat to a well–lived life."

I balled my hands – his own *mother* had noticed my courage. "I know it is far easier to accept a drama long buried," my eyes flashed, "than one that is a live, twisting snake." Soon as I spoke I regretted it.

"Come, come," John said and slapped Echo a little hard on the back. "Some philosophic debate with our art? Shake hands and come out friends. Look, there are the lights."

I glanced at Echo and pursed a little smile, but he was silent and physically distant for the disturbingly un–magical second half.

"You know, Jeanne," we stepped out onto my balcony, brandies in hand, lights of the skyscrapers on full display behind us. "Please don't take my words tonight too harshly." He sighed staring into buildings. "I hadn't thought about my father... thought about sharing him for some time." He turned to me. "Still tonight I enjoyed myself – as always." He outlined my cheek.

Diffused light from all the windows, the calm energy from his hand, it all softened my doubts and brought back the black.

"So tell me," he rolled back against the railing; the Financial District looming behind his head.

"Tell you what?" The warm light, the mild night, his voice, the city hum far beneath, it all lulled me.

"Tell me again why you really want to write this story. Make me believe you."

Slowly I set my arms on the railing next to him, "There are a lot of reasons." I see dead people for one; I want you for another.

He crossed his arms.

I stared at my Macy's mittens, now paid for on the Visa perhaps by him, and I thought about Cariña, the twin powers being seduction and possibly love – and that Clive would say a source should never be in a reporter's home.

"Fact is, Echo," but up from inside bubbled Moman L's, *we don't keep our place by being open and free.* My voice solidified, "Echo, profiles remake legacies. Don't you owe your dad – especially if someone's stealing his work?"

He acquiesced with a sidewise nod, but kept his eyes on my apartment rather than me.

My hand tightened 'round my mug. "Besides both of us having pioneer ancestors who *knew* each other… we are in some way old friends." It surprised me how hard it was to hold back the truth – about Cariña, about how much his story meant to us.

His eyes lingered on me. "I was nine when the feeding frenzy ended, but I felt ninety. It devastated our family, almost destroyed my mother." His eyes glanced behind me. "It's why we left the States."

My face tightened. "I thought there was little coverage."

"There was plenty in the science press," he said. "My father was incredibly dumb."

"But he was a world–class physicist."

Echo laughed and tapped his head. "He was a physicist dedicated to proving points that were not scientific."

"Oh Eric, come on."

"All right," he pulled me to my small, mottled glass table. A gust of wind hurried us to sit close to each other. "Science requires we are external to the experiment." He took off his Cartier. "Einstein said a physicist is like a man trying to understand the mechanism of a watch with no way to open it. So he makes reasonable explanations based on the ticking of the hands, the winding process, the numbers on the dial, the weight of the thing."

His second hand clicked with Swiss precision. And I thought this method could apply to trying to read sources.

"Inside the atom every observation affects it. By simply *seeing* a wave or a particle, we change its reality." He snapped the watch back on.

"So how do we actually learn about anything subatomic?"
"This wasn't lost on other theoreticians. Just my father."
"Or," I countered. "We look for methods that can observe a particle without changing it." The same for a source.
Echo spoke sharply. "There is a reality beneath our five senses. But we can never think of its nature. We are caged by our very thoughts, which are born of time and senses. We can't think our way to an answer. So he went beyond thought." When he said this, a chill ran down me. "In the end, he lost everything." His hand played with the ear of his mug.
"Is it true there were no remains?"
His eyes flashed. "I was eight, watching him shrink away."
The magic of the night floated away over muffled traffic. Féy's death had been fast, at least and left little carnage behind. We moved back inside.
"Echo," at the door I leant forward. "Do you know any of your father's website guys? I can't get them to respond to me."
He shook his head.
"Are any of his files left?" Somewhere there must be a clue.
He dropped his shoulders. "Friday night?"
That long, "Yes." My fervor maybe showed, as he grinned.
I lifted my hand to meet his, willing my fingers still.
Now Echo smiled broadly, "San Mateo Airport. North of Half Moon Bay. An hour before sunset. Don't be late. Good night, Jeanne." He kissed my hand, his thumb lingering. When he kissed my lips, I held back. But each place he touched, as before on my palm, echoed after he'd gone.

The next morning news had come from Tulane – mention of a Lilla Cadot who'd gone out west. Being a fourth daughter there'd been no letter from her, but her elder sister Genevieve had mentioned her migration, her marriage to a prominent citizen. She would translate and send registered snail mail – they didn't feel comfortable sending cross the Internet. I hit reply.

Nine

Monday through Thursday passed by as in a dream. No news from Eric, Tulane, Max Conrad or Annie French – though now I had Kris looking for her. I found no accounts close to any of my numbers in the wire transfers – and besides, none of them had yet been made. So who the heck had made mine?

Friday I rose at dawn. After a frustrating hour with the card companies, it turned out that just because someone had paid my bills didn't mean I had the right to know who or where from. That would impede on the depositor's right to privacy. Their investigation was ongoing. If they found anything illegal they'd certainly let me know. I asked if the source accounts were Swiss. Their silence was readable as either yes or I don't know. Same as it was when I told them where I worked.

My first stop was the historical library. Though placed smack dab in the metallurgy section of old town, the hotels and museums stayed firm. I searched through large archival photo files without luck. Every time articles, letters or journals mentioned a "Negro" they'd rarely mention a name or only the first. There was even less on the Peruvians. After an hour I went entirely to the Kincaid's.

There were newspaper articles, stories in letters, even a ship registry of the *HMS Lawrence II* with Kincaid as owner. Finally in a picture of the Bank of California directors, there was an indistinguishable black man behind Kincaid, identified only as Jim. It could be my – Lilla's – James Collins. I ordered an enlargement of the photo.

Off the Bay Bridge, the water sparkled blue, dotted with sails. Windows on Alcatraz, trees on Mt. Tam, numbers on the face of the Campanile, all stood in high relief.

Fulani, one of the men I was going to see – Berne's former boss, had called his work "pure garbage" before firing him. He wasn't the only one. It had been called "pandering," "misguided," "bordering on science fiction" and "softer than social science" in reputable physics journals.

So my heart rate rose with me up the Berkeley hill to Birge Hall. Cold crept up with the wind and the sun already hung above the horizon. By 5:20 it would seem the middle of the night. I was to be with Eric on the coast at four. Anticipation rippled through me. Tonight I'd come hell or high water, I had to get his "yes."

But now my hope was Michael Coomb – Enrico Fulani's younger colleague. Berne had been his thesis advisor and they'd worked together for years. They'd written together on teleportation, the science and the science fiction. But in the end Coomb's allegiance had swung – and to his betterment. Scientific American had said of Fulani and Coomb's recent experiment:

"We are one step closer to large–body teleportation – the Star Trek form of travel that enables objects to move from place to place in an eye's blink without wasted resource, wasted time or stress. To date it's been science fiction. Heisenberg's Uncertainty Principle prevents it.

But new photon teleportation experiments by Enrico Fulani and Michael Coomb may pave the way for computers that could eventually allow for exploring just that."

Approaching the steps, I sucked in a lungful of cooling air, yanked open the double door, and bounded up the few steps into the stuffy, stale, sweat odor of the Physics hall.

A man with blue jeans, cowboy boots and tan suede jacket opened the windowed door, "Office hours are Tuesdays." A wizened old man sat reclined behind a desk layered with papers, gazing out a window.

I showed my press pass. "Jeannie Cadot. With The Sheet. I spoke to your secretary. We're doing a piece on likely local Nobel contenders – 'Teleportation: Science Fiction or A Nobel Dream'."

Coomb widened the door and extended his hand, "Michael Coomb."

I smiled, "She said today would be a good time to get you?"

Coomb cracked the door more as he turned to Fulani who swiveled from the window with bright eyes, his mouth stern, his face lined. He looked as if he were used to getting his way. His hearing was still fine as he said not without affection, "Get out, get out, you monkeys. Give us a half hour, will you?" Coomb opened the door and several undergraduates – all thin, acned, white, Asian and one black – hurried out glancing at me, papers clasped to their chests.

Fulani stared at me as I came in, and then he and Coomb exchanged looks.

Coomb said, "We can give you a few minutes. Forgive the mess." He walked over and pulled out a chair at a messy round table. "We're preparing for a conference."

I nodded at him as I walked over to Fulani. "It is an honor to meet you, professor," I extended my hand. A curt nod was his only reply.

I set up my tape recorder on his desk. "We're focused on the 'science fiction' history of teleportation and how you two made it science. For instance, there's a fellow," I looked down at my notes, "Edward Berne. He worked with you. But his work was–"

"Ed Berne is not worth our time," Fulani spoke in a voice refined in lecture halls. "His ideas were ludicrous, his science more like ideology. He distrusted science in the end. He's really nothing more than an embarrassment."

"But why was it so nuts...so we can say why yours isn't."

Coomb's glance checked Fulani. Then he shrugged. "We'll do our best."

"I've read some of your work on quantum teleportation. Zapping objects through space."

"We do not 'zap'." Fulani sighed, "We swap identities."

"But we've only 'zapped' photons – light particles – we're nowhere near large bodies yet," Coomb added. "But maybe one far, far, far day."

Fulani scoffed. "You must forgive him, Miss. He's a romantic. That *is* science fiction."

"Well," I said, "it's what Berne was working on. Entanglement in large-body objects."

I heard a practiced, mellow twang in Coomb's voice as he turned to his boss," Let's give the lady *some* content."

Fulani revolved back to the window pressed back in his chair.

"Berne's theory was not entirely mad. Most, if not all, of the great theoretical physicists and mathematicians have searched for the primary equations explaining the universe, Einstein's Grand Unified Theory."

"The big T.O.E.," I said flashing on Eric's coil on my palm. Coomb nodded. Fulani just stared at a paper he held.

"But Newtonian mechanics doesn't work at the speed of light *or* inside an atom. To theoreticians this means that Newton, relativity, and quantum mechanics are subsets of some larger truth." He stopped and I wondered – could he be the tipster?

Coomb smiled. "Once we got inside the atom, we didn't have any way to see. Light waves – our main investigative instrument – literally can't see a particle. A wavelength is much longer than a particle." Coomb drew an arc of one hand over the other.

"So eventually, instead of using light, we bombarded atoms with particles. Based on how they bounced we interpolated the structure." He paused. "But when we bombard a particle, we shoot to heck either its position or its momentum – our most fundamental Newtonian measurements. The more precisely we know one, the less we know of the other."

"Heisenberg's Uncertainty Principle," I said. At the window Fulani sighed, obviously hoping to embarrass and hurry me.

But Coomb ignored him, "So we can't study anything at a sub–atomic level without changing its material nature. We can't say for certain where it is. We don't know really where it's going. We can't even really know that it truly existed prior to our bombardment."

"Sub-atomic reality slippery," I jotted thinking it explained a lot of mine.

"That compromises one of the basic requirements of the scientific method – objectivity."

"The observer doesn't affect the observed," I said. "Einstein's watch."

"Very good," Coomb said. Warmth flowed from his shy grin.

But Fulani sneered, "The quantum mechanics algorithms produce extraordinarily precise predictions of sub–atomic activity – despite these flaws. So our more practical students focused on solving *specific* problems, rather than tackling *irrelevant* paradoxes."

But Coomb grimaced and said, "Berne, like Einstein, wanted an objective reality to underlie sub–atomic theory, just as it underlies Newton's. But best as we can tell on the level of an electron, the world is a chaos of transformation. Electrons turn into photons, matter becomes energy and vice versa. Particles from our apparatus morph into electrons in my fingernail.

Billions of times each second. The Cosmic Dance," Coomb's words brought a flash of being spun by Echo. "The randomness drove Berne nuts. God doesn't play dice with the universe. As Einstein said." Fulani scowled.

"So Berne thought discovery of the sub–atomic world with its own laws and limits proved there are multiple levels of reality. He envisioned these levels extending to infinity. Further, he thought that just as with levels of human experience – biological, psychological, social – each level influences those adjacent. Each level of reality reflects or mirrors the others. The microcosm reflects the macrocosm.

"He called the level we live in – what we touch, see, hear, smell and feel – the explicate order. He proposed it is only the reflection of something deeper – a level on which all things we see as discrete are actually one. He called this the implicate order. There exist none of the dyads that characterize our level of existence: living and dead, past and present, matter and energy, even life and death. Here you would see all the connections between entities and events that look discrete to us."

Fulani snorted, "A scientist's Heaven."

Also, an explanation for my visions.

Coomb walked over to the chalkboard, erased some complicated equations. "He had a famous experiment to demonstrate the relationship between the realities. A kind of bundt pan of two concentric glass cylinders." He drew two circles, one in the center of the other.

"He filled the space between them with glycerin, a fairly gluey substance. Then he put a drop of ink in the fluid and turned the outer cylinder. As the fluid moved, the drop was drawn out into a thread that eventually became so thin that it disappeared from view. Berne said that when the ink was *enfolded* like this through the glycerin in a million little particles, it possessed a hidden connection. Much like separate phenomena in our world possess a non–manifest link."

"Wait a minute," I said. "So things that look separate to us 'cross time are really part of a whole?" Like the dead that keep hounding me?

Coomb clapped the chalk off his hands and came back, "Or across space. Even systems and events can be linked in the fundamental level. Berne set out to prove these hidden connections could be exploited by science."

"For time travel? Visits from the dead and gone?"

Coomb shrugged. Fulani chuckled.

"So how do we know what's connected?"

Fulani turned from the window. "Can we wrap this up?"

Coomb cast a look his way. "All right. Look." Coomb cut the air with his hands. "The scientific approach is one of analysis – breaking things down into smaller and smaller chunks. The goal is to find the smallest possible components of the universe, and the relationships between them. OK?"

I nodded.

"But Berne knew sub-atomically there were no separate entities. He began seeking ways to experiment from the inside–out, not the outside–in."

"We have the whole universe within us," Fulani waved his hand over his hand.

Coomb spoke quickly. "So – and here's where it gets nuts. Edward thought he could experience the quantum dynamics of the universe within his own *form,* and through controlled, subtle, muscular movements *sense* the laws that govern it."

"Ha!" Fulani's dry laugh turned into a raspy cough. Coomb paused until he sipped from a glass on his desk just for this purpose, judging by how quickly his hand went for it.

Coomb went on. "Certainly to think you can feel all the phenomena of the universe inside your own mind and body was crazy, but his mathematics always solidified, verified, even made elegant, the findings he'd bring back from his 'excursions'."

With Fulani getting antsy, I figured my time was getting short. "Do you know anything about his final experiments at home?"

Fulani shot a look at Coomb, "Professor?"

Coomb bobbed his shoulders once.

Taking a deep breath I said, "Wait a minute. You called it garbage. In Physics?"

Fulani's eyes shrank to slits, but he spoke casually, "Later in his life Berne did some strange work with holograms. I never understood it. Holograms are made with lasers. Lasers are just concentrated light – and as we already know, light doesn't penetrate an atom."

"But you use lasers to create entangled pairs also, don't you?" I ruffled out their article.

"I am familiar with the process, Miss," Fulani barked.

I made a note to talk alone with Coomb who now easily hid a smile by speaking, "To make a hologram, a laser light is split into two beams, one of which is reflected off an object onto a photographic plate where it interferes with the second. On the plate, the recorded swirls of the interference pattern appear meaningless and chaotic. But the pattern possesses a hidden order and when it's relit with the first beam, it produces a three–dimensional image of the original object."

"So the hologram is the explicate order," I murmured. "And the plate contains swirls of implicate order."

"Right! But a hologram, of course, is just a representation of matter. If you put your hand in it, it would swipe right through the image."

"An illusion," Fulani said. "Just like Berne's 'science'."

I wondered if my pioneers were like holograms – would I swipe right through them?

Coomb continued as if he'd not heard Fulani, "A remarkable feature of a hologram is that if a holographic film is cut into pieces, each piece produces an image of the whole object. Though the smaller the piece, the hazier the image, the explicate picture is manifest in the smallest divisible piece of the plate."

"But so what?" Fulani had had enough.

Coomb nodded without looking back. "If even the tiniest part of the universe, say an electron, has encoded in it – even faintly – the picture, if you will – of the entire universe – a universal footprint. If we could tap into this footprint at the right level, we could release the secrets – and power – of existence itself."

"You mean like time travel?" Relief flooded me.

Coomb nodded, "I mean like the end of death – traveling to and from heaven like we'd go to Bermuda. Breaking the barriers between everything: life and death, male and female, young and old. This is what extended his reputation to poets, scholars, hippie–activists, early computer fans, and seekers, and dreamers."

"You all know about the websites?"

Fulani turned to us again. "Ideology drives science straight to hell. No standards of factual rigor any more. Berne was one of the pioneers of faux physics."

"Now hold on, Professor," Coomb interjected. "He was not an ideologue."

I took a deep breath. "What about the rumor he was nominated for a Nobel prize?"

Fulani exploded, "There is no Nobel prize in mathematics, which was Berne's strength."

"I meant for his work on entanglement. Lasers are used to create the entangled particle pairs necessary for teleportation." I asked casually, despite the hammering of my heart, half-expecting him to throw me out.

"Yes, yes. As you said, lasers can create entangled photons. But whether Edward Berne was working on teleportation, or not, doesn't rank – does not matter. His experimentation was driven by imagination and intuition. *Science* is driven by measurement, mathematics, and logic."

"But," I pressed, "I thought he was a great mathematician?"

Fulani said nothing. He'd given up.

Coomb interjected, "The problem is more in his method."

"Brilliant, don't you think?" Fulani once more interjected. "We have just developed the most predictive theory in history and Berne says any prediction we make is an illusion. He abandoned his profession. He thought only of his own obsession and became mentally undone. I remember him once describing how he felt possessed by the will of God after giving a talk. He was high for a few hours then he crashed for a week."

I noticed Coomb watching Fulani. "So he was destroyed by his experiment. How?"

Fulani smirked, "Probably mis–set one of his lasers in his obsessed haze."

Coomb turned to Fulani and said, "You don't know that." He turned and shrugged, "Could have been equipment failure."

Fulani looked at him sharply, "Berne was *sick*. It was his choice not to come back to the world of engines, apples and billiard balls. It cost him his career."

"It cost him his life." Now Fulani glared at him.

Coomb asked if I'd like a glass of water. When he left, I asked Fulani, heart pounding, "So Professor, I wanted to ask you this alone. And I apologize for the gossipy nature, but our readers will want to know. Was there any tension there between him and his semiconductor in–laws?"

Fulani's eyes flashed just for a second before he looked over his glasses. "Young lady, his choice of in–laws does not mean he was working successfully on teleportation. He hated them, you know. Never did see the need for ownership of science. His wife was caught between." He lowered his gaze at the mention of Anna. "He worked mostly on pure theory – after the plasma."

"But why then would he need a lab?"

Fulani sighed again and raised his hands.

Coomb returned as I asked, "What did his wife think?"

He spoke gruffly, "I didn't know her well. She was always charming, worried at the end. A lonely woman I think – straddling two opposing powers."

"Those were?"

"Purity and practicality," Coomb's open palms reminded me of Eric's hand face up on the table, inviting.

I swallowed and nodded. "Do you know what Dr. Berne was

working on at home?"

Coomb snuck a quick glance at Fulani as he set the paper cup down. "I'm not familiar," he spoke slowly. "It had to do with the same. Didn't it, Professor?"

"I lost touch with him once he resigned," Fulani looked down at the pen he rolled between his fingers. "And now, Miss," he patted his desk. "Time for you to go. We must get back to our work. Eh, Coomb? We've our own prize to strive for."

"Whatever you say, Professor. Did you get enough, Miss Cadot?"

"I may have a few more questions," I rushed, happy Fulani had no idea I knew of his relationship with KinCo.

Coomb smiled as he said, "Let me *know.*"

"Thank you, Professor." His grip was firm and tight – too tight. I glanced up then stared. His eyes were as bare a cupboard as Eric's sometimes, something open and pleading in them. It lasted only a moment, like an electric shock.

I stammered something over my knocking heart, walked over to Fulani. "I appreciate the time." I extended my arm. Fulani bent his head but offered no hand.

I turned and held out a card to Coomb. Two fingers grabbed it. Fulani watched with an artifact smile, until I brushed Coomb's wrist.

Then as usual the black came and took me to a small, dark room, a phone booth, with hard plastic pressed to my ear – an old style phone. "All right, I'm in."

Despite the lack of twang in the subdued tone, I knew it was a younger Coomb. "Okay, it's done. I'll tell him." He stood close to the dark wall outside as hung up the phone. Then the scene dissolved into the white windowed classroom and Coomb's now averted gaze as he escorted me toward the door.

Ten

Racing the sun to the coastal mountains, I called voicemail.

"This is Annie French. Ah– you can reach me at...."

I redialed immediately.

"Annie."

"Annie. Jeanne Cadot. We met on the plane about 4 years ago. I'd come from New Orleans."

"The dot.bomb journalist. How's it been?"

"I graduated school. I work for The Sheet."

"Hunter's rag. He ruined you yet?"

"Not so far God help me." I hadn't seen him since the party. "Ever heard of a hacker group 'round here called the Grey Hats? I mean in specific. I remembered your Grey Hat pin when we met."

"You a recipient?"

"A recipient?" My pulse warmed.

"Listen, seeing as we're both working girls, I'm going to tell you. But you can't use my name, right? You do and I can make your life miserable. Promise?"

"Yes." My heart rose then dropped. Was I going to be able to quote anybody in this story?

"Vague SoMa rumor has it there's some self–styled Internet Robin Hoods, virtual Butch and Sundance. Yeah, I know its silly, but hackers love all that mythical cloak and dagger shit. Rumor says those who get hit are all under SEC indictment for corporate theft. Their offshore accounts are hidden, so they don't want to mention it."

"So these hackers are stealing from them?"

"They got tired of waiting for justice. Plus, shutting down eBay is a punk move. But hitting Swiss banks? Making all those monies come back to the people? This is the ultimate hack."

Perfect for a Swiss financial genius who was playing me – I choked the steering wheel. "Who are the recipients?"

"Think they're talking? Not yet. But enough banks get strange deposits and something will be done, even if done in secret. Now it may be a few stings, but a swarm of bees could kill you."

And that swarm was coming Feb 15th. "Have you ever heard of Eric Berne—Kincaid?" A pause.

"Can't help you there. I gotta go. Good luck." The phone died against "Annie, what do you do?" I called back. It rolled to voicemail. Thinking she reminded me of Anna – as elusive and probably as in the middle – I dialed again.

"Hey boss," I rapped to his terse 'Clive.' "You won't believe this. How about modern Robin Hoods? And I'll bet Anna's son's involved." Of course I'd no exact evidence of this.

"Yeah? Did you find more recipients?"

"Not yet, but I've got account numbers and there's rumors they're folks injured in corporate scandals current and past." I outlined our conversation. "And I talked with Fulani and Coomb, the accused physicists. Coomb reached out. I'll contact him next. I'm headed now to get Anna's son."

"Good work, Slugger. Keep moving forward, but be careful. Call Susan."

At her name, a mini tornado raged in my chest, "Yeah, Clive – you know – I never told her about this—I wanted to see what I could do first."

"I told you—" then he paused – we might now have a story we could use for our own leverage here or somewhere else. "Don't make going behind my back a habit or you'll be pounding pavement, got it?"

"I got it boss–man." For the first time since the call with Susan my smile about Clive was genuine. It simply didn't cross my mind I'd still not told him I'd danced with the main suspect.

Eric jogged over from a small, well-kept bi-plane. The rips and tears of his washed–out denim jeans were no doubt real, but topped today with a soft white shirt and a fur–collared vintage pilot's jacket. I smiled wryly. Let the games begin. "You look good enough to eat."

He offered a bow. The small airport just north of Half Moon Bay didn't seem very busy. Two mechanics in blue uniforms inspected a propeller on the north of the tarmac.

"So did you know Fulani and Coomb?"

"Did I say yes to an interview and miss it?"

I blushed, fell back a step from him as we walked briskly toward a bronzy–orange plane.

"She's a Cessna 172 Skyhawk."

"Orange used to be my favorite color." I touched his elbow and suddenly the tarmac rippled green. I let go. "You been flying long?"

"Most of my life," he said. "My father was a pilot in his youth."

We approached. We were going up the coast, at twilight. Over water, in the dark. When he touched my shoulder at the door my vision rippled once again. The plane morphed into golden grass woodland. I heard the rushing, smelled the old sewer.

Suddenly Féy crossed the grass in her bone sheath toward

me. I could imagine the dress flapping up 'round her waist as she fell to the middle of the sea. "Jeanne," she reached out as if to touch me. "Not all the Ten will be good to you. You must learn to use both powers." She reached out to touch me.

And I reached forward, letting her ghostly energy swirl 'round and through my forearm. There was no physical connection, but her words seemed to come through my pores. "I'm sorry, *dauphine*; I should've been with you back then — I did it for you — never for the money."

The inky wave crashed in as if I'd called it to me, which I had not for this was another of those memories I kept buried.

Still I let it break into the waning full moon rising above the Mississippi banks north of the Port where Moman L, Féy and I stood before the Mississippi Queen, grand riverboat set to sail up to Memphis and St. Louis.

Spring's sweet olive lingered in the air, but I was sullen. This year she'd not gotten out of bed until four or five pm and some days she hadn't left her bed at all. Two hours late to my birthday celebration, held in our own parlor, and her gift was an old silver, soft-hair bristled brush that would never work on my small curls.

Now Féy squatted in front of me on the hard ground, soothing my forearms. Moman L's still strong hands held my shoulders. Féy eyes *had* teared up, "Well, *dauphine*. Now we must say goodbye." At that word I began inexplicably to cry.

She reached out to smooth my hair. "You're to be heir *dauphine*, didn't I tell you?" Her eyes flicked. Her flawless skin, paler this year, showed off her red rosebud lips, eclipsing her eyes heavily lined with brilliant blue on the lids like the sky'd kissed them — all to hide the fact that they'd become yellowed around the edges. She paused then chuckled. "Now I'll just be Féy." She tossed her head and scorn lit her tears.

"Jeanne," Moman L's no–nonsense tone cut through, "You stay here. I need to talk to Faye." She lengthened the A so it reminded of Féy's given name.

They walked a little way and quarreled hushed in the dark.

Féy signed some thick papers before she sidled back over. She squatted down and pecked my cheek. She took my hands, opened their palms and laid in them her slip of paper and her peridot earrings. "I've read the past and seen the future, Jeanne. And I know," she looked down, "we'll never really be apart." She closed my fingers over the gift, stroked my cheek, "Do you remember that day on Royal two years back?"

I nodded, petrified to reveal my secret obsession.

"Well, you're not to be scared of them or me, *dauphine*. Don't fear your destiny – or the twin powers."

"That enough Féy," Moman L scolded, "Stop fillin' her head with fairy tales."

My heart beat louder than the cicadas, but I could not move. The full moon played in and out of clouds as I watched her board. The boatmen cast off. My mind clenched off the memory of what came after to keep me up to snuff.

But instead Féy's visceral voice pulsed again, "Always know that you're stronger than I was then. Jeanne, don't fear the dark."

But now the black wave forced my feet back and I stumbled. Echo's arms came 'round me. Into my ear he murmured, "*Mon chere*...The things you'll do to get into my arms."

My heart's thud grew hollow, but the tarmac reappeared and Echo's laughter bubbled against my back when I spoke. "It's a childhood thing with water. I don't swim. Usually it doesn't come up." To date when I was awake on solid ground, neither had Féy. But had she just warned me about Echo?

Echo watched me. "Still want to go?"

I scanned the plane. "Anna" was stenciled on the plane's tail. Recalling how even Fulani had bent his head in respect to her, I smiled and nodded though I could not will words past my incisors.

"Just hold onto me, *chere*. You'll be perfectly fine. No swimming, I promise." With one hand he poked inside. From a storage compartment behind the rear seat, he pulled a pair of gloves, army surplus earmuff, and another bomber jacket, this one smaller than his. "Will this fit? It is Maman's. Anna. This is her namesake."

"So your mother was a flier as well as an equestrienne?" I asked sliding my arm in the jacket, wondering if it would imbue me with some of her strength.

"In her youth my mother did a lot of things."

"Do tell?"

"Get in," he held my elbow as I lifted myself onto the ladder. Then he walked to the front of the plane to spin the propeller. Lord, he looked good. But what if he knew of all my debts? And God knows what else.

Echo got in and began flipping switches, checking gauges, making notes in his log. The two–person cockpit was loaded with LCD screens, digital readouts, mini–computer keyboards and what looked like equalizers, as well as the switches and dials. In front of me was a control stick topped by a horseshoe with its points up. I took a good look 'round to see if I could make sense of it. "I guess you know a lot about computers?"

He shook his head. "Idiot savant – good with equations, not code. I can use all these though, don't worry."

My pulse, disobeying, began to knock at my birthmark. Was he lying straight to my face as we were about to take off?

We sat my knee to his rump, both cross–buckled in. He handed me a headset with microphones, explaining, "So we won't have to shout." I held tightly onto my seat as we taxied to the small runway. "Your control yoke – stick – is locked, let me know if you want to play with it."

"I won't be doing that."

"Ah, you'll miss the best part." We began to roll.

Moments later we rose above the mustard grass cliffs and Torrey pines heading north out of Half Moon Bay. We flew up toward a high, thick cloud layer. Where the sun sank the light at sea was vibrant orange. I looked down. Rocky, winding coast ranches, parks and small communities bordered the narrow dark ribbon of Highway One: Miramar, Pillar's Point, Moss Beach,

Montara – town names from a romance novel. The thick vibration of the propeller enveloped us.

No time like the present to call up the past. I put a hand to Eric's hip.

Sure enough I thrust into black to the same loud propeller sound, my competent hands working fast an older array of panels and screens. Someone else had a hand on my thigh from behind, a man whose voice hollered in my ear, "Anna, I can't. My career's already on the brink. Do you want me to lose everything?" The voice sounded like Coomb's.

My throat, Anna's throat, caught and I yanked a power switch with unnecessary pressure, but compensated with my hand on the control yoke. Keeping the horseshoe true against driving wind, she – I – pressed the nose down to sea and drove it out faster and faster.

"Anna," the voice pled, the hand scrabbled like a branch at a window, "Anything else just ask – but not this."

Something in the voice got to Anna – and she – I –leveled out the plane.

"So what did you learn from Fulani and Coomb about my father?" Eric asked through the headphones cracking the past.

"Entanglement," my voice was muffled in the wind. "Hidden threads of connection thru time and space. The universal dance."

"The Cosmic Dance," Eric agreed, "Inescapable."

The sky darkened to red. We flew over Pacifica. "Listen, Echo. Did anyone ever come between your parents?"

Eric didn't respond, but I could tell he was listening.

"Because Enrico Fulani and Michael *Coomb* told me about the tension between your," I paused, "mother's family and your father's beliefs – that must've been very hard to bridge."

We flew in silence over the Cliff House and Seal Rock. The crashing waves below looked gentle from here. When we came 'round the split cliffs of the headlands, the Golden Gate Bridge came into view – sparkling orange in the last of the sunlight.

It took my breath away to see it in real, waking life. My head swiveled to catch every last glimpse.   At the cliffs of the Headlands just north of the Golden Gate, Eric banked the plane west, toward the nearly done sinking sun and the broad ocean.

He pointed the nose down into an incline, just as his mother had done, just as Féy had in my dream. We headed toward the twilight blue ocean – the exact color of Eric's eyes. "Eric…Echo," I tried to speak calmly, "what are you doing?"

He kept his eyes pinned ahead and the nose at 8:00. "Let's see what we're really made of."

"I want to live Echo," I said as the sky whizzed by and wet darkness sped toward us.

"I need to you to understand, Jeanne. If we do this story, I'm going to have to go where I don't want to. So you're going to have to go where you don't want to also." He peered out to the sky, his voice still as a midnight pool. "How much of yourself are you willing to risk?"

I bet he'd not take his own life. "I can go wherever you can Eric."

"Good, close your eyes. Hurry."

I couldn't tell how soon we'd smack the ocean.

"Are your eyes shut?"

"Yes." Unbelievably they were.

"Good, now what do you feel. In your chest. Inside."

Must everything be a test with this family? "How about abject terror?"

He laughed. "What else?"

The engine seemed to get louder. The plane's shudder rippled through me. This must be similar to what Berne had felt. "A ball spinning."

"Good. See if you can spin it the other way. See an image in your mind's eye – a tornado or a whirlpool."

Without thinking I reached forward, lifted the protective cap, flicked the switch and using the same pressure I'd learned from Anna, lifted the control stick as little and straight and gently as possible. The plane responded. A few shadows hulked outside.

We passed them steadily by.

A long minute passed without him saying anything.

I exhaled, loosened my grip on the controls. "I felt something. I did."

"All Cretans are liars." He banked the plane and climbed in a broad ellipse, heading back.

"Beg pardon?" I gripped the wheel again – forced myself to look down. I might somehow have to land this thing.

"The first paradox – 200 B.C., time of Pythagoras – uttered by a Cretan named Epimenides. Honest or lying, either statement contradicts itself. It's an un-resolvable riddle. My father could not accept such fallacies in reason – he believed there must be a path out – a way to resolution – to purity. But contradiction is the base of life. In life there's death, in good there's evil, in evil, good; in death there's..."

"Life. Lord, Eric – most times things are just as they seem, don't you think?" And it seemed he'd just been trying to kill us.

After closing up the plane, we walked back to my car.

"You didn't tell me you knew how to fly," he tossed it off casually, but voice rose at the end.

"I don't really."

"Really? You took quite a chance."

"I did the least possible."

"You know Jeanne, my father believed that by living a life devoted to the quest for pure knowledge, the mathematician's soul becomes purified until glimpses of true arithmetic and geometry can be reflected in it."

"Then that's exactly how I knew how to fly – I got a pure glimpse with my pure soul. But did you ever go flying with your mother? Did she take folks up with her?"

He smiled, and his eyes telegraphed knowledge – as if he knew *exactly* how I'd known what to do. And I thought again, could he be a male *mambo*? But he changed the topic, "The media only ever focused on my father's humiliation. I *am* the last one able to affect his legacy."

"Let me come to you... to your family home. See his papers.
Your mother's diary. She mentioned she had one." I stopped.

He laid a finger 'cross my lips and wrapped a leather arm
'round me. He smiled, "I'm nearly ready."

When his millionaire lips came near, I thought to hell with
Clive and Moman L, hooray for Anna and Féy – as I sank into
his long kiss in the now dark and empty parking lot.

But that night in my dreams Féy didn't come to me.

With three weeks left until February 15th and the big
distribution, every spare minute the following week was filled
with leaving messages with folks who'd lost everything in various
corporate lootings and might have been "recipients".

The day before the first interview with Eric, the registered
letter came in from Miss Carmela Peters at Tulane. "Per your
request I translated..."

> The youngest of us four, Lilla, went off to San
> Francisco in 1869 despite *Popa's* wishes. Said she
> wouldn't perish in Storyville when good money
> awaited. In the beginning she worked for high
> wages as a cook, Creole cuisine being much in
> demand. She met a Mr. Collins, son of a most
> prominent black millionaire, real estate and ship
> owner. I'll tell you this set our eyes to light: their
> whirlwind courtship, over the course of several
> fine dinners, parties and balls; then marriage in all
> the French fashions – nice as in New Orleans.
> They are going in on a ship with several partners,
> one of them a white man! Out there she says
> there are as many abolitionists as rebels. She
> would cook and he steward, they were to have
> music and dancers ferrying folks between San

Francisco and the Gold country. Service trades *were* the gold and silver bonanza for most colored folk by then. But we never heard again from Lilla. After the war, having lost so many, we dared not send out another to find her. But we never stopped praying for her to one day come home.

So there had been a ship, partners, dancers, music, and a white man – and a lost ancestress.

The entry on the Ten was brief and from Marie, namesake of Moman L's *moman*, "When the line whittles to ones, devil birthmarks and hid shames will mark she who can bring the Ten–into–one, repay the Eight and remove the curse." But there was not a word about any twin powers or any real living. I wrote again to Miss Peters.

Eleven

The whole next week of no visits from Féy I took more risks, as I imagined Anna might have – I saw her as Féy without the disgrace, and somehow since hers was less obvious, without the despair.   Friday, after no luck from Tulane, nor word from any credit card company or bank contact, nor response to any of my 50 phone calls to Coomb, Annie or Max Conrad or the folks who lost it all in corporate scandals, I could not wait to hit the road – I'd an interview with Echo at one.

Before I left, at the historical library I found the *HMS Lawrence II* fell off the registry after 1875 without any explanation. But in Collins's Black newspaper, *the Pacific Appeal*, in September there was an outraged letter.

A George Washington Dennis wrote – immediately I thought of Verna Dennis and her nephew, Walter – that Alex Kincaid, co–signer for a non-white group unable to get credit without him – had secretly and unlawfully used co-signed assets for collateral on a Comstock silver mine that went bust.   It was one of several mines that caused the August 1875 stock market crash, the subsequent run on Ralston's bank and his consequent drowning. In the day's panic, the institution's remaining directors needed to pay off its most influential creditors first. To do so it had seized and liquidated this property – on which the rightful owners had paid nearly in full – along with a slew of others from less important account holders, all of the black and brown ones, but some poor white ones as well, all of whom had needed co-signers to get their loans.

Yet this particular action would never come to trial the author lamented, as rather than fight, this particular group of families had fled, with their property to a place not-here-revealed but believed to offer more free justice to the races. Sad irony for America given the ban on Negro and Indian testimony had finally been lifted in 1863. If we didn't stay and fight for our rights, then did we truly deserve to receive them?

It could certainly have meant the *HMS Lawrence II* – perhaps they went north to Vancouver as many folks of color had done in the late 19th century.

If the piece was about them, then Eric's relatives on both sides – one an owner, the others his former servants – had betrayed each other. Only to be reunited three generations later in Anna and Berne. A coincidence? Did she know who Berne was? If her parents had gotten a notion of his true identity, surely Berne would be undesirable. But could old revenge be a motive for murder?

Driving up to the bridge I stopped at a light on old Rincon Hill and a black bird circled before my window. The wave came and lifted then washed me over to the corner of California and Sansome to a gray and black wool suited crowd with bankbooks and papers thrust up in their hands toward a gray stone building.

Its grand plate-glass windows and bronze doors were thrown open to reveal heaps of gold and silver coins high upon marble counters, being piled into withdrawals by nervous fingers of tellers who kept glancing up at a massing crowd. Uniformed men were pushing at the massive doors to shut them.

Off to the side, near where a performer played an annoying march, stood our two couples, nervously craning their necks. They didn't dare to march into the contentious crowd – half were for Ralston, the other half against.   But all were loud and shouting.

A car horn behind me blared and the past deliquesced leaving today's sun to blaze through finally dispersing cloud cover. 'Crossing the bridge I found there were 14 W. Dennis's in the city. I'd have to call them this weekend.

This interview was really just a cover for me. It got me access. How I'd ask the real questions I'd not yet seen. Would there be, I wondered, any confirmation of my visions in Echo's home?   Any notion that Berne knew of his family's past involvement with the Kincaid's. Or, if I hit the jackpot, I might find Anna's diary, see something linking Eric to the Grey Hats, or find Berne's last physics secret – or something showing the whole thing was a ploy in the old feud.

But my heart feared another agenda. Seduction seemed Eric's main interest. Today, at his home, I was certain the ante would up. Worse, the thawing heart in me wanted it to. I hoped this would not be the time Féy or Moman L or pioneers would show up.

On one of the few blocks behind the Claremont left undamaged by the Oakland fire, one or two wrens sang and early afternoon sun filtered through the winter cool, and the thick canopy of mature pines, maples and elderberry trees. A perfect spot for dogs and children, but I didn't hear or see any – still, not the neighborhood of a typical man worth $97 million. I'd parked between an Altima and an Alfa Romeo. So Eric didn't live as my vision of an owner, he lived like one of the rest of us. Again, Féy seemed to be right.

On the high side of the street, 'cross from a yard of prize–striving roses, the burnt yellow stucco home rose like three-story candy box above a ground floor garage. Dark chocolate strips crisscrossed the facade like medieval marching soldiers above two Hershey's-square garage doors. Eric had told me to come up the brick steps 'round back through a cozy cedar and brick patio to open sliding glass doors with driftwood handles. You could see clear through to the bayside windows. "Hello. Eric?" The wood-paneled house was cool and still.

"Take the stairs beyond the kitchen," came out of the open upstairs window.

A stove more fertility-figured than pot-bellied, lived in the back's left corner faced by a sturdy brown leather couch and recliner punctuated by spindly brass floor lamps. Heavy glass ashtrays sat on top of T.V. and stereo console further in. On the right wall black bookcases filled with physics texts and covered with locked Plexiglas too past a hulking black file cabinet that was also locked. But a round table with two chairs sat in the space formed by them should the locks ever be opened.

I walked past the stereo and small dining area into the kitchen, took in slowly the chrome toaster and blender – as it could have been in 1965 when Eric was three, but for the microwave. I laid fingers on the speckled Formica kitchen table, just as it had been in Anna's memory. But now the curtains over the double sink were white, not orange. Beyond the second kitchen entrance at the back, stairs ran up the left front of the house.

Upstairs four tinted French–paned Mylar's ran along the house's bayside. Three doors dotted the bare white, eastern hall. This floor had been repainted. No family photos anywhere I could see, but the first door was open. "In here," he called.

I scooted down a narrow hall in past a glass–brick wall behind which presumably lived a bed. To my far right in front of walls as dark blue as his eyes, he sat at a black drafting table set to look across the room and out floor–to–ceiling windows to his garden. Hanging perpendicular to the windows he had four monitors: the New York, the Pacific Coast, the NASDAQ and the Nippon stock exchanges. Black metal shelves held thick reference books, CD–ROMs and discs, and miscellaneous computer parts.

"Welcome," he glanced up from his flat monitor with a distracted smile.

"Wow." Facing him the room had been extended 'cross the length of the house. A bar and tables sat in the far right corner, a basketball hoop high on the west wall past a door to bathroom. Metal racks of the Wall Street Journal, Barron's and Forbes sat behind a blank blackboard. "Did some remodel?"

"Had to. There is a sort of a mystery surrounding this room. Would you like to hear it?"

I tossed back an encouraging nod as I scanned the shelves.

"I redid this room to a totally different feel. I had to." He lowered his voice. "Sometimes, in those windows," his voice softened, "I used to see my father sitting at my desk, standing in front of my blackboard, studying, assessing my progress. Pretty crazy, don't you think?"

So he, too, had visitations from the dead. "Your father thought there were multi dimensions, past and present all continuing on at once. And metaphoric wormholes between them – hidden connections."

"Yes," he spoke rising, and raised a hand. "Let's go back down for this. I prefer to keep my father downstairs." Clicking off his screen with a flourish, he lifted his coat from the back of his netted office chair.

But before we went down he showed me his sister, Heather's, old room, behind the last of those other hall doors. Four–poster bed, dressers, a wardrobe and a vanity spotted with pictures of the family mostly out–of–doors. I ran a light hand over the brushes with soft–as–silk boar's hair, a sterling silver hand mirror, and comb, just like Féy's old gift. He'd kept all as it had been – like an eerie shrine.

Did he feel responsible for his sister's death? Or was he just holding on to whatever family he had left. Cariña flashed into my mind. Our calls had been awkward lately – I'd not felt comfortable sharing all this with her – nor comfortable that she might already have seen it despite her assurances to the contrary.

"Heather always preferred to live in style." His smile turned down at the end in sadness. I glanced at a picture. Anna, young and beautiful, beamed as a woman beloved, her arm wrapped 'round a frail–looking girl with a petite version of her father's nose and shoulders; Eric, young and kneeling beneath them with his mother's eyes and bearing – his father no doubt behind the lens. Like me he was surrounded by dead. Could that be a sign of the Ten? I was thankful my immediate dead seemed to have taken the day off. Right now, his folks seemed more promising.

When we sat with two cups each of espresso at the round wood table, I took a sip. I had to start carefully. "So where would you like to begin?"

Eric's eyes sparked and I prepared for his throwing it back to me. Finally he said, "When I was a child my father would talk to me about a light strong enough to reach the stars. A light so intense that it would transcend the visible and ultraviolet into some unknown spectrum beyond; so powerful that it would penetrate all matter, every level of existence."

"I know he worked with lasers."

"Inside the circuit, with the right intensity, they can burn a hole through metal or skin." He snorted. "Well, he's dead."

My voice softened, "What do you think happened that night?"

Eric stared for a long moment as if looking back in time. When he spoke his voice was cold. "His search for 'the Great Truth' was like staring into a fire's flames. If you don't look away, after a while you become mesmerized, even paralyzed. He began it as a way to...find the truth. But instead he got transfixed. In the end, he was consumed." He cleared his throat. "His eastern teacher, Krishnamurti, said 'truth is a pathless land' – meaning we each must find our own way out of life's grand paradoxes. Quantum physics at heart is mired in paradox. But like so many, I believe my father needed something in the way of a map. He'd have been happier if he'd stayed within Newton's world."

Even when you sometimes had a map in life, as I did, you couldn't – or didn't – always trust its routes. And how was I going to get him to be more specific without pushing him.

He placed his hands on the back of his neck, leaned back in his chair, and stretched out his legs. Then, looking at me, he asked, "What do you think happened?"

I took a breath. Eric saw his father as the enemy – something I well understood. "The police and court files are sealed," I slowed, skipping over 'juvenile involvement'. "Frankly, there's not much press either – that's suspicious...but they didn't find any forced entry, accelerant paths or a note. So it looks like an accident. But then, you saw the tip."

He watched my lips before he looked away reminding my heart to jump. "He was working with laser holography."

"Do you know if a laser expert examined the rubble?"

He laughed. "A laser expert? It was 1973. There weren't many of those around."

"What he was doing with holography?" Was he trying to touch the past? Or create something that would destroy his in-laws?

"I was only nine. I understood only some." He drained his first cup, his face and body already taut.

"Was it a terrible shock for you, your sister and your mother?"

"He'd stopped listening even to her. We'd all come to hate him." He dipped his voice with his gaze.

A moment of silence seemed appropriate. He'd not told anyone this before. And he was telling me more about his life than Moman L or Féy ever had done about their own.

"In the final month he retreated here to his laboratory where twice a day we brought him food. Once he didn't come up for 10 days. That seventh evening I brought his dinner down instead of Heather. I walked down the stairs and saw him seated on a stool at a lab table, a lamp knocked over below him throwing eerie shadows on those steel walls and ceiling above him.

"His grey face stared at his calculations on the blackboard, as though they would provide him some answer – some answer he wasn't getting from life with us." His voice sounded smaller and younger than I'd ever heard it. "His clothes were wrinkled. He sat on top of his old metal stool. I don't think he even noticed me. After that I asked not to go down again. Maman agreed."

Leaning forward I touched his hand, but he shook me off and went on. He'd looked like that as a boy in the photo – fiercely independent, contemptuous of help or hindrance.

"Eventually she had to call in the doctors. One doctor after another—they still made house calls then—brought him upstairs, often out into the yard, tapped his knees, ordered him to raise his arms above his head, to cough."

Though this sounded more like 50's than the 70's, and wasn't getting me any closer to what I needed, with each word my sympathy for the family's predicament grew. "But why was he down there? Was he depressed? Obsessive?"

"All of them said, 'there's nothing physically wrong with your husband.' They would tell her he needed sun and some exercise every now and again – perhaps a psychiatrist. Some said, 'He'll come out of it when he's ready.'

"Once a kindly, physician scratched his balding head and said to my mother, 'If I didn't know better, I'd say he was suffering from a broken heart.'

"My mother blanched, but said nothing and had me show him to the door."

Ah, so there *could* be infidelity on Anna's part, but Eric had no knowledge of it. I wondered if his sister had. And whether it might not have contributed to her passing?

"The night before he died, my mother said he left his study for the first time in two weeks. She watched him go into my sister's room and mine, kneel at the foot of our beds like a spectre. Never saying a word to her, he went into every room, opened every closet and cupboard door; finally, after the backyard, he came in to kneel by her side of the bed. 'Please forgive me Anna. Please forgive,' he broke down crying. Feeling perhaps things were on the mend, she soothed him until she fell asleep. When she woke he was gone back to his lab.

"The next night, a Saturday, Maman took us to the movies. We saw "Live and Let Die" – I'll never forget that Tarot Queen, so beautiful and so trapped, like ma mere, like all of us – like even you, dear Jeanne."

But I refused to get distracted now he was finally opening up.

"When we returned, we could see smoke and a glowing light from under the garage door. We ran inside, but the cellar doorknob was a hot poker. Maman kept us outside and called the fire department. The fire never touched any other part of the house. He'd lined the walls and ceiling with sheet metal. The reflected fire eventually turned the small basement into an incinerator. We had to replace the floor, two walls and the ceiling, but there was only minor damage otherwise."

"Were the walls singed?" I nodded to the kitchen remembering the char behind Anna's head. That very night she must've reviewed Berne's journal and that passport – I flashed on my last vision – those passbooks held by the withdrawers – they had looked a lot like a passport.

"Its back walls have been redone," Eric's tone was flat. "But I can still smell the smoke." He stopped.

"I'm so sorry, Eric."

Eric snapped. "They found a pile of ash in the center of the room. Do you know what that means?" Eric asked impatiently. I shook my head.

"He was in the center of the explosion. He set himself on fire."

I raised my eyebrows. So, like Lily, he believed it was suicide. No wonder he hated his father so. "Did your father ever have anything to do with Kincaid Corp?"

He narrowed his eyes, wiggled his shoulders, "Why?"

I shrugged. "Semiconductors, computing."

Eric toyed with his sugar packet. "As far as I know, she was cut off officially from the family fortune when they married."

I stifled my inhale. Well, that would throw some leeching plans asunder, wouldn't it? It might make one's death the only way to get the revenge money. On the other hand a boy would hold onto a suicide theory rather than know that his mother and her family had had his father murdered.

I wanted to shake Eric and say, "Where is your mother's diary? Your father's last journal," but I couldn't risk alerting him again to my targets. So I said, "Wouldn't your father say he'd just gone back to the implicate order?"

Eric snorted, reminding me of Fulani.

"Okay," I said taking another plunge, "I tried to open the police files. They're sealed. I need your testimony to ask the court to open them. You game?" I held forward the petition form for his signature.

He just looked at it. Then he stood up. He walked to the window and looked out at the back yard. He said. "Don't get sidetracked."

I see-sawed my head – that damn profile cover story. "Are these all his records?" I gestured behind me.

Eric crossed his arms and fixed me with a steady gaze.

"Echo, you've just told me you believe your father committed suicide when all the official reports say accident and someone's told us murder. I have to find some proof as to his state of mind at least."

He kept silent.

I slapped my hand against my knee. "We need a break." I had to decide whether to come clean about the wire transfers.

He paused. Then he smiled and said coolly. "How about a bike ride?"

He grabbed my hand playfully and pulled me out into the mid–afternoon light.

We rode out 'round Lake Temescal and then up Snake road. I must've ridden Anna's or his sister's bike, complete with water bottle and helmet. We wound up and up until I blessed my very occasional riding with Chuck. Atop Grizzly Peak we stopped at a bench and looked out over the smoggy fog. I'd not had a view like this since I'd arrived. And I caught a few turkey vultures circling here and there – but no condor.

He spoke first through heaving breaths. "God, it's peaceful up here. A few years ago I promised myself that I wouldn't die until I'd had a moment's peace."

"And have you?"

The rise of his eyebrows took my pulse with it. "I'm working on it."

"You're not the only one."

"Jeanne," he came and sat next to me.

"Yes?"

"Jeanne." His hand touched my face, as the use of my French name, heretofore only spoken by family, touched my soul. I startled, but remained and this time there was no cool black rising, but all red–hot, bubbling blood.

He put his hand behind my neck and pulled me in. At the moment our lips met, his other hand went beneath my tee. Cars behind us wouldn't see. He kissed my throat, my birthmark. Just as he was about to lift his hand up, I grabbed it, pulled my head back.

"What is it?" he breathed.

"It's . . ." I huffed, holding back Cariña's name, "...I can't."

He sounded stunned. "You can't..."

"Oh shit, I'm sorry." I pushed myself back. "I really like you, Eric. It's just ...with this story and all," I wanted to scream frustration.

A minute later, Eric murmured straight forward to the view, "No one need know what happens between us."

My heart's trot accelerated into a canter. I shook my head, "But it's not right. I have a duty to the public."

He considered, "Acts of love in any form are always right. Not so for acts of fear." Love and fear – the ultimate twin powers – love drove straight into my resolve, cracking it.

"I'll tell you what," he went on. "Let me take you to the cabin this weekend. I have a place below Sea Ranch, or rather my family did, I do now. Our hearts' home, we used to call it. There are a lot of photos and memorabilia there. They'll bring back more things. Might even be some more of those pioneers. I'll take you sailing up the coast like we always did with Dad."

"Hmm," My heaves slowed. Out of town no one need know that we were together. And who knew what Eric would tell me. "That sounds intriguing. We'd need to meet somewhere discreet." A twinge passed through me – I sounded like Féy – but I was in too deep now to back out.

"No problem." Eric said.

"And I'd need my own room," I glanced at him.

He went on, "Whatever you want. But if we're going to do this story, pry into the dusty crevices of *my* past, I want to get to yours, too. It's important."

I smiled, "You drive a hard bargain. But okay. Let's do it."

"Good. But before we agree, tell me something about you. Something no one else knows."

He watched me sit back down with a burning in my chest.

"All right," I spoke slowly. "Remember our relatives?"

He indicated yes.

"Well, the four of them I think worked with Alex Kincaid the first. I've not found any proof yet, but it looks like they owned a ship together." He rocked back.

"There are pictures of him at the cabin." He said, then stood and adjusted his helmet. "I'll arrange it, ok?" he added.

I was relieved. "Can I do anything to help?"

"We can do it all going."

"Sounds great," Perhaps I'd find the diary, the journal and the old story of the Ten in one fell swoop. But bring them into one what? One story? One meeting? And what would that entail?

The sun began to sink.

He reached out his hand, "Come on, I'll race you down."

"Oh no, this will probably be the end of me."

He tucked a tuft of curl behind my ear.

In the end we didn't go away that week. We didn't even talk until I called Eric on Friday.

"Eric Berne," a work tone responded to the ring.

"Echo?"

"Yes."

"It's Jeannie."

"Oh, Jeanne, oh hello. How are you?"

"Fine. I'm fine. Been working like a pit bull this week." Awkwardly I dashed to the point. "I'm calling about this weekend; I've cooked up a few things."

"This weekend. *Merde*. Blast. The cabin," he sounded annoyed. "Look, Jeanne, I'm afraid I can't go. Something's come up."

"Oh," I said. A voice in my head howled.

"I was going to call you tonight," Eric continued. "We'll have to postpone."

"Yeah," my tone spread distant and flat as a Midwestern plain. It had been two and half weeks now and I had nothing.

"There's nothing I can do about it."

I brightened mechanically. "These things happen. Will you have time for an interview?"

There was a moment of silence. "Afraid that won't work either," he said tersely. "I'm going out of town. I'll call you next week."

"Jesus, Echo. Can we talk now? My deadline's on its way."

"Oh, no, not now," he said as though this made a difference. "Rain check. I'll call you next week."

Shit, was all I thought as we hung up.

Friday night I staked out Conrad's place, but he was gone

when I arrived and never returned. Saturday I dragged through errands imagining Eric robbing banks – and meticulously reviewed our cabin conversation. I went to his home in Oakland, but his car was gone. That night, first time since I'd met him, I curled up with *Live and Let Die* and *Angel Heart*, a large bowl of buttered popcorn and a small bottle of the Mark.

Monday, Clive flayed me for missing a key obit and plugging in a wire blurb at the last minute, and for good measure he also badgered me about the Grey Hats piece. By the end of the day my head pounded like cops on doors.

Eric called on Tuesday morning. "Jeanne?" his conciliatory accent tested on the other end of my work line.

"Echo?"

"Echo, Echo, Echo." He jested. When I didn't laugh, he asked more sedately, "How are you?"

"I'm fine," our silence stretched like elastic.

"Fine. Well, I'm fine, also...Well, that's...that's a fine start."

I let a quiet "ha" escape.

He went on, "Meet me for lunch at Justin Herman Plaza? I'd like to see you."

"How do I know you'll actually be there?"

"I'll actually be there," he assured.

"I've got a lot going on today." Perhaps I'd not been hard enough to get last week.

"Oh come on," Eric chided. "You have to eat. I'll bring some salad. Think of it as a peace offering. We'll sit on a bench and watch the squirrels fall upon the pigeons."

A vision of Eric refereeing a squirrel–pigeon skirmish caused me to smile. "Okay," I said softly.

"Okay…. Then you forgive me?"

I took a breath. "You're on the right track."

"I'll see you at noon," Eric breathed, "Don't be late."

"Yeah, right," I laughed harshly as I hung up the phone, "You're only 6 days late," I said to no one. But I was pleased.

He still wanted me.

We met in the wide plaza filled with lunchtime eater's three BART stops from my building. Eric was right on time with a Greek salad and large bouquet of yellow roses.

"Hello Jeanne. You look good enough to eat," he said obviously trying to please and cajole.

"Hello, Eric," I said coolly, glad I'd worn my sling–backs and a gauzy peach midi. Still when I looked at him I was pissed. All I saw was a stranger. If it wasn't for this damn story...you'd be here anyway, something in me reminded.

"I hope you'll forgive me for last week," Eric presented the roses. "Something unavoidable came up."

You keep saying, but I replied, "Well, Echo, they're beautiful. But I can't accept them... because of the story. As I could not accept the last." I exaggerated my pout.

"Well," Eric said, holding onto the flowers awkwardly. "How was your weekend?" We walked to an empty bench.

"Fine. You know, Echo," I continued as he placed the flowers next to him. "I've only got a few weeks left on this piece. I hope we can move ahead."

"*Mea culpa,* Jeanne. Truly an emergency," his voice trailed off.

"Was it your mother? Is she all right?" My hand jumped to cover my mouth, as my heart double clutched in worry and then guilt.

"She's still hanging in. Fine as can be expected. No this was...something else – a client." He looked down at his salad, but didn't move his fork.

"Echo, this really isn't any of my business, but are you still seeing Marcia?"

Eric stabbed some lettuce unsuccessfully. "Marcia is not really your concern," he paused. "But I will tell you that we are very old family friends."

"Did you see her this weekend?" I rushed.

Lettuce finally secured, he stared straight ahead at a pigeon. Then he half–smiled, and said, "Matter of fact, yes I did." He took his bite as though it were a prime cut of meat.

"Oh—" Blood sprinted to the surface of my skin. I steeled my lips like a concrete dam.

"But since I've moved, we're both seeing other people."

"Oh. A *good* family friend." The back of my eyes burned. To think I was feeling something similar to what Féy may have.

"It has nothing whatever to do with us." He ignored the discomfort I worked to conceal with small movements. "Shall we go out Friday night? I want to spend some more time with you and give you more on the story." Even with my head bent to my tomatoes, his eyes tugged at me. I ignored them.

"Let me think about it." You might think I'm being school-girlie and peevish, but with his recent broken promise, this seduction didn't seem so light-hearted anymore. Certainly not something I'd ever want Cariña to see. "How do I know you won't stand me up again?"

"I suppose you'll have to trust me," he chuckled.

"I suppose you'll have to earn it." That stopped his laugh.

"You've decided not to pursue the piece on my father?"

A moment later, I spoke in a warning tone, "If Friday's about the story, I'll go. But that's it."

"Absolutely," Eric said firmly, "But that's a two–way street, remember?" I nodded over a tight throat. For a few minutes we ate our salad listening to the random shrieks of blue jays.

On Muni going up Market, I imagined the conversation. "Clive, we've got trouble."

"Oh yeah?"

"Yeah, access to this story is blocked except through Anna's son, but he demands that I go away with, sleep, with him. So far we've only made out."

I could not see that talk happening. I had to get something else. I could go back to Anna and have her what, order him to give me the diary. But I doubted the maid would put me through or let me in. Besides her very approach implied the diary was beyond her reach.

Back at work I avoided Clive and tracked down Walter Dennis. Turned out George Washington Dennis, who'd written the editorial on the *Lawrence II*, had been a former slave who'd bought his freedom from his father and had made his fortune in real estate. He'd been one of my American Dream pioneers. No wonder they'd looked at me funny when I'd rattled on about them. But why hadn't they said anything? Perhaps they'd lost it all. And then with Mrs. Dennis giving away what she had.

I dialed through the book, until at the third W. Dennis an elderly woman answered, "Ye–es."

I gave my cover. "While a student I lived with Verna Dennis. Now I work for The Sheet, San Francisco. We're looking for descendants of prominent early city residents for a special on the city's ability to create wealth multi-culturally."

"We–e–ll, my son's Verna's great nephew – and my great granddaddy was George Dennis, so I guess you want to talk with me."

"Terrific," my heart beat against my neck, "Truth is we know most of the early fortunes were lost over the years one way or another – often unfairly, sometimes dumbly. However, we've found some descendants have recently regained them."

"Through the computers?"

"We–e–ll, actually...for some it seemed," I crossed my fingers as I spoke, "to just appear."

"What on earth do you mean? Like from thin air?"

I smiled, "Almost ma'am, almost. We're trying to find out. Thought we might add you—"

"You mean like a nice surprise in the bank account?"

My heart's heavy pounding stopped a moment.

"Ma'am? That's exactly it. Did something happen to yours?"

"Not mine..."

But it had happened I could tell. "Ma'am, when did this occur? What can you tell me...?"

"I can't say anything else. I don't know anything else..."

Her tone itched with protectiveness. "Is it Walter's account?"

"Walter," she said and my heart leapt.

"Where could I find him these days? Be great to see him."

Silence answered.

"When's a good time to reach him?" But she wouldn't implicate her son-in-law. "Would you like me to add you to our list? Let you know what we found out before we go public? That money could be stolen."

"Y–yes."

"All right, I'll do that Ms. Dennis. And why don't you take my name, in case your son would like to contact me, an old family friend." She wrote down the information. "Ms. Dennis, we don't know yet of anything illegal. But...to be on the safe side, I wouldn't spend that money. Order a trace on the deposit. Write down that you've talked with me today. Just to play it safe." I jotted a record of my call to her. Once we hung up, it dawned on me I should have some trace info by now. A few more calls and I was ready to talk with Clive.

"Hey, bossman," I swung easily into his chair. "I've got news."

"I'm an old man Jeannie, I don't need foreplay."

"I found another 'recipient' and the connection at least to me. The *HMS Lawrence II.*"

"The what?"

"It was a ship in 1873 owned by a group of black San Franciscans. Don't know what happened to it, but a descendant of at least one of the other owners, had a bank account filled."

He glanced at me, sat back. "Are you kidding?"

I shrugged, "Could be a coincidence. I've calls out to the others I could find. And guess what? My payments? All also came from a Swiss bank – though they're not among the transfers I have. They can't give me the account number as it's not in my name. But it all looks legit – at least no one in either bank complained. Though in all my cases the amounts would have no tax trigger." It dawned on me how widespread such a scheme could be. Most folks had under 10,000 in debt. Less than 10,000 was a non-taxable gift. There were a hundred 10,000's in a million; 100,000 in a billion.

"So who's doing it?"

I sighed. "If I can find enough folks, we could do a class action to get a court order to reveal the account name." I doubted that would occur – who in their right mind would come forward to give back free money?

"Or go direct to the bank."

"Want to fly me to Switzerland?"

He smirked, "Let's start with a phone call, Slugger." He picked up his receiver and dialed, "Todd, meeting's off, call me." A weight lifted from me as he spoke. He must've seen it in my face as he rushed, "Don't spend your eggs yet, Jeannie. But good work. Keep going.

"Yes, boss man."

I left and ran straight into Susan and Todd.

"Jeannie."

"Susan, Todd." I kept on, but Todd said, "Come join us."

I walked back in serenely, intending to improve upon any watery memory of me. Clive looked up from his phone startled. Todd waved him to finish and took a seat in the right chair. I waved Susan into the left. No way was I sitting with her standing. She descended gracefully as a butterfly on a reed.

Clive said to the phone, "Call me when you get it." Then without a beat I turned to Todd. I couldn't wait to see how he played this—now that we'd a real story.

"What's up Clive? What's the exclusive piece?"

"Jeannie?" Clive turned to me, "Want to tell them?"

Almost swallowing my spearmint gum, I rushed, "I thought I had something on a large local name, but..."

Susan turned to me, "Fell through again, Slugger? Research can be so tricky." My heart's thump signaled a black wave of escape, but none rose. Perhaps with uncontrollable dark memories I was done. Perhaps I'd mastered some power.

"Confirmation hasn't come in," Clive interposed. "And we don't want to start anything until we know for certain."

Todd narrowed his eyes, "So why'd you call us?"

Clive rushed in before me, "I jumped the gun – I was sure a lead would pan out. I was wrong."

Todd was already standing, buttoning his single–breasted jacket. Susan's eyes still swiveled back and forth between Clive and me; with him I didn't dare to make eye contact.

"We'll let you know soon as we're certain," I assured Susan's stare, "We've more leads in the pipeline."

She smirked as she rose to follow Todd out – she was going to be trouble. And yet in her eyes again I sensed something more – some way in – I just had to find it.

Todd turned at the door, smiled back at us, "Let's reschedule this for next week some time alright?"

Susan scratched a note. "Great," she grinned.

"Should be fine," Clive and I spoke over ourselves and then when they were gone, he and I laughed together, the first time in ages.

Twelve

Wednesday night in my sleep, I flew low again, this time myself the condor speeding 'cross the bay – as we had in Eric's plane – over the white caps heading toward the Golden Gate, back-dropped by the wispy clouded, orange–lit sky.

A small white dot stood outside in the bridge's center and grew as I neared. It was Féy, this time her bone white sheath glowed orange-red like the bridge, and she stood outside the rails, as if she were going to jump. Her arms were spread up to the sky as I flew up and over her, her voice riding the wind from behind, "Jeanne. You've started well with the powers. But you must move on. You have to want *me*...to want real living..."

I circled back once more to see her press her reaching thumb deliberately against her wrist and all went dark.

Till a voice vibrated into me, a low rumble, "You're a bad tramp, aren't you?"

Hot leather covered my – Féy's – face and body; my arms stretched behind to rings against a brick basement wall, my legs were restrained, but I – she – liked the tension holding me.

"Suppose we need some light now, slut, don't we?" Alfonse sounded wooden with the words, but he wouldn't swear in his own language or in French – only in English. And much of him would prefer not to do this at all – it was a remnant of a much harsher, shallower man who had not yet experienced adult love or loss. Yet every time he played this now, with the woman he was coming to love, he felt more of both.

A bald bulb blazed. I – Féy – was standing in a smooth black leather brassiere with metal clasps atop each mammilla that raised in me a strange, unsettling sensation.

My voice and lips seduced, my skin pressed forward against my restraints, "Have mercy...Hit me, Alfonse." The blow at least for a while would knock out the guilt of leaving home, leaving me, Jeanne, for a craving for love so much bigger than her talent; and now her longing for surcease. Sustaining this old practice of theirs, begun for fun, she now continued for rehab, for penance, but she knew it had been cursed as a cure.

A bell thrust me into black. Before I gathered all my wits about me, the phone rang again.

"Hello?" My body vibrated between remembered flight and restraint, and beneath them both lay a fear of why she'd picked this night of all nights to show this to me.

"Oh, you're sleeping," Eric's voice dripped discomfort, I thought at waking me, but also contained a challenge and subdued pleasure.

Relieved it wasn't Davis or Jacqueline, I stretched back, "What time is it?"

"11:30 or so." His low tone rolled behind my knees. "I'm in your neighborhood and wondered if you wanted to go out?"

I sat up on one elbow, rubbed an eyebrow ridge. So had Féy had warned me again of him?

"There's something I want to show you." His voice rippled through static.

I pushed myself up, "Well, where are you?"

"Just coming up on your building."

"Great," I beat my comforter back, "I need 10 minutes."

He hung up.

Exactly 10 minutes later I answered the door in a red silk kimono with a golden dragon stitched 'cross the back. It was tied to reveal a touch of cleavage.

A peck on his cheek revealed his usual cool cinnamon cedar odor. I waved a toothbrush toward the living room and a small rolling cart near the office stairs. "You can make a drink over there. Check out the view. I'll be back in a flash."

At the door to my bedroom, I turned back and checked him. A black leather jacket with long angled zippers made him broader, stronger, more dangerous – energy swirled up my spine. "What's the attire?"

"Leather. Lace. Black." Eric gazed out the bay windows bringing back memories of Marcia against his windows upstairs. Entangled or not, our relationship was founded on dark space.

But when I came out in black hose, black lace miniskirt and shimmering peacock–green bra under black mesh top to match Féy's peridot drop earrings, his challenging, twilight eyes caught mine in my reflection. And suddenly I saw the watery girl I'd left in the Mississippi – the night Féy'd left for the last time. The last time I saw her as she was tucked deeply inside. He saw her, too, though, judging from his stare, which knocked the wind from me.

He set down his drink and walked over, watching the rise and fall of my chest, his eyes outlining my curves. Then he laid his hands on my hips, just where they join the thigh. One at a time, he slid them behind, to pull me against him. And we kissed. His calm touch was now overshadowed by warm pinpricks as though limbs fallen asleep were waking.

Against all professionalism I wrapped my arms 'round his shoulders.

He nuzzled into my neck. "This observer wants you to know you've been seen."

I tingled down to the star he'd no notion lay just beneath his hands. Still he moved them up, catching my skirt as he kissed me. Without thinking I opened my lips and with them the darkness in me welled up, out and all through me. His one hand moved up my back pressing me in. He murmured, "I couldn't wait to get here," and for a long while I swam in the dark of our kiss.

Finally I broke back, "Let's go *now*."

His chuckle rumbled through my jaw to behind my knees.

"If I can walk."   Water now seemed contained in my shoulders, in my voice – as though I'd just aged through a kiss.

The dark and windy streets were deserted except for the occasional late night worker, so Eric snaked the Citroen fast and close 'round each curve. "So where we going?"

He smiled. "Beyond thought. Beyond judgment."

"Into fairy land?" But a familiar quiver ran down my spine.

"There's this club tonight. A good example of what my father studied."

We pulled into a parking lot just south of the 101 near Tenth Street. "Here," Eric handed me a small black mask.

"What's this?"

"You don't want to be recognized, do you?"

I slipped on the half mask as the night wind bit, clenched my jacket lapels, and ran a bit to keep up with Eric's pace.

"What's this place?" I whispered as we approached a black door and a waiting line of people.

"The Bondge," he replied with a small smile.

"Short for?"   As we passed the line, eyes startled and appraised over leather vests and jackets with studs, zippers, snaps, dark eyeliner, pierced lips and noses, and bare arms painted with tattoos.

"Bondage," Eric squeezed my hand between his arm and his chest. "Short for the Bondage a'Go–Go." Fear sliced briefly down my chest to my belly, but I shook my doubt off. When we joined the short line at the entrance, I stood back a bit from Eric with a cocked hip, though I still gripped his elbow.

"You come out here a lot?"

He shrugged. "It's really a nightclub with a Bondage theme. Two," he barked at the ticket seller who just nodded. No money changed hands – so they knew him here. Dark and driving heavy metal and a blue light came from behind black drapes.

"Hey man," the bouncer nodded to Eric as he pulled back the cordon. Then he looked at me with a wicked smile, "Have a good time in Heaven."

Eric said nothing to my questioning eyes. So I stepped through the drape bracing myself.

But the room beyond looked like an ordinary barroom. We entered the length of it. To our right was a pool table with a dyed and pierced crowd standing 'round. Scattered throughout were pinball games – mostly in use. At the far left was the bar, an opening into another room. From here the music drove. The space glowed blue.

Moving toward the bar nearly everyone was in black, from head to foot. Women wore leather corsets or mesh shirts over tight leather shorts or mini–minis. A dog collar loomed in the corner of my eye; a woman led a man on a chain. A few wore masks, some much more elaborate. "Nice," someone whispered in my ear. A hand brushed my rear. I turned. A woman with short, auburn hair, small leather cap and halter shaped like a Confederate Cross, grinned at me through a Cat Woman–style mask. She had those black bead eyes – the condor's eyes. Panicked, I turned to Eric. He laughed, "Everything's consensual here. There are rules."

"Of course." These were large–scale objects governed by clear laws – Newton's world. But Eric had said his father's world was here also – the world of chaos and of time connection. "What are the rules?" I kept my voice low to hide any shaking.

"Respectful treatment of all others. Only consensual play. No nudity outside the pit. No penetration. No exchange of bodily fluids. Except kissing, of course." He ran his finger under my chin. "Exchange of matter and energy," he said. "I think you'll find this place does that well. It always energizes me." He ran his finger down over my nipple, and tweaked it.

"Stop," I scolded, but it primed all my nerve endings.

"What, Jeanne?" He ran two fingers along the mask's string 'cross back of my head, resting on my neck and sending warmth down my back. "Want to stop seeking to know the story despite where it might take you?"

"*Au contraire*," I said, barely noticing the French, "But I do want to know how this place links to your father."

He grinned. "Well, what else have you learned about him?" Eric turned from the bar and handed me a drink. "Bourbon, rocks?"

I grabbed and swallowed, set it down and while I waited for the drink's familiar warmth I took in the posters announcing branding sessions with Mistress Paula. What would Moman L and her Ladies think?

"Let me give you a grand tour," he said. "This is just the foyer." He grabbed my hand and led through the blue–black mouth before I could get my second drink.

Inside, the height of the club and the fervor of the crowd doubled, trebled. Music boomed, mirror balls sprayed light like paint drops everywhere, and lasers roved the filled dance floor. Here and there a nipple hinted, shoulders gleamed, a thigh showed – all twenty– or thirty–something, every ethnic group, writhing en masse. Behind this, on a stage, a black cube framed a pale, thin man with long, fine, white–blond hair. He sat like a meditating ghost and the music pounded 'round him.

As I was about to ask Eric what was up, the woman who had touched me at the bar mounted the stage. She pulled a whip from her waist. The crowd continued to dance, their energy heightened. "Come here," Eric said. I followed him up onto the back stairs. At the landing we looked down on the stage as the woman approached the man.

She cracked the whip three times over his head, and then hung it on the cube. From one side, she loosened a black strap, grabbed one of the man's wrists and roughly tied it. The man swayed, opened his mouth. She kissed him. Then she strode to the other side and tied up his other wrist. She leant down and whispered. He nodded, swayed back and forth between his binds like a bayou reed, his eyes shut tight. The music drummed and pounded. The crowd now danced toward them.

Donning black leather gloves she pulled out a jar with a wide cork and needles stuck into clear liquid. Next to her, the ghost writhed.

Eric spoke. "Sterile piercings. It's a rule." By now the woman had the needle poised above the man's chest. His head was thrown back. The lights strobed as the woman stuck the needle below the nipple into the man's flesh. She ran it under his skin an inch.

"Aargh." The ghost released. There was no blood. The woman crossed to his other side with a second needle. She pierced him again only this time she turned the needle after it was in. Still there was no blood, but the most exquisite expression on the ghost's face — like beatitude. Eric leaned toward me, "Come on. I want to show you the pit. It's upstairs."

I was grateful to be tugged away. I wanted to be led in this place. True I'd craved the redemption of punishment in a way coming out here. But feeling I deserved actual, physical pain I could not see. On the stairs a man and a woman were playing with each other's pierced tongues. I looked away.

Along the rear of the club upstairs, dark windows fronted a loft overlooking the dance floor. Into an area behind them flowed a stream of light and humanity. Eric led me through the crowd to a section where a rope guarded three apparatuses. Behind them a bearded, somber man in a leather apron paced.

"Who's that?" I asked.

"The pit boss," Eric replied. "He makes sure everyone follows the rules." I glanced over. A thick man leant over a narrow vault horse. "Iron Butt," Eric whispered in my ear, sliding his hand to my belly button. "The Web," he turned me to a thick, black nylon web stretched from ceiling to floor.

A woman lay on it face down, eyes masked, plug in her lips. A man stood below taking her breasts in his kiss, other times brushing them with soft leather or a long–tailed brush. Eric slid one hand down to the soft top of my thigh. I forced myself to stare at the webbed woman in the mask, willing her to reveal to me the secrets of this kind of sensual love. At least it seemed like love – in her I didn't feel any rancor or anger.

Sweat gathered in the hollow of the web girl's neck, her back and neck stretched in ecstasy each time her partner touched her; or her body shuddered. Echo's lips on my neck, his heat warming my back, thumb of his second hand below my breasts brushing them, and the usual smooth velvet of his touch surrounded me. The bass boomed. The crowd swarmed. I could taste smoke in the back of my mouth.

"What's this to do with your father?" My voice floated out.

Eric growled low, "Krishnamurti said that man has built in himself fences of security – beliefs, judgments, and identities – thoughts that divide man from man, man from truth. That truth could not be contained, spoon–fed or read; that for each of us it has to be experienced directly, seen anew. Are you willing to feel first, Jeanne? Not think, nor judge, simply experience?"

In the last station a woman had electric circuits attached to her aureoles. Another woman had the controls. I steeled myself to watch, tried to think what Anna might do – she'd go for the adventure I told myself. As had Féy, and for me it was now or never, regardless of Cariña watching in. Were she in this situation herself – at my age, I added, just in case she could somehow hear this – I'd want her not to fear it.

Despite the Peeping Toms the women saw only each other. And I, like those 'round me, saw only them. As if they had invited in each of us – which in a manner of speaking, they had.

When the partner turned and threw the switch, the shock stung me. Sweat now beaded the hollow of my neck, just where it had on the woman in the web. It seemed Eric's soft lips were everywhere. *Truth is a pathless land. Women bare less than you think, dauphine. Beyond thought. Beyond judgment. Seek to know...*I lost myself in quotes from different voices in different times.

Metal burned. Black rose. Faces morphed – swapped identities – and as had happened at the dance, green vapor rose.

But instead of pioneers, this time Moman L waved into view. "Jeanne, I truly loved you. Never doubt that."

I burst into tears. "Moman L, why didn't you tell me you were sick? I could've come to see you."

"Buried truth's dangerous as a flood, dauphine. Most folk do well enough without it."

I lowered my head, "I didn't mean to let you down."

Her tongue clicked. "Jeanne, I forgave you the moment I passed. Your mother was right you know, there are things you needed to know of the world. After death we see everything.

"Now I know, Jeanne, we could have been together all those years. But my hard judgment came from hard experience. But now, Jeanne – now, you're ready to learn to love past the harsh, kinky truths – something your Moman and I never could do while alive – love to the soul."

She pressed my thumb against her wrist, just as Féy had and sent a real tingle up my arm. Before I could react I was in deep black, then in Cadot's storeroom against the metal shelving along the back wall, seeing Moman L grip the shoulders of Alva, her best friend – and Jacqueline's *Moman*. Alva was turned away, her shoulders hunched, her face in her hands. A hand, narrow, long, light in skin, Moman L's hand, my hand, reached out to Alva and turned her chin.

Her face looked forty years younger, a study of pain, and not just for the bruise that ran below her right eye – the one she'd been hiding.

"Alva, my dear. You must run from him."

"He loves me in his way."

"Love doesn't slap or punch."

"I've just got to get with child. He'll calm down." Her

desperate eyes searched mine.   Her hands pressed against my
sternum. My chest swelled.   I could see beads of sweat above her
lip, a faint red arc along her left cheek.

Next thing I knew I traced that arc and then kissed it gently, my
lips soon found by Alva's, as soft as hungry.   We kissed.   And I
touched her wrist – saw Alva being beat and hit by a towering,
angry figure.   Then time broke apart and the whole world was soft
grasping until someone cleared his throat.

We broke up, hands and minds scrabbling back to
consciousness.   Cold air rushed in.   Through the metal shelving in
the doorsill stood a bearded man I knew from our footed family
albums, Moman L's father, Marie's husband, Marcel Merciér, one
of the handful of surviving husbands dotting our line.

"There you are," his tone sagged with disapproval.   "Alva, your
husband's out here.   I expect he's wanting to get home to dinner.
Laetitia, you've a customer out here *and* a daughter."   He left the
door wide behind his scowl.

Then it went black.   The club's smell of warm, spicy sweat
rose again.   But then I saw the black condor's eyes, glancing at
me. I blinked. It was Annie – Annie French from the plane. She
pulled off a mouth ball. She'd been the one on the web.

I shook my head clear. Echo was gone. But Annie pulled on
a deep red tee shirt.

"Annie? Annie French?" I struggled to focus. "It's Jeannie.
From The Sheet—the plane..."

She came out from under the cordon and reached out an arm
to steady me. Reality rippled. My head didn't want to settle, even
though Moman L was gone and there'd been no burning metal or
green air.

"Jeannie, I remember. What are you doing here?"

"I'm with Echo...my friend," I mumbled, leaning.

Annie craned her neck behind me. "Oh," she eyed me with
raised eyebrows. "Are you alright?"

"I just...need a little—" My knees didn't want to stand, "What
are you doing here?"

"Here, come with me." She ushered me through the cordon, flashing a sign to the pit boss. Next thing we were through a door behind the pit to the room with the darkened windows. You could feel the music here more than hear it.

"What is this place?" I asked Annie. I saw three ponytails behind me monitoring screens.

"She's okay guys," Annie shot over her shoulder. "She's with Eric Kincaid." One or two of them turned to peer at me. They looked for a while until Annie opened a bottle of water. "She's a virgin, all right? You're all jaded."

I took the water and turned, my eyes adjusting, perspective settling, head rush subsiding. On their black screens vague green code and numbers flashed. What they were doing had nothing at all to do with bondage or submission—I was certain of that. And certain I'd stumbled into another piece of the thread – no doubt why Echo had brought me here.

"Feeling better?" Annie knelt down concerned. "So you know Eric?" She shrugged, slanted away her eyes. "He's kind of famous around here. Made the club its share of cash last year. Now we own this building."

"Are you all the Grey Hats?" It was out before I could think or stop myself.

Annie blushed and glanced behind me again. "I don't know what you—?"

But one of the guys behind her said, "He wouldn't have brought her here if he didn't trust her."

I sat up as if someone had rung a clear bell.

"But she's a journalist," Annie hissed.

"Yes, and he did bring me here – he said he had something he wanted me to see." I scooted closer to their set ups.

At some invisible sign, the screens went blank. Annie rose and grabbed my arm, "Jeannie, he's probably looking for you."

"Okay, okay." Dang, I hadn't brought a card. "I'm at The Sheet – on line. You can reach me...well, you know how. Can I expect to be prosecuted?" I hoped they understood my meaning.

"Someone will get back to you," the furthest fellow spoke. Though his face was shadowed he was Japanese it seemed.

I smiled. "This week," I said shaking off Annie's pull.

"Soon. We promise."

At the door Annie said, "I'll be in touch."

"Nice to see—," but the door slammed in my face. I picked my way out of the pit much like I'd picked myself out of the Mississippi mud – eyes on my carefully placed feet, happy to been there, happy to be leaving, a bit disbelieving at I'd been altered by those flashes of Féy, Moman L and even Annie.

Eric was staring at me from behind the stream of humanity at the back wall with his arms 'round two women.

As I made my way over to him, a short man came up to me and said, "Top?" I waved "no" but this time he didn't scare me at all.

When I got to Eric, he said, "Well, ladies, this is my girl. Jeannie? Ladies. Darling, where've you been?"

"Oh, she's pretty," purred the twenty–something girl with pigtails. She licked a pink lollipop.

The thirty–something, brown-skinned woman said, "Can you both come and play?"

"In the web," the younger one pushed her face forward, "I'm going up next."

Her lips pouted forward until before I knew it I kissed them and she, after a moment's surprise, kissed me back, tasting of beer, lime and sugar. Coming to my senses, I withdrew, leant against Eric, surprised at myself, imagining Féy's laughter, Moman L's shock, surprised her lips, though soft, hadn't felt that much different than a man's.

Echo must've read my face and laughed. "Sorry girls. Anymore and my love here might explode." Had he just said love?

The young girl pouted like she'd just lost a hot toy, but a young man sidled up to her saving the day.

"You coming to the meeting?" The older one asked.

Eric nodded. As we left the club, he whispered only, "You want inside my head? I want inside you." In my new state, that pleased me.

Later above him in my bay windows I imagined myself on one side of a web, him on the other. When Eric kissed my breasts, the dark well in me reared and Annie's sweat, the women connected by their nipples, the young girl's candy lips, the white ghost, Moman L's secret passion, and Féy's desire for restraint and pain – they all circled in my mind on waves I rode slowly. I finally landed in a deep, dreamless sleep.

I woke with my head resting on the window seat, in the late morning, wrapped in my comforter, with grey covering the sky. I found a note stuck to my window, "What was true last night? What was connected? What do you think was real?"

Well, the whole night had been a setup. But now a woman of the world, I was eager for another test drive.

Coming in a little late Thursday morning I walked past Todd taking Marcia Witt to the elevator, "Oh, Jeanne, we just came down to see you..."

Marcia declined her red, virgin wool beret and murmured, stepping into the elevator.

"I'll be back with you in a minute," Todd said and turned back to Marcia.

At my desk my cell rang. "Jeannie," Annie's early morning voice was hoarse, "Come to the Cave, 8 tonight. Your questions will be answered. Nice work." She clicked off.

I sat down. The Cave – Echo's spot, I should run to Clive. But Todd's Polo cologne curled into my nose; his ruby school ring appeared on my cube edge. "Todd," I stood.

"Jeannie, haven't heard much from you."

The crispness of his shirt and richness of his deep navy pinstripe Armani with 24-carat cufflinks brought out the awkward girl in me as if finally standing face to face with Alfonse. To keep my mind here, I kicked up one faux–Jimmy Chu, kept one hand somewhat casually on the desk, "What can I do for you?"

He smiled slowly – his teeth glinting. "Let's go to lunch today." His gold Cartier gleamed, "I'll pick you up on the back corner at 12:30. But let's keep this between us."

"I'll rearrange my..." I tossed the words at his coat back.

The red Lamborghini sat idling by the curb in T–top style. "Hop in," Todd leaned over and popped open the door before he went back talking to his wireless headphone. He was only 10 minutes late. What *had* Marcia said?

Driving through the streets, Todd never tired of barking at someone on the line and he had two cell phones Velcro-ed to his dash, so I concentrated on the 12–speaker sound – Gangsta rap mixed with Yardbird Parker's jazz saxophone. I calmed my beating chest with slow, steady breaths.

As we pulled in the high-up circular drive – the elegant bricks rising to the spire, Todd said, "We're done. I'll get back to you." He hung up. Then he asked, "You ever been here?"

"Can't say yes." Couldn't say I'd ever been at lunch with the big boss either.

"The view is spectacular."

"We're going up?"

"All the way to the Top of the Mark. No need to worry about you though. You live in the Tower I understand?" He handed the keys to the valet.

I nodded. "Marcia mentioned it?"

That slow smile again – those strangely grey eyes – like Annie's hat pin or the Grey Hats. Could Todd be connected to the Ten?

"She might have," he held the hotel door open for me and on the elevator made a show of turning off his wireless headphone, forwarding his calls.

When the doors opened, "*The very thought of you*" on piano swept me back a moment to New Orleans and Cariña – reminded me who I was fighting for.

The view from the cozy, mustard room with plate glass windows stretched over the white, grey and blue city. We were led to a white-linen table that looked out at the Golden Gate Bridge. I stared at it daring it to ripple. Todd reviewed the wine list. The scene stayed perfectly still.

"So Mr. Hunter," I lifted my icy water glass, "To what do I owe the honor? You doin' this for all the candidates?"

"Welcome to the Top of the Mark," a fresh–looking Latin man said, in a crisp, white half apron over black pants. "Something to start?"

After he'd gone, my questions still hung in the air. I waited.

Todd settled his Bluetooth then folded his hands, "I didn't tell Clive about this meeting."

My heart froze.

"Don't get me wrong – he's a veteran journalist – a master of his craft and a great editor – an eye for important stories. It's just The Sheet's L.A. strategy," he eyed my boobs and I grabbed a piece of sourdough to cover my persimmon v-neck, "has been to hit the youth market. We are young, brash, hip: sizzle and truth."

"Clive's hip." And sizzle and truth were two powers.

"Clive's classic. We're new millennium. And so..." he leaned in, "I'd like to keep this meeting just between us," he covered my hand, his ring heavy against my finger, "just as I'll keep your reporting methods between us."

I moved my head in a way I hoped might imply nodding, but could later be denied. Luckily our Nicoise salad and Mark Club sandwich came.

"You know I met Pauline Kincaid many years back," he said putting his own mayonnaise on the bread. My head turned instinctively to locate the tympanic boom. Though now I couldn't hear anything but Todd's voice, the clink of our utensils and glasses muffled like when part of your hearing goes out.

"I was a young editor then and she'd headed KinCo for 10

years.   I was covering high tech.   I heard her speak at the
National Association for SemiConducting.   I had a mean mother
and three tough sisters, but I'd never seen a woman equal her in
union ball-busting.   I met her.   She'd known my father.   I dare say
now she'd remember me.   More wine?"   He raised a bottle and I
covered my still full glass with my hand.

"Busy afternoon," I said.   "Why don't you just tell me what
your point is?"

He chuckled, wiped his mouth carefully as he had on the
boat, "Believe it or not my father then was a union foreman.   A
few years later he was an unemployed, cuckolded drunk."   His last
words hung as dead in the air as the image must have in his life.

"If any in that family – say her son..." his stark glance told me
he knew just who it was I'd danced with that night on the ship,
"had something to tell, The Sheet S.F. would certainly welcome
it."   His eye glinted.   "I'd like you to keep me informed on any
big developments in the story."

"Wait a minute, Clive's pro unio—."

"*Sizzle* and truth, Miss Cadot."

"Jeannie, please."

"Jeannie," the grey eyes smiled.   "I'd like to be the silent
check on any major tactics or events.   Maybe I can help."

"You know all my reporting's done free–lance.   I'm officially
still just an E.A."

His smile was more deliberate.   "If it's created on our
equipment, or with our direction, we share copyright."

"I've got my own computer."   This was true of my desktop –
at home.   "This has all been done after hours," I lied, leaning into
the sizzle, "And what about their advertising?"

He raised his brow.   "If this is a real story – they won't be
advertising anymore.   Another reason I need you to brief me – or
Susan.   Or if Clive gets any notions to drop it – come see me – or
her if it's more discreet."

"And you'll keep my...methods...private?   Otherwise, deal's
off?"

"No one would be more pleased than me to welcome you to the Dream Team," he raised his glass with his left hand. "I'm not who most folks think I am, Ms. Cadot."

I see that, I thought sticking out my right palm. "I'm already reporting to Clive. And Mavis. They stay in the loop."

"Keep me secret." He grabbed my hand too tight, reminding me of his grip on the dance floor. But I must have satisfied him, as over his slight smile, his grey discs were closed vaults again when, releasing me, he clicked his cell phones open.

The rest of our lunch he was on the phone. By two, he dropped me off at the corner. I stepped out casually, not even waving to his distracted nod, trying to look as if I'd nothing special on my mind.

At 8 o'clock the Cave was more crowded, even a few leather jacketed Mohawk-sporters with skateboards hung in the alley. This time I scanned for cameras, saw two on either end of the bar. I strode to the back without even turning to the mirror where eyes watched me. Though I'd pulled out one of my most casual suits, folks in them here this late were usually looking for trouble.

At the last booth, the one I'd sat in with Echo, four young men sat in fashionable haircuts, dark t–shirts and jeans. "Jeannie?" the one against the wall asked, indicating I should sit down. I thought I recognized him from last night. "Please turn off your cell." His smile stayed closed until I showed him the dark screen. He indicated a position in the middle of the table where I slid the dead piece.

"Don't suppose I could get you fellows' names?"

He smiled. No smiles met him 'round the table. Goatees, sunglasses, but no tattoos, piercings, and only small earrings marked these men.

The same waitress came up. "Bourbon and water," I said.

"Unh huh." No doubt this was their regular booth. No doubt she knew all about it, all about Echo. She sashayed away.

"Gentlemen?" The oldest, vaguely Japanese fellow said. The other three pulled laptops from next to them, already powered up. "Miss Cadot, do you believe in divine justice?"

I fumbled in my pocket to turn on the mini tape recorder.

"Only 3% of the S&L funds were ever paid back. And probably less of the current stolen funds will even be returned. A small network of folks got tired of all that. We decided to help God." There was a lot of that going 'round, I thought.

The hackers' fingers began clicking. "We can't stop corruption. But we can hit the bastards in their privates—bank accounts that is. Swiss, hidden and full of ill-gotten funds."

A screen came up on the laptop next to me. Written in German it seemed.

"Taken illegally as determined by you?"

"By the SEC's indictments. Don't you think most people would say corporate crooks' money should be returned? To the people from whom it was taken?"

Hell, yes. "So, you give back to—"

"We've not given to anyone yet."

"But what about the wire transfer pages you sent me?"

"Transfers?" They glanced at each other, shaking heads and frowning, "Well, everything's set, but we've not yet paid out anything. But the program will start with their credit cards, any overflow will go directly into their savings in two sums – one for any tax should they get caught."

I pulled out the card and email, "Ever seen these?" The leader frowned, "These are not from us."

Because they're from Echo, but I held my tongue, "And who will your recipients be?"

"There are shareholder and employee lists if you know where to look."

"Whose accounts do you hit?"

"Executives from Enron. World.com. Tyco. Goldman Sachs. All the corporate crooks." He looked at the screens. "Show her." I noticed he wore black gloves. They all did. They acted like spies, which, if their story was true, I supposed they sort of were.

They turned their screens; each had a wire transfer screen flickering, in both German and English. They each had amounts filled in in Deutschmarks: One million, one million point five.

"Would you like to click?"

"No thanks, go ahead." I tried to memorize the account number. I got 11235813...before he nodded and simultaneously they all clicked and the screens went dead.

"Whose accounts were those?"

"Fastow."

"Koslowski."

"Anschutz."

After a number of other clicks, they began closing windows. The whole thing having taken only minutes, it seemed like a hoax. Still, the notion of having Cariña, of having no more worries, just like that, intoxicated me as much as bourbon. "Why do you tell me?" I rushed.

"We have a big distribution coming up."

"But why would you want press?"

"You're recording this, right?"

Reluctantly I nodded, pulled the recorder from my pocket and set it facing him.

"Regular guys like us built all these systems. The elites then rig the laws to take the spoils from us, through our own 'children'. Well, our minds made them rich, they can also unmake it. Proving everyman ingenuity wins out every time."

One of his compadres broke in. "Did you know they still don't know how Vladimir Levin got the money out of Citibank?" Levin was a hacker who in 1995 had tricked Citibank computers into spitting out ten million dollars. He'd been caught, most of the money returned and Citibank's encryption made even tighter. "Someone might spread rumors about who did this, what it was."

The leader broke in, "Annie says you call him Echo – not many know that name – only friends. What did you tell him about meeting us?" He whispered to one of the other men.

My ears perked up, even though my hand itched to shut off the recorder. "He says he doesn't know you."

He listened then shook his head – he had an earplug in. "Is that Eric on the other end?"

"He knows nothing of this. Not from us." His tone implied I'd run to tell him, but still he went on. "It's for his father."

"Berne? Is *he* on the other end?"

He grimaced a smile.

"Why for him?"

"We can't tell you that."

These guys had read way too many books. They popped cards out of their computers, gave them to their black turtle-necked leader, then swapped empty decks and packed.

"Wait. I don't have your names." I grabbed and tried to discreetly turn on my phone.

Their leader smiled. "I don't think you want to ambush us, Ms. Cadot," he said, "If we can get to the Swiss..." I took my finger off the power button.

He stood up. "You have the names that you need."

"But why would you meet with me – blow your cover?"

"Truth, Ms. Cadot. You're a reporter for the people, we're told. If a story comes out, we need someone who can speak for them – for us. Who knows what lies they might spread? And we won't be able to say a word then, of course."

"But if we publish, won't they go after your recipients?"

He chuckled, "We're willing to bet no one will even contest the theft – they'd have to explain the hidden money, the security breach – it would cause questions and ripples far too public. Remember, all the transferred funds are *illegal* gains. Swiss banks and the ultra rich believe in discretion more than truth."

"Is Walter Dennis a recipient?" He gave no response. "Well, I need some proof." My racing pulse wasn't just for the story.

He considered a moment then nodded. "You'll get it."

"Tell me at least a screen name."

With an enigmatic smile and shrug, he followed the men who were already gone into the crowd. I stayed some feet behind. Outside they walked to 9th – to the studio of Berne's website administrator, Conrad. There I shot a distant picture of their backs. I waited for a few hours, but no one came out and there was only the single buzzer to which they wouldn't respond. Could they possibly be telling the truth?

Clive roared when I told him about the hackers, "Why didn't you tell me? We could have had a photographer shadow you."

"Oh Clive, these guys are too smart."

"Well, what do we have now?"

"Though they deny sending them, we have the emails, the wire transfers, my tape of the meeting," though someone could be trying to frame me and I'd a good idea who.

"On the record?"

I shrugged. "They won't risk their anonymity."

"We need more. We need the source or destination of those emails or transfers."

"I'm on it." I needed time to think.

"Go talk to Blowhard Carruthers," Clive said. "See if he's heard anything – millionaires talk."

My mouth puckered, "Yeah, all right."

The Pacific Stock Exchange on Sansome at California where Ralston's bank had been, had imposing statues in front of it, marble stairs, wide white columns, and a heavy, stacked roof, but my press pass got me through the metal detectors, new since 9–11 – and the past stayed down. I found Blowhard hanging 'round the press desk above the trading floor. His usual lasciviousness awakened upon seeing me.

"*Ms.* Cadot, to what do I owe the luck?" The sound was deafening with guys in blue cotton coats over white shirts fighting for the best deal.

"Mike, I need a favor."

"Oh, really?" He turned, leaned against the waist–high wall guarding the floor.

"I wanted to ask if you'd check for me into a Swiss bank."

"Which one? There are a lot."

"Oh…Banque Geneva maybe."

"Check for what?"

"On whether some accounts exist or not."

"Accounts."

"We got a silly tip. Waste always flows downstream. I'm just checking it out."

"And they send you out here in the middle of the day?" He stood up.

"We–ell," 'I was in the neighborhood' I was about to say, "You know I'm reporting some – on Fridays."

"Yeah…" He placed his hand on the wall, deciding whether to believe me.

"Well, could you see if you could find anything on these accounts?" I handed him a list of just the account numbers. "So I can escape my sad, sycophantic profiles."

"Hey, Jeannie, you know my mouth…it's been trained on the Street."

"Well, make it up to me."

"Hey, this about that other thing last week?"

"Keep it to yourself or I'll deny it." I left him there watching my ass walk.

By Friday I made my way down to Pier 27, the wharf where Walter Dennis owned a vintage boat repair. Despite being next to the site of the old ship, the old city stayed at bay once more. Perhaps the past was calmer now I was on the track. I approached the small office 'round the back of the pier as we'd agreed. Walter was outside smoking – I remembered Verna's glossy cheeks right away.

"Walter, how nice to see you – Claudette and the kids all right?"

He nodded, taking a drag of his Dunhill, "Sorry I never got back to you."

"How've you been? And the girls?" His tight shrug showed he still resented that Verna gave so much money to the scholarships – and blamed me. Still his alligator shoes and Panthers leather jacket, and the brand new Harley whose seat he leaned on, showed he was doing all right, was well-connected.

"About the story on the 'recipients' of the Grey Hats. It's not my intention to get you into trouble. I know someone well who's benefited herself – a lot."

"Oh yeah?" He stared at the dock while the winter wind bit. "One or two?"

"Three. Thirty grand," I leaned in and whispered.

His face went shocked, then disgusted and he moved away, "Aw..."

"Did you get more, Walter? How much?"

"I got to get back in – break's over.

"You didn't get one of these?" He blanched at the email, but still held back. "Any of these account numbers look familiar?" I held out the list.

He looked down at them, angrily flicked his butt, knocked on the iron grill, which opened to let him in. "Don't come here or call me again."

How much had he gotten? Immediately, I stopped by the ATM. I glanced at the receipt, and my hand crumpled it. My balance was $10,030.65. The Grey Hats sure had hit me, but at far less than Walter Dennis's face had implied. So, what gave?

At O'Malley's Irish Pub on Union Square that evening, an hour before I was to call Echo, Mavis sat hands folded atop a high booth's round table.

"Someone just deposited almost ten grand in my bank account."

"What?! Your guys? Did you tell the bank?"

"They were closed." I tossed the receipt 'cross the table.

"Jeannie, do you think?"

"I asked the hackers for proof the other night."

"So you think these are..."

"Stolen funds. Yes. That's not all. Todd took me to lunch yesterday. He wants to be kept appraised through Susan."

"Oh shit, Jeanne. You tell Clive yet?"

"He doesn't want Clive to know of his interest. Thinks Clive's too old – not you, he didn't mention that – but he wants The Sheet to be young and hip and sizzling."

"Clive's hip," Mavis chided.

I waggled my head. "We have to save him. Todd said you could talk to Susan for me. It gives us more wiggle room – for coummunication breakdowns."

Mavis reluctantly acquiesced.

"Nothing until I verify the wire transfers, right?" We clinked on it. "The second set of bank records Kris decoded showed dozens of transactions not yet activated; some for amounts far greater than mine. Luckily none of my cards were in the batch."

"You know Jeannie, I've been meaning to say, don't let Mr. Great Legs fool you. I'm not sure his family is all that benign."

And the Grey Hats had said they were doing this for his father, but I didn't want to share that yet – she'd probably freak out. I sipped my Mark on the rocks, "You're telling me."

"Blowhard nixed a story on them a while back, before we were the Eye. They had some henchman, an executive vice president of Pauline's. He scared the bejesus out of him."

"I don't think there's much love lost between Echo and the Kincaid's. But do I need to tell Todd? He doesn't know of my debts yet."

After replaying the entire event, we chose to wait a few days.

Soon as Mavis hopped in a cab I called Eric. When he answered I said, "How about I come by?"

I parked down the block without noticing. The Grey Hats seemed to be protecting him, so I had to make him relax; to want to tell me. So inside the door, I kissed *him*, welcoming the spark down to the star at the bottom of my torso.

We moved to the worn, but still well-padded, brown leather couch in front of the lit, graceful wood stove. A silk rope lay on the coffee table. "What's this?"

Eric ran the cord through his startling hands. He said, "Looks like a present." He wrapped it gently 'round my wrist.

"Echo, let me ask you again – have you ever heard of the Grey Hats?"

In reply he took a bite of my neck and I took a deep whiff of his spicy wood scent. I let him take off my coat, then my shirt. Once I lay on the couch in my bra and panties and he smiled, leaned down and pulled out more soft, satin ropes.

"Oh," I scooted into the couch's heart, keeping my mind on the prize – or the price of admission. "Because the Grey Hats are certainly looking to help you out."

He smiled and laid the cords along my leg. When he reached my face, our breath was jagged. He held himself inches above and blew cool air, as he had when we danced and suddenly I was back there again with he and the pioneer faces pressing in. I blinked. "Help your father I mean – you sure this won't hurt?"

Surprise crossed his face. He lifted back, "Don't you recall? Where women are honored, there the gods are pleased, but where they are not honored no sacred rite yields rewards." Then relaxing, he traced my face. "I only enjoy myself if you do. That's the point, isn't it?"

I covered my discomfort, "Yes, that's right. You are too good to be true, aren't you?"

He smiled and nipped my ear, "And you're delicious." He yanked his shirt off, grabbed a cord and wrapped my ankle. He ran his hand up my thigh. My leg would only give a few inches. I didn't find it quite as inspiring as Féy had.

He traced up from my belly through my bra's cups then 'cross my right shoulder. "How about this," he asked, as from near my ear, he lifted my wrist above my head. I flinched.

He stopped. "After all we're practically family. And you know where I live."

"Eric, please." A black wave rocked up bringing clangs of concern, as if the old Moman L somewhere banged from behind a cellar door. This was not how I'd imagined this night going. I'd suddenly become his servant. I glanced around for a video camera, but saw no red light anywhere.

He wound cords gently 'round my crossed wrists and lifted them above my head. He moved and murmured, gentle, solicitous. He felt he was serving me.

Once this was clear to me, there was nothing more to do but stretch out, allow him to use the blindfold – and later peppermint, eucalyptus, soft lips, hungry but kind fingers, strawberries and chocolate – searching tongue behind my knees, at my elbows, releasing me over and again. I bit my lip and drew blood.

I finally drifted into sleep with my blindfold half on, one leg still bound. And I slept through the night without a single dream.

I woke rested and by myself. The house sat quiet except for a small music sound coming from upstairs. For a while I lay arms wrapped 'round my chest. Today I had to face all I'd put off – forward the story without arousing suspicion. I rose to find Eric at his computer in hazy light.

"I'm working," he said, not harshly, but without turning, in response to my nuzzle. Then, "You slept well?" in a kinder tone.

"Like a baby. Thank you. I'm surprised. And today I hope to surprise you about your father." He grunted.

But after I showered, he pulled himself from his screen and led me down to his father's study 'cross from where I'd spent the night. I could smell incense, as if ingrained somehow in the Oriental rug on the floor.

"He kept scientific diaries from age 13."

I ran my fingers over the spines, curled into him when he circled me from behind and kissed the chord at the left side of my throat. "Is it possible to see his lab?"

Echo stiffened, then, "Yes, of course."

He led me by hand down stairs wearing years of cobwebs and a slight basement must, but I couldn't smell the ash odor he'd griped about. A bald 60–watt bulb flickered to life revealing Eric's car, an ancient weed–whacker and a rake.

"Where *is* everything?"

"We never had the heart to fill it back up." He shrugged as I inspected the brick wall that rose halfway to meet a bare wooden frame.

Eric patted a stud. "My father's steel lining cost a fortune, but in the end it encased the fire."

"Part of his experiment – do you know what it was?"

Eric shrugged. "Seen enough?"

"Did you ever hear they found no human remains?"

"What do you mean?"

"The journalist at the Herald told me. There were ashes of burnt papers, destroyed lasers, but no organic remnants." He walked 'round the car. "Perhaps the fire was so hot," I offered, "Hot enough to melt metal."

"I went inside the next day. Ash everywhere and chunks of melted metal here…here. The heat singed the wood walls *above* the ceiling, so it was burning like hell in here. But they didn't even find teeth. Nice thing for a son to know about his father, isn't it?"

"So maybe he wasn't here?" But if he was hiding from his son – that would crush Eric.

"Read his work. This weekend I'll be at my desk." He paused. "But we might eat together tonight." He brushed his hand 'cross my hip making me feel my own skin.

I turned and took his face in my hands. "I'll be sure and have something sizzling for you, then." We kissed again. It certainly seemed that Féy had been on to something all those years.

Thirteen

While Eric returned to his office I thought about calling Annie French and going again to see that Conrad fellow. But Eric always worked with his windows open so he could hear everything. So, I pulled out 30 small, textured black books with white drawing paper inside, all covered with equations and barely understandable abbreviated prose.

An article of Berne's lay tucked between two pages. On it, scrawled by hand was, "Bell–State mathematics the best I've ever seen. A. Einstein." Albert Einstein – but no pages were attached. Yet on the left page beneath it, without a single abbreviation, lay:

> *Somewhere in the dark - of the atom, of ourselves,*
> *Way beyond light and time,*
> *Or the scalpel of thought,*
> *There lies the place where physics and love are one*
> *Mustn't it be from there all life comes and returns?*
> *Seek to know the truth, despite where it leads.*
> *E. Berne, 1973*

Written the year I'd been born and Berne had burned up, 100 years after the pioneer ghosts had bought their ship.

So the years connected us – and all the marriages – matters of both physics and love. And Berne longed to know the place where all these hidden ties were revealed – that place which being known, all else is known – his implicate order – our Heaven.

And Eric couldn't understand how that could consume him? Well, my idea of Heaven was being with Cariña and I was consumed by that – I suppose Eric had never let himself feel such.

14 pages were ripped out from the end of this book, and all the rest was drawings. Expanding three-dimensional spheres and cubes, each arc and angle laced with equations and degree annotations.

Flipping back to the start, I translated, "What are the impacts of Heisenberg here?"

On the following page, best as I could tell he'd scrawled, "Creation's the movement of the unknowable essence of the whole, not the expression of the part. The fragment can never understand the totality. Krishnamurti." The man Eric had said was Berne's teacher that night the Bondge. Beneath the quote was scrawled the number 31.

31, my age then, but more important, in front of me there were three stacks each of 10 journals – perhaps the 31st contained the answer. Perhaps it was the black book Anna had held at the kitchen table. Methodically I searched. Also for the passport – or passbook – she'd held. I ransacked the drawers and shelves.

Finally, removing a dusty encyclopedia volume number 31 from a top shelf, a glint caught my eye. Pulling out a few more, I saw against the wall behind them what seemed to be a large, dust-covered rectangle of silk.

Carefully lifting the hanging out, I shook the piece softly. Dust came off in a piece revealing jewel–like gold. Shaking harder, then laying it on the circular black table, I blew clear a tiny emerald Buddha of unique expression and delicately posed long hands. I brushed wider to reveal a sapphire demon with bulging red eyes and sea blue scales, behind him a ring of stylized ruby waves. Grabbing my Pashmina scarf, I cleaned off the middle to see two dark sapphire figures entwined in....carnal bliss.

It brought back last night with Eric. Here the act was captured in jewels. And oddly last night's seduction felt to me similar. It engendered no guilt – perhaps because there'd been no Féy, no anger, perhaps because it had had to be done.

Surprisingly, I felt more Cariña's mother than ever – more capable of protecting her through anything. Musing on what she might be doing, to the low hum of a distant jazz saxophone, I lost track of time.

Until hands slid down my chest and I leaned back and looked up into Echo's twilight eyes.

"Mm," I said as our upside-down lips met, "Perfect timing." He turned my chair 'round and sank down.

Later, as we lay on the Oriental rug, I rose and hung the silk painting on the filing cabinet. Echo had just locked all this up and ignored it – just as Moman L and I had done with all our bad memories. But they never really went away.

I grabbed the drawn journal from the desk, held the book up, "What are these, Echo?"

He opened one eye, sat up on an elbow.

Gesturing between Berne's drawings and the hanging, I said, "Both telescoping in: circle, square, circle, square and circle – the same five-level structure. And geometry is the spatial representation of number."

"Very good Cadot," Echo's voice was flat, "Mandalas. Buddhist meditation guides. He got them from Krishnamurti."

"That looks like gold." I pointed out the outline of the innermost circle.

"Illuminatory materials," Echo sounded tired. His eyes were half closed.

"And how do you use them?"

"Why don't you come back here and I'll tell you all about it." He patted the space next to him.

I lay back down and settled in.

"Well," he pointed at the mandala, "I'm no guru, but do you see the center circle – the one back-dropping the divine lovers? It represents the Monad – the unity – the unknowable source." He traced my bellybutton. "Pythagoras said it was parent of all numbers and shapes. From the one, the circle, comes all else in our universe, yet it never alters the identity of whatever it meets. One times one times one times one times one is still one."

I rolled toward him. "Some sort of Godlike mirror?"

Echo spread his fingertips out from my stomach's center, "The circle offers the most space with the smallest perimeter: cups, cans, pizza or womb. The center is nowhere that expands equally in all directions like ripples, craters, or the rings on a tree, until along the circumference there are infinite points. Still inside it contains no differences."

So inside the innermost circle was Heaven – Berne's implicate reality – the world from which we all came and to which we seemingly return, if Féy, Moman L and the dead pioneers were any evidence. "So a mandala's a path to heaven?"

He smiled and ran his hand up to draw a slow line across my chest connecting my breasts. I shivered a bit. "The line, like those two gods, represents the two – the reflected source. To stave off loneliness, the circle duplicates, shifts a few inches off-center, but still overlaps itself, the union of the two forming–," he ran his hand up the middle of my chest, over my heart, "the *vesica piscis* – an almond–shaped middle – the realm of paradox."

He fingered my right areole. "The center points, the ends of the line represent the polar opposites: negative and positive, attraction and repulsion, man and woman, black and white, good and evil, rich and poor, light and dark," he outlined my jaw.

"Other and self. As all oppositions – they are connected by a continuum." He smiled. "But the ends can't exist without their opposite – a line without end is a circle. And both opposites long to reunite with the source then separate from it over and again – as man longs to reunite with woman and then pull away. From this dynamic tension between them comes all creation. Inside the dance of the two, the ground is hallowed – the ground is life."

He lifted me up and over him. He ran one hand down my stomach. "What do we find in the almond–shaped intersection of the circles of thighs?" he said moving into me, "We find the gateway to the past and future, good and evil, man and woman – the mandala." His voice faded out and his eyes closed. Letting mine follow suit, I fell again into our blank space, black and thick and safe.

His voice trailed in as through a pinhole, "Pairs of opposites with some third to bind or catalyze them, become a trinity, a 'tri–unity', three–into–one – a knot – one of the strongest and oldest forms in the universe. Proton, electron and neutron become an atom; two hydrogens and one oxygen become water."

His hands moved my hips, but I swirled in solar systems, cloudy, pastel nebulae, and planets' rings.

"Sellers, buyers, and money become an economy; man, woman and sexual attraction becomes a child; the initiate, the mantra and the mandala become – enlightened."

His final push shot my eyes open – I hadn't refilled my diaphragm. But then I fell back – through stars, twilight blue and clouds above the beautiful, fecund earth. And I sank onto his long, lean frame, filled with ice floes and broad deserts, cool redwoods and calm oceans.

After Echo returned upstairs, I reviewed. Berne would have come together with his mantra and mandala in a physical way. He'd have built some crazy teleportation machine to transport him to the One. And this was the science KinCo's IPO was after?

But Berne's pursuit of Heaven had become an act of betrayal to his family. As had Féy's. And if I reported on the Grey Hats and Eric was involved, I, too, would be betraying someone I lov...owed.

Fourteen

Monday having told Annie I'd received the Grey Hats "message", and leaving another of my own for Michael Coomb, I took Berne's journal and mandala in. Now in February with only days left, I finally got word from Max Conrad that he'd see me that afternoon.

"What's that?" Shel Goldberg asked after I lay the journal open in front of him. Shel's cube had five years of articles, press releases, and other documents stacked in and 'round it.

"A mandala," All I saw in Shel's eyes was my own reflection.

"This is science? I've never seen anything like it."

"I found them in Berne's work," I shrugged.

"Take it to Liz," he suggested.

Liz Clark, fine art critic, glanced up briefly from her computer surrounded by glossies, rolled prints, lithographs and Xeroxes. "Hi, Jeannie. I'm on deadline. Whatcha got there?" Liz squinted at her screen.

"I wondered if you knew anything about these." I flipped the hanging 'round.

Liz glanced, "Looks like a mandala."

"Exactly," I beamed.

I could practically see her pulling from the stacks of information in her mind, "Earliest ones found in India, but also seen in China, Japan, Tibet. They're used as guides in meditation. They represent the homes of deities. You can see the divinity. Here." She pointed to the center. "The circles and squares outline the architecture of the palace – complete with gateways and gatekeepers." Her finger outlined a break on each side of the innermost square that framed the center figure. A figure guarded each gate. "And grounds to pass through to enter," she drew the three circles expanding to the paper's square edge.

"They're like sacred temple blueprints. They can be painted on silk, but also sculpted out of the fine materials like jewels, or even sand and talcum powder." She leaned back from her keyboard and crossed her arms. "They're..." she sought for a word. "Esoteric knowledge. Their use and meaning are only revealed to the initiates."

She leaned over and wiggled out a note–sized piece of paper from the stack her neighbors called Pisa, which they reinforced their walls against. She examined it. "Byoung Lee. Asian Art Museum, specializes in Sacred Tibetan Art. Now g'way," She winked, "Mandalas demonstrate impermanence."

Before Byoung Lee and I sat down in a room in back of the Asian Art Museum early that afternoon, I produced the wall hanging and extended it.

Byoung took the piece between two reverent fingers. "A mandala *thangka*. That's real gold. All hand drawn – even these tiny skulls and spirals." He pointed to a belt and a stylized dragon's fiery breath. "It's a beautiful specimen. Old, but what we call contemporary. Maybe the mid 19th century? You should consider showing it. At least cleaning it. It's probably worth ten thousand. Such a large one could be worth up to a hundred thousand. May I?" I let him take the piece.

"On the simplest level," he stood up and held it without looking back at me, "it is a 'floor plan' of a particular divinity's sacred temple palace. But it is also a cosmic map, a blueprint to enlightenment." He circled over the center with his index finger. "The initiate allows the perfect spheres and swirls to bring to life the temple world in his mind in precise detail. As he does so, a shift in consciousness, neurological consciousness we now know, causes a moment of enlightenment, of pure seeing. Nirvana."

"And what's the significance of the two in the center."

"It's always the joining of opposites — in this case the joining of the masculine and feminine aspect of the deity. This is a Nepali Vajrashakti mandala — the god Vajra with his consort, Shakti. Not Tibetan."

"They both believe the same thing?"

"They both come from a source 5000 years old — the Vedas. Our tradition believes that," he lifted his palms up slowly, "there are many levels of reality or dimensions — but there is only one level of pure bliss, the pure land — Shambhala. Similar to Western heaven or Eden. Mandalas are gateways — the meeting of opposites. By forming the temple full and alive in one's mind, one cuts through the layers of illusion to the universal dance that underlies all of us."

"So who are these two?"

He steepled his fingers to his lips. Then he stood. "Come with me, if you will."

At the end of a back hall lit by high windows, he brought out a full key ring and unlocked a door. Crates and boxes stacked the height and width of the long, narrow room. Against the far wall, there were two empty display cases bookending a doorway. Byoung walked toward it.

He used two more keys, and then fluorescent lights flickered down on a table running the windowless, small room's length, full of gold encrusted bowls, scrolls and small bronze Buddha's. At the far end Byoung stopped. Two stylized gods in gold consorted, *inflagrante delicto*, on a pedestal of jeweled circles. I whistled softly.

"This Vajrashakti statue, circa 1200 A.D., was taken from a temple in Khatmandu in 1962, and locked away in Beijing. We have only just retrieved it.... Do you know why they kept it for so long?"

I can imagine, I thought and gave a sideways nod.

Byoung inclined his head. "The Cosmic Dance," he lovingly touched the piece. "This is the highest Tantra practice. Only for eyes of initiates, traditionally," he bowed to me. "The Cosmic Merging. The Buddha represents wisdom; his consort shows us passion. Together they create a purified circle of *com*passion. Do you know about the Tantra?" Shaking away visions of Eric and me, I concentrated on wisdom and compassion as twin powers – a world without paradox.

"The Tantra sect was first heard of 6 centuries before Christ. The Left Hand school is in the great tradition of the *kama yoga* – high pleasure as a path to know God. Tantra channels crude desire into a finer consciousness. Tantra believes that every sense can advance from the gross and crude to the subtle and fine."

Gross to fine – that's what had occurred last night.

Byoung leaned down to the piece, "In the ecstatic climax we experience a moment of enlightened bliss: the collapse of duality, the merging into one, a moment of sublime compassion and awakening. It is a most subtle and divine religious practice; only the most enlightened of our monks are initiated. It is often misused."

"What's this?" I pointed to a fearsome head with ruby eyes, rising out of the pedestal. Perhaps that was corruption, or sin.

"Ah," Byoung said. "The Goddess, Tara. The destroyer. Every sacred space has a protector, a guardian. Most mandalas have four doorkeepers guarding the doorway to the temple. In this statue, it's there, beneath them." He pointed to a thick–bordered square enclosing the locked couple. "You have to get past the four guardians before you can gain nirvana."

It wasn't until we walked back to his office that I asked, "Do you know if mandalas have ever been used in science?"

Opening his door, Byoung considered, "Many physicists believe that vibration and rhythm are the ties that bind all in the universe. Particles have characteristic vibratory movements and rhythms. Cells pulsate, as do molecules, organs. These vibrations create bioelectrical currents that stream continuously and generate energy fields. Some believe even our mental and emotional states generate specific vibrations that alter these energy fields."

"Do you know of any scientific study of this?" Following him in, I picked up the mandala from the leather chair's back.

"There have been biofeedback and neurological studies."

"Have you ever heard of someone using them to," I gazed at the intricate puzzle. "Is it possible," I asked, "are there recorded cases of someone using a mandala to...transport or...teleport ...themselves," my face crunched, "to this pure land or other universes, other dimensions?" Even as I spoke I regretted it.

When he spoke this time, his voice had the same pleasant tone, but his eyes narrowed slightly. "Please, Miss Cadot, we are monks and scholars, not magicians. As I'm sure you are not a 'The Star' reporter." Then he sighed and cocked his head at the large hanging.

"It is said that if you dwell in – that is meditate on – the Kalachakra palace well and long and often, that they will come for you at the moment of death to take you to Shambhala – the Buddhist heaven. But attaining the temple of enlightenment takes years of mental discipline. Not many experience true bliss before death."

"What's this?" I said, flipping the piece over to brief words written on the back, ignoring the strong beat in my chest.

"It's in the old Nepali language. The mantra," Byoung said. Seeing my quizzical expression, he added, "Of the deity."

"I see," I said. "You chant it to..." I searched for a word, "invoke the temple?"

Byoung's eyes flashed. "This information, Miss," he said through his now concrete smile, "is of the highest value in our culture. "

"Esoteric knowledge."

He acquiesced with an Indian–style nod. "As I said, Tantrika are holy men, not black magicians. Thank you for the interview," he stood and bowed.

At the office door I turned to thank him, but the door was already shutting on his smile. I couldn't blame him.

On the way to Max Conrad's, I left a message. "I hesitated to call, to intrude on you again, but I'm having trouble following up on what you asked of me. I do believe I have found the one you wanted to save before it was too late." When my cell phone beeped I saw it was Anna Kincaid calling back. "Hello."

"Yes, Miss Cadot. No, leave that and leave me. I'll call in a moment. Get out now I say." Something clattered. "How can I help?"

I remembered her red satin sheets mastering that great black bed and went right to the heart, "You know I think I've discovered why you picked me. My ancestress Lilla Cadot was married to a business partner of your great, great grandfather, Alex Kincaid, the first."

"Ah," so she'd been expecting me to find out.

"But Eric is...focused on me studying his father's work. And I understand why – I found the mandala, I found the drawings," I took a deep breath and crossed my fingers, "I know about the teleportation machine." There was no sound on the other end. "But I've found no diary. If you could put in a good word – or give me something – he knows we met."

"Toying with you is he?"

"Well, ma'am, I wouldn't say that..."

"Means he's enjoying himself," she sounded pleased. "I've not talked to my son in 15 years."

"Ms. Kincaid?"

"We had a falling out." She began to cough.

"I'm so sorry to hear that ma'am—Anna. Take your time." But when she stopped I asked, "Was the fight over...your husband?"

"Was over a lot of things. But it was years after my husband died. So you see I'm afraid I need you to help me. But you might try Gstaad. Thank you for calling Ms. Cadot." And she hung up.

Gstaad was in Switzerland near Eric's business. I left another message for Coomb.

Max Conrad's was above blacked out store windows off Mission on 9th. 'Round here were small recording studios and artists groups. I finally got let in when a small, non-descript guy in a navy hood came out after my buzz, and I went in up two stair flights. After 10 seconds or so of pounding over loud music, I heard locks go and the door cracked letting out the smell of closed rooms, empty beer bottles and unwashed clothes. But beneath clean hair, clear eyes looked at me, "Yeah?"

"You Max Conrad of Newphysics.org?"

"Yeah?" Smile battled with suspicion on his face. "Who wants to know?"

"I'm the reporter with The Sheet?"

"Unh huh?"

"You called me?"

"Yeah, what do you want? You left me like a million messages."

"You ever heard of the Grey Hats? I tracked some of them here last week. I'm a friend of Eric Kincaid's." I held up the card I hoped he'd sent me – with the holograms.

His eyes sparked. Then he opened the door to reveal beyond his left shoulder an empty plate and fork atop cardboard box. "Want to come in?"

"Thanks." Within seconds we stood in his bare light–bulb hall. "Don't mind the mess," he said, suddenly leading me through a living room where it seemed a pile of clothes had exploded over a saggy brown suede–like couch and easy chair. Two folding chairs sat at the end next to a monitor on a table used as a desk.

I pulled three un–decoded pages from my bag once we sat, held them out so he could get a look at them.

He whistled. "Where'd you get this?"

"From an email."

He glanced at it, "You trace it?"

"Couldn't. Some sort of worm." I put the pages back in my bag.

"Nice," he nodded his head and sat back on his computer desk. He was lying I was certain.

"Well, what about these fellows, the Grey Hats – we made it, we can break it. What were they doing here?"

"You recording me? I want a record. You gonna mention the site in the article?"

"Yeah, yeah." I pulled out the recorder from my pocket and clicked it on. Did he miss the memo on the top secret security? Then he probably wasn't a recipient, but did he know any names?

"My name is Max Conrad. Spelled like it sounds," He smiled, his hands on his thighs, elbows akimbo. "Edward Berne knew the first programmers at M.I.T. and Berkeley back when assembly code was created. Like most engineers he always considered himself a peasant, not an aristocrat. Rumor's been he convinced them to hide some secret word in the assembly code compiler that would give the people the power to act hidden from the powers that be – a Robin Hood hack – but he never released it."

But his son might. "So how'd they get it now? And wouldn't others find the code? You can read these compilers can't you?"

He shrugged, "Programs can be pretty complex. And stuff can be hidden. They're locked now to most – and hardly anyone knows how to use it anymore – not well. Those fellows last week gave me an interview about it. Warned me to be careful, to wait to publish it *after*. Can I look at those?" He was looking hungrily at the pages. This might be his first chance to see any sign of this Holy Grail.

I held them back from him, "Where'd they get the code?" I took hold of a page and waved it, "Got a name?"

Max shrugged, but his eyes didn't leave the page, "Michael Coomb."

So I'd been right. "That's great Max. Just one," I extended the last page fully. The hologram card caught on it and fell on the floor.

"Aw, you're no fun." Glancing at the card, reluctantly he lifted his hands. "Those guys said Interpol's been sniffing 'round. You're temptation walking," he said, "To my mind, you've never been here."

Driving into Oakland, still shaking off Max's comment, which brought back the Faucheaux boys and their calls of *sorciére* and who exactly I was trying to become out here – my cell phone rang.

"Jeannie?" the voice on the other end demanded. "Did that boy suck you into that house over there?"

I winced just as when she called me *piti* on the cruise. How the hell did she know where I'd been? "Hey, Mave – I was in. Just mostly I've been out looking for Anna's diary."

"Listen, you heard from Blowhard?"

I checked my phone. No messages. "No."

"Word is he got taken in for questioning at the Exchange."

"What?!" Automatically I checked the rear view. No one followed.

"His assistant – Taylor – said some foreign guys came and took him down a back hall. They stopped him from following. He was supposed to be back for an editorial meeting two hours ago. No one's seen him."

"What's Taylor's cell?"

She gave it to me. "Listen, Jeannie. You saw him yesterday. Was he working on your story?"

"How would I know? I've got to talk with Taylor."

"Well, be careful. A breather might be in order."

"Have you told Clive yet?"

"I didn't have to."

"Can you tell him I'm about to have an interview that could blow open the whole thing."

Taylor knew nothing more than what Mavis had reported. Todd's line went blessedly to voicemail – I told him I'd no confirmation Blowhard's questioning was because of me.

I went immediately to Berkeley and ran throughout the Physics building. But there was no one of note there – school was not yet in session.

On my way to Eric's, I called Cariña, who said unprompted, "I hear you're doing well, Momma. Maybe it will be sooner than we think."

I held back my tears, but could not speak for a bit.

Upon arriving in Oakland, I didn't see Echo's Citroën in the driveway. As usual I parked down the street, let myself in the house, and went straight to the study. I pulled apart the office to find Anna's diary. At some point my cell rang.

"Yes," frustration broke through my voice.

"This is Michael Coomb," the soft twang said. "This Miss Cadot?"

"Yes," I shot a prayer. "Thank you for calling, Professor."

"I got your messages—."

"Yes, Professor Coomb. Have you ever heard of the Grey Hats? Or Max Conrad? Because they've heard of you."

A pause. A sigh, "I called to tell you to stop calling, Ms. Cadot. Until after the declaration at least." The Nobel Prize for physics wasn't until October. "Then I'll call you."

"So you have heard of the Grey Hats?"

"You need to stop with these questions."

"Sealed records, missing newspaper files, a hostile family, a rogue group, no media coverage. Plenty of folks have stopped –

all of them. But what about Berne? He left a legacy that's nearly destroyed his entire family. And perhaps he was murdered for math now getting Nobel credit. And I, a stranger, give a damn more than his most famous protégé soon to be profiting from all this again — yet doing something in the background to make it up — in secret. That, my friend, is not a little, light corruption. That is something much worse."

His sigh held a sob. "Just a few more months."

"Dr. Coomb, are you really this comfortable stealing his life?"

He breathed sharply once, twice, "Juvenile involvement's a cover. They're really classified. Like all of Berne's work."

"Classified?" Work on teleportation and mandalas and the Pure Land. Before I could ask my next question, he said, "Leave sleeping dogs to lay, Ms. Cadot. You do, and after the prize we can talk." He hung up.

Well, no way I would wait that long.

When Echo arrived past eight, I had the journal laid open to the stubs of the missing pages, "Did you know your father's work was classified at the end?"

His fingers paused almost imperceptibly before he said, "Must have been an oversight."

"I don't think so. And I hear he created some secret code that unlocks the hidden powers of assembly language?"

He fingered the pages, "What did you discover about mandalas?"

"Echo, I'm trying to tell you there was more to your father's work than you know."

"So you've not found out anything?" The twilight eyes challenged, but his sadness was back again. I'd not seen it for a while and my heart gave a twinge.

"Mandalas are a map that provokes and guides a journey to heaven or nirvana. Five levels each preceded by a gate representing a test, an initiation. Each test is of increasing challenge and danger to the psyche. Each test requires greater mental and emotional strength."

Echo, sitting on the desk near me, asked, "What are the tests?"

"The first gate," now I traced the mandala with my finger, "awakens the psyche – an event that opens, surprises and arouses curiosity," I paused.

"Like our dance," Echo chuckled. I smiled, traced my finger in to the next circle. "The next gate opens into the *vajra* circle. *Vajra* means diamond. It stands for clarity, strength and fearlessness. This might be a series of challenges that build knowledge and courage."

"Like learning quantum physics or flying into the sea?" He stood just behind me. "What's the next one?" he asked softly. He reached 'round me, brushing my shoulder with his hand, and traced the third telescoping circle. He whispered just millimeters from my ear. As I spoke, fire leapt into my throat. I willed it gone.

"The purifying fire of wisdom." Echo gently brushed my bare collarbone, but made no comment. I continued thinking of Byoung, "Passionate, blazing, enflamed – burns away the old so something new might emerge."

A finger slid underneath my spaghetti strap and down the facing skin. "And the next to last gate?"

"The tombs – symbolizing the eight states of consciousness – gaining awareness of your thoughts, your ego, your senses and life force or soul."

"Sounds interesting," He ran his hand back up and lifted the strap off.

"But it is the most dangerous and costly of the rites."

"Why is that?"

"Your father wrote that to confront yourself, to probe the electrons – the negative charges – of your own soul – your shadow – takes rare courage. Our deceptions, lies, and betrayals we see as the price for success. But every deceit eats at the pure center. It must be purged...or it kills...Because the worst betrayal of all," I turned to him, "is the betrayal of yourself."

He kissed my forehead, let me go and grabbed his coat from the chair.

"Echo." He turned back. "I've scoured this room, and other than these diagrams, I haven't any solid proof on what he was working on at the end. Pages are missing, what's here are in a hidden order. The number 31 is written in one book, hinting at it completing the totality of these 30 journals. Maybe the missing things have the hidden code, and whatever was classified."

He raised an eyebrow.

"I was wondering if there might be records anywhere else. Your cabin. Gstaad or Saanen? Your heart's home?"

He stopped, half-huffed surprise then smiled. "What's the last gate of the mandala?"

My gaze hardened. So he'd seduced me just to get the chance to teach me all his arcane philosophical notions? I glanced at my notes. "The lotus circle – an open state of devotion. In it you must defeat the four angry doorkeepers who guard the temple."

Echo paused, his eyes darkened. "I've no doubt you will." His quick, sad smile just pissed me off.

Still I smiled back, "Well, then I'll just write the same old piece that was written back when he passed away – with just a little more explanation about why his experiment was so nuts – because it was based on pretty, poetic notions about wormholes, dimensions and entanglements across time – the stuff of science fiction. Or I could find his math – for which he was renown – the sequent to his plasma equations that now underlay most of solid state physics. To my mind that would be a more interesting angle, but perhaps that's just me."

Echo walked backwards towards the stairs, "You've learned a good deal. Maybe it is cabin time. Tomorrow."

I breathed audibly. "I think I've earned it."

He smiled and turned to dash up.

I immediately called Clive, "Boss man, this might be it."

"Best to get you out of town for a day or two anyway. Call me the minute you get something. Try and be good, Slugger."

Fifteen

"God's Palm," Echo pointed 'cross me to a hundred feet or so off the rocky northern California coast. There raised a number of rocky crags in a thick, closed horseshoe. The scent of redwood filled the air. The woods were close 'cross the highway behind us, blocking out any highway noise. But here it was treeless and bright. "It marks the meeting place of two tides, and a deep crack in the tectonic plate beneath it. When the winter moon is full and above it, there is a large whirlpool in its middle."

"Wow," I said, willing myself to dispel the well of fear I felt rise in me. Far to the right a turkey vulture circled low over a hilltop.

"Dad used to sail to it when I was a kid. It's a vortex," Echo said. "If the boat still works, we can come here later. Moon's full."

I nodded, but didn't speak. I wouldn't even think in advance about getting on a small sailboat. Those crags must be massive…I shuddered to think.

We got back in my car – I'd thought taking it would be lower profile than taking his Citroën – and quickly we wound through a small, forested canyon, like a corkscrew through a cork. Cicadas replaced the radio; wood squashed the smell of exhaust.   I strained to glimpse a house. Echo drove into a clearing at a cliff and stopped. I still didn't see a thing.

Out of the car, you could hear no engines. I inhaled the deep scent of pine.

"It's down here," Echo stood at a staircase going down the cliff next to a "No Trespassing" sign. I jogged over.

"Oh my God, Echo." Hanging a few feet below the cliff, like a bird clinging to the rock, was a driftwood roof with numerous skylights, some of them open.

I climbed down behind him. "Father knew an architect. Girders are stuck 70 feet into the rock." He unlocked the hatch door and smiled at me. He inclined his head, "Come on in."

Inside we hit redwood and dry must.   At the bottom of a circular stair – like one you'd find on a freighter I imagined, we stood in a round foyer.   Off it, a narrow hall with four doors ran north and five doors ran south, three of these facing east into the rock.

A tile floor led ahead to a kitchen to the right, who knew what on the left.   Echo turned 180 degrees.   "Bedrooms are downstairs. This floor has the living areas."

He pulled me back to the winding stairwell. Downstairs he led me down the hall to the right. Here the walls were peppered with photos.   Young people dressed for tennis, riding or an evening event, carefree. Despite their glassed-in smiles, down here it was cold. Despite the windows on either hall's end, it was dark. I cradled my elbows, and strained to see.

Echo turned on the light. "The hall of ancestors." He swept a hand.   "For what it's worth... Maman's family.   Dad's colleagues." He looked at me. "Well, you know. Don't you?"

I nodded and looked harder – so we'd spoken of this in that lost hour? Cheeky Prep school kids in tuxes in front of limos, a large group of happy faces in black tie toasting each other with martinis. Rows of faces in business suits posed in front of columned buildings.

Echo unlocked the door at the end of the hall. Cool air blew in. "The caretaker has opened all the windows to air the place out. I haven't been here recently." So had he ever brought Marcia here?

The little room's light revealed a few cobwebs. The spread of the sturdy bunk bed sported an anchor. He pushed open the navy curtains and closed the porthole window.

"Let me guess," I said. "Your room."

Echo shrugged. "My father was an expert sailor," he said.

Behind the second door an abstract orange balloon print bedspread matched lake green pastel sheets beneath a matching canopy. Instead of a desk, a stuffed rocking chair covered with white lace sat next to a round table with a lamp under a gauze–curtained, four–paned window. "Heather's room." Echo said.

The last room on that wing and the first on the other were guest rooms, comfortable, but bare. Echo led down to the last door. "Master suite. My mother's."

The room was very cold. Echo walked through deep baby blue, a feminine version of his condo, past elegant kelp–like fronds waving up the walls. He shut the large porthole window 'cross from the head of the four–poster high off the floor. An old oak trunk with ornate brass borders rested at its foot, holding buried treasures.

I crossed the light Persian rug and touched the ocean quilt. Pictures in little silver frames sat on the ash wood bureaus and table, simple wood frames hung on the walls.

"Once you said you wanted your own room. Take this one. Do you want to unpack? Change? I'll go upstairs and make us a drink. Why don't you meet me up there? There should be towels in here." He flicked on the suite's bathroom light. The modern dressing room's two circle wall lights faced a mirror above a white counter and two parlor chairs. The thick carpet was gold.

"This was Maman's sanctuary." Echo murmured. But he

didn't walk in.

"Which room do you want?"

"Don't worry about that," Echo assured.

I dropped my faux Coach bags on the foot of the bed.

"I'll go see about putting our food away." Echo said. "Meet you upstairs."

My blood rose – alone so soon with Anna's things. A sign he trusted me. Or was there just nothing here. "OK."

"You may want to put on a bathing suit," Echo's eyes traced me.

"It's almost night in January."

"Still gets hot upstairs," he turned and opened the door. "Pot bellied stove."

I ripped my case open, but as soon as he was gone up the stairs, I stopped and looked 'round. On the sea–green table painted with delicately designed fish, a few books leaned against a rearing ceramic horse on stone – Miss Manners and a dime novel. I touched the mother–of–pearl, sterling hairbrush with soft, white bristles, and picked up the matching comb.

Same as Féy's gift – even down to the silver frame 'round a picture of Heather, Berne and Eric on a boat named Heart's Home – what Anna had said. Be just my luck the diary'd be hidden there.

It made me think of Cariña. She'd been missing my phone calls a bit the last few weeks, but I'd not said anything yet. I'd been so caught up in this story – it was taking me away from the important things in life. She would love to hear about this place. I brought out my phone, but there was no signal.

The closet held only hangers and a few old cardigans, a Mackintosh and boots. I was rooting under the bathroom sink after checking its cabinets, when Eric caught me.

"Looking for cleanser?"

"No…I thought I heard a leak."

"A leak?"

"Must've been in my mind. I don't see anything." I stood and brushed my hands against my trousers.

"You're not dressed yet," he said glancing back at my unpacked bag.

"I was looking for that diary."

"No luck under the bathroom sink? I brought you a scotch and soda, sorry no bourbon."

"Thanks, that'll do. I'll be up toot suite." I took the highball. After he'd gone I quickly used the lime green phone in Anna's lounge to call Cariña – who wasn't home.

"So we've never really talked about your mother. I take it you two weren't all that close?" We sat on an enclosed patio in two redwood chaise lounge chairs by the left of a blazing stove. Through the inevitable plate glass windows, floor to ceiling clear, as they most all had been since I'd met him, the night and the ocean rolled in.

The walls behind us were covered with built–in bookshelves. And yes, I was wearing my bathing suit – beneath a robe. I had to admit, I loved the danger of it – the unexpected arousal.

"In Europe – that's where they met you know – aside from raising us, she raced horses, took flying lessons. Volunteered for the Socialists. Once we got here she replaced that with Junior League, the scientists' wives…later work with KinCo."

Ah, KinCo. "So your parents had no interaction with the Kincaid's when your Dad…"

"Lived? She hated them at the start of my life." His tone was dry.

And now she lay in their stronghold dying. Anna'd said it'd been 15 years since she and Eric had spoken. So they'd fought a decade after she'd returned to the fold.

Eric walked past the ping–pong and pool tables to crack the deck's door and turned on an outside light. When he came back, he sat on the edge of my chaise and slid his hand up my thigh.

I moved his hand gently away before pulling the enlarged old photo out of my briefcase, which sat on the rug next to me. "With the money due you," I said.

"What?"

"That's what the email said. With the money due you. I didn't lose anything in a corporate scandal at least not recent. But back then they did. I figure you must've known. And you used your Daddy's hack to pay my debts, so I wouldn't have to claim it as income. But I'm not the only recipient and you're not the only broker. The Grey Hats are going to—"

"Who are these Grey Hats?"

"Oh, come on Echo. You must have given it to—" Suddenly I paused. "Eric, did you know Michael Coomb?"

"Fulani's flunky? Is he still in science?" He reached for my suit's bra strap. I wrapped his hand with mine, pulled it away.

"He's up for a Nobel Prize with the esteemed Fulani. Supposedly off some of your father's classified work."

"Who said?"

"Remember the hologram card?" Could his anger toward his father really blind him this much? I eyed a curling stair at the end of the deck. "Does that staircase lead down to the beach?"

"Mm hm," Echo nodded. "Want to go down?"

When I looked over, the black Mississippi loomed. Echo sat watching me. I took a big breath. "You know I think your mother sent it. When she asked me to find her diary. I think she was trying to make something up to you." This was not necessarily a lie.

"So that's why you were under the sink."

"You know who I am. What I'm doing here."

He spoke through shut lids, "If there was a diary it might be in Switzerland."

"Saanen, outside Gstaad." My heart stilled.

"Where Krishnamurti lived for a while." He sat back on his lounge, his eyes half shut, his voice dreamy as if I were losing him to sleep.

"Do you go there a lot?"

"Not for years. Come over here."

"Wait, can I just ask you—."

His voice sounded tired. "Tomorrow, okay? Tonight just come here."

Finally, I moved to sit on his thighs, with my knees at his hips. He opened eyes filled with pain, kissed the warm skin of my chest and pulled off my wet sticky pink suit. When my body finally slipped over his, I fell again into the black. But this time I heard drums – or maybe it was just my blood. We moved in unison – Annie, the web and the gold entwined gods circling through my mind.

Then the drums – no, not drums, a fast thwacking, a motor – grew loud. I turned. 50 feet outside the picture window, a helicopter leveled and hovered – blades spinning.

"Damn Mendocino tourists, getting their money's worth today," But Eric hid most of his face behind my shoulder.

I just stared disbelieving, in my confusion ecstasy slowed, but still rising. After a few moments the helicopter flew away and we climaxed then separated with a gasp, followed by emptiness – like having the wind knocked out of us.

"Shall we eat?" he asked. We burst into laughter.

After a shared porterhouse and Cabernet, crawling out of the thick, warm down of the four–poster bed, I opened the window. Outside the Pacific Ocean rolled and spumed. He murmured something and I scurried back to bed. He whispered into my ear, "'whatever is thought or said, I am in you and I am you.'"

Impulsively I replied, "And also with you." He nipped the back of my ear. I threw my arms 'round him in a rush of warmth. It was as good as an "I love you." After our talk tonight I was convinced he was totally in the dark on this story – it had been Coomb's brain child – perhaps under orders from Berne. It truly was impossible for him to think his father could have had anything of value to offer at the end. My ecstasy morphed into sleep so deep I didn't even notice him leave.

I rose early, refreshed, but immediately in unease. I was alone and I'd wasted the entire night doing and thinking things I'd no business to – getting distracted – I didn't need Moman L's voice to tell me that. I discovered Echo in his childhood bunk bed, asleep. I began more closely reviewing the pictures dotting the hall.

When Echo wandered into Anna's bedroom in blue pajama bottoms I was ready. "Good morning. There's coffee upstairs. When was this taken?" I pointed to the silver frame – beneath a wallet-sized shot of he and Heather playing in the kiddie pool, was Echo, Heather and Edward on the single sailed Heart's Home. Berne was at the helm. His brow was pale and drawn. His eyes troubled, but his lips smiled lightly. And Echo, sitting in the helm, was looking away from the camera, staring at his Dad, shoulders rigid in dislike or worry.

"Ah," he wandered over. "Our last family trip here," he yawned. "The summer before the....the incident. Coffee—"

"You must've been tired."

"Unh, worked late last night."

So he must've been up while I slept – probably hacking away. "Cream or sugar?" I moved toward the door.

Echo grunted, "I'll take a shower."

While he did, I scoured upstairs. I tried the doors that opened into the cliff – all shallow-shelved closets except one at the end that was locked. The door matched the wall so it took time to notice it. Perhaps all the plumbing and water heaters were there – I heard nothing with my ear against it.

Still I ran to the desk in the room across from me and found a large paper clip. After several tries the door opened. Inside a small storage hole, stacked on the bottom were two large photo boxes. Carrying them into the den I opened the first: letters, ticket stubs, old photographs, birth certificate – the humble but detailed remnants of Edward Berne. Locked up just like his home study.

In the second box, right on top were ticket stubs from Peter and the Wolf, and the Firebird. Halfway down the three-quarters full contents was a photo of Estella Berne – Edward's mother –

who had been dark–skinned with brown woolly hair, and a bit of a wild eye. This photo wasn't framed in the hall – no wonder. But I found no extra journal, no ripped out pages. But at the bottom lay the same picture as mine of the *HMS Lawrence II* and a roll of dog–eared papers.

Echo called, "Jeanne?"

"In the den." I unrolled the fountain pen and ink pages.

Echo poked his head in.

"Look what I found."

He came forward and picked up the shot in front of the *Lawrence*. "Dad's boxes. I thought they were out here." But he averted his eyes.

I read, "On this 6th day of July 1873 in the great city of San Francisco, of California of the United States of America, we the undersigned do agree that:

    ℥ 1. I, Alex Kincaid I, acknowledge on this day receipt of $6,000 in equal shares from the following: James R. Collins, George Washington Dennis, Thomas Taylor, Thomas Bundy, Edward Cain and Benjamin Harris and families.

    ℥ 2. Said funds to be deposited in Bank of California this self–same day in collateral against a material loan of $12,000 for the *HMS Lawrence II*, sea-faring passenger vessel, U.S. Registry #3329.

    ℥ 3. To be held as regular bank funds, and as such to enjoy 90% of any interests and dividends acrrued from investments of said funds. Any such gains shall be applied to the loan's balance until paid in full, as recorded in bi–monthly statements.

    ℥ 4. Upon satisfactory repayment of the remaining $4,000 plus an annualized 6% interest, title to the *HMS Lawrence II* will be signed over to the above shareholders.

Not only the principals signed the bottom, but also, unbelievably...William Chapman Ralston as witness. I handed him the sheet, and watched his lips draw together as he read.

"I wonder what happened?"

He drew in his cheeks, "Well..."

"There are only a few records I can find on a ship named the *HMS Lawrence II* – shows it was owned by Alex Kincaid, the first." I summarized George Dennis's editorial.

But he didn't watch me. He picked through the other photographs, held up the 1965 Firebird ballet ticket stub.

"Your father never showed you these?"

"No."

"I think the Grey Hats, this tip on KinCo, it's all somehow to avenge these people and this ship. What can you tell me about what happened between your father and the Kincaid's?"

He frowned. "They disowned my mother for marrying him. He died before she got officially involved with KinCo. Of course they met once or twice early on."

"So your dad never worked for Alex." If my theory was true, he must've planned his whole life how to get close to Kincaid, as his father must have planned before him.

"My father wasn't interested in capitalism. You ought to know that. Wait, I think..." Searching the box he pulled out a photo – young Edward and Anna sitting at a thick carved table with a scowling, cigar–smoking man. Berne was watching Anna, who was smiling at the lens. Eric looked at the back. "This is when they met."

"So Echo," I made my tone gentle as I could, "There's something in her diary that explains everything. And I apologize, but I have to tell you," I took a deep breath, "It looks like some large transfers were made 'round your father's passing."

"You mean my mother got paid for my father's murder? That my life's been funded by blood money?"

I recoiled. "No, no Echo. It's not certain."

"Is this what you really want? To drag me now through the

mud? Me, the last one. Maybe it's time to go."

"Echo, Echo, remember me? We go way back." I put up the *Lawrence II* photo again. "My whole career is riding on this. And you may have noticed I've done a few things I'd prefer to keep quiet."

His face tensed before his shoulders slightly relaxed.

The sun was breaking through, "Want to go out?"

20 minutes later we strolled along the dirt cliff above his home. The ocean roar was constant and light glimmered from it. It reminded me of a photo in Heather's room... a slight, ethereal woman in gauzy white standing on the beach at sundown, in the shallows. The light reflected, so it looked like she was walking on the water.

"Tell me about your sister?" I asked gingerly as Echo tossed a stone. "She died so closely behind your father."

As he turned I caught sadness in his eyes. "The only person Heather was tied to was my father." He bent down for more rocks. "By nature both would see things upside–down and backwards; they'd create fantastic worlds where dreams are real." He squinted against the now suddenly cloudless light.

"But frequently in the evenings he'd sit her on his knee, nestle his chin in her hair and remind her, their worlds were only make–believe. That here in the real world there are dishes and rules, laws, and the need to remember what it is you are doing." His voice trembled.

With all his people dead, memory had become his life.

"Father's forced retirement hit Heather hard. She read and clipped each article into those Oakland files. It's probably she who organized and hid those boxes there.

"At night with him in the basement, she'd review them shaking her head, searching for some crucial word or image that would solve this impossible disgrace of her *preux chevalier*, her champion."

He stood. We began to walk the cliff's edge. Occasional vultures would soar just below eye level. They always caught my breath as did the steep drop just a foot away.

"Only one thing – other than our dad – kept her attention. She'd spend hours with wildflowers, watching the sea, clouds, an anthill. She said she understood the ants – they thought they'd make up in numbers what each lacked in size."

Echo raised his voice. "Heather never cared whether she actually completed schoolwork, chores or artwork. She'd use her not–quite–right theories to draw funny, futuristic worlds: toasters, televisions and Jack–in–the–boxes with human arms and legs."

Hanging his toes over the edge, he tossed a stone and kept his eyes on its descent. "Drawn along the Golden Mean – very aesthetic. And the creatures spouted formulas. But she littered unfinished projects behind her like breadcrumbs. Maman would bring her books or lunch to school from the backyard or odd spot on the floor where she'd simply left them, forgotten."

He cleared his throat and lobbed another. 200 feet below I saw a flash of movement where it hit. Two birds rose.

That's as far as Féy fell, I thought suddenly. I'd not thought of her for a while.

"After…the incident, she began to act as if she were one of her own human limbed robots. Her face became hard. She spent more time at the anthill with lines etched deep in her brow like an old woman.

"Maman would force her to bathe or wash against wild protest. She'd wear the same dress for three days. She began leaving things all over the house, saying crazy things. She was a danger," his voice flared, "to herself. That's why we moved back to Switzerland. It's why we rushed the investigation and sealed the files."

Coomb's "classified" pushed against my throat. "But—"

"Classified was probably just some favor from Opjie or someone – out of pity. In Switzerland, Heather seemed to calm down for a while – B–plus or higher grades, a few roles on stage."

All the love he didn't have for Anna he placed in his sister, as I had placed mine for Féy in Cariña, Moman L had placed hers for Alva initially with me, later with Cariña as well. Somehow displaced love seemed a power – taken from one, and given to another.

"But Heather began to run with a drugs, motorcycles, and shoplifting crowd. Her attendance and grades dropped. Her doodling stopped." Echo paused. "One day she went for a ride through the Alps on the back of a motorbike and was thrown when he skidded in a patch of black ice. She was not wearing a helmet, so she landed like a rag doll, breaking nearly every bone."

"Echo, I'd no notion."

"She followed her 'champion' to their heavens where they could dream their worlds in peace," he spat. Then he threw a final rock and gazed out to sea.

"I can tell that you loved them both."

He nodded, corners of his lips slightly rising. We listened to the sea, the gulls and the wind – giving them all our love and attention.

Sixteen

Late that afternoon I looked through Berne's most treasured correspondence kept in plain brown storage boxes. Back in the Oakland study, all but the journals was type-written. Up here were all hand–written. I held a letter gingerly through driving gloves.

Dated October 1954, sent to Brazil, in it Einstein discussed Berne's alternative quantum theory. "If anyone can do it, I am certain it will be you," he wrote, "to succeed in navigating the depths of the atom where others, including I, have not." He followed with a critique of Berne's recent experimental findings. He ended, "You must never despair, Edward, nor doubt the direction in which you walk. The end result of all scientific research is the religious experience. Whether or not the world knows, we do. Yours always, A. Einstein."

I called for Echo without response, so I ran through the enclosed patio out to the small landing. It was cold, but there wasn't much wind. At the bottom, a small boathouse sat at the end of an ell–shaped pier. On the beach front of it Echo sat watching the red sun sink. He turned and waved. Leaving the letter inside, with a smile I went down the long winding staircase.

He grabbed my hand without turning to me. "Tonight we're eating out. There's something I want to show you."

A flock of gulls darted 'cross the deepening sky.

Echo announced, "Tonight we're sailing to God's Palm."

I willed myself to a deep breath. I'd been in a plane, a bondage club, down in a Cave, up at the Mark, surely I was ready to be at sea in a small sailboat. "You know Echo, you saw what happened the only time I've ever been on a boat."

A black shadow flew past my eye – the condor.

"A few times our family went night–sailing," Echo said. "My father taught us from here." He gazed out, then pointed up the coast 10 miles to where the land reached a point. "Merchant's Point," he said. My pulse quickened – he meant to take me to that whirlpool. "Our destination."

Under dock light the black water crinkled like homemade paper. Suddenly it rippled. Along with vapory green air, a burning metal smell rose.

A wavy Echo stood, stretched his arms out, and took a deep breath. My heart pounded like a bass drum. Out of the ocean, sodden and dripping, came Féy, in her white dress. She smiled at me, "Dauphine," she scowled down at the beach, "I can't keep them back. Are you prepared?"

Suddenly I saw pioneers coming up on the beach, up from the sea – four of my five plus others – presumably all the owners and their families. An awful stench rose.

Then soft warmth pressed my own. I turned to see a young Anna standing with one thumb on my wrist, the other on her son's, "You cannot go out on that boat tonight, Jeanne. See," she harshed before all went black and I thrust into a tight space with stairs going down behind me: Echo's house – the stairs to the basement.

My hand on the darkened banister trembled. My head turned back to watch an eerie gleam. I saw nothing else, I heard nothing down there – not even breathing. Turning back in silent sobs, my left hand ripped thick journal pages. Tears streamed down my – Echo's – cheeks along with small gulps and bent shoulders of a nine year old. I was terrified to go forward and my head jerked back. My vision went to black.

I turned to Anna, "*What* did you do?!"

Eric, blurred, turned, "I just said the moon is about half and half tonight." The moon wavered behind scattered clouds as I knew it would.

Anna said, "Don't you make the same error."

"Who are you to advise on family?"

Féy interrupted, "Dauphine, you cannot go out on that boat tonight. The child must be born – the curse lifted."

"Preparations must be made," Anna's voice sounded grim.

I had less desire than a pig in a poke to understand what they were telling me. My pioneers did not gather this time; rather my bearded white man lingered with my Incan woman, helping her up from the beach, shooting occasional glances up. I didn't see James or Lilla.

"Jeanne, what are you talking about? I just thought we'd go for a sail," Eric said frustrated.

Despite a sudden nausea, I said, "I don't believe you." But I wasn't clear to whom I addressed this.

"Jeanne, you must first go to Switzerland," Anna said gently and she tightened her grasp on my wrist. I began to breathe too fast and felt the migraine's warning even before the pioneers faded. My hand found the pier's first post, and I sank gratefully to my knees.

"Jeanne – use the two powers – I'm not sure who's lyin—" Féy said before a bald condor with black bead eyes filled the sky and I blacked out.

When I first woke I thought the night sky was ministering to me. The headache was abating, replaced by a full body warmth. I was beneath a thick comforter. The bed rocked. Moonlight was shining through a skylight above me. I could hear water below. I was in the boat. I panicked. A shadow emerged from the dark. A knee. A leg. A cigarette ember. "Where are you taking me?"

"You seem to have a habit of collapsing on me," Echo's familiar, restrained tone eased my fears.

"I–I must've blacked out. I'm sorry." I elbowed myself up and hit my head. The boat was tiny.

Echo stood and flicked the cigarette out the skylight, sat on the edge of the bed in the moonlight and took my hand. He smoothed my hair.

"Thanks for saving me again. Where are we?" But I knew.

Echo kissed my palm. "I wasn't thinking, pushing you...us like that."

Suddenly Anna came back to me along with Féy's final doubt. I kept to the back of my mind that there'd have been my ten out there if you didn't count Berne or a life inside me. "Are we in Heart's Home?" Moving was surprisingly hard against the ocean's give. But for the moment no nausea surfaced.

Echo leaned down to me and I instinctually inhaled his scent. "We're still docked," he said. "My folks used to sleep in here sometimes."

"Did they love each other very much?" asked the part of me that was the little girl shocked into awareness first.

I only wanted him to say, yes, but instead he said, "You're far too romantic a mind to be a reporter." That got me up, but before I could search the ship, he herded me back up the stairs to jump down from the boat, hanging in hydraulic hold a foot or more from the dock, never on the water at all. Imagining him heaving a groggy me up onto his cherished boat, raised in me glimmers of fear. He was stronger than he looked.

The next morning when I woke, Echo was already gone. I went up thinking perhaps he was making breakfast. But when I reached the empty foyer, I saw him coming in from outside. "I already packed the car," he said. "You almost ready?"

I searched his eyes, but he didn't meet mine. "I can be very shortly."

"Good," Echo said, shallow, unreadable, "My mother died last night. I've got to turn off the power."

I averted my eyes from his. Anna'd died while I was passed out on her ship. "Echo, I'm so...'

"Can you get ready fast?" he said walking down the hall, leaving me stunned with the fact that one seemed to join the group of Ten when one died – and that I was about to attend my first funeral for a passed mother.

As we wound back to the coast highway, the wonderful weekend, knowing that Eric had taken his father's journal pages, seemingly lost interest for me last night after I'd fainted, and that now, as with Verna, the woman who'd brought us together, had died – once again it all felt stolen, illicit, foolish. Echo made little effort to communicate. "Do you know if she went peacefully?"

"I don't know anything. Grand Mere tried to reach me. No cell reception on the pier."

I gathered strength. "Echo," I touched his arm. "I'm so sorry. Losing a mother – even an estranged one – it isn't easy. It never leaves you the same. But you do reconstitute – eventually."

He kept his eyes on the road and sea, tapping his fingers on his thighs to low music from the local classical station.

No way I could tell him that I knew about Heart's Home. Or that our dead mothers had told me last night that I was pregnant with his child. Or that he, Eric, might be trying to kill me. That our ancestors had visited.

I suddenly felt Féy's tinkling laugh warm my skin. So I might be losing my mind 'long with my immortal soul. Still, today I had to finalize Anna's obituary. And I had to look into going to Switzerland while trying to forget her hand on my wrist last night. So to Shostakovich and the gulls' damning shrieks, I formulated sentences while Eric drove.

Seventeen

Back at my place Eric stood motionless by the fireplace; his hand rested near a framed picture of Cariña, but his unseeing eyes fixed on the floor.

"You hungry? Why don't you sit down? I'll make us something." My fingers itched to grab down the photo, but I supposed I'd done enough, so I laid my hand on his shoulder as I powered on the stereo. I moved to change the old tango, but he raised a hand to stop me.

After laying a second ineffective hand on his tense shoulder I walked straight into the kitchen. Moman L seemed with me as I chopped her Holy Trinity; boiled water with garlic and her not–so–secret ingredient – Tabasco and balsamic vinegar in the rice and beans. "The dead aren't always as far gone as they seem, *dauphine*," Féy's voice rang and for a minute my vision rippled. Though her tone relaxed my neck and back, I still beat it away with a rhythmic clack of a stirring wooden spoon. Today I had to keep my wits about me.

When the cornbread and baked fish Creole simmered in the

oven, Echo sat on the red couch with his eyes closed, his breathing not changing even when I set down a cup of coffee with chicory.

"Eric, do you want to talk about Anna? Anything? Your mother was a remarkable woman."

"She's dead." His voice was barely audible.

"Eric?" His lips shut tight as if worried what would come out. I couldn't badger the man – I'd already kept him from Anna's side at the moment of her death when she'd decided to reach out and forgive him. Would he have gone to her? Now clearly he was in shock. After a few moments I left.

I called Jane Kennedy, the new obits intern, from the bedroom and asked her to cover for me, since it was the day before my fourth, approved out–of–office Friday. Keeping my voice low I told her I'd send the final Kincaid profile in an hour.

Clive had sent me an email. A Saudi sheik had complained to AP reporters about a theft from some Swiss accounts. But most folks took him as trying to strong arm the bank, which refused to speak since doing so would confirm or deny his account and subject them to potential imprisonment by Swiss law. Mike Carruthers might know the fellow. I left him a message that we needed to catch up, feeling a slight twinge I'd not phoned before.

Anna's obit ended with a quote from our initial interview, "Whatever I did, I did to keep my family." I'd shared it with Eric, though I doubted he'd even see the piece.

"Marie?" I asked to an efficient, lightly accented, "Kincaid residence."

"No, this is Claire," a voice clipped. The service would be the following day at a local church.

I had just hung up when Eric's head came up the steps. "Hello," his still sleepy voice rumbled.

I turned, using my back to cover the screen from him.

"You working?" He yawned and scratched the back of his head.

"Almost finished. 15 minutes. Till food, also."

"Good. I'm going upstairs to take another shower. Then I'd like to go back home."

"I've got a feast ready. We might want to stay here. The service is tomorrow."

Eric reached out to pull me up, wrap his arms tight 'round my waist. "I've one last thing to share," he whispered into my ear. Against his still spicy scent my heart pounded. So he wasn't through with me entirely.

Suddenly I saw black, smelled Chanel, and became lightheaded when I glimpsed the bone white sheath in my corner straight backed chair. But, begging destiny for eventual forgiveness, I clenched my jaw, rattled my chin and she vanished.

In Oakland, all Eric grabbed was a projector he set atop a filing cabinet. Then on the wall above the couch he'd tied me to, a young Anna, scarf askew behind her ears with a boy of 7 or so who must've been Eric, in front of their chocolate door garage, shoved an old Coleman cooler into the back of a small "Woody" Chrysler station wagon.

When they finished she held a hand to reddened cheeks beneath dark-circled eyes and waved a palm to scat the camera away from her wrinkled, white midriff on which it seemed to focus. A little girl, presumably Heather, tried to dance with the dour boy. His eyes were fixed on his mom with occasional glances at the cameraman.

"We were going off to the Grand Canyon that summer. First summer we got back from Switzerland…" He trailed off.

"Your father was filming?"

"Yeah," his brow knotted together.

"Did he always have you two do the heavy lifting?"

Eric sighed, "I told you he wasn't helpful."

"How'd your Mom feel about that?"

Eric's eyebrows went up in annoyance, "You're the reporter aren't you? You figure it out." And he left the room. A moment later I heard his bedroom door slam. I crossed to the filing cabinet. There were nine movie reels labeled by years.

So, while eating a plate of my red beans and rice, I surfed up all I could on Gstaad and Saanen, while on the wall, a seemingly tense, tired or irritated Anna put food out at birthday parties or Thanksgiving dinner, unpacked picnics at the shore, in the boat, or loaded and unloaded the car. Always she waved the lens away – but he never wavered. Eventually, she'd continue with tight shoulders. Her husband never once entered the frame. The way the lens followed her, she almost seemed like one of his subjects.

It was this he'd wanted me to see. On a whim, I typed in Saanen and physics. Up popped a conference – the Quantum Theory Conference in Gstaad – this week. Fulani and Coomb were noted speakers. I'd nearly missed it. My face flushed as I picked up the phone to tell Todd.

On the wall behind me, Anna, with a kerchief on her head, scowled at a sink of soapy water and dishes.

I spent the night making travel plans, as if the idea'd been approved, glancing now and again at Berne outings and vacations. Nothing much changed. Heather's smile denied. Echo brooded.

Cariña's jealousy of my relationship with Moman L might have pushed her to drive me out. But what if Moman L had been jealous of Féy's relationship with me?

I slept that night on the couch, Berne family dynamics projecting above me, but my own Cadot ones flickering inside.

First thing the next morning I called Blowhard. "Mike, are you all right? Any more visits?"

He laughed. "I carried it off. I didn't give you up."

"Mike, I really appreciate that."

"But they were barkin' up an empty tree, weren't they love? I'd no idea what I was looking for."

"Did they get anything?" Quietly, I held my breath.

"The arsewipes wanted to know what *I'd* heard. You heard about that Arab sheik?"

"Yeah? I mean yes, of course – that's why I asked you."

"Ah...Well, hot lead. I told them all I was after was a routine sniff out job, which netted exactly nil. You know you can't have a numbered Swiss account as an American citizen. You've got to disclose any relationship you have with a foreign bank to your state Treasury.   And U.S. institutions must report any international transaction over $5000 unless it's a long–held account designated 'exempt' by the bank. That's why folks fly to the Cayman's with traveler's checks or loads of cash. Unlikely any American did this, if it happened."

But an expat Swiss forecasting genius would have one of those "exempt" accounts, wouldn't he? It brought to mind Eric's unexpected trip out of town. "Blowhard, you're not so bad."

"I'm actually great, darling. Care to find out?"

"I already am, Mike. I already am."

The following day at a late brunch at my home, I spoke casually, "Did you know I met your Grand Mere, Pauline?"

"That so?"

"Yeah, when I met your mother."

He nodded.

"She didn't take to me very well."

He laughed.

"She ran me out. Warned me to go away, never be seen again."

"She'll do that."

"So about today."

He regarded me with those truth serum orbs – the eyes that had rescued me continually and without a word.

"I mean of course I'll go."

He returned to his Branola dosed with brown sugar.

"But maybe I can just sit in the back, on the side...not with you. Pour no salt in the open wound."

He paused then nodded.

"But after...I assume you'll be going with them back to their home?"

His head shot up. "I haven't seen them for years."

I said softly. "It's time then. Don't worry; Anna's spirit will protect you." I hoped Féy and Moman L would not bring up anything today I could not handle.

Driving out 280's pine, oak and laurel woods the moon's ghostly sliver cupped the sky's pale blue above the mountains – outline of a nearly closed, lash–less eye. It'd be a dark night tonight, but I feigned brightness, "So what do I need to know about your grandmother Pauline?"

"She's a bitch. I scarcely know her," he muttered, as morose as he'd looked in his childhood videos.

A broad-winged buzzard circled above the Santa Cruz Mountains. I took a breath, "You know I've never been to a funeral before – my mother never had one and I was out here for Moman L's."

He glanced sharply at me.

"Don't worry I can handle it. I'll be killing three birds with one stone." His face was stone. I drummed fingers on the armrest. "Sorry."

Eric sighed, his tone soft but terse, "It will be one more thing we do together. But the story's about my father. You promised."

"Of course. But you want the truth, don't you?" Perhaps I should tell him of the wire transfers – especially if I was going to confront Pauline.

He shook his head, "Whose truth?"

Our son's truth. We exited on the same off ramp I'd used to Anna's just weeks ago.

Eric walked up Woodside Congregational's white walled interior filled with as many locals as business folk, judging by the work and formal attire, to the altar dripping with lilies. Grande Mere Pauline, her grey hair pulled back tight, her skin powdered porcelain, her lipstick and smile tight, nodded coolly at Echo as he approached and took her hand with great formality.

Grand Mere met his eyes briefly, before they swept behind him. He shook his head. No doubt she'd been expecting Marcia Witt.

Sitting next to Pauline was a stocky European man, an aging athlete, bodyguard or soldier. He most certainly could've been Mavis's henchman. He and Eric exchanged nods.

From where I sat a few pews cattycorner, I could see his eyes were black, small and prying. Condor eyes always signaled danger past and present – perhaps the bad half of the Ten. Perhaps this was who had got into it with Blowhar—Mike Carruthers.

But soon as Eric sat next to the bodyguard, the pastor rose. Eric and his grandmother, now the only two of that family left, were not even sitting together. I couldn't help but think of Cariña – I'd missed our call yesterday – out of honor to Echo. Discreetly I snapped a shot of the bodyguard's head inclined toward Pauline's, Eric's held erect, away from him. Here you could see the difference in his toasted skin color. Something you could not when he was on his own.

Sitting on the warm wood pews brought back Moman L's white–gloved hands and short–sleeved, flowered silk arm warming mine at St. Louis Cathedral, morning sun bringing alive the stained glass windows as we rose from prayer, "And also with you. Amen". I'm sure they'd said that at her service.

Through the long ceremony I thought of Féy. She'd killed herself just as Anna'd claimed to have done. Still Eric was here. I could have honored Féy some way back then. She'd given me Moman L, Davis, Cariña, Cecile, Lilla and all. Echo had only money left – and Pauline. If I was pregnant I had to tell him.

There was no sign of Fulani or Coomb who'd no doubt already be in Switzerland, but a row behind Pauline I saw the maid Maria who glanced back at me then shyly smiled.

After the service, once the crowd thinned I headed to the family, still gathered with their staff at the closed casket altar taking in the last well wishers.

As I approached, Eric leant to his grandmother who held a teacup and saucer, and spoke in her ear. Then he stood with a crooked smile.

I took a deep breath, flashed on Sid's, "Tougher than a witches' tit."

"Ah, here she is, grandma." Echo's light accent had changed into a bright, hollow American. So he hid his real voice from his Grand Mere?

"Mrs. Kincaid," I extended my hand, "May I offer my great condolences. Your daughter was a remarkable woman – that was easy to see." Without taking it, the old lady nodded. She accepted a filled blue and white teacup and saucer from Maria.

Echo dove in, "Jeanne's doing a story on my father for the paper, Gramms. A *positive* profile. She already wrote Maman's–."

Our eyes met briefly.

"I told you not to use anything from that interview." She slowly lowered the cup. It was a few seconds before anyone spoke. "And how did you two meet?" She looked casually at her grandson, but Echo's complexion suggested he'd rather look down the barrel of a loaded gun.

"On a dance floor actually, Grand Mere." A bit of his accent came back.

Thick silence ensued. Then the barrels turned, fully loaded, "So you're stalking the entire family, young lady? Plan to suck us like a tick?"

I straightened myself. "Well, it was my editor's idea initially, Clive Jones?" I was pleased to see recognition in her old eyes. "He likes to write about folks who got a raw deal...were, er, maltreated by the press. We try to set the record straight – give them a voice with which to fight back. Clive thought Berne would be a good candidate seeing as it's almost the 30th anniversary of his death."

"I didn't much agree with your take on James Cooper." My heart began to dance. "I know him," Grande Mere continued, "as much more of a son–uva–bitch than you people said," she held her hand up, "Some of us are not meant to have great power, young lady." Her gaze deigned upon me, "From those to whom much is given, much is expected – and much more is taken away. At any rate," Grande Mere sighed, "It is my policy not to discuss family matters with the press." She lifted both cup and saucer to Maria who caught my eye, and held it a bit. Grand Mere put a hand on her chair's joystick. "I'm sure you'll get everything you need from Eric."

I rushed forward a thousand confronting questions on my lips, "Ma'am, the timing I know could be better," glancing 'round I saw a couple of slouch-backed reporters leaning against the church side door, so I said, "There are rumors about their marriage being one of convenience – about how he died. We'll probably print it. Now's your chance to give your take on Berne and your daughter." Eric watched her closely also.

Grand Mere drew her fingers into a fist. "Anna was a wonderful girl, to whom life dealt a harsh hand. Yes, young lady, even the rich can have difficulties." She cast a look at Eric. "She made the best of it."

"You mean after the...fire." I winced, "when she retook the name Kincaid and joined you at the firm?"

"We Kincaid's strive to be an asset to our families." Eric's throat tightened, but she did not notice him. "But this story isn't about me or KinCo – is it?" Her eyes let me know this wasn't a casual question. And Eric's gaze was also on me, as was that of the reporters at the door.

I straightened up a bit, looked casual, "You two worked together for more years than she was even married." Grande Mere acquiesced with a sideways nod. "How would you say she felt about her husband, their marriage, his work, *his* passing?"

"Then we talked mostly about how to protect our family from the *rab*–ble." As if on cue her bodyguard busted in past the stringers and pointed his arm outside to a black limo. Grande Mere smiled sweetly, "This day of all days I'm sure you understand?" She began to roll.

Eric and I walked on either side of her. Catching my eye he leaned his head as if to say "Told you so."

"My daughter, Miss Cadot, was a private citizen, as am I, as is my grandson." She began to roll ahead.

As will be your great grandson; I jogged a step, and reached down to pat her hand, letting the momentum slide my fingers beneath her wrist.

This time I dove into the rising black tide. Late summer warmth burst in with the smell of jasmine, and a linoleum patio lay behind a cement fence on a busy corner where I sat at a metal lipped glass table looking onto a black-haired Fulani and somber, colt-like Michael Coomb. A young Anna sat next to me with her head down. My hand shook her elbow – we Kincaid's did not show discomfort in public. "He was never of right blood." The harshness of my tone belied the quick beating of my heart.

"I beg your pardon," sliced through the dark. Suddenly my hand dangled in mid-air. I paused as if trying to recall, "En–rico Fulani and Michael Coomb? You know them?" Grande Mere gave the slightest flicker. "They said they knew you—"

Grande Mere interrupted, "I know every physics professor, and many of the chemists and mathematicians in the Bay Area. But then I know most of the judges, DAs, police chiefs, supervisors and *publishers*." As if dismissing a maid she turned to Eric, at the chapel's front threshold, "Now Eric, please tell me — how is our lovely Marcia? When will you bring her to see me?"

I started a smile upon seeing her flushed cheeks, but before Eric's response, nausea came over me and I excused myself.

On my way out of the lou, a hand stopped me, "Ah, ma'am."

"Maria." She looked younger and more frightened.

"This is for you. I promise Miss Kincaid." She darted inside.

The envelope was heavy just like the other. Inside in an old woman's old-time print, it read, "Seek to know the truth in Saanen." All the tips had come from Anna Kincaid.

Eighteen

"Jeannie," Clive barked on my cell as I drove back up to the Kincaid's, "Where's my goddamn story? It's been days since we've seen you."

Child on board I wanted to say. "I know, I know. I just came from Anna Kincaid's memorial. We're just driving to the house."

Clive snapped, "What, you're with the son?"

"Oh, yes, you're right. She did a lot for her world." I smiled at Echo.

Clive was silent.

"Well," I lifted my top lip like a cat. "I'll let you know when we're done."

"Don't hang up," Clive growled just as I moved to hit end. "I need to see you right now for lunch."

"Clive," I sighed. I chose my tone carefully. "Let's plan something early tomorrow..."

He cut me off. "Unless your appendix bursts, we *will* meet now, today – after you drop him off. Do not go into that house,

Jeannie. If you want to stay on at The Sheet, that is."

That was fast. I wondered what he'd heard. "What's up, Clive?"

"Not on the phone," Clive barked. "Meet me at Mama's on the pier at 12:30. Don't be late and don't be in too much of a hurry. I want the full download."

"Yessir, massah," I said and flipped my middle finger as hung up. My mind worked the scenarios. None of them were good. After explaining what he'd heard to an increasingly peeved Echo and dropping him off, promising to catch up later, I called Mavis, but the message said she was out of the office today. At least that meant she couldn't have told Clive anything.

I arrived beneath the Bay Bridge at Mama's a little after 12:30. I crossed myself before entering the shack on a pier that looked like it could sink away at any moment. The place smelled of oil and salt water, but was full of early diners.

Clive sat at an ancient picnic table beneath a grimy window at the far end of the garage–sized room. I went to order a cheeseburger fries and a soda from the battered wall menu for $4.40, which was why newspapermen loved it here, but my stomach gave a lurch. I just ordered a chicken burger with a garden salad. Clive fixed me with a meaty gaze as I made my way with eyes everywhere but on him.

"Clive," I breathed as I leaned down to airbrush his cheeks.

"Jeannie," Clive nodded. "Glad you made it." He took a sip of water. I took a seat.

Clive's eyes checked me. "How was the service?"

My voice was steady. "Pauline sends her best. Didn't much like Susan's piece on Cooper." My laugh stabbed silence. Susan had taken the Belinda Wheeler information and turned it into misunderstood millionaire trash. "She wouldn't talk, but guess who our tip was from?"

"Who?" I handed him the note from Maria. He read it and I could see his shoulders relax. "So you found her diary?"

I shook my head. "Pretty sure it's in Switzerland – outside Gstaad." As I said it, a busboy dropped off Clive's special order grilled onion burger.

"G–what?"

"Gstaad, in Switzerland. As it happens, the city of Bern, an hour or less away, is a physics hub. So there's a physics convention out there this weekend." And I almost missed it. I placed the downloaded web page in front of him, "The International Applied Quantum Theory Conference."

My plate arrived, but my gaze did not leave his face. "Fulani and Coomb who worked with Berne, whom the tips called thieves, who I'm pretty sure knew her mother Pauline, were preparing for it when I interviewed them. And Coomb's almost ready to crack. Clive, why did you call me here? Right when a ton of sources are in one room together?"

His gaze was hard, wiseass, "You think that would have been a good place for you to probe? Letting everyone see? Get things good and out in the open?"

He had a point. "I didn't tip my hand at the funeral."

"You see why I want you to have a handler?" My silence acquiesced in more ways than he knew, and he accepted it. Then he said, "So what happened at your high class lunch last week?"

After a beat, I spoke softly, "I wanted to tell you. I just didn't know how to bring it up. After our dance that night, I slept in Eric's guest apartment – upstairs in my building. We got together after that for a thank you drink. Over a series of dates we started talking. I know how you feel about those things. But then Marcia Witt visited Todd to share – and I saw them together. He didn't tell me what she said, just that he would publish it if there is something. He's testing all of our limits. And he swore me to secrecy."

Clive grimaced with his final swallow; held his school–ringed hand up as he finished his coke. "Have you slept with him?"

"No." My eyes felt big as saucers.

"You told Todd about your debt?"

I shook my head.

Clive took his time using the wet nap. "Hey, Slugger. You danced with and wooed a high class source you were about to escort to his Ma's funeral. You go to lunch with Todd. I hear none of this in advance. You making some kind of end run?"

"Clive," my desperation leaked in, "I'm just trying to keep my job. Like you with me and Susan. You know I have a daughter? She's eleven going on twenty-one. Cariña. She's with her dad."

Clive's face was a study in curiosity. I think he already knew, but why was I coming clean now?

"Shameful secrets are a habit of my kin. I'm sorry. But it took five meetings and three weeks to get the son to talk. He may be revenging his father through those Swiss transfers to the tune of millions. And nobody is paying attention – still."

Clive bounced a quarter between thumb and forefinger, deciding what to decide about me – as he'd done many times about many young flatfoots. "You got a passport?"

I nodded, "I got one before I came out west," in preparation for my *succés fou*.

"I don't care what Todd said, anything over $1500 you're paying yourself." He rose, "One thing, Slugger. Since you never told me you danced with him? This is strike two. From here on out, no more secrets. Call me if anything looks suspicious."

I pursed my lips and nodded once.

"And," he wagged his well–manicured finger in my face. "I'll have talked with Todd and cleared this whole thing up. *I* want the first phone call the minute you get back which should be," he checked his watch.

"End of Monday." Once he'd left, I devoured my lunch.

On my way back home to pack, my heart did a mambo. I just had time to leave a message for Mavis, before packing and calling Cariña. "Darling," I lilted, "What's going on?"

"Oh, Momma," she sounded surprised.

"What is it darling?"

"What? Nothing. I'm fine."

"School all right? The boys?" I dragged us through the litany. All her girlish verve was replaced by teen churl, so I announced, "I'm off to Europe, darling, for work – Switzerland."

"That's good," she said distracted.

"Did you hear me? My first time overseas."

"It's not Paris."

"No, no, that's true. But it's for work, darling, Momma doesn't get to pick."

"Oh."

Try as I might, from monosyllables she'd not budge. Soon we hung up. Could she know already about her brother?

Eric was not in when I phoned.

The flight to Bern, Switzerland seemed to take days. I'd nothing to do but pace and think about how I really felt about Eric and Anna, me and Féy – or think about the baby. I should get my period here or – I braced myself for history's resurgence.

A fun-loving, large couple going to Switzerland for the first time to visit their daughter sat next to me, overfilling our row. Not far in front of us sat an older man with a wiry beard, and two younger men, one with glasses.

Midflight I wandered past and saw the young man with glasses reading American Physics and the older man the Journal of Quantum Mechanics. But as I caught the youngest's eyes under a baseball cap, I thought his mother probably was never knocked up by two different, otherwise involved men, and I glanced away.

Back at my seat I pulled a picture out from my bag – the one Echo had found. A very young Anna and Berne stood behind a well–laid dinner table with Anna's father, Alex Kincaid III. The older man smiled broadly 'round his stogie, and his hand was raised to back–pat Berne who had his head lowered toward Anna who stood between them. His eyes weren't clearly visible. Anna's head just reached her father's shoulder – her eyes caught the camera over a proud, lightly smug, smile.

I ran my fingers along the wrinkled photo, as I had Lilla and James's as a child – willing the scene to come alive.   I willed Anna to come to me now as she had at the ocean – to show me something, teach me something she'd learned. With each breath I conjured her more. I welcomed the acrid smell, the dark.

Finally, the wave caught me. Then candlelight bounced off the crystal glassware and began dancing in the latticed windows framing the front door.   Anna's laughter bubbled over the tinkling forks and knives against the Spode china plate; the glasses gleamed.   A Souza march played in the background. Kincaid's hand slapped down onto Edward's back, inciting in him a violent and funny gulp.

Suddenly, everything froze.   Anna stood and walked toward me. "Marches were his favorites," she began. "Jeannie," she sounded underwater like the voices rushing back on Royal, "Don't be frightened. I wanted to tell you when we met, but Pauline came and you weren't ready...When I met Edward Berne..." I held my breath, scared to exhale and fade the scene. "My father had particular ideas of what and whom his daughter would or would not be. And I doted on him...."

"So, young Edward," the leather squeaked as Mr. Kincaid leant back in his chair.

Anna spoke directly to me again, "Edward and I had met in my...club and Papa had asked me to invite him to dinner."

Kincaid watched Berne carefully and chewed on that cigar he held in his right hand. "I hear there might be some use in industry for your plasma experimentation. The stuff of stars here on earth – creating the fourth state of matter. That's quite something."

Edward – who wasn't smoking – shrugged and shifted in his chair. "It shows promise for speeding the production of silicon chips. But it's not confirmed. It needs a team of engineers and machinists to make it work."

Mr. Kincaid's chair creaked a bit, "I understand that if a plant implemented your plasma process for preparing the silicon, they could double their production in just a few weeks."

Edward sat back. "Theoretically," he pronounced each syllable. "But it hasn't been done yet. It hasn't been produced."

"Edward Berne," Mr. Kincaid put on his closing voice – soft and serious. "I've been hearing about you – one of Oppenheimer's Golden Boys. At least you were," his eyes glanced at him, "Well, I've got an opportunity for you to be golden again." He leaned forward, "Let's you and I develop an exclusive contract," he pressed his hands together. "Together we'll triple our production, halve our costs, and take over the industry. How's that sound? I'll give you the finest machinist and engineering team available. We'll renovate the entire facility to exploit your process." He sat back again.

Edward's nostrils flared. Kincaid didn't notice. He continued, "This computer trend is a revolution. I am as certain of that as of anything in my career." He raised his hand to acknowledge his success. "And that's peanuts compared to what our collaboration could earn. We could lead the way, son...to the future. Forget your ivory tower. Put some muscle behind your ideas. Help us really change the world. Put food in folks' bellies, shoes on their feet. Working in the economy, my young friend, getting your hands dirty," he clenched his fist "is the noblest profession. What do you think?" He smiled at Edward, enjoying himself.

Edward stood. He raised his glass toward Kincaid. "To you, sir," he said quietly. "And to your smart and lovely daughter." Here he nodded to Anna, "*A votre sante.* It is my honor to meet you, sir, believe me."

Anna interjected, "As they drank I am sure I breathed – at least once."

After the sip, Berne went on. "Which makes it that much harder to say I cannot work with you ever, I'm afraid."

Kincaid swapped the cigar with his weight to left side. "Tell me son," he chuckled, "why not the father? You seem to have no problem working with his daughter?"

Berne spoke through red cheeks, "Science belongs to the common man,' Edward said. '*Pro bono publico.* It is a tool for all men to raise us out of the dark. It is not," his voice tensed, "something to be exploited or used for the gain of an individual group. Nor am I. That is neither my nature nor purpose." His chest rose, his face reddened.

"I see," Kincaid cogitated over his Cubano. His eyes never left Edward's face. For a few seconds, time stood still, and no one moved. When the maid pushed the door open, Edward clicked his heels, bowed to Kincaid, then to Anna, murmured "Good Night", and made his way out the door.

Anna broke in once more. "He left us there like that over unfinished brandies. It was a few minutes before Papá spoke."

Kincaid rose from his chair. "Well, Anna," he said gruffly, "we must have your friends over for dinner more often."

"I was too scared to laugh, but he went straight to bed and I ran straight outside. But Edward was gone. I was left breathless. I knew I would certainly see him again."

The scene or hallucination faded.

Back in my plane seat, still holding the photo, I felt a bulge and turned it over. "First meeting, 1956" in block letters crawled across a raised square. I ran my finger along the side. The backing was loose. I brought the photo up to peer inside. There was something in there. My index nail worked back and forth until the side was open. I tapped it against my palm. A piece of folded paper fluttered out. On it was written:

March, 1973

$$\oint\!\!\!\oint \prod\left(\sum 4\sqrt{7\beta9}\right)\!\varpi$$

Arcane algorithms filled the page. A thrill raced through me — it was Sid's missing proof. I'd forgotten I'd been chosen to solve this. I grinned at the other passengers while we waited to deplane.

Nineteen

Down at baggage claim I stood by my learned men; one in his late 50's with smart guy beard and rumpled dark grey suit; the fellow with John Lennon glasses in his 30's. The baseball cap kid was very early 20's – an undergrad I imagined. He stood in a dark, green tee with washed–out image, black jeans and heavy, black boots at the carousel, which wasn't yet turning. The grad stood a few feet behind him. No time like the present. I smiled at the older man. "Going to Gstaad?"

He seemed startled for a second, "Why, yes," he said with a very light German accent. He assessed me. "And you?" By now the other two had noticed our conversation. "I'm going as well. Covering the conference for The Sheet, San Francisco. Jeannie Cadot." I extended my hand.

"Oh," the man shook my hand without meaning it. I colored. "A science journalist?"

"Actually, I'm in Metro. I write about City Heroes and I'm here to cover..." I stopped. "Well, it's my first science gig. I've been studying up on quantum computing. As you know, some of the early breakthroughs came from Berkeley, so I'm here," I shrugged, hoping to look innocent.

"I see," said the scientist, his face softening. "So this is your first assignment?" He shook his head, "I would have thought they'd send someone more experienced to such an event."

My stomach lurched. I rushed, "Well, it's an exposé of the key physicists in the development of quantum computing: Fulani, Coomb, Berne." I tossed off the last name, but watched for signs of alarm. There were none. "Actually," I continued, "I'm most curious about Edward Berne. He discovered quantum teleportation years ago, didn't he?"

The physicist's face clouded. "I'm not familiar with Edward Berne's work."

His be-spectacled middle companion placed a black bag at his feet. "He was Oppenheimer's Black Sheep. Eighty–sixed from Los Alamos. Brief renaissance at Berkeley in the 60's with our esteemed Fulani." The older gentleman's eyes acknowledged the reference. "Known as more of a mystic than a true physicist," he chuckled. "I didn't know he was into quantum computing?" He looked questioningly at the older man.

"Hmph," the professor mumbled as if he'd ruined an experiment. When he spoke again his accent was thicker. I could scarcely understand him, "I know nothing about it."

The youngest scientist looked perplexed. "I've read everything ever written about teleportation theory from Aspect to you, sir. And I've never heard mention of Berne." He paused to consider. "When did he publish?"

"Ah, finally, my luggage. Come, young Paul, Andrew, let's move. We must meet the others in one hour." Then, as if he'd gathered his thoughts along with his luggage, "Young lady. I wish you luck. One word of caution, science comes from repeatable observation, not vague sensations or conjured visions or some such nonsense." I glanced taken aback at the older man who'd initially lied straight to my face.

Back with the dark khaki luggage, the young men stared at him. He explained, "Berne was a fine mathematician, but his physics notions were rubbish – pure rubbish – attractive to young, undisciplined minds. You'll do better to focus on Fulani or Coomb's work. Men who moved the field forward."

With that he turned past the young men, and they were off. The suggestion that we share a cab died in my throat. His youngest companion gave me a sheepish shrug as he dragged the older man's bags on the cart backward.

The familiarity of the taxi meter's digital readout comforted me as I watched the Swiss landscape fly by during our 45–minute drive from Bern to Gstaad. Pine trees haired snow–skinned Alps. Swiss chalets like iced gingerbread homes in villages with complicated names – Schönried, Saanenmöser and Gsteig–Feutersoey – polka dotted hillsides sensuous beneath 5–foot drifts. And it was well below zero. A half to bursting moon rose above the high rounded slopes. And yet we weren't too high here, maybe 3500 feet. After a long rise we came into a valley. The tallest Alp, Finsteraarhorn, rose at the far end, dwarfing everything.

Lights clustered at the bottom, Gstaad – cozy chalets, a small lake and lit castle – the Palace Hotel. Destination of the rich and famous for centuries – Rousseau, Lord Byron and Dumas had visited here. I rolled down the window, and inhaled the freezing, crisp air. Who'd have thought it all those years ago on Royal?

Dadaist paintings and sculptures studded the ultra–modern exhibition hall at the Palace. The swirling chaos of dots and rivers of paint seemed very fitting for discussions of quantum physics with its particles, matter–energy dance and invisible connections. All up and down the wide hall small pockets of scientists spoke quietly or gesticulated in short, eager bursts.

I approached the Press table. Out of the corner of my eye saw the two men from the airport. The older was looking at me as he spoke to another man. For a moment I thought he was talking about me, but dismissed that as the hostess asked me to sign in. By the time I was done, the men were gone. I frowned down at the conference map and schedule. The first plenary session wasn't until tomorrow morning. This evening's festivities were check–in and cocktails. My task tonight was to identify the players. Once done, I could build my game plan.

Walking into the Exhibit Hall, a cowboy strode up. He stuck out his hand.

"Professor Coomb," I smiled, warmly taking his hand despite his tight smile. "A pleasure to see you again. This is quite something."

He studied me, "You surprise me."

"Really – hard–headed, I think." Together we turned and gazed 'cross the great ballroom studded with booths and intricate posters 'round which small knots of attendees gathered. Quantum, Teletronix, QC Solutions, Next Computing, CIA, FBI, and the booths went on.

"To them this place looks like a pasture of Jersey Herefords. Only the milk these animals produce lines their pockets, as well as their bellies." Coomb's eyes weren't laughing when he turned to me. He glanced at the schedule in my hand. "Know where you're going?" he asked casually.

I looked down at my list. "Just trying to discover what's when."

"Ah," Coomb turned back to the indoor meadow. "I'd check out the talks on quantum theory," Coomb said. "I think Hawthorne is leading one. John Weinstein, Richard Furynmann, Tom Chaulkin. There's a panel on teleportation..."

I regarded him, "Aren't you giving a talk?"

He fidgeted in his pocket. "Actually Fulani will be talking. And our young friend does the poster board, so I'm..."

"Available?" I beamed. "I'd listen to *anything* you had to say." I laid a hand on his arm.

Sadness came into his eyes. He nodded.

I asked gently, "Is there anything you'd like to tell me, Professor? Tell the truth and shame the Devil?"

Coomb closed his eyes. His shoulders bent and for the first time he looked middle aged. It was a long moment before he straightened like shaking off a mood. He forced a smile and the color came back to his face. He shook his head. "No ma'am."

He held my eyes.

"You were at the Watch with Berne, weren't you?"

"Um, yes," Coomb began shifting back and forth. "In the last years of his..." he paused, "tenure."

I thought back. "Didn't you write the Free Radicals column in the lab's newsletter?"

Coomb stopped dancing. But when he spoke, he looked often at his feet. "I was a bit of a hot head back then. Wanted to set the world on fire. Shake it up. Berne's lab was the place to do that. We saw the concept lessons we were learning in physics had broader applications – to the social order, organizations, even the psyche." He looked up.

"Freshman year in 1967 I saw Edward Berne speak outside of Sproul Hall. One of those afternoon rallies. He said just as it was time to overturn outdated social policies based on false assumptions of blacks," he paused and colored again, "I mean African Americans," I waved his discomfort gone. "...as being other than us, we needed to overturn our assumptions in science that what we observe is separate."

Here we go. Should I tell him of my dead, my Ten?

Coomb continued wistfully, "Berne said he and his group were beginning to believe that all matter, space, and time were part of a single order. That separateness was an illusion created by thought. That reality was much larger than our minds could grasp and we would never get a glimpse of it via conventional methods."

"So, he went on to meditation and holograms and visions and impulses – and possibly teleportation."

"He urged us to abandon all our preconceived notions and

embrace the other, the other student, the other race, the other society, the other language." He paused. "I mean here I was interacting with, heck, seeing types of people I'd never known before. To think that we were somehow all connected gave me comfort." He smiled ruefully. "Well, I finagled an invitation to the lab. After that I spent most of my waking hours exploring Berne's truth, helping to prove it in whatever small way I could. It helped me sleep better to feel part of something rather than swimming alone in it."

"Did you know his wife, Anna?"

Coomb started and seemed to pull back into himself. "I met her. Berne would have dinners every semester to celebrate graduates and new additions. She would hostess them."

I nodded. "I hear she was quite the pilot."

Coomb looked away and said, "I don't know about that." I had an instinct that actually he did, but I had to make the most of my time.

"And in your estimate, what happened that night in his lab?"

When he spoke his voice was soft and hoarse. "Berne had no politician in him. When his colleagues turned against him, he only knew one way to fight. He went home to prove irrevocably that he was right – that his new method brought traditional results. Unfortunately it didn't work."

"So you do know what he was working on that night?"

Coomb shot a quick sidewise glance, and then spoke lightly, not meeting my gaze, "Something to do with holography and non–locality, I guess. He wouldn't let any of us in to see him. He severed all ties, he wouldn't publish anymore. None of us knew what he was up to. Not even Fulani."

"Did I hear my name?" boomed a voice from behind. We jumped, and turned. Fulani was nearly on top of us. "Come, *Professor* Coomb," Fulani stressed. "Have you finished explaining to this lovely young laywoman – or lay person – is that what you folk now prefer to be called?"

Not waiting for my response, he addressed Coomb, "Let's

prepare." Coomb dutifully escorted the slow, but stately Fulani down the steps. At the bottom, crowds of physicists drew toward the two men like metal shavings to a magnet.

I watched them proceed through the great hall. After the dead Five, Anna, Féy, Echo, Berne, Coomb must be the tenth in our thread. Then was his life in danger also.

That evening, after the movie, I walked the car–free cobblestone paths before bed. Full laughter pierced the cold, clear air. A frozen river snaked its way beneath rebuilt bridges. I walked the banks. Tomorrow I had to locate Eric and possibly Anna's old home or at least the site of his business.

At the bridge, sitting in a well-lit café a man paid a bill. He looked just like Eric. I blinked and then he was gone. I laughed involuntarily. A sudden low–grade burn – as if all of my cells howled in a single tone – made me shiver and draw my coat. Come on, girl. Now everyone is looking like him.

No Eric Berne lay in the phone book. I reached the Palace so deep in thought I didn't stop the elevator doors as they slid closed on a poor man leaning down to press the button.

Upstairs I called Echo, but hung up without leaving a message. It was too late to reach Cariña, but I left a brief story for Clive. "Everything's fine here. I attended my first session today. No news yet, but Fulani sure is prickly and Coomb is cracking. Don't worry, I'm being careful. I'll try to call back again tomorrow." When I hit the pillow my head was full of twilight eyes. It didn't take long for them to guide me to sleep.

Twenty

Next morning at 7 am I threw open wooden shutters to the bright snow and inhaled slowly. I inhaled until I could feel my pulse at neck and wrists. I would see Fulani and Coomb at 9:00 for their plenary speech. 15 minutes later I jogged out of the hotel for a run along the river.

My breath made clouds, but many people made their way to open cafes and the warm smells enticed, though I ran on – I'd have breakfast later. I wasn't especially hungry yet. Perhaps that meant I wasn't with child?

On my way back, 'cross the street from the hotel, I saw Echo walking down its entrance steps. It was Eric or his twin – getting into a cab. Panicked, I scooted behind a delivery van. Was he following me? He didn't know I was here. So was he here for Coomb, for his business? But why then stay at the Palace? Once his cab took off, I ran for the next.

"Follow that cab," I said, and realized how silly it sounds when you actually say it. The driver looked at me quizzically taking in my American voice, dark skin, matching running suit and shoes, my roused bosom and flushed cheeks. I wondered if he understood me, but he turned and released the brake. Suddenly I flashed on the elevator and the man I'd seen as the doors had shut – it could have been Eric. I leaned forward between the front headrests, pointed out each lane change and maneuver the cab made. About two miles outside Gstaad, the cab turned into a steep lane. At the bottom was a sign: *Maison de Santé*, Saanen.

"*Maison de Santé*," I repeated out loud. "*Maison de Santé*."

"*Das ist waf für irre,*" the driver circled his finger above his ear. "*Irre,*" he repeated. "Bird over Cuckoo Nest."

"Crazies?" I said.

"*Das stimmt,* cra–zee," the driver repeated nodding vigorously.

I tapped the man's shoulder. "Drive, drive." I didn't want to run into Eric, not here away from everyone. The sanatorium was most likely a client. But could Berne somehow be in there?

The driver said, "*Mademoiselle?*" and raised his hands in question. I had him pull over and after a few minutes ran in, though the reception would not tell me anything or let me in. By the time I came out, it was ten minutes to Fulani's talk. "Palace," I said jumping in the cab.

Back at the hotel, I asked to leave a message for Eric Berne. "Herr Berne," the attendant said, "Certainly, madam." He produced a pen and paper. I wrote, "Sorry to have missed you. —C." Let him figure that one out. I watched the attendant swoop it into a large cubby marked "Jungfrau Suite."

"He's in a Suite."

The attendant smiled, "Herr Berne prefers the view of Jungfrau." The hotel's brochure heralded their spectacular views. Eric was staying in one of the best rooms. Their last single room had cost $375 for one night. The suites ran close to $1500. My smile was small and tight. The attendant didn't seem to notice.

It sounded like he visited a lot. What was he doing here?

An hour later I lurked the halls hoping to find one of my

targets moving between sessions. Alain Aspect, the discoverer of something called non-locality – the phenomenon enabling entanglement, exchanged looks with me as he was hurried through a door.

Fulani's presentation was in a large, amphitheater–style classroom. It was already crowded with buzzing scientists by the time I entered at the bottom. I saw Coomb 'cross the floor. To my questioning eyebrows, he shrugged.

The crowd was very attentive as the men ascended the podium and the lights dimmed. A slide came up on the screen hanging from the ceiling. I sat back. 45 minutes later when the lights came up for questions, I sat in the same position. 45 minutes on entanglement and how it enabled teleportation. Even a slide with a proof similar to the one hidden in the photo was discussed at length – but no one mentioned Edward Berne. Even though yesterday Coomb had admitted how indebted they were to him.

When the lights came on, I tapped toes against the seat in front. Clive's exhortation, "loose lips sink stories …and reporters," repeated until the place began to clear.

Then I stood, took measured steps down to the stage. My eyes pinned on Fulani, breathing moderated, hands clinched. Just as I was breaking into final approach, Coomb appeared, suddenly in my face.

"Well, hello there," he said. He tipped a black cowboy hat.

"You didn't even mention Berne. Is it that classified?"

"I know, I know," Coomb raised open hands chest level.

I seethed, "Get out of my way. I'm going to show that pompous airbag once and for..." I held the proof and picture.

Coomb grabbed my elbow with a grip just tight enough to show he meant business. He moved me to a side door and spoke in a loud voice, "You're right, Miss Cadot, there are tremendous barriers to being able to teleport anything larger than a few photons. We don't have the computing power to conduct a Bell state measurement of even 10^7 atoms." He held the door open with his foot. I jostled to break free, but his grip tightened and shook a bit. I glared at him as he pushed me through.

Soon as they closed, I wrenched my arm free, "Get your hands off me. How dare you."

"Shh," he put a finger to my lips, and then looked up and down the hall. And he fixed me with such a stare I nodded once. He exhaled audibly, gently pushing me down a service hall. "Follow me."

We went 'round a corner and found an unlocked storage closet. Coomb opened the door. Once inside he squatted right next to the door and yanked me down by the wrist. I searched his eyes. "What the hell are you up to?"

Coomb hissed, "Did you ever think there might be a good reason — or maybe a real bad reason no one mentions Berne's name?" He glanced at his wrist. "Now look, I don't have much time. He'll get antsy if I'm gone too long."

"Fulani?" I pulled my note pad out.

"Off the record," he demanded. "You can't use my name." Once I returned my pen and pad to my purse he let his head and hands droop for a moment, then sat back against the wall and sighed. "Look. Edward Berne was the first to understand that change in spin was the key to harnessing entanglement."

I nodded, squinting so as not to miss anything.

"All right," Coomb continued. "He did apply his theory. And his experiment worked. At least it seemed to. I was there with him." He faced his palms to the ceiling, "He achieved a successful teleportation in 1970."

"What?" Could it possibly be that this scientist, this learned man, was telling me a passing brother teleported himself to another reality?

Coomb must have known because he whispered. "I still don't know how to make sense of it. He sat in the midst of this contraption — a prismatic mandala."

"A hologram?"

Coomb shook his head. "A large laser circuit. Just above him 486 violet beams fed into a computerized prism that spread the combined light into an intense field 'round him – but each laser spun precisely through the entire spectrum, simulating the reflective properties of a cut diamond. At the controls 15 feet away, I watched him through safety goggles.

"Inside the field, photons would collide and release quanta – packets of energy – that excited any free field particles to a pure quantum state which would excite the next and so on – at least, that was the idea. But that state's never been stable with more than a few photons. Berne would stabilize his system through meditation. Quanta don't jump further than a few millimeters, so the laser circuit was close – the smallest movement would burn him. Still, by then, he refused to be strapped to the narrow rod to support him – said it constrained him and damaged his freedom.

"We'd done 3 trials – each 5 minutes – over 5 hours. Inside the reflecting light he looked tireless, the image of heaven. Outside, he seemed to age 15 years before my eyes. And though he'd never complain, I could see him squint from migraines.

"I'd made up my mind this would be the last trial today and forever. I glanced over at him and he flickered. Of course that's impossible. A manifestation of my guilt and all the crazy light that required goggles, I was sure.

"But then light seemed to swirl all around him, centering in his chest – he seemed to be lit from inside – to flicker, to reflect.

"The odd light extended to the entire room then was gone quick and the machines began beeping – for 5 seconds there'd been static on the biofeedback tape, straight lines. Now the levels were back…changed, his blood oxygen heightened – a lot."

He paused for chatting passersby. "We shut down immediately. Without speaking to me he began scribbling equations: simple, elegant, concise, precise, using 10 dimensions. Bell State mathematics for large bodies. He wrote for about an hour – as long as the elevated levels remained. When he finished, he took Demerol and slept for about 12 hours. And we had our proof." Coomb paused.

"Did you copy them?"

"Unh unh. He made me swear to tell no one about what had happened until he published his paper. He tried to enlist me in helping him do it again. But I declined." Coomb paused. "He aged seven years in those few minutes. His blood pressure remained 15% higher. I worried if he tried it again, he'd die. I worried he might be making me insane along with him."

He whispered with regret, "I told him to just report the math, but he wanted to share the whole experiment. Fulani already wanted to dump him." Coomb shook his head. "I transferred advisors." He held his hand up to the question on my lips. "I was young, ambitious, scared of it being a lie, terrified of it being the truth.

"A few weeks later, Edward submitted to Fulani a paper he wanted to publish on how he used heightened consciousness to control the polarity of his *own* entangled electrons – to teleport to his own large–body through his multidimensional thread. And he included the brilliant mathematics."

"The would-be classified proofs."

Coomb's first response was a sad, slow nod. "If it were true, what Berne had found would be beyond space travel and have implications not just for industry and the academy, but even the military. Today there are claims that China has children who can teleport small objects through walls."

"But that's nuts," I assured us both. It couldn't be real anymore than my visions could.

Coomb shrugged. "It was the math. Berne's mathematics are the basis of our work today. But Berne – he practiced *pro bono publico* as you said. So he resigned and used his family fortune instead. I warned him against it. I pleaded he play ball." Coomb continued flatly. "So, Anna came to me. Her mother had suggested a way she could get the mathematics and a lot of money from KinCo."

I whistled.

"Anna was terrified for her future, her kids, as was I. We grew close – very close – too close. With my third child just born, my wife overwhelmed, my mentor imploding, everyone needing a hero...I just ran with it. I thought a sacrifice was required."

A sharp voice came down the hall, "he went this way, Professor?" Fulani's stentorian boomed, "Coomb."

"Now I've got to go, you stay." And he rose.

"But professor, why did it take 30 years for you to use the proof?" But I'd seen the answer, Eric ripping out those pages.

He cracked the door then turned back to me, "Not everyone it seems, Ms. Cadot, is so easily bought. Berne only left for us the final equation, not the steps of the proof which we needed for the set-up."

"Wait," I grabbed and brushed his wrist – nothing. Perhaps the curse *was* turning. "So the Kincaid's killed Berne in cahoots with you and Fulani."

Only I could hear the slow whirring of my micro cassette recorder I hoped. Still, he wouldn't answer, turned to go.

"Why are you telling me before the prize?"

His face caved. For the first time I saw his age. "Life's funny, isn't it? I've worked so hard for so long to get tenure. And now I have it. Fulani made it happen for me." He smiled a bit. "But I've got something else, too. I have prostate cancer. I'm dying, Miss Cadot."

My breath caught in my throat. I pressed his hand.

The wistful smile stayed, "Maybe it's karma, Miss Cadot."

"I am so sorry Professor," I shook my head not knowing what else to say.

"My family's all set. I'm a tenured, endowed chair at my alma mater. Can I tell you something, Miss Cadot?"

"Please, call me Jeannie."

His silence focused my eyes. "One thing haunts me. What

was it in me that let me participate in betraying my mentor?" His voice caught and dropped. "At the time, I told myself it was practical to go along. That success required true sacrifice, but what if it was something worse than human nature, something more personal."

He worried his brow, shook his head, "Sacrifice has a tendency to snowball. So be careful what you choose. Before you leave Gstaad," he held his hand out for my pad, "Go and see this woman. She's in the sanatorium in Saanen up the road." I looked at him in shock. "My sacrifice," he gave me a pained look, "put her there."

"Who?" I asked vaguely, still stuck on his advice to choose carefully.

"She's been in a psychotic state for nearly 30 years," he shrugged and handing my back my pad, said slowly, "Her name's Heather Berne. If I were you I'd spend the night in a Saanen chalet." He stood up, brushed his hands on his pants and casually opened the door. He walked straight out whistling, left me there on the floor trying to catch my breath. Heather was alive.

While my heart and breath regulated, I replayed what Coomb had said. In his lab Berne had flickered, just as my pioneers and Féy had all these years. And Anna and Eric had kept Heather psychotic for 30 years. And they'd lied quite elaborately and convincingly to me. Well, Anna hadn't.

Suddenly, the memory of Eric's small fingers ripping out pages in agony, returned. He'd been a machinator even then.

But stuck in my craw was Coomb's story of damned sacrifice. Perhaps God had punished him, perhaps his own conscience had. That was something Féy might call real living. But as Coomb had learned the hard way, I wanted no part of it.

Back at the hotel desk, my message was taken and Eric had checked out. Even then I was calm. I stayed calm on the railway to Saanen, and in finding a small chalet overlooking the river.

After dropping my luggage on the floor, I sat on the edge of the small bed. I toed off my shoes. A window looked out on the long, thin, iced-over river. Village lights twinkled on the other side. Large snowflakes splooshed against the pane.

Their soft dampness brought it all back — the blank looks about Fulani and Coomb, that long song and dance about Heather's death, about Berne's last days — and my foolishness in the compromising sex, my silly notions of our destiny and Féy's visits, and my innocent questions on his family, and then taking him at his word — and getting knocked up by him. I *was* too romantic to be a reporter.

Crouched beside the mini–bar I saw Johnny Walker Red & Black, Dewar's, Canadian Club. No Mark. I emptied the Walker Red over a bit of ice. As I lifted the tumbler to my lips, my hand shook slightly and spilled the liquor onto my new white blouse — on my belly. My temples pounded like a bass drum. I poured the drink down the sink, filled the glass with tap water and pushed the chair to stare out to the storm. In the windows my reflection faced me.

I ripped the scarf — tied in the choker–style I'd copied from Anna — from my neck and regarded my brown cashmere turtleneck and black wool pants. Beyond them a bird circled — surely not a condor, but still, slowly the gently lit, snaking valley, rippled.

It would end with Féy and maybe the old Five and I was sick of them driving me. As Coomb I wondered if it was Cadot nature or something more personally damning.

So I dammed the black wave and no one appeared. Through the long window behind my arm-wrapped legs was just the night — foreign and dark. But I liked it. It reminded me darkness and me were family.

Eric had played me, but until the cabin I'd lied to him, to Clive for three years, to Chuck. I recorded most everyone without their knowledge. I was lying to Todd, to all, except for Mavis — even Cariña. I lied about who I was — a failed mother, a cursed *sorciére*. I was keeping everyone out of my core.

And still Eric had given me clues all along – clues that had got me here. He tried to teach me something. My heart drummed. Unbelievably, I still cared for him. He was the most exciting man I'd ever known – might ever know. But still, it was that longing I most needed to staunch – that I couldn't afford as a reporter. That I could no longer carry on this story.

I knew where my own excitement – my own drama lay. So after some minutes I finally brushed my own wrist and let the black rush over me, sweep me back to my perfect, *café–au–lait–*skinned, green–eyed, Cadot–nosed, Cariña, whom Moman L held by my Jefferson Parish hospital bedside when I awoke from my first post labor sleep.

Standing there, with my tiny cherub still red from the womb, in her arms, Moman L told me she thought "Cariña" an odd name, "I'll call her Corinne."

Not mentioning the Spanish name was vague revenge against Féy and Alfonse, I said, "With the soft "n" you can never snarl."

"And we'll say she's Féy's daughter. Right Jeanne?"

"No! No one will believe that she never died – just ran away."

"Of course they will Jeanne. Things happen all the time. You're much too young to be a mother. It will ruin your chances. Corinne should have a sister – you of all girls should know how lonely being an only child is." And she smiled down to my darling daughter, now become her best hope.

Pain had ping–ponged then between my temples – a migraine from the epidural. By the time the pain was controlled a few hours later Moman L'd already moved forward with her plan. And so, eight years later, I did the same with my own.

But now the black rose again, this time like a tsunami that swept me further into the dark than I'd ever gone before.

Back to that night in New Orleans so hot, even past midnight, where the lazy ceiling fan in the second floor, red parlor created the only, thin breeze. The night I'd snuck out after being sent to bed early to give Féy and her *placer* Folies choreographer, Alfonse, a wide berth.

By now Féy lay collapsed 'cross the chair, chest heaving, one of her sparkly nipples escaped. The young, low–voiced man, without rising from his overstuffed burgundy chair, burst into hurrahs. Féy sprang up and ran to the one who didn't clap, a hard–looking, handsome face back against the brick fireplace. In front of him she bowed.

By his hand a small glass of pasty green liquid—first time I'd seen prepared absinthe. They shared an exchange I could not hear. Next to the seated man, on the myrtle end table a green sugar cube dripped through a slotted spoon.

I thought, Moman L will have a fit if the sugar eats through her varnish. My throat clucked. Wouldn't you know it was a break in the song?

The lean–and–mean man – who must be Alfonse – peered into the darkened hall. I scooted back from the banister, realizing too late I was in my new white birthday gown, a gift from Moman L.

"Who is *this?*" His words, curious, vaguely growled. I backed up and stood against the wall.

Féy glanced up, face bright with exertion. Without thinking at first she smiled. She strode toward me, arms spread. "Jeanne Marie. What are you doing up, *dau*—" Glancing back to Alfonse, she paused and clenched her neck. She waved a finger before settling her hands on her hips, "You little thing," her cheeky voice warned.

I could not stop swallowing. I wanted to run, but I raised my chin as I'd seen both Moman L and Féy do. My fingertips pressed against the wall pushing me up.

Féy's face dropped. "Jeanne Marie. You return to bed *tout suite.*" And right between her breasts I saw a five–sided star like mine. I shifted my eyes to the handsome iceman. *"Popa?"* escaped me as though it had a life of its own. I was mortified soon as I said it. The man in the chair coughed a laugh and now sat up; Alfonse glared.

He crossed the floor in a step. "Why you little woolly–haired *negressa* …Well, *I'm* certainly not your father. Why would you think?" He turned slowly to Féy, raked his gaze down her resting on her mark. My hand went to my throat and encountered the gown's high lace collar. Still I didn't move. I couldn't take my eyes off Alfonse and Féy.

She turned briskly, "My second cousin, Jeanne Marie Cadot. From my mother's youngest sister." She hoarsed, "Abandoned. Moman L raises her as my sister. Poor thing…" She swiveled back to me with a begging smile, "but she won't be poor long. She's on her way to grand things, isn't she? Upstairs now, Jeanne." Féy spoke the last in a submerged growl.

I rose slowly. I paused, looked at her. "Good night, *Auntie* Féy." If she was telling the truth, why did we have the same birthmark?

"Monsieur Alfonse; Monsieur Pierre." The man in the easy chair raised his glass to me.

I nodded and turned to walk up, but I slowed.

Féy was saying, "That poor child, she just simply destroys me. Moman L is so good. I help best I can, of course. Send money. Visit to ease the load. Show the girl some fun. One day I hope to bring them to see France. Shall we have a drink to orphans?" The murmurs acquiesced and another tango scratched. "Dance with me Alfonse…."

That night I'd first dreamed of flying from the orange bridge. But that flight took me through yet another, biggest yet dark wave.

My heart beat louder than the cicadas. Out from the black the full moon played in and out of clouds, and sweet olive filled the air. Féy looked into my young eyes with her yellowed ones. Her fingers smoothed my hair as if it were straight as her own, "Do not despair, *dauphine*. As the poet says, 'we *all* eventually return to the sea…the stream of time, the beginning and the end.'" She'd been warning me where she was going. Then she kneeled down to me.

"You are daughter to an African king, *dauphine*. Descendant of an ancient empire whose descendants still rule in northern Nigeria... a scholar and a gentleman. One day, you find him. I have of his a ring and some other things." And she tapped the peridot earrings. But I couldn't think. I stayed paralyzed and watched her board, no longer swaying.

Frozen there, my hands holding those earrings and that tiny slip of paper, the Mississippi Queen began to disappear 'round the crescent, with Féy and all the light and magic and love I was afraid I'd ever see. I started with a lurch toward the bank.

"Jeanne," Moman L shouted. "You come back...Let her go, child. You'll do better not knowing her. That's not for you."

Still I broke into a run. "Any mess you make you'll be adding to your chores *tonight*, Jeanne, 'long with your repairing your jumper."

I ran to the far end of the bank through low–hanging myrtle. "*Moman*," I burst onto the soggy shore. "*Moman*, come back. *Moman*." I dodged the long–wooden fence of a boatyard and my feet sank into mud. My cry died. She would never respond. After all, we are Creole ladies, aren't we, *dauphine*?

The river slid Féy—laughing with enchanted fans in front of her white–suited band—away from my swallowed wail, on the bank, in the dark, the Mississippi's mud water now claiming my patent leathers. I sank to my knees, came close to my tear-ruined moonlit reflection. The boat's wake rippled it into a blur then the black and an image of Féy's bone white sheath flapped up as she fell 200 feet. I saw her death in the Mississippi's waters. Turning, I made my way carefully back to Moman L's now comforting scolds.

Scolds that years later had run cold upon seeing the white pills with the large V on their face sitting in a neat pile on my dresser – I'd only taken three – just after I'd told her of Cariña.

Her sandy face ran white, her every extremity drew in tight – she grabbed me by the elbow and didn't speak until we got to Mercy General, when she told the blue-shirted nurse, "This fool girl's taken my sleeping pills – and she's pregnant. I ought to have let her die – now she's no better than her mother."

From there had grown Cariña's hatred of me and my acceptance of it; my hidden impulse to take that last step off the Golden Gate – or let my guard down and trust somebody else – someone different than them all, someone risky – in this case Eric or Echo Berne or Kincaid. Like me, even his name was a trick. I was after all Jeanne Cadot Merciér.

For a while I just watched flakes of snow hit and often melt on the outside of the tall window. The drops ran down until they froze – a glimpse of water – so innocuous. Yet water took Féy's life – and it was water we came from – one of Eric's paradoxes. I suppose we all did return to the sea as Féy'd once said.

Even my watery past – full of dirt and shame as it was – had propelled me here to watch Swiss snow melt. Knowing of Sophie's babe had driven me to my Invisible Heroes. Féy's denial of me had made it easier to ignore once she'd left then died. It had taken both Carina's and Moman L's scorn to get me out to San Francisco and onto this supposed destiny. And a trail of others' shames had led me here to Saanen. My consciousness let go. I dropped into half-sleep.

"*Dauphine.*" Féy said in my dream – her voice for once without any lilt. She and I were flying together back to Coit Tower. "Now you see the twin powers. You've almost turned the curse. You've almost your *succés fou.* It's just a matter of physics."

"What do you mean? Entanglement? That the dead aren't as far gone as they seem? And now you all have come back for me. But to do what? To write the old story? And why use you? You left me."

"I would rather have not."

"Then why did you go in the first place? And in the middle of the sea? So we couldn't bury you with us."

There was a long pause. "That wasn't me, *dauphine.* I'm not truthfully dead. It was Laetitia's idea. She didn't want you ever finding me. She could be much crueler than me."

"Oh, come on." Moman L had always said they'd never found her body – she obviously hadn't wanted us to – and that was why we'd never had a funeral.

"I'm in Paris, *dauphine*. I have been all these years. First I was sleeping when I came to you. It took years for me to learn to get here even awake – or for this long. The couture was from me. I've kept up with you since before you could ever see me. I've other things never sent. Letters. Postcards. Even your popa's ring."

So the African King was true as well. "You're alive?"

"Always, *dauphine*."

"Why didn't you ever tell me? And why did she lie – my whole life?"

"Part of it was habit, I guess. But I was no good for you then, Jeanne. No good for anyone, but Moman L was – even at that price. I knew I'd be with you again – once we were both grown. I began working for it from that very day I left you. I'm sorry, *dauphine*. You were left at the stoop, but you were never abandoned."

I wanted to rage and scream, feel indignant, but my newfound thought of paradox held me. Only time would reveal Féy's truth and it's meaning for me, and for Cariña. Better to move on while I had her. "That night on the ship when you came into me to dance with Eric – what did we tell him in that lost hour?"

"Everything, my darling. We told him everything." My dream face must have shown reaction for she rushed, "Ah, *dauphine*, don't you know he is your soul's foil? The one for whom you risk all? For whom you sacrifice everything? The one who holds the key to the new world? *He* knew even then. But that is not as important as what you tell him now – and when." She pointed to my belly. "As you're learning, we can't always see everything for ourselves when we need to."

I tried to sleep the rest of the night, without much luck.

Twenty–One

The next morning I woke, fully cramped in the easy chair in front of the window that now had solid snow packed in its corners. A migraine threatened. I stood up slowly and put my hand over my left eye. "Damn," a nerve jabbed at my temple. I popped two Tylenol with codeines.

From my prepaid cell phone, I spoke to voicemail, "Clive. Almost home. Lots of progress – may find the answer today."

For a moment in the taxi, heart softly thumping, my mouth dry, I thought about driving straight to the airport.

But as if in slow motion I tapped the window and signaled the cabbie to pull over to a flower stand at the side of the road.

Picking a bright, vital bouquet of orange roses, yellow tulips and baby's breath I remembered the yellow roses that Eric had brought me to apologize after missing our first cabin excursion. He said he'd been with a client in New York. I wondered if he'd really been here.

The sanatorium was a long, solid, four–story structure built close against a small, but steep Alpine foothill. Manicured lawns swept 'round a U–shaped drive in front. A thick forest of fir and birch covered in snow grew all 'round the building, so that it was hidden and whatever was behind it was completely shielded from the wind. It was as close as I had ever been to a manor house, except there was no sea and we weren't on the cliffs of Dover. I appraised it for a moment, felt a rumble in the hollow of my stomach, and then as if I were about to climb Jungfrau, I started up the stone steps.

At the front desk a possibly Turkish man studied a computer screen. "Delivery for Heather Berne?" I queried in English. Without a beat, after a scant look at my bouquet and white running suit, he said, "1192." He continued with a subtle accent, "Follow the hall all the way down, then right, all the way back," even as his eyes returned to the screen.

Heather must get flowers a lot. As I walked down the white hall, walls heavy with Mondrian's, Kandinsky's, the subtly well–dressed visitors didn't glance or offered small, forced smiles.

When I turned right into the last hallway, the yellow door at the very end rushed forward: 1192. I set off down the hall, an itch in the hollow of my feet.

Echo's long recollection of Heather's life at the edge of the cliff – the two birds his thrown stone had dislodged from the tree, I should have known they stood for secrets: his and hers. Flowers sat on matched stands down the hall – lilies and cymbidiums reminded me of that decayed smell in Anna's room.

I rapped on the door. A Southern voice responded. "Who there?" She swapped the "r" with an "uh" – a Southern tone.

"Jeanne Cadot," I replied with what hoped was good cheer. "I'm a friend of Eric Berne's. I was just in the neighborhood," I colored. "I mean at the conference – the physics conference in Gstaad. Well, anyway. I'm just here to drop off some flowers. To give my best to Fraulein Berne, if that's possible." After a bit of silence, a few locks turned and the door opened into a hallway bathed in natural sunlight.

A heavyset, dark black woman with a brown unfiltered cigarette in her mouth, and a load of clean laundry in a basket, leaned back and regarded me through an unwrinkled face. She could have been 64 or 84. Her white uniform hurt my eyes in the sunlight.

"Hello," I said in what I hoped was a warm voice and inclined the flowers. "Is Ms. Berne at home?"

"She's in there," the nurse used the same two-beat pronunciation and tossed her head behind her before she pulled the door to. She sat down heavily on the bench just to the left of the door. "You go on in if you like." She put her load down and brought out a lighter. "Put them," she gestured to the flowers, "downstairs. Don't stay long. Not that you'll want to," she chuckled, stretched to return the lighter to her pocket and blew out a formless puff. "Good luck." She settled down to smoke.

I turned back toward the door. Slowly, I pushed it open.

Down one side of the dormer ceiling, sunlight spiked through four skylights to bounce off a bone-white hall. A delicately bow-legged side table perched on one side of the hall, just next to a large Persian rug. The facing wall held a painting covering the whole of it – a clockwise swirl of bold strokes of vivid reds, oranges and lavenders – a spiral, a sunset or a forest fire. Past it opposing, curved stairwells appeared – before the hallway continued on into darkness.

Sunlight scampered down the wide, left curving stairs. Large bouquets dotted both sides. I stood at the crossroads for a moment. Flipping a mental coin, I walked down the right side. I banged into a wall.

"Mirror," a heavy German voice came up from behind. Sure enough – I'd smacked into my own reflection. I laughed and turned. "Aren't these lovely," a thick arm thrust forward to touch the bouquet. The accent lightened, "There's room at the bottom of the stairs. I won't be a moment," and she clambered to the left into the darkened hall. I squinted down the hall after her, but couldn't adjust to the extreme contrast. So I began to descend the flower–laden staircase.

At the bottom a large room with golden light from a long wall of windows on the left bordering a thick forest garden was directly 'cross from a large fireplace with a heavy brick mantle. The fireplace made the fourth side of a square of a sofa and two easy chairs. Behind the couch – toward me – was a tall Queen Anne writing table in beautiful condition.

Every open place was already covered with flowers – mostly forget–me–nots, but also daffodils, roses, lilacs, even amaranthine. They covered the sprawling round dining table off to the left, the ample coffee table, even what I supposed was a counter to the kitchen. It was all antiques, golden light and flowers – easy to imagine Berne and Anna sitting here.

I was interrupted from behind, "Tuber roses. Have you brought me tubers?" Then, "Oh," as I turned 'round still holding my vase. She stilled the hands patting her chin and studied me. Dressed in a faded, shapeless blue tee over bare legs, beneath unkempt hair, she still looked 18, though more ghostly than ethereal.

"Who are you?" the girl asked over carelessly slumped shoulders. Small bright eyes – the same blue as Anna's – peered through her clean, disregarded, curtain of hair. She shifted from one foot to another on the rug a few feet away.

I held out the vase. "I'm a friend of your brother's." After a minute I put the vase down on the floor. Once I stood up, I began removing my gloves. "Jeanne Cadot," I stuck out my hand. "You must be Heather?"

Heather looked quizzically at me, and then looked at my outstretched hand. "Is that diamond fire? In your eyes," her hand flittered out like a hummingbird, and grasped mine tightly between bone–like fingers.

"Nice to meet you," I smiled. "I'm a great fan of your father's."

Heather just peered through her bangs with sky blue eyes. I loosed my hand slowly, waved at the room, "Such lovely things."

I moved slowly. "I am a friend of Eric's," I repeated.

"I see fire in your eyes." Heather stared at me surprisingly clear, before she up and twirled away. I rose, my heart beating like a cat's.

I followed her at a distance as she spiraled 'round the room, quickly touching pieces here and there, eventually landing on the hearth at the right side of the fireplace, near some shiny figurines. I settled on the nearest sofa. "I'm here," I lay my gloves against each other, "because of my admiration for your father."

Heather said nothing, but stared at a tiny metal figure with a boxy middle, conjuring Echo's talk of her toaster robots — perhaps it hadn't *all* been a lie?

"I'm a journalist," I said, "a friend of your brother's. I'm doing a story on your father," I paused. Heather still said nothing. "On his death." She picked at one of the fire pokers.

I shot a glance over my shoulder. No nurse yet. "Not a mean piece," I continued, "a kind story this time."

"Papa's in the temple," Heather said trying to balance a figure on one foot.

"Yes, I know, Heather," I said. "I am so sorry for that. I can't imagine..."

"Did you see the fire? It's hot." Heather jabbed the piece against the brick.

I glanced over my shoulder for the nurse again. "Yes, the fire," I gushed. "What do you know about it Heather?"

"The diamond fire. It's on the path to the temple." Heather punctuated each sentence with a dash of the tiny figurine.

"The diamond fire," I whispered, "Oh, yes. It's beautiful."

Heather turned burning eyes toward. "Oh, yes," she echoed. "Papá took me there the first time. Now I have to go on my own," she held her pert chin up, her eyes doubling her defiance.

"You've seen your father?" She turned back. "Heather?" I rose and came over next to her. "I want to talk with you about your Papá."

"He's in the temple," Heather said a bit frustrated.

I touched her hand, "Heather," she looked down at our hands, studied them. "I wanted to talk with you about the fire at your home. Do you remember that fire?"

Heather leaned forward and plucked my middle finger like it was a guitar string. She began rocking back and forth, quietly singing. I couldn't quite hear. I bent closer.

"Papá's in the temple." Her slate blue eyes were bright. She begged in a sing–song, "Papá's in the temple. Make him let me in. It's me. Tell him it's me, *dauphine*. Tell him. Quick – before the doorkeepers hear."

Stifling a gasp, I put my hand on her shoulder. "It's all right Heather, it's fine. It's me, *dauphine*. Who are the doorkeepers?"

The girl's eyes went wide. "No, no," she begged. "No doorkeepers." I took both of her hands, avoiding her wrists, and looked her in the eye.

"Heather?" I asked in a soft voice. "Do you want to say anything about what happened to your Papá? You can tell me anything. Now's your chance, dear Heather." I gave her hands a little shake. Her mantra continued.

"Heather, we think someone killed your Papa."

At that Heather grabbed me, "Number 31 is locked inside the tomb. Get it out. But watch out for the Doorkeepers. Seek to know the truth, *dauphine*..." Her volume increased with each word. She continued rocking and singing. I was scared to move. The Swiss German nurse came running down the stairs.

"What did you do?" she blazed past.

"I don't know," I said, pulling Heather's hands off my own. "I'm a friend of her brother, Eric."

At this Heather let go, "Eric's keeping me out, *dauphine*..." Then the nurse grabbed her, cooing.

"She can beat the doorkeepers. Let me go. It's hot. It burns. Get me into the temple." She began pulling at her tee.

"You better go," the nurse said through tight lips. I swallowed and mouthed, "I'm sorry". As I climbed the stairs I could hear Heather's screams, "She could get me into the temple.

Let me go. Get me in. Papá. Papá." When I got outside the door, I leant against it, breathing heavily.

The black nurse sat folding white laundry. A cigarette burned in the knee–high sand ashtray by the stone bench's side. "Whew," I sat down heavily next to her and wiped my brow with my hand. "Is she always like that?"

"Usually she's quiet as a mouse on the hunt, 'cept with strangers."

"Oh," I looked at her as my bosom subsided. "You been her nurse long?"

"Thirty–seven years," the nurse spoke slowly. "Guess that's long enough. What d'you want with her? Who'd you say you work for?" She turned wary eyes to me.

"The Sheet out of San Francisco," I said reaching for my card. "I'm in human interest stories. Berne was a local hero — and it's coming up on the 30th anniversary of his death."

"Hm," the nurse said reading the card.

"Jeannie Cadot," I stuck out my hand.

The woman continued folding. "Carmen Dumileh."

"So Heather is sometimes as she used to be...before?"

"That chile always hung on to reality by a thin thread, but she was all right after her Daddy's...accident."

I stared. "So what brought her to that?" I nodded back toward the door, brought out the tape recorder.

"I ain't sayin' anything on the record," Carmen said. "But that girl was wake as she'd ever been after her Daddy died. She was spitting mad, but her mind was tracking. It was my day off, but Eric called, said Heather was grabbing knives, jabbing at them. Then the day after, her Momma called Miss Pauline then asked me to give these men who worked with her Daddy some time. They might have something to help calm her down. So I sat right outside the door like we're sitting now. I heard her Momma pleading with her. After about five minutes, the door opened and out they came — the men — Anna and Pauline." So

Eric wasn't there.

"The head doctor, he gave me a bottle of liquid, 'give her one milliliter of this every day.'

"I figured I'd read the bottle later and decide for myself if I'd give it to her or not. But I asked, 'for how long?' That bastard looked at me and said, 'forever – or else the next time she might not miss.'" Her eyes filled.

"What was it?" I asked, lulled.

"A–mi–trip–ty–line," Carmen pronounced it through smoke. "An early form. Can't think. Can't see. Can't remember. Body gets hot." So she was trapped in fire, just like her papa.

Carmen used two fingers to pick tobacco from her lip. "At first, I tried to reduce the dosage, but she broke her brother's collarbone. I'd no choice but to keep her on it."

"Is she ever lucid?"

"Only little bits," Carmen watched the smoke curl up from her Black and Mild. "Lucidity brings back the anger."

"And Anna never tried to rehab her?"

"Hmph," Carmen scoffed. "Anna went back to the U.S."

I squinted. So Anna was worse even than Féy?

"Always sent flowers and expensive gifts, but never visited." She shook her head.

I tried to keep my tone even, "What about Heather's brother, did he visit?"

"Hmph," Carmen said characteristically. "With his dark face, his dark mood, you get the feelin' he's watching, watching everything. But he doesn't say 'boo'. He just takes notes in his head. Doesn't even write 'em down." She chuckled. "He always been the connection between his Momma and his sister. He never did care that without the drugs, she'd have killed him."

"And now?" My lungs released a pint of air.

"He comes here once the month," Carmen waved her hand. "Most times brings his gal with him." The blood drained from my face. "Sends flowers every few days. That's who I thought you was early on – one of his deliveries."

She smiled at me and my face replied in kind, "his girlfriend?"

"That Marcia. They been together ever since I've known them. She's been coming here since the accident." My mouth went dry. Images of them jet–setting through boutiques and long lunches left me nauseated.

"Did you ever hear her mention a diamond fire?"

"Papa's in the temple," Carmen chuckled.

"Yes, what does it mean?"

"Now you know that, don't you, *piti*?"

"I beg your pardon?" Could Carmen be one of my Ten?

"Said I've no notion what it means," her eyes stayed steady.

Seeing as my dreams could no longer drive, I changed the subject. "And you left your home and family and have been with Heather ever since." I spoke more to myself than out loud.

"There were 15 of of us Dumileh's altogether." Carmen said. "I go back once the year at Christmas. Vacation to South of France each year with Miss Heather. I might not look it, but I've seen...oh, I've seen a lot of things, Miss Cadot." She smiled.

I felt drawn to her. "You didn't lose your accent?"

"I'm still a Georgian. I'm just all the family Heather's got now regular, and Eric's made a nice way for me. One thing I will say for him and his Momma. The money's never stopped. Don't guess it ever will."

"When did you all get here?" I said.

"Right after that fire, after those men."

"Which men visited that night?" I asked.

Carmen didn't answer right away.

I reached inside my bag, pulled out the conference program and turned to the Presenter's page. I pointed to Fulani. "Is he one?"

Carmen's eyes clouded. She looked away and spat.

"Carmen," I said softly. "I hope you'll consider letting me put your story on the record. A living crime like yours and Miss Berne's should not be pardoned nor forgot." I nodded to the door behind me.

Carmen chewed then nodded judiciously.

"Call me collect, anytime – day or night.   Maybe it's not too late for Heather."

"Hmph," Carmen blew smoke from her nose. "May been too long to help now."

"Next time she wakes up. Call me collect. Tell her it could be her last gift to her father – to save his name. And to herself – to save her will to live." I rose, "Carmen, you ever find any diary here? Anna told me she'd left one. Asked me to find it."

She plunged her cigar into the sand. "You mean those black books? Eric took them back with him last time he was here." She looked hard at my frozen face. "Better be careful, young blood. Sleeping dogs sure may lie, but they can still bite when they get up." Coomb's words again, "What do you mean?"

But she turned back to her folding and wouldn't look up.

Minutes later I rose and walked slowly, carefully, down the cigar–laden hall.

Outside, still forcing calm, at first I barely noticed the black limousine. It wasn't huge or ostentatious, just black and gleaming like my old, pre-mud patent leathers. Simultaneously I registered it and a hand vise–gripped my arm. "Fraulein Cadot," a heavily accented voice said. "Please come."

The back door to the town car swung open as we approached. Inside sat Grande Mere.

"Pauline," I said as I ducked into the car. Her henchman bent in behind me. "To what do I owe...?"

Grande Mere used a cane to tap on the thick window separating the front from the back. The driver lowered it. "To the airport..." she looked at me, "Which airline?"

"Lufthansa."

Grande Mere nodded to the driver. He powered the window back up.

Glancing 'round for weapons I saw none.

As we drove along the winding valley road, Grande Mere

spoke without looking at me. "You're to be congratulated Miss Cadot. I also see you have built a 'relationship' with young Eric — where many more have failed. Franz?" Her man threw pictures on my lap. Through Eric's open office window we kissed. Damn, I thought.

"Franz spotted you yesterday at the conference," Grande Mere went on.

"I didn't see him."

Grande Mere dismissed with her hand, "We prefer to keep a low profile. I'm sure you can understand — the spotlight's so common." She nodded again to Franz who went to his jacket pocket. I eyed the door. The inside handles seemed to be missing. But Franz brought out a small book from his pocket. He handed it to Grande Mere who handed it to me. It was, as Anna's had been, a twilight blue passbook — Swiss and anonymous, with a balance of $100,000.

Grande Mere looked right at me, "Though your extraction methods are most cheap, Ms. Cadot, your investigative skill is has earned you this offer. For your silence — and a reward for your success — from old pro to young one. This is a numbered Swiss account in your name — Jeanne Marie Cadot Merciér, yes? Untraceable from the U.S. On this day, for each of the next nine years, this account will receive another deposit just like it." She studied me a moment. "Provided the story never appears, of course. We'll send you a portion of the negatives each year." She turned and looked out the window. "You'll have them all plus one million tax-free dollars by the end."

My mind wobbled for a moment. I looked at the passbook: $100,000. Nine more just like it without lifting a finger. Here was the *vesica piscis* to my Dream. I just had to wed myself to the big lie. Something I'd been mightily familiar with until now.

"Of course, if you don't accept our offer," Grande Mere continued, "or if you tell anyone about it. I'm afraid we'll have to let these pictures out. I do hate to shine the spotlight on anyone. But, it's been so long since I spoke to Todd. It'd be nice to see him."

So she wasn't beyond carrying a grudge for decades, just as Sid had said. But she wasn't willing to hurt her grandson either — she wasn't threatening to drum me out. Perhaps she knew Todd would never cave to her.

We drove through the idyllic Swiss countryside. Since Echo'd been lying all along to me — I could certainly return the favor. Action and reaction perhaps was another form of real living.

At the airport, Grande Mere turned and said, "Don't tell anyone — especially not Eric. Not Todd. I'll know. I always do." My face was stone. "Have a safe flight," she concluded, "Think about it. You'll make the right decision. Chances like this don't come along every day. Play ball and more stories could come your way. Good day, Miss Cadot."

The door opened and I was out on the street with my bag and photos before I could find any words to speak.

Twenty–Two

On the flight home, Pauline's photos lay in their open manila envelope beneath the front seat. Warmth zinged down me at the sight of Eric and me in an embrace. Shots showed me leaving the house early in the morning, looking furtively over my shoulder getting into my car parked so carefully down the street. There was even one of me straddling him in the enclosed patio at their "cabin." I rolled my eyes remembering the helicopter.

Inside the envelope was also the passbook winking at me – so like Anna's back when. And Heather's strange words lingered – 'she can fight the doorkeepers.' Clearly Pauline was a doorkeeper. But Heather had said Eric was as well – so had Féy.

30 seconds later, I got up and went to the lavatory. My period had not even hinted in Gstaad. After sliding the lock shut, I looked in the mirror. My face looked drawn, but I could see some glow that brought back my term with Cariña.

I put my palms under the cool water. The memory of Sophie Benvenue's child rushed in. I was no longer an orphan. Féy said she was alive, had been all these years – without a word to me. If it was true, that meant most everything else had been as well — I was not crazy and there were now three Cadots, enough to be a knot — a family — perhaps soon to be four — a firm foundation. No matter how unresolved I felt about Féy, I had to keep the family together — else the curse would not be lifted.

I closed my eyes and leant back against the mirror. My probable son could not hate me as Cariña had. I had to get to *ssucés fou*. I had to get back on that sailboat to find the diary. To do so I'd probably have to let Eric back in my body. Honestly, part of me welcomed the chance to play him again — and another part just wanted to hold him.

Off the plane, I powered on my cell and called Mavis. "Hey girl," I said warmly.

"Hey, back at you. Where you been? You been holed up with Prince Charming?"

"Not exactly, Mave," It felt so good to hear her voice; I suspected I could tell her anything. "Look, can we meet for lunch?"

"You ok?" Mavis sounded suspicious.

"I just need to talk with you today. Can you meet me at Mama's?"

"Sure, honey, I guess so," Mavis drawled.

"OK. I guess I'll call Todd."

"Clive's been pacing for two days and I believe he's filled up your voicemail."

"I'll call him next. But don't tell anyone?"

"Roger, Mata Hari." Mavis's silence accepted my biting laugh.

"And I've got to call Todd. This is material info."

"I'll let him know."

"See you in a bit."

At the boisterous Mama's, I ordered a chicken burger, fries and a Crystal Geyser, and then found a seat in the back. No one paid me any mind. I sighed. If I were lucky, they weren't following me.

Clive and Mavis's thick winter coats – both black per S.F. fashion – blotted out their surprise till the four were on me.

I rose and extended my hand, "Todd, Susan, Clive," who leaned in for a cheek and shoulder hug. 'Mavis." She nodded coolly as she appraised her seat for leftovers then sat gingerly in her muted-pink stubbed wool coat.

"Thought we'd hear for ourselves," Todd took off grey leather driving gloves, turned his chair backwards and sat open–legged with his arms crossed atop its back, reminding me of Féy's stance, "We don't have long."

Susan leaned an elbow on the table. Clive sat at table's end on my left, both black gloves in fists on the yellowed Formica. It flashed me back to the original Five. This group could be the ones living who avenged – a sight better than the Berne's. "Well, I didn't find the diary yet – the main proof, but I may have found something better."

I pulled out my recorder, played a few seconds of Heather's "Diamond fire." I looked to Todd then Clive. "I found Eric's sister. Heather Berne – she's supposed to have been dead for 25 years. She's been drugged and kept in a ritzy clinic outside Saanen. She's not lucid, but she and her nurse confirmed there's a diary and the son brought it back here. I know him – Eric," mercifully both Todd and Susan kept still, "and I'm pretty sure I can get him to show it to me – soon."

Clive slipped a manila envelope on the table. "Police file on Berne."

"But it's sealed."

He shrugged, "I called in a favor." I grinned and cracked it – black and white eight by ten's and coroner's reports.

"How do we know it's exclusive?" Todd asked after giving Clive a nod.

I pulled out the photo with the proof sticking out, "I got this from their vacation home. This is the main teleportation proof Fulani and Coomb have up for the Nobel Prize. Only this was written 30 years ago – about the time of this photograph and Heather's 'death'. Took me three weeks to get it. Eric – you know, I danced with him." A small silence, "Yes – that's helped. He's not talked to the press all this time – he lives usually in Switzerland. But he let me find this. He'll let me find the diary."

"You seem sure."

"I've had some help from his mother – before she passed."

"Don't let word get to anyone," Todd rose as did Susan. They shared a little smile.

So now they both wanted this story – to avenge Todd's father. As I wanted – was taking – revenge against Eric – just as Eric had taken revenge against the Kincaid's.

The waiter arrived with my food, but I was nauseous.

"Well, well," Clive turned back in to me and Mavis, "Seems you made a conquest."

Mavis reached over for a fry – I pushed to her my plate and launched into almost the whole shebang: Berne's classified mathematics, Coomb's confession, Heather's house, Grande Mere's threat, the Swiss passbook. I ended, "My house might be watched."

"Stay with Mavis," Clive said immediately. "And don't come in the office."

Mavis looked at me. "Do you think you can trust this Eric?"

"I trust him," I held off her eyes. "And I think I know where that diary is." I'd better figure it out – fast.

"I want to hear from you often," Clive said. "On a land-line. If you don't call me, I'll find you. OK?" He looked at Mavis. "OK?"

I punched a finger into the manila envelope. "These are of Berne's crime scene?" I snatched up a photo. The detritus in the picture certainly inspired the image of an explosion. I looked at another, brought them all out. "There's no ...remains," I said softly.

"Hm," Clive took one up. "Maybe they were removed." Then he grabbed me in a tight hug and murmured, "Be careful,

Slugger. You got it?" He hissed. Aloud he said, "I'll give you three more days. Good enough?" I nodded even though my mouth was dry.

Mavis went to my apartment that afternoon while I went by the drug store. She didn't see anyone when she picked up the few things I had requested. But when I asked her to grab a man's jacket hanging on the door with the monogram EKB, she made disapproving throat noises.

After the expected pink strip results, dinner and a long phone call with Cariña, who said, "Maman, we welcome him," sending spasms through my heart, Mavis and I did our toenails in front of the TV to the first Bachelor. Mavis dabbed on a coat of Fire Opal, "So what's really going on with Eric? Hm?"

"Oh, Mavis," I said. "I sure can pick 'em, can't I?"

Mavis said, "Why don't you tell me how you got knocked up?"

A burst of tears replaced my surprise. I jabbed at my nails with the brush. "He looked me dead in the eye and lied. He even cried. That kind of contradicts the true love thing I was figuring on."

"Yes." Mavis began another toe. "I hate to say it, but you know, I told you...."

I winced, "Yes, Mave. You did." I stared blankly at one of her perfectly done toes for a few seconds. "You also told me something else about him that turned out to be true."

"Really?" Mave stretched out her finished foot and turned toward me. "What?"

"Heather's nurse told me he visits with Marcia – the woman from the cruise – every month."

"Oh, my," Mavis said. "I am really sorry, sweet pea." She reached out and clasped my hand.

I knit my brow and focused on the next foot. "You know what's worst of all?"

Mavis cocked her head keeping one eye on the television

screen. She loved her reality shows.

"I miss him," I said. "Right now. After all the lies. I'd love to see him. Be in his arms." Mavis put down her polish and turned both eyes on me.

"Jeannie," she said slowly. "Being alive is stepping in shit, being aware is looking down, being adult is cleaning it up. You think about that life inside."

I laid my head on my knees. "I am."

We watched the rest of the program in silence.

Before falling asleep, I checked my home messages. There were two from Eric – finally – just when I didn't want them. The first was a late night booty call; the second sounded more concerned. Both in the past two days. He must've left Switzerland right after I saw him. I took a deep breath. Tomorrow he wouldn't take calls until two or three in the afternoon. With my heart pounding so loud I was sure I'd barely hear over it, I picked up the phone and dialed his number. He picked it up right away.

"Hi Eric," my voice sounded surprisingly soft.

"Well, hey beautiful," he said. "Where've you been? I thought I'd lost you."

I waited a beat as I pushed back the tear in my voice. "I had to go out of town for a few days. I just got back."

"Oh. Business or pleasure?"

"Business," I said. Then in a split second decision, "I went to Gstaad for a physics conference, the IQTC."

There was a pause. "Oh." Another pause. "Was it helpful?"

"Sure," I drew out the word. "It was very educational. I now know more about quantum mechanics than I'd ever intended. But it was worth it."

"Unh huh," Eric said. I could hear him typing in the background – already multitasking. I rolled my eyes.

"What have you been doing?" I asked.

"Oh, nothing much. Mostly working. I took a business trip."

"Really. Where?"

"Back to New York again. Those clients are demanding. But the money's good." He laughed, "When are you coming over? I missed you." His voice dropped. Inadvertently I groaned.

"I missed you, too," I said. "What about tomorrow? I've got a few more questions."

"Tomorrow evening," Eric said. "At my house. I want you to myself first. After that, I'll answer all the questions you like."

I smiled. In spite of everything I felt relieved. "You do have a way of making a girl feel wanted."

"Because I want you," Eric said articulating the last two words.

"Aargh," I said falling back on the bed. "I'll see you tomorrow. Don't work too hard."

"Don't worry," Eric said. "I'll save myself."

I hung up and feel asleep once more to his eyes.

When I got back to the office, I found a manila envelope postmarked "Puerto Vallarta." I ripped it open and pulled out an 8 x 10 with a stickie, "Kid – hope this helps. –Sid."

The photo was a much younger Grande Mere, Anna, Fulani, Coomb and Franz conferring at an outdoor café. Sid or someone held up in it *The Montclarion* newspaper dated in Oct 1973, two weeks before Berne died. I kissed the picture, and picked up the phone.

Sid's voice sounded less slurred this time – full on the hard–edged reporter in the tropics. "Sid," I began. "Jeannie Cadot here."

Sid said, "How's it shakin' kid?"

"Just great," I said belying the twisting in my belly. Though I'd eaten hearty this morning I was hungry already again. "I just got your package."

"Rock your world, kid?" Sid's gruff voice teased, "or had you already sussed it out?"

I forced myself to smile. "Pretty interesting photographs."

"Nice to get it off my chest. But you'll need more than that to open up the case."

"I've got more. I got pictures of the crime scene today."

Sid was silent.

"Only the remains had already been removed. Just like you said."

Sid chuckled. I waited. He chuckled again. "Sid?"

"I'm sorry, kid. Those are the photos. I remember seeing them before everything was sealed. I told you that bitch was powerful."

"Sure, she can make entire bodies disappear," my heart danced in my chest.

"Gotta go," Sid hung up the phone before I could get the name of his source.

I stared at the pages. A few moments later, I packed my stuff and walked to Mavis' desk.

"Mave. Meet you at home later. I've got to go to Eric's."

Mavis had daggers of concern in her eyes.

Lips tight, I pivoted and walked away.

Twenty–Three

At Eric's that evening, as a brisk wind blew under my pink cotton midi. I was thankful for the seasonal bite – I'd have an excuse to cover my trembling. I held the faintest hope that I might pull this off. There might be a perfectly innocent explanation for Eric's lies and omissions, for that young image of him on the stairway.

Waiting downstairs, he drew me into his arms and kissed me. I pushed away a little after I should have, but what was wrong with the baby getting a little taste of joy between his parents. "I missed you, baby," Eric slid his hand down my belly, over his hidden son, tracing my hip socket with his thumb and squeezing.

"Eric, stop," I said faintly.

"I want to taste you," Eric whispered, so softly it was almost inaudible, as his mouth brushed by my left ear. I inhaled cedar and soap. I breathed in deep and sighed, "I missed you, too. But, first let's catch up."

"Why?" Eric breathed taking my belt and tugging it open. My knees went weak.

Goddamn, I thought. He's not gonna let up until I give in. Besides, he could get suspicious. When he ripped my shirt open, I enjoyed the sound of the buttons popping.

In the wee hours, I propped my head on my hand and looked at Eric, taking in his high cheekbones and the sculpted lines of his face. Would our child look like him? Like Cadot, a Berne or a Kincaid? Eric slept and I crawled out of bed and tiptoed into the hall.

Downstairs, in the now familiar study, my eyes caressed the reference books, the bound journals, the scrapbooks, albums, Berne's scientific notebooks and my pad. My eye lingered. "Papá's in the temple." Heather'd been describing a mandala.

"Diamond fire." It must've been the hologram. She must have seen it. I ran upstairs to her bedroom.

On a beveled glass tray so reminiscent of Féy, so reminiscent of the set at the cabin. Something caught my eye in the mirror — one of the framed pictures near the bed. Anna, Eric and Heather sitting on a deck, heads close together, all smiling — laughing actually — at the camera.

Suddenly I remembered the crate of "books" Eric had stashed in my trunk when we went to visit — right after his return from his unexplained trip. They'd had a small stamp, "Suisse."

"Oh my God." I squared my shoulders and began formulating a plan.

The next afternoon when Eric came down to begin his day; I was in the living room watching movies of Anna Berne. This particular reel captured a sailing trip. They were rigging the mainsail. Anna poked her tongue at the camera as she tugged the sail up the mast.

At first I didn't turn 'round when I heard Eric. A few minutes later he said, "You like these." He said it as a statement, not a question.

"Oh," I started. I turned 'round briefly. "I didn't hear you come in."

Eric stood by the side of the couch and watched the screen. "We used to sail a lot as a family up there on the ocean. I forgot about this trip though."

I stole a sideways glance at him. He was fixed on the screen. I took a deep breath, and then said, "Sailing is all about physics, isn't it?"

Eric nodded, "Yes."

We watched in silence for a bit. When the film switched to Heather's birthday party, I said, "Eric, I've been thinking. Maybe I can learn to sail as well. I mean – I'd like to try again."

Eric turned with deliberation and let his eyebrows rise. "What are you trying to say?"

"I'm saying," I said rising and walking over to him, "I want to try again." I held his shoulders and took in those blue orbs, "I'm saying, I want to go to God's Palm. This time I'll try and feel the flow."

Eric fingered my waist, "Umm."

"I mean, I'll be terrified," I rolled my "r". "I'll be scared out of my wits, but I want to do it and I know you'll take care of me. You see I am learning."

"Mm," Eric pulled my shirt over my head.

I turned my flinch into flint and said, "I'll take that as a yes."

Eric barely mumbled. Reflected in the black file cabinet behind us, Heather held a mast and stared out to the sea.

The next day dawned beautiful, just like a month before. I went by the bureau in the morning to update Clive and Mavis. On my way back to my desk I ran into Susan in the hall. I beamed.

She smiled back under curious eyebrows, "Your Echo behaving?"

I just tipped my chin and walked on.

We met at a deserted stretch of Ocean Beach where we could leave a car for a while. Anticipation and dread drummed through me as he gunned my roadster. This time we took the less scenic, faster 101 north. Driving 'cross the Golden Gate I looked out to sea. Sure enough a black spot soared.

Neither of us was particularly playful – both our mothers' fading death scents lingered in the air – along with our secrets.

We planned to get up there, settle in (and look for the diary), then start a trip early the next evening. Once we left the Bay Area, the sky grew cloudy. Thick clouds gradually darkened. Weather had said there was rain coming. Good, I thought. Maybe we wouldn't have to go – though in my heart, I knew better. And I had to go as far as he wanted – I owed that much to him.

The house looked squatter and little more dusty, rustic.

Eric carried his things straight downstairs. "Shower," was all he said. Then, "Coming?" he asked to my silence.

"I'll be down in a minute," I said. "I'll make a drink first. I want to relax."

He laughed. "Don't be long." He continued down.

I walked out on the enclosed deck. The ocean was serene. The floor to ceiling view still inspired awe and vertigo – in front of them we'd created little Dumileh. He would never see the place where he was conceived – unless one day I showed him the stolen picture. At the sound of the shower, I went straight to Heather's room.

Here as well was the hairbrush set and behind it the photo of Edward and Heather on Heart's Home – with Eric with his intent eyes. Anna must have taken it – one of the few if not the only one without her in it. I grabbed the pewter frame, loosed the back, the old wood square popping out to reveal ripped journal pages filled with equations in the same scrawl as before.

The shower turned off. I closed the frame back up best I could and shoved the pages into my pocket.

Then I jogged upstairs and headed into the living room to the rolling bar. I opened the liquor cabinet and made two drinks, mine just soda with only a splash of bourbon for color. Just as

Eric opened the bathroom door, wearing a brief towel and drying his hair, I handed one to him. "I've had a head start," I twinkled, raising my glass to him.

"Love your outfit," I continued as Eric gulped his drink down.

"Ah," he put down the emptied glass, released his towel and pulled me toward him.

As always, I invited the passion, I willed his secrets through his tongue, his lips, his breath.

"Jeanne," he finally pulled back, "You are so much more than..." he stopped.

"Hmmm?" I said as I tried to move from my desire.

"Forget it," he said briskly. "Let me get dressed, and then let us eat."

"OK." Soon this would all be over anyway.

While Eric changed, I hummed and searched kitchen drawers and cabinets.

When he came in, I had water heating, salad in prep and a sauce bubbling. "Well, well," he said, "Feeling industrious?"

"New York steaks, potatoes au gratin, cheesy broccoli and cauliflower, butter biscuits. This is what I do with my nervous energy."

"Remind me to get you nervous more often."

"You," I pointed at him with the paring knife, "don't need any help."

He chuckled and poured an '88 Cabernet for himself at the counter. "You remind me tonight of Maman. When I was younger." He popped an olive into his mouth. As he chewed his smile faded.

"Guess we'll really see the difference tomorrow."

"I guess we will," Eric said. He thought for a bit. "Jeanne, about tomorrow. I'm really glad you came. I've always wanted someone to see this place – to see God's Palm from the sea."

I stopped mid–slice and looked at him.

Something flickered behind his eyes, shifted the balance of

his shoulders.

"Eric, what is it? Is something wrong?"

"You're just right for me," he said in a soft tone. And suddenly a little, light corruption began to feel heavy. "When do we eat?"

"In an hour."

Over dinner he drank a lot of wine and I pretended to. After dinner we sat on the cold brick in front of the plate glass windows, no fire behind this time. Eric had not touched me since the first kiss.

"So where are you now with Dad, Jeanne? Did you learn anything in Switzerland?"

I swallowed, nodding. "I believe I've learned almost everything – about your father's end."

He, leaning forward across his knees, picked at a shoelace.

"Coomb admitted your father worked inside a prismatic laser mandala – meditating to stability to let the accelerated energy rise him into a pure quantum state. People in the government were after his results simply for – as you suspected – the math. In took them 30 years to recreate the missing 14 pages – the ones you all hid in the sailboat photo taken by Anna. You did a nice job on that."

That stayed his hand.

I brushed his back, "I'm sure he would've been proud of you."

For a minute his back tensed. We just sat the sound of the ocean muffled 'round us. When he spoke he sounded young – the boy on the stairs.

"The first time I went down into his Lab was at Maman's request. Though Heather went often, as I said I avoided the place. So my father happily watched me nervously case his notes, tracking logs, and journals. I think he knew right then."

Itching for my recorder, I worried I'd lose him if I moved.

"As I looked, he began to tell me of his mother's father – a wise man who moved from boats to fixing trains out of Oakland

– who'd once given him a locket and letter signed from the man you saw in that old wedding photo, Benjamin Harris."

I stifled my inhale.

"Seems my great grandfather had been Cati's son of dubious paternity, and the note explained why they must leave him behind – all because of Alex Kincaid. Then he produced this letter and showed me the loan contract, the picture of the *Lawrence II*. He told me that his whole life motive, as his mother's father before him, had been one of justified revenge."

"A lot of that going 'round."

"But when push came to shove, my father couldn't find a revenge that was honest, fair, on the side of justice. And he'd heard Maman on the phone earlier and knew of her plan, had known of her relationship with Coomb, and through him, Fulani. That's when a new vision came to him."

Eric turned to look at me, "You see, Jeanne, he truly believed in Shambhala – that if he set his lasers higher, past the safety bounds of Coomb, that they'd teleport him there – to Heaven, to Eden, to God's palm."

I wanted to interject, 'But he wasn't the last fool, Echo. People bought his math. And yes, your father, he truly believed in purity, in heaven. That's why his heart broke upon learning about your Maman and Coomb. Why despite it being an accident, or even the blood money from Grand Mere, actually, truly, it was a suicide. Why it's ever harder to live with that money, why you'd have to dispose of those funds.' But I kept it shut like a good journalist. I kept it shut and I put my hand on his back.

"He enlisted me to come back in two nights to help him finish the configurations, and to keep it all a secret from Maman – whom he'd come to love. I could say nothing until she was dead. This was the best way – he said.

"The second time I went down he'd already placed the journals and proofs in an envelope. I helped him input the final laser settings. After, holding me for the first time in years, he whispered, 'Already, I'm proud.' Those words still taunt me. I hope someday to make them stop." He laid his head back on his knees.

I ran my hand up to his neck. "But you and I Eric, we're made of stronger stuff. Suddenly Cariña flashed in my mind. "I have a daughter, Cariña – back in New Orleans. She's 12 going on 73. She was my biggest secret. But not anymore." I grinned. "I told your Maman of her. That's when she told me of her diary. And your Heart's Home."

I leaned against him. From the moment we touched the black velvet grew. I would never, ever forget that cool, arousing touch.

Still when he fell into soundless sleep, I snuck out, grabbed pants and my coat, a flashlight from the hall closet, and headed for the deck. I reached for the key next to the door. Heather had said, "The book is near the tomb." Only one thing out there looked like a tomb to me.

The wind whipped against the cliffs as I scurried down the circular stairs. This time there was no ripple of the air as I approached the small pier. I took a breath and stepped my right foot on the weathered board. No ripple, no smell but seawater, no green tinge. I walked 15 feet to the left angle and straight to the boathouse door without looking down – breathing deep to avoid dizziness. The lock stuck but I managed to wiggle it open. I found a switch on the wall to my immediate right.

As my eyes adjusted to the bald light, I picked out deflated lifeboats, oars and life jackets, binoculars, and hats all hanging on the walls, covered in dust. The boat hung a few feet in the air, but didn't rock. Down its far side was a small workbench. At the end of it were garbage cans and a hand truck. I edged on the foot wide board 'round the boat. Next to the hand truck, half covered by a sheet without dust, sat a crate marked Suisse in small black stencil.

I stood there for a few minutes. Then I moved down the ledge.

The crate was nailed shut. I scanned the walls. There – a crowbar. I lifted the ancient device from its hook, jammed my foot against the box for support, and crossed myself.

I leaned on the bar once, twice, again – no give. My air came in gulps. I tried again, this time using my foot for more leverage, trying to keep my weight against the wall. All I needed was to fall in beneath the boat and the dock and get trapped down there. Slowly the lid began to lift. Perspiration bloomed on my brows. I continued to concentrate and push – the nails came all the way out on one corner. A few minutes later with the lid on the floor, I stared at curly strips of brown paper that gave the impression of thick brown hair. I closed my eyes and sent out an inarticulate prayer. Then I dived in.

The first thing I touched was a stack of statements from Banque Saanen. I put one in my pocket to match the accounts later. The crate was filled with statements. I had fifteen stacks scattered on the bench next to me before my fingers touched the unmistakable feel of the hard–backed cover of a book. I pulled it out. Five black bound journals tied with a ribbon. My heart did a screaming merengue. I heaved my breaths.

I undid the ribbon. Diary of Anna Taylor Kincaid: 1955–1957 the first title read. She had lovely penmanship, of course – a more rounded, happier version of the hologram card. I upended a bucket, and sat down next to the crate, water lapping inches below my feet and for the first time I didn't pay any attention – there was no vapor, no wooziness, no metal smell. I opened the second book. The date: 1958–1960. Anna would be nearly 18 – just when she met Berne – my heart punched. I began to read.

1 Sep *Papá* insists a London season is still *de rigueur* in the *bourgeoisie*. It will provide excellent fodder for my travelogue. And we brought my Durango, feistiest steed this side of the Sahara.

Luckily, my partner–in–crime, Marlena Witt must

go through this *horreur* as well. She's been here twice before. Our days are spent in ridiculous teas where we receive instruction on how to curtsy, set a snooty table, and play bridge. We commit to heart the lineages of London's most snooty families.

The day's events are the price we pay for the nights' plays, dinners, and balls. The girls' escorts come along.

7 Sep There is a scientist who certainly seems a *homme d'esprit*. Edward Berne. An American professor at London College. He says the same ideas that govern the planets and the stars guide our own atoms and ions, and that matter is spinning and whirling all through us all the time. *Sic i tur ad astra...*

"Such is the way to the stars," according to my college Latin, stars symbolized immortality. Absently I rubbed my birthmark and thought of Eric's hand 'cross it, teaching me. The journal continued.

15 Sep Yesterday Papá forced me to entertain his crusty businessmen at his dinner gala. His hopes to interest me in one of the young men were low and obvious. They've all buried their consciences so long ago they've forgotten where. But I made polite conversation and tried not to choke on my minted lamb as I watched them guzzle Moncrief '25 through their self–satisfied smiles. I was finally able to escape by engineering a spill of red wine on my silk blouse. I simply never returned after leaving to clean up. Instead I went to the stables to check on Durango. He is nearly ready for our next competition. He took the jumps today like a *preux chevalier*.

"Brave knight," it had been in one of Féy's fairy tales.

Sep 23   Edward took me to a scientific
salon. The men there had worked with Oppenheimer
of the atom bomb. Edward did at first, but he
couldn't bring himself to wreak mass destruction and
got out.

He is searching for the Holy Grail of the universe
– that which, once know, all else will seem to make
sense – not seem so harsh. Next we are to hear a
guru from India speak. India, dear diary – where
father forbade me to ever go. Edward says it will
open my mind.

Sep 27 The meeting was outstanding, *mon cher
journal. A la belle étoile* in a beautiful garden out in the
country where the universe filled the sky and our
senses.

After the lecture we met the great man who told
the story of the Gautama Buddha. Of his awakening
to the world of suffering and then to the eight–fold
path. As he spoke I felt chills.

The master guided us through a meditation. The
first sensation was simple numbness, followed by a
body awareness that swelled and left in its wake a
great calm. Edward and I sat on the lawn for hours
afterward. *Vis vitae.* I am reborn.

Sep 29 Edward has told me that they are planning
meetings called 'Gatherings' very near Saanen, outside
Bern. Edward says young people from all over the
world will attend. He says old restrictions are
breaking down. Class, race and nationalism, even
physical divisions of waves and particles are being
transcended. He says young people of today can no

longer support the status quo. I will definitely attend.

Yet she'd ended under blood red satin covers wanting to see my gait.

> 1 Oct I have determined what I must do. The way to save my eternal soul. As a modern woman, I so clearly see I must leave my cloistered world as the Buddha did before me. And I will open my eyes to the world, live like one of the people.
> I will go to Saanen. I will eschew all earthly goods, even my beloved Durango, – just as Buddha did – for we are all part of an illusion and our attachment to anything is really a shackle to suffering. Let them go and the shackles will release. From this emptiness, *l'avenir. Vox Populi, Vox Dei.*

L'avenir – the future. Voice of the People is the voice of God. So she'd become a socialist. And I'd become a vixen.

> 10 Oct I have fled the palace. The past week I have abandoned the debutantes and joined with Edward to organize this year's Gathering. I have seen Edward nearly every night. And tonight he's told me a secret. His mother's people escaped from slavery to California. The only thing Papá ever escaped from is taxes – and regulation!

> 20 Oct Papá has sold Durango! I tell myself the tears I shed all night prove I'd too great an attachment. And Father has invited Edward to dinner. He has discovered that something that Edward is working on is very important.

> 23 Oct Oh diary. At our dinner tonight, Father

of course tried to buy Edward, but Edward walked out on him. No one has ever before dared such a thing. Edward was my new *chevalier*. He has won my favor, my admiration and, most importantly, *cher journal*, he has won *mon amor*.

It must have been the night of the photo where the equation was hidden – my first external confirmation of a vision. If this were true, then perhaps so was everything from Sophie's baby to Féy's being alive to a young Eric on the stairs to Dumileh. And Berne contempt for the Kincaid's ran deep.

25 Oct A *contretemps*! Edward will be leaving by the end of the month for a post in Switzerland. He. He has asked me to marry him. *Satis verborum.*

10 Nov – Secretly, we're engaged! We daren't tell anyone. Two interminable weeks to my 18th birthday and my freedom.

23 Nov *Entre nous*, Edward and I have eloped. Marlena was our witness. We'll be leaving for Switzerland end of the month. I haven't told Papá. I'll let him hear it in the open air. By then I'll be gone. *A cause cèlébre.* It will be good for the movement.

Anna fled to Switzerland. As Féy had to Paris. And I had to San Francisco. Where would Cariña flee. Or Eric?

30 Nov Papá is furious! I spoke with Maman on the phone. She said Edward would only bring me sadness. But he brings me the greatest joy. As usual when *Papá* doesn't get his way, it was thunder and lightening, but with Krishnamurti's teaching the

words hurtled through the air, and not touching me. Papá already has his people working on an annulment. There's nothing for it but to flee. *Coute que coute.*

"Cost what it may." Féy's phrase when Moman L complained of her choices, of Alfonse – and when she'd left me. They both were willing to pay for love. Was that also real living?

1 Dec Papá can't imagine anyone surviving without the killer instinct. Well, we will show him wrong – I'm sure of it.

I turned the page so intent, I never registered Eric standing silently at the dock door for a good long while before he turned and walked away.

15 Dec The past few days have been wonderful and terrible. My proletariat state is official. I'm cut off. Penniless. Destitute. We celebrated with a perfectly good table wine at a small local *fondue* shop. With Edward, my *preux chevalier*, by my side I feel I can weather any storm.

10 Dec On Edward's income, we can't afford help, not even once a week. I'm having to learn to cook and clean. Now I wish I'd paid more attention to the maids.
Hearing my parents' door slam behind me no longer rings. Edward is so calm and gentle. He says we'll start a family soon in this University junior faculty flat.

Following this the entries stopped entirely for a while. 'Round Christmas, I read...

23 Dec *Au desespoir.* The mountain of housework simply won't go away. My hands are now red and blistered. Living as one of the people is not what I expected.

Perhaps it is not what Edward expected either. He gets terrible headaches and sometimes is dizzy when he works. It is not surprising. He works such long hours. Often upon arriving home at 10 at night, he collapses in his study chair. He perks up only when I engage him in political discussion. I worry I am a disappointment to him.

25 Dec Miraculous news. I'm pregnant. Edward is thrilled. It is the best Christmas present. I feel my old *vis vitae* returning. I am sure it is a boy.

I paged ahead.

20 Sep 1963 1:40 pm Eric Daniel Berne. 5 lbs, 6 oz. Premature so small, but he looks already like Edward when he smiles – infrequently these days – so that I wanted to name him Edward, Jr., but Edward would not hear of so much attachment. So I will call him Echo. He will always remind me of my love for the man his father was when I met him.

The entries continued on in compact bursts of Eric's activities and progress, the birth of Heather, finally, the move back to the United States. No more of the French and Latin–laced, romantic prose.

Upon their arrival back in Berkeley, Anna mentioned that Papá had sickened in the intervening years. There were mentions of Maman – I supposed this meant Grand Mere Pauline – with the 4–year–old Eric and 2–year–old Heather. By the time Anna stopped writing about their reintegration, Mother was mentioned in nearly every entry – more than Edward himself. The final series of entries began in July, 1973.

7/13 Edward refuses to go to the HCI Conference, he's so upset over the Nobel Prize. Michael – who is still here and still our friend – Thank God – tried to talk some sense into him. But Edward says he does not want to talk with naysayers anymore.

7/17 Michael called me today. Edward has been forced to resign! He now is locked down there in that basement lab of his banging on things. Once in a while Eric checks – he is such a good boy. Not like his damnable sister! He says Edward is building some sort of machine. God knows what. I just hope it will not blow up the house. Thank God for Eric. He's become the man to replace his father!

That line sent shivers all through me. He'd just been nine.

7/20 I stole a look at the books. We have only got two months of savings left. Papá has expressly barred me in his will, and Maman has not moved him around it yet. I just pray Edward has this thing figured out before the two months are up.

9/25 Yesterday the accountant called. If we do not start getting an income by December, we are going to lose the house. That will be after we have used the kids' college savings, including their Savings Bonds. Edward has spent all of our money building whatever is in our basement. If it wasn't for dear

Echo, my rock, my *petite chevalier.* I tell him all and he advises me. I feel most calm when he's by my side. We've decided tomorrow I'm going to Fulani.

10/1 The plan worked. Have found allies. Fulani will come over and talk some sense into Ed. Then... Well, I'm afraid *mon cher journal* – that must be my secret.

10/10 Fulani says time for the next step. All we have to do is have Heather remove her father's notebooks. Since Echo stopped, she's down there every day. I will speak to her tonight.

10/13 Heather shut her eyes, hummed and waved her chin from side to side at my every attempt to speak. instead. Only Echo can save our family.

10/27 Echo's done it. My darling boy. He brought all of Edward's research material up. He says he told his father he was making him a study. He is so strong for his sister – and me. I tell him he is my hero. But he's so quiet. His teachers say he is an exceptionally smart boy for his age.
He understands. Their future is the most important. Fulani says I cannot write anymore. He says we must have no evidence and he is right. I will give you to Eric tonight. As soon as this is done I'm sending him to the best school money can buy and he'll take you with him. Tomorrow night we go to the movies for our usual family outing. Fulani will take care of the rest.

This was the last entry, the night before the fire. I sat stunned. There it was in her own hand as promised. Anna,

Coomb, Fulani and Grande Mere had murdered Edward Berne. And Anna at least partially orchestrated it, and dragged Eric into it. Eric had hidden it all these years, as he'd hidden so much.

I exhaled. With the wire transfers, Heather's existence and this, I could get this published, possibly the case re–opened. But while it would certainly redeem Berne, it would destroy what was left of Eric and Anna's reputations. I sat, rubbing the journal back and forth under my chin.

Finally, I repacked the crate, stood up with the final diary, took one last look 'round. I walked back thinking that a sea accident might be a better way to go – than by the hands of your own family. Then, next to the door, I caught sight of something. I pulled the chain again on the overhead light.

Tucked between two beams was a weather–beaten old sign. I pulled it out – the *HMS Lawrence II*. Had Echo known of it, too?

Just before 7 a.m., I crawled back into bed. Eric's regular breathing told me he had slept through the night, but when I snuggled up next to him, he reached out for me.

My eyes filled. One more time I told myself. One more time, and then I'll be fine for years. I let him tie my hands to the bedposts, cover my eyes, and nibble me from head to foot. By the time we were done I didn't even feel him stand at the end of the bed, nor did I notice him leave.

I rolled over to embrace Eric shortly after four pm.

He wasn't there. Slowly through my half–sleep, a figure came into view standing next to the window. He was dressed in a thick sweater and jeans, a steaming cup of coffee below his lips. For minute I thought it was Edward Berne.

Then the figure turned. "Time to get up," Eric said in a funny–sounding voice. "Wind's up this evening. I made coffee." He held the cup out to me. Then, coming over to the bed, he leant down and whispered, "Is your courage up?"

I looked into his eyes. So it was to be the scamp today – presto–chango from aggressive lover to sad, mischievous boy. I could have used the man today. Still I was certain the final journal was on that boat and he was finally ready to show me. And give me his true confession.

The soft, round images sharpened into edges and glints. "I'll have breakfast for dinner," I said as Eric pulled me up, and out of bed.

In the bathroom time felt surreal. I steeled myself in the mirror. I wanted to scream, to flee, but I refused to let Eric get the best of me.

Downstairs, my shaking hands made a mess of the eggs, but finally got the shells out. "Breathe, girl," I told myself in Mavis' voice. "One step at a time. You can do this." I glanced at the threatening sky outside and looked for a radio. It'd be good to get a weather report. It would be good to call Cariña.

When Echo came down, I said, "It don't look so good – out there I mean."

He glanced outside, "It's perfect."

I peered at the sky. Clouds covered the dimming horizon. But fog didn't usually mean rain. If I demurred now he'd suspect something – maybe take back the book now hid in my luggage. I breathed deep and felt my heartbeat regulate.

After eating, we packed up then walked 'cross the patio. He slid open the door and the cold wind whipped in.

If I left him here alone, surely he'd come after me – or go on the side of Grand Mere. And if I suggested we both bail on the whirlpool he'd talked about wanting me to see for weeks, he'd do the same thing. If anything got dicey out there I'd tell him of Dumileh. If he confessed everything I'd tell him for certain. "So your family used to sail quite a bit?"

Eric said nothing, his face was braced to the night wind, waiting for me to step out the door.

"I mean you know how to sail in bad night weather?" I pointed, "There's rain." A blur marred the center horizon.

"Yup," Eric said, and began down the stairs.

"Is it safe to sail in the rain?" I stepped out and held the railing.

Eric stopped and turned, "Now you don't trust me? Crabbers are out every night. And I'm a master sailor." Then, he turned and continued down.

"Aye, aye, Captain Berne." I told myself this was him ushering me through the door to the new world – I would get at those last hidden records tonight.

Down at the dock, Eric showed me how to lower the boat then rig the main sail. He explained that he would be helmsman, and I would be crew. He showed me the difference between a cleat and a winch. He showed me how to use the radio. And I saluted him. He explained with mock seriousness that the crew would need to follow orders from the helmsman. I replied that I was ready to serve. Eric smiled at me. I found the water didn't scare me so – even when the air thickened and rippled, turned green, it held at bay as though a great atmospheric bubble surrounded us.

Just before we set sail, Eric showed me the safety kit. "Life jacket," he threw one to me. "Phosphorus flare," he showed me how to shoot the gun. He told me to be careful – it could blow a bad hole in the boat at close range. Though my heart was pounding I refused to faint or go into the black or show any weakness.

We set out into the rough ocean. I sat in the helm, not too close to the stern, and watched the trees and cliffs – not the storm or the smashing sea.

The coast was wild and scrubby. Before it, jagged rocks jutted out of the water. Waves broke and drenched them with spray. Eric explained leeward and windward.

"Isn't sailing mostly about physics?"

He winched the mainsail, "The family business."

"And your father taught you all you know?" I ventured.

Eric kept his eyes on the seas in front of us. "You're right," he said. "He wasn't so terrible."

Water slapped the side of the boat.

"There it is," he pointed ahead. We were close to the point.

The waves broke against large rocks. "*A la belle étoile*," Echo said.

"What does that mean?" I asked casually, remembering that phrase from Anna's diary.

Eric turned 'round. "Under the stars, in the open air. Maman used to use it. Just past that those," he pointed to the largest crags, "is the whirlpool." The air rippled.

I sat back against the side. This area could be riddled with rocks under the waves.

"A whirlpool lasts as long as the full moon shines directly over the meeting of the tides. 20 minutes." He pointed behind my head.

I turned 'round and looked out to sea where the clouds had gone. The full moon hung in the far Western sky – nothing but lightly green air between it and me. It illuminated God's Palm halfway and suddenly I saw the ship – the HMS *Lawrence II* running at us. The blood drained from my face. The wind picked up as we neared the crags. We had to raise our voices. We both spoke at the same time.

"Eric."

"Jeanne."

"No, you go." This was it. My heart pounded.

He waited a beat. "I want you to know I really appreciate your diligence in telling my family's story. You've changed nearly everything as to how I feel about them – about him."

"I'm just so sorry his life ended like it did."

When he spoke next, his voice quavered almost imperceptibly. "I wanted you to know," he stopped for a minute, "that there are no hard feelings. There are only," he turned and smiled weakly, "some very warm ones. I am truly grateful."

"Eric," I began again.

He slammed the tiller away from his body. The sail jerked over to the right. I ducked. It flapped noisily above the roar of the ocean before it caught. "It took me a long time to find you, Cadot Merciér."

After a sharp look at him I stared at the water. The angle was taking us right into God's Palm. It was getting rougher as we approached. I felt whirling now in my chest. Instinctively, I braced and placed a palm on my belly.

Eric continued. "At first it was a game. But then your optimism, your enthusiasm, your hope – I had forgotten these things." Without realizing it, I began inching back from him, looking for a weapon without him seeing me.

"You were right about so many things, Cadot. Submersion in the past pulls the plug on life. I needed someone to know the truth. I needed to lighten my load. At first it worked. But now I find that since someone does know the truth, I don't feel any better. If anything I feel worse...."

The water stormed, lurching, but I was scared alert beyond even nausea. And then on the far side of the rocks, the *HMS Lawrence II* as lighted and bedecked as the ship Féy'd sailed away on, was struggling in the waves and a group of folks were on deck, eight of them, just as I'd seen them that night on the Creole Queen. I searched for the bone sheath.

"Anyway," Eric spoke heavily, "Our relationship has fulfilled its original intent."

"Eric, what are you talking about? You're scaring me." I grabbed the rail of the boat. We were caught in a side current driving us toward the large rock. It looked like we'd get jammed between two of the spires.

He leaned over and popped the latch on the side hatch next to him. He opened it and stuck his arm inside. He pulled out the flare gun. I glanced over to the struggling ship – two figures came into view: Anna and Berne on the one deck above water. A darker, thin, older man appeared behind them and placed his hand on Berne's shoulder; then pierced me with those impossible dark blue eyes – Berne's father? Of course, a hidden one of my Ten – Eric's grandfather. I turned on the recorder in my pocket.

Echo waved the gun, "I only expected an entertainment, a diversion, a pleasure, cat and mouse. It looked to be a lovely game. Especially when I saw you all hot and red at that

Christmas party. Or flustered on the phone call after. Yes, that was best."

I gulped. As if he'd read my mind, Eric continued, "I mean I'd hoped for more, but hadn't expected it really. After all, the beautiful, misfit reporter that championed lost causes wasn't getting much real estate." Eric let his voice drop on this last line. "The dead and dying didn't seem to be selling at today's Sheet."

On the sinking ship, Lilla, James, Benjamin, Cati and Alex joined the three Berne's along with Henry Collins. Alex's right hand lay on the elder Berne's left shoulder – and they held themselves with the same rigid posture. With us and Dumileh, there were twelve figures on the sea.

Our boat rocked and creaked insanely as it wedged itself against the rocks, the ocean behind me now pouring 'cross its hull, a little of it coming inside, but the hull turned, lifted, settled. Beyond it was the whirlpool. The sound of the water was deafening as the moon rose.

Eric was shouting against the rising sound, "Seeing your note in Gstaad - that surprised me. I never imagined you'd find Heather. Or..." He brought out a book – Anna's final diary. He must've found it in my suitcase. Bu where was Berne's journal?

My eyes flew wide. I looked over the side and wondered whether to dive in. But my stomach came up in my throat and I turned back. The phantom ship was down to the last deck, the apparitions sinking.

"It's been delightful. I have truly enjoyed...watching your progress. But as we've met our original goal, I'm afraid it's time to end it."

I crouched against the port seat. We were at least a half–mile from shore – a half–mile of dark ocean water churning through a forest of rocks. I put up one hand, "Echo. Eric. Don't do anything crazy. Please. We can work this out." Tell him about Dumileh, ran through my head – but to offer my son so cheaply to a man who might not be at all what I thought?

But Echo wasn't listening, he was talking. "But I was

surprised.   Pleased." he continued, "That last night — this morning — you found the diaries. *Touché.*" He touched the gun to his forehead. "A real *coup de grace.* Take the helm," he threw the lever to me and stood up.

I jumped to grab the tiller that wanted to move wildly in the roiling water, and held on tight.

Eric laughed and flung his arms out when it began to rain. "This is perfect," he said. "Perfect weather." I gauged whether I could leap to get the gun or knock him off the boat. He must have read my face because he pointed the flare gun at me.

The wind howled and the ocean rocked. "I didn't expect so much. You've done a good job, a fine job." There were tears adding to the rain on his face.

"Echo," I began, "Where is your father's...."

"Now it's time for me to talk, then it will be time for you to choose." Eric stabbed the gun at me. "Everyone gets a moment of truth in their life, Cadot. A moment to show what they truly are made of. This is yours. You've come this far, but can you go all the way? Do you have the heart?"

His mother's question — so had they really been in cahoots, as he had obviously been with the Grey Hats? Then he would now kill me no matter what I said. Copper tasted in my mouth, and my blood drummed; the gun barrel suddenly rippled. On the ship behind him Kincaid, soaking wet Ralston and the bone sheath finally appeared. I heaved a sign of relief — I'd never been so happy to see my mother. Alex went straight to Cati.

"Echo, when you've someone to love it can change everything."

Eric continued, "Jeanne, listen to me. There's not much time. The whirlpool doesn't last long." A chill ran up my spine. He punched the air with the diary. "Don't talk to me of love. I killed my father, Jeanne — just as if I'd pulled the switch. Everything that's good in my life, everything fine, everything I love — I...destroy. Still want me?" He snarled the last words.

"Echo. You were only eight years old. I forgive you. God

forgives you. And so will others." I placed one hand on my belly, willing him to see, to find his instinctual love.

His head bobbed, but it could just be the motion of the boat. Behind him the spirit ship sank beneath the waves, Alex Kincaid's arm supporting Cati whose black bead eyes were irreversibly on me. She was telling me – despite Lilla, despite destiny – she was the one who'd brought the whole group to me. We were the Ten and we were about to be united, unless I mastered the twin powers.

I rushed. "Think, Echo. Your past has taken down everyone that you've loved. Anna, Heather, your father." I pleaded, "They loved you. Don't let the past bring down your future. No one wants that." Tears stung the back of my eyes. Don't be the last fool – you have a successor – yet still I hesitated. I wanted him to believe me.

"Don't let my past take me down?" Eric repeated.

"Yes," I yelled through the intensifying rain. "Think of your future." I'm carrying your son. For some reason the words wouldn't pass my lips.

"You think living in the past is cowardice, Jeanne? What about living *without* it?"

My stomach lurched.

"Do you know where your mother is, Jeanne? She's in Paris."

I just stared at him.

Eric continued holding the gun eye–to–eye with me. "Did you know your mother has breast cancer, Jeanne? That they've given her eight months to live? But I guess since she's *dead*, she's not doing so poorly, now is she?

"You're not so naive, Jeanne," his face softened again as the storm eased. "That's what I like about you – one of the things." He considered then sighed. "I leaked my father's assembly bug. I knew where to do so. They'll prosecute me."

"Not necessarily. No one even knows about the bug."

"You'll tell them. They'll talk eventually. Did you know

Féy's been clean for 10 years? That phonying her death sobered her up?"

I shook my head. He couldn't possibly know this. The gun barrel still eyed me.

"Marcia Witt's son – now a Grey Hat was in your first class with Clive. You wouldn't know him – he slouched, sat in the back and didn't do very well. But he watched your performance. He even watched you at Café Rosso – with Chuck? When I told Marcia and he about what I planned to do with the code – the money, he suggested you. And when mother mentioned your name – I did some research.

"I was upstairs in the house that day you came to see Anna. I saw you look up, give Maria your card. I think that's when I first decided it would be you." In me a cold wave rose.

He went on. "Why do you hide your daughter, Jeanne? You hate your family as much as I hated mine," he seethed. "At least I have the courage to know that means I hate myself." He formed a cadence with the last three words, "and act accordingly."

I blinked at him. "You know Echo, before I met you, I think I agreed with that – except I always loved my daughter, Cariña, even when she didn't love me." The calm of my voice surprised me, as if the cool of Eric's touch had rubbed off. "That's the power of the one beneath the two."

He winced. The hand holding the journal dropped closer to the deck.

"Remember that photo of Lilla, James, Cati, Benjamin, Alex the first and Ralston? Well, Ralston may not count, but the other five, I've found are the first half of a Ten – a group foretold in my family letters. The other half is to be completed and brought to fruition by me. Do you know who I think they are?"

The twilight blue–black orbs stared confused, angry, hurt, desperate.

"Remember the *HMS Lawrence II* I showed you. After Ralston's bank failed, the owners fled from the Bank of

California, who was thought to be taking back the boat during the 1875 Comstock collapse and bank run. Well, I think out here they caught a snag and went down. They were never heard from again – nor was the boat ever seen."

"So what?"

"Well, somehow your father knew – that's why he built your house overlooking God's Palm. Why do you have blue eyes Eric? How in a black man? Did you notice your Alex Kincaid's blue eyes, Eric? And your father's? Your grandfather's? I think they were lovers, Eric – Alex Kincaid and Cati. That your grandfather was not a son of Benjamin's at all, but a Kincaid.

"And the feud after three generations is still going on – by you, Eric. You and Anna, Féy, me, your father, your sister, those Lawrence owners – but we all came together for one." I looked down. "I think I might be pregnant with him. He's yours – all of ours." I looked up.

The journal fell from his hands into the helm.

"Do you remember the meaning of the Ten, Eric?" I moved toward him. "I looked up Dr. Schneider."

He sank down to a squat. The lurching for the moment abated. I went on, "The Ten raises each numeral to a higher order without changing its basic self. It represents the divine order, 'cross color, caste, class and even time." I touched his free hand, relishing even its cold, before taking the diary. "It's your father's thread – the perspective from Shambhala. Perhaps this child is from him."

Eric shook his head, "It's not possible. It's not...I'm dry...it's never happened."

"A pregnancy test says it has."

A long while passed. "Will you publish our story, Jeanne?"

The passbook and dreams of first class travel with Cariña flashed, "Of course yes, Eric." His nod was curt. "But don't you want to know your impossible son?"

He bared his teeth. The surf thundered behind him. He stood up, shaking. "What did Heather tell you about me?"

"She spoke of a mandala – and the temple."

"Go on."

"She was trapped outside. You were a doorkeeper she said."

"So now you see."

"But of course you're her guardian."

"No!" The force sent a chill through me. "You *must* see."

Eric was guardian to them all, his dead, just like me – only till now he'd been the only one. I had Cariña.

He chuckled, "My father's end – it doesn't matter."

"Eric, I don't see—" I gulped oxygen. I had to think.

"I have lived with this for so long, Cadot," he said, "My complicity in my own father's death. I profited from it, allowed my sister's life to be destroyed, lied, and violated National Security – most of this before I turned 10.

"Now I will kill for it. Isn't that the inevitable end for a doorkeeper – letting folks in? One door closes, another opens?" The steel of his tone raised my hair on end. He jumped out of the helm. The boat lurched and I jerked the rudder. I looked out again at the angry, swirling water as I stabilized the back end. "The time comes, Jeanne," he walked backwards, keeping the gun on me, hanging on the various sail lines. "When you have to pay the piper. And now is that time. You see," his beloved eyes seemed to sink. "I can't spend the rest of my days in a jail cell or on the run." The boat was only 18'. "Did you ever find the truth about the twin powers, Jeanne?"

"It's the power of the Two – the eternal physical dance – coming together and then moving apart again – the inexorable linking of every opposite – as you've showed me."

He sneered and despite paradox the tension was unbearable, so quickly the dark wave knocked me back to that sea salt and polished mahogany scent of our first, forgotten, conversation.

In the well-appointed captain's quarters on the *San Francisco Belle*, he placed me on a plush Creole green settee. Then he sat and I leaned my head against his velvet lapel, my eyes closed. "Mm," I snuggled in, "you smell rich and beloved."

He chuckled, "Do I? That's odd."

"I want to be rich and beloved," I whined a little.

"Better to be rich in love."

"No," I shook my head with drunken vigor, "The American Dream."

"It's not what you think you know — the real dream isn't money. The real American Dream is love and mercy."

"Love, mercy and family's all a crock. Money, well-invested, stays and money earns you respect — and wings."

"Without love you fly into the sun. Sometimes even with it."

"Better than being in hell...But I've got the Cadot curse. And success will give me the power to lift it."

"Outward power may not be all that's needed."

"Spoken like a powerful man."

"Spoken like a man who knows true power. What you have."

"Yeah?" I growled in a child's tone, "Mother gave me to my Grand Moman at birth. Cursed me with others' shames at 10, denied me at 11, killed herself at 12. My Grand Moman hated me when I had my girl at 18 — unwed. My 8 year old daughter called me a whore before I left. That's what I have."

"All of that — yes. And your father?" His tone masked interest.

I threw my head, "West African, medical student, son of a chief — never met him — doubt he knows I exist."

"So you see, from their sins, you're free." He regarded my nails with kind, seemingly vague interest.

I shook my head, "No, no, I'm exiled and cursed full of shame," I turned my palm, "and not just my own."

"With all that shame you must feel great mercy."

"I don't understand the way you talk." A yawn rose.

"You will. I'll show you."

"Let's never bring it up again." And nestling deeper in, I fell asleep. The ebony wave washed me back to Heart's Home where Eric's eyes watched me with comprehension. Again he knew what had just occurred.

"So do you understand yet, Jeanne? Do you still think I'm rich and beloved? Still think you're full only of shame? Well, Pauline was right about one thing. No one lives a rich life without sacrifice – the more of one you get, the more of the other you have. At its root, life is paradox – the bad pulls against the good, always. Purity cannot long survive."

"But Eric, what's the alternative?" Our dance flashed – the seductive, velvet darkness. That's what he wanted – despite Eric's backbone – his heart's home – his most intimate core of faith – was gone – taken from him by his mother before his first decade. He'd no reason to ever love or believe in himself or anyone else ever again. But without it, the Cosmic Dance – the constant, violent rip tide of life – was killing him. He was getting pulled into the dark sea – and meant to take me with him.

I glanced behind him to the whirlpool, the green ship already sunk, remembering Féy spinning, twirling on the old ship's dance floor and me dancing with Cariña in our haute couture. And my fingers gripped Anna's book. "But what saves us is using love and faith as verbs, like a muscle. They carry us above life's back and forth." As I said this I rose.

"As any *maman* must respond. But some things cannot be forgiven or let go – fathers know this. Some things cannot be escaped. Some pain cannot be taken. And I've only one thing left to share with you – an experience of the real temple – of shame and mercy and paradox – your 'real living' – and my nightmare."

My eyes winced closed. Féy, Moman L and especially Cariña filled my mind's eye. Silently I asked for their forgiveness. I should've known better than to come out here.

Pop–whiz, pop–splash and then the boat rocked.

My eyes flew open. The first flare rocketed up to the sky. I edged to the stern keeping my hand on the tiller. Eight feet from the ship, above an awful orange, red glow from his chest, Eric's lifeless, twilight eyes reflected red sparks. His body thrust against rocks with awful force. My mouth flew open and I screamed.

Twenty–Four

My grip strangled the rudder for a long, lost moment till I pushed back hysteria. Stabilizing the rudder to a cleat with a bungee cord, I ducked down into the tiny cabin, flipped the radio switch on and shouted into the handset. "SOS. SOS. Heart's Home. Stranded at God's Palm." I flicked the dials to the marked emergency channel and repeated the message.

Sure enough, "Roger, Heart's Home. Gualala Coast Guard. Saw your flare. Help is en route. Sit tight. Any injuries?"

Next to the radio were two pictures I'd not seen before: one of the old *HMS Lawrence II*, the other of a boat being nailed together by Berne and Eric who stared taciturnly at the camera. Heather spun on the beach in front of a pile of new lumber. Old lumber sat in another stack. Atop the heap lay the *HMS Lawrence* sign. So they'd built Heart's Home with some of its old wood.

And Eric had known all along the shipwreck had been his parents' heart's home. Bracing myself against the curved counter, I pulled down his impossible eyes – behind them sat an LCD screen above a keypad – a safe. Heather had said, number 31 is locked inside the tomb. The boat lurched to the port and now water rushed down the stairs. It didn't stop coming over the transom. "We must die before we live, *dauphine,*" Féy's voice wisped.

I punched in 1973, 1873 and combinations thereof. Nothing worked. I stared at the two framed photos – my pioneer five in one, the four Berne's in the other. I dialed in 10-2-1 – but no click. I tried 10-2-31 – no luck. The water kept coming. This time I really was wet up to my ankles.

"Five is the shape of life," wafted through my head. So did all Eric's talk of numbers. I plugged in 10-02-05-31-01. The safe popped wide.

Inside I touched a thick manila envelope, locket and letter with Jeanne scrawled outside in what must be Eric's handwriting.

Quickly the darkness welled up. I left my cold, shivering frame, fingers still poised to grab. Up from God's Palm, strands of light coiled, mingled and separated through filmy clouds – the diamond flames of Eric and Anna, Berne, his father, Cati, Benjamin, Lilla, James and even Alex Kincaid. All down the coast, other ribbons wisped up – from shipwrecks and suicides or murders. Untold diamond fires flickered up from the cliffs.

Above Coit Tower the condor circled, and ribbons rose. Mary Ellen Pleasant, the *voodooienne* cook become boarding house millionaire who hosted governors, politically aided escaped slaves, and won desegregation of the streetcars but waited over 30 years for its enforcement; Bridget "Biddy" Mason, the real estate mogul, and her ruled "free forever" family of 13; Edmonia Lewis the sculptress; and William Leidesdorff, 1850's "most valuable resident". Then the dead nine showed me their final memory.

"Cati, it's over. The bank now owns the boat."

A second story salon – walls covered in rose velvet lamé, girls – mostly French from their colony at Lima, a few Chinese, one frail mulatto – lounged with suited guests, jackets discarded and shirts open, on rose velvet divans and settees, large gilded mirrors and thick–framed paintings like gilt jewels on the walls. This must have been how our parlor had appeared 135 years back.

Kincaid and Cati stood outside the languid scene in a darkened, pale jade hallway. The close space between them rippled with angry sexual tension – as of a tango. Cati was a *cholo*, a mix of Indian and white – but her white had come from white Creole – known then for their sensual and to many, obscene, dances. Cati herself had been a heart–breaking dancer – she'd used that to win enough fortune and fame to lease this space and to present her first girls – all of whom danced wonderfully as well. That's how she commanded the highest rates and the best neighborhood – Pike Street, today Waverly Place, behind Union Square. Carriages of the best houses rounded her small alley every night and they had for eight years.

Now Cati wanted to move a step further – and it wasn't just because of the quiet babe with Bertha down the hall – a babe she couldn't acknowledge for its coming strawberry blonde curls just like Alex's. Hair Benjamin hadn't really gotten mad at as yet. And hair that would ensure the baby's future after she and Benjamin departed and Alex took him away. But Cati wanted out of women's work, women's life entirely – out to the sea which she'd loved ever since she'd sailed on Captain Mann's schooner up from Lima. Cati'd long ago paid him off, as she had the man who'd bought her upon docking.

But now this man Kincaid, so recently her tender lover, her hope for the sea dream she'd held secret for 23 years, a dream now so close – and now he was telling her the dream was gone.

"They can't take it," she hissed through her still–thick accent, "We own it. We paid it all off."

"Yes, you paid me, but..."

"But?" Small insistent beats pricked against her chest.

"Well, it is complex," the powerful man looked down. "With the stock crash, then the bank run – the funds were technically at risk – invested. Consolidated Virginia." She'd heard the name discussed between the men – one of Ralston's Nevada Comstock mines. After great investment there'd been no return.

"You lost the funds."

Kincaid only nodded, "Fell off 50 points."

"You lost it all?" No sense bringing up he'd not asked permission to risk their boat, their whole hopes, in his own silly wagers.

"It sure seemed sure, Cati. Look, on this, I've lost everything. If I didn't have..." his eyes began to wander the fixtures – *his* fixtures as Cati just let her rooms – before he cleared his throat, "the family home."

Cati's eyes had shrunk to tiny, black beads. It was the only way she could keep herself from leaping on this man, scratching his eyes out. But as he drew his thumb down her cheek, through the anger an idea grew – a solution.

The bank was tied up with the run – all was chaos – there might be a way. So, she nodded and patted Alex on his way out, assuring him with her usual grace all was okay, accepting his fervent assurances that in two hours his carriage would come for their son.

Soon as his carriage pulled away, she sent a boy to fetch her own from the St. Francis 'cross the square.

"Gentlemen and Lady," Cati emphasized the last in her harsh voiced authority, "we've only one option – we must move and we must do it tonight. The bank won't dare take it before the Inaugural sail tomorrow – scared of another riot."

"There's a full moon tonight and the ship's stocked for tomorrow." Benjamin added, "Cati just brought me from there."

"How do we know it's not already too late?"

"As of when I left, no one but our Jake was there."

"You mean leave everything?" Lilla frowned in concern. "And everyone?"

"We can't risk any leaks or any time. Vancouver awaits – they won't know which direction we've gone if we don't light the lights until we're well out of the Gate."

Lilla looked at James who circled the hat he held in his hands. Feeling the pressure of her eyes, he glanced up – his face so young, so worried, it practically hurt. Finally he shrugged, his brows high, "I can't think of another way. Lilla, we'll lose everything."

Lilla flashed on all the long days, the back–breaking work, the nights of abstinence, except during her floods, to ensure they had no babies. And now she'd missed her last two months' floods, but hadn't told him yet.

They shared a moment's eye contact without speaking and then James looked at Benjamin, then Cati, then his father, Henry, and nodded.

In the end getting their belongings packed and aboard without raising suspicion had been the most difficult part. They'd left most behind and claimed they had to attend to a relative's sudden illness in Sacramento to those few they saw.

Maneuvering out at night was only possible by the full moon, but they weren't the only ones using it – a few ships lingered in the Gate – still drawn here, despite the fall.

The group breathed a sigh of relief when they rounded the headlands and passed out of sight.

They waited a good hour before they lit a few candle–lamps in the main cabin and then, their narrow escape, the sudden change in their circumstances, the partial light made them giddy and the three couples danced, drank champagne and ate caviar all meant for the following night – for the mostly whites they would have carried. They even danced beneath the huge Inaugural Ball banner.

Henry Collins was in the bridge. But he'd never been up the coast – he'd been a river and inland man for years. So who could blame him if he got curious after two hours of smooth sailing – curious to see the magnificent cliffs up close – not too close, but closer than he felt was perfectly right. Still, they'd never be coming back here and with the laughter and stomping rising up, he was pretty sure he was the only one here appreciating it.

And then realizing there were little coves all long – he thought once they got far enough they might be able to pull over for the night. Not just for safety, but also to see this magnificence during the day.

He'd been looking for sites for about half an hour when they hit the snag.

The ship caught, the engine strained for a second then lurched forward with a horrifying tearing metal sound before he shut them off.

He'd seen the dark shadows sticking up – but he hadn't watched for undersea ones, not a ship's length away. Now there was a rushing sound, an awful, loud sound of water filling the hull three stories down. And then a crash as the current slammed them into the up thrust rocks. And from below now James – his son, the engine man – yelled, "Sir, what happened? You see anything?"

"She ran a snag," Henry hollered back, turning the bilge on full and offering up a quick prayer. Then he hurried down to the others to see about evacuating.

They were still ½ mile from the beach and none of them knew how to swim. Judging from the rushing sound, they had a half an hour. Henry had heard the same explosion with his first *Lawrence*, but that was on the Delta – they'd all made it out – still the ship had been ruined.

Downstairs all was quiet – the women had gone to get their things – the men wrestled with the lifeboat. There were two, but they could all fit in one. Though there were no lights ashore that Henry could see, he knew there were little encampments all up and down this shore and there was a beach directly south of them surrounded by steep cliffs. But down below he could tell the rushing sound wasn't just from them.

With the full moon high overhead, there was a whirlpool created behind the rocks thrust up like a palm. And it was getting bigger – water was flooding into the boat, ripping apart its undercarriage. To get to the beach they'd have to get 'round it somehow, yet the eddy's outer edges ran the length of the 63' ship. They'd have to go in from the down current side and paddle their way clear.

The first boat out included three gentlemen, one of them James, Benjamin stayed back with Lilla and Cati. The men soon learned the problem of the whirlpool. All currents – top and undertow align and the waves swirl powerfully into the black hole center – the hole to take you to Berne's heaven I imagined.

This center caught the tiny dinghy quick before they could attach to a crag with a line from the ship – to help guide the second and third, larger boats. Watching them go down, Lilla and Benjamin and the others who remained thought, sure death either way. So they chose to go standing on their last investment in the world, on the top deck.

Suddenly, water nipped at my hip and a helicopter's blades whirred, a light flashed across the stairway waterfall and a loudspeaker boomed, "Heart's Home – US Coast Guard. Prepare to be boarded."

A thud and the boat jolted. I shouted, "In here." Grabbing the threshold, shoving the contraband in my coat, I pulled myself up from the small sea to the watery deck.

Wind numbed the closeness of my rescuer as he quickly belted me in to a swing hooked to a line from the helicopter. I nodded my okay.

As we lifted high above the now sinking boat, the dark sea, my former self and Echo, I knew how I'd died – I'd left below young Jeanne with the curse, with my Ten.

They Five had risked all to not be cheated or exploited and to not cheat or exploit, simply to contribute – to live without any chains of denial or corruption, even through rough seas – and for a time they'd succeeded in doing well by doing good – succés fou – the highly elusive, eternally hoped-for, increasingly rare American Dream. And I nearly had it.

Twenty–Five

Overnight at Santa Rosa General for observation, after a two–hour interrogation with the Gualala sheriff, a severe chill, slight fever and an armed guard that Clive somehow made happen, I rested fitfully. Early the next morning Mavis and Susan arrived to collect me.

"Well, my dear," Mavis gave me a good, long look after a bear hug. "You can thank Susan here."

Susan smiled, "Todd said Marcia Witt called from her honeymoon – told him all about the cabin and how strange Eric had been when they'd last spoken."

Her *honeymoon?*

"Everything's fine here," Mavis mimicked me in a high voice.

Susan stopped her. "Girl, are you okay? The baby?"

"Oh Mave," I cringed.

"I had to tell her."

"I know pregnancy when I see it. From the look on Mavis's face I knew something was going on." Susan sounded concerned. "I'm a single mother myself. She's seven."

Her smile suggested she was open to a truce. Perhaps we'd both misjudged. I wasn't surprised. The woman I used to be now seemed so young. I was sore all over. "He seems fine." I just wanted to get out and go home.

"Clive got the confession," Mavis said as we drove home. "It's with the police now."

"What?" I said.

"The confession. It arrived in the mail today. From Eric. Says you were innocent of any wrongdoing; that he off'd himself out of guilt from helping murder his father and incapacitate his sister. That it had all been planned. And you were his witness. It will make great copy. If you survive, your future's made." She saw me look for the thick envelope, "I stashed your evidence."

She held out a plastic bag of my clothes; manila peeked out of my jacket. "Mavis, you're underpaid."

"He said you'd been profiling his father and that he'd invited you up. The police found your things in separate bedrooms."

Relief clogged my throat. He must've moved them when he took the diary. At least the pictures weren't released, yet.

"Anyway, I guess the Oakland police want to talk with you about the elder Berne's death, too."

"Ah," I said and watched the landscape roll as we drove the 150 miles back to the City.

It wasn't until I got home that I could open the safe's envelope. Inside were: impossibly Grand Mere's photos and negatives; a leather–faced journal; and a twilight blue passbook with 12 entries, each for $1 million from 1972 to 1975. Gingerly I opened the 31st journal. There were only a few entries.

Aug 15. New laser equip arrived! Michael and I prep teleportation experiment. Using neural monitor. Expect to test whether quanta in laser gas can generate a pure quantum state – or affect a large–body in any way.

This must be the experiment Coomb had mentioned.

> Mar 26. Eureka! After many hours of straight experiment, first QTP success!! have been to wondrous soul of the universe!! Exhaustion/reduced resistance a critical requirement?? Hurtled forward – dozens (hundreds?) of images unroll like film. One frame per potential reality?? Gravity–like force tugs as I pass → entangled body inside?? Back in Lab – a proof burned in mind's eye. A diamond laser hologram will create pocket to pitch anyone into QTP! Krishnaji's "pocket of sacred time"? Must prove.

What followed were lines of pure gobbledy–gook to me. But I saw the similarity to Fulani and Coomb's proofs. He never wrote of achieving teleportation again. In fact, the rest of the journal was mostly blank.

I refilled my glass of water and fingered my tile. At nine Eric had had the presence of mind to tear those pages out, hide this book and save his father's name – though it hadn't worked. And his whole family had been destroyed – almost all.

Bringing my blue–tinted Mexican glass back to the counter, I stared at the white envelope addressed to me. Eric's twilight eyes burned in my brain. His handwriting was spare and aesthetic.

He had scratched his signature 'cross the bottom of the filmy parchment. It had been notarized the weekend of his unexpected trip.

I dropped the letter. If only I'd told him of his son a day before...perhaps things would have ended differently. Reverberating through my mind was my promise to Eric, "I will publish."

My fingers scurried through the zippered side pocket in my purse. Behind my Gstaad receipts, I found the passbook. I pulled it out and before I could change my mind, I ripped it up. Then getting out Anna's old passbook, I checked the account number against the source account in the first 2003 wire transfers. They matched. Eric had given all this dirty money away. Whether any had truly come from Fastow and Koslowski I bet even the Grey Hats did not know. I'd skip being the last fool. Without a complaint, the story no longer merited following.

The next day, using the confession, I petitioned a district judge to open the files. By the following afternoon by special dispensation I sat with the file in the police archives.

The arson report described the fire starting via explosion in the middle of the converted garage then quickly spreading throughout the room. The room had been loaded with accelerants and retardants both – most of them used in chemistry: alcohol, ether, even sand – typical equipment for a chemist, not a physicist. The report suggested that the laser devices were on. The fire scene report tersely noted "no remains. Accelerants and melted steel could have created a fire hot enough to melt any."

That night I called Clive. I told him everything, even about the Ten and the revenge – and about Dumileh.

He listened without clicking his mouse. "Send the diary stuff ASAP," he said, "I'll run it by Todd."

"Will do," I said quickly, belying the wave of fear deep inside. I included Berne's mathematics in his own hand, bits of Eric's confession, Anna's diary, the old and new passbooks, the wire transfers and the photo of the conspirators.

I included nothing about my paid debts or the Grey Hats. I could not be that ignoble to Walter, or to any of the finally repaid.

Valentine's Day came and went with no outcry and no card from Cariña. She was out when I phoned. The next day I sent in the exposé. I waited to hear Clive's howls.

On the last day of a dreamless, visionless week, I got

something from Trout & Cie. The key and deed to the coastal cabin transferred to me, along with those to Heart's Home, with another very short note from Eric. "They're no Swiss bank account, but you know their secrets. I leave them in your care. E." The old warmth swirled. All his Swiss bank records were out there. In his way he had not betrayed me.

Right away I phoned Saanen. "Miss Cadot," the thick, smoky voice said. "This is Carmen."

"Carmen," I swung into my blue easy chair. "How are you? How's Miss.... how's Heather?"

"Just a minute," the phone scratched and Carmen whispered as it shifted hands.

"Miss Cadot?" The voice was still tiny, but stronger – not so fragile or spacey.

"Heather," my voice crumpled at the end.

"I wanted to say thank you, Miss Cadot," her melodic line reminded me of Féy. "I read your story. My brother's confession. How you stood up to Anna and Eric and Franz and Grande Mere, and I wanted to thank you. Thank you. Thank you. The doorkeepers are dead. Poor Eric is dead. He's dead...."

The phone switched again. I could hear a Thank You, He's Dead chorus echo.

"That's enough now, Heather," Carmen said off the line. Then to me she said, "She loved her brother, she just don't know what to do with her grief. Since she read your story, she asked me to switch her off that medicine. It's slow, but she's been working hard. I think she may have a chance. Miss Heather!" When she came back she rushed, "Ah've got to go, we just wanted to say 'thank you'."

"You are so welcome," I said. "Listen, Eric gave me his family cabin – I want to give it to Heather." I heard something crash in the background.

"You just keep it, honey. She ain't never goin' back there I don't expect."

"I'll keep it in trust for her – anytime..." but Carmen was

gone. I sighed as I hung up the phone, which rang immediately.

"Slugger?"

"Hey Clive," I sat slowly back down in my desk chair, noting the sound of the speaker.

"You sitting?" Todd asked.

My heart thudded. "Yes."

"Good. Now don't fall over—" Clive warned.

"Just spit it out."

I heard a mouse click. "Welcome to the Dream Team." Todd said. "We're going to run it front page Sunday – to introduce you. You're going to be the first one profiled."

"I—I..." Words wouldn't form so my throat just clicked.

"I see I've finally left you speechless – about time," Clive coughed. "You got your byline, Slugger. But the police will probably need that passbook. Now, did you mention you found... wasn't there something else – some artifact?"

Like the baby in my belly? Or a box full of Swiss bank records? "I found – uh – a locket with some pioneer hair."

"Right, yeah, that was it. So, now you're a science journalist, I've got three letters for you: D – N – A."

Despite Clive's use of our signal – 'do not ask', meaning he'd explain later about why he kept my secret and his next ulterior idea, despite the ludicrousness of my being a science writer – now that the dead had indeed brought me to *succés fou,* to mastery of the twin powers, to the one of the Ten, and the turn of the curse, thoughts of Cariña, her African grandfather, the second heart beating inside me, and now alive Féy who linked us all – rose up like a shimmering, diamond thread.

From behind Lilla and James' old wedding photo, I loosed Féy's strip of numbers. I knew when I picked up the phone to call Chuck before I dialed New Orleans – they were the digits to Féy's Paris phone. And Cariña and I were finally about to call it.

Half Tanzanian, half Scottish-English-Irish American, Staci was adopted into the 3rd generation of a black Californian Gold Rush family, one of a few thousand who came out West to find their freedom.

After a Harvard A.B. in Anthropology and a Haas MBA in Organization Behavior, Staci listened to 300 or so of America's diverse, 25 million professional women. They taught her that they hope for something beyond wealth – a contributive, noble American Dream – with a healthy dose of romance, adventure and sense of their place in history.

Multiple visits to New Orleans and research into the past of both cities have revealed this historical group, predecessor to today's modern pioneers who continue to migrate to the coasts to transform their own and our American dream.

To reach Staci, go to: www.narrativeedge.com